STAY ON
TRACK

Anton Philip Noël

Andrea,

Thanks for your support. I'm glad you enjoyed it.
I appreciate you. It's an honor to know how much my
work grasped your attention.

Dedications

- My Lord and Savior, Jesus Christ

- My family and friends
  -Your constant love, support, and pressure for me to succeed are greatly appreciated.

- Joi
  -You're the motivation behind this book. I thank you and I love you.

- Every writer that I've developed a bond with
  -Our craft is more than just an art; it's our way of life.

- Mrs. Leslie Greene, Dr. Carolyn Knight, Mrs. Deena Barlev, and Mrs. Drimmer
  -For contributing to the development of my literary skills, and helping me to push my writing to the next level.

Disclaimer

This is a work of fiction. It is not meant to depict, portray or represent any particular persons or real life events. Names, places, characters, incidents are a product of the author's imagination and used solely for the entertainment of the reader. Any resemblances to actual persons, business establishments, events or locales are not intentional. Any real names used are based on the author's admiration of that particular individual or organization, and a showcase of respect for their character.

STARTING LINE

The decisions we make in life are a representation of who we are. The people we associate ourselves with, the clothes we wear, our hobbies, goals, and the things we express interest in become our identity. The outcome of each decision could be beneficial or detrimental. No matter what you do, make sure you choose wisely.

My name is Charmaine. The story I am about to share with you is a prime example of the aforementioned philosophy regarding decision making. This philosophy is something I experienced firsthand a long time ago. The year was 1995, a beautiful time to be alive. If it wasn't the music we were blessed to hear, it was the TV shows that weren't flooded with garbage and actually taught you something. Clinton was in office and people still went outside to socialize. However, in this case that different time and setting proved to be a gift and a curse.

I was on my high school track team. I didn't take it seriously; I only joined because my best friend wanted me to join with her. Her name is Shayna, we're more like sisters. Shayna was the epitome of a track star. She was faster than anybody that was put up against her and had a room full of medals, trophies, certificates, and awards to prove it. Her track meets usually drew a crowd that resembled the crowds seen at our varsity boys basketball games, sometimes even bigger.

On one particular day it was about 85 degrees with a light breeze; perfect temperature for a track meet. Personally, it was

1

the perfect weather for me. I served as an alternate for the team so I usually just sat back and relaxed the entire time. I didn't mind; it gave me extracurricular activity credit, and gave Shayna confidence to know that she always had a form of support. I usually sat in front of a portion of the bleachers that was adjacent to the finish line waiting for Shayna. I was sitting in front of some guys on those very bleachers and heard some of the most foul, disgusting, and disrespectful comments about the female runners. I usually brought my CD player to track meets, that day I had my Pete Rock & C.L. Smooth *The Main Ingredient* album. I put my headphones on and turned the volume up to tune them out.

By now you may have deciphered what their comments entailed. For those that are not aware, track workouts and routines have a tendency of shaping the body. The results are of course more pronounced in the legs, thighs, and glutes. This was something that was very evident in Shayna's figure. Either she was the hardest working track runner in the world, or just naturally blessed. It became very apparent when she ran in her events due to the size of the shorts we had to wear. The shorts would inevitably ride up as we ran; another reason I didn't mind being an alternate. Shayna on the other hand would disregard the shorts issue entirely. She was more focused on getting a scholarship; it was our senior year. Most guys won't admit it, but gazing at the girls was the only reason they came out to the track meets. The guys on the bleachers behind me were a perfect example.

Shayna had just finished running her signature event; the 100 meter dash. I met her at the line to congratulate her. As I was giving her a hug, those same three guys that were making distasteful comments popped up right behind us. That was one thing I had a problem with at our track meets; anybody was allowed to walk near the track. It wasn't like the other sporting events that had security or rules to prevent people from walking onto a court or field. I asked the three of them if there was something we could help them with. In my experience, there's always one main clown that serves as a mouth piece for the accompanying clowns. In this particular occurrence, the main clown stood in the center of the three of them and said "Yes, you can!" He removed his hat in an attempt to be a gentleman, but that ship had already sailed.

He requested that we allow him to introduce himself. He said "I'm Key! These are my boys, Stack and Intellek." Shayna and I gave each other a puzzled look. I could tell we were thinking the same thing; these guys couldn't be serious. Instead of embarrassing them, although they made it very easy, Shayna asked the other two if they were incapable of speaking for themselves. Intellek replied, "Not at all. How you doin', sweetheart?" That brought a smile to Shayna's face. Key must have gotten jealous because he immediately intervened; "Since we're all acquainted and comfortable..." That's when I cut him off and told him that we were not comfortable, and we definitely weren't interested. I wasn't going to give him the time of day if he saw women in the way I heard him so vulgarly describing us. He was quiet for a second before building up the nerve to tell me to loosen up. At that point Shayna and I decided to walk away.

The 100 meters was Shayna's final event so we decided to get our stuff and sit on the bleachers until the meet was over. As we sat, I explained what I was referring to when I mentioned Key's vulgar comments about her and the other female runners. Shayna did what she always did when she heard those types of comments; she turned the left side of her mouth up, rolled her eyes, and waved her right hand as if to say "Whatever!" We both had our own methods of ignoring the ignorant boys that attended Jackie Robinson High. To be fair, they weren't all like that. The track meet was over and Shayna's mom was waiting for us out front to drive us home. We lived on the same block three houses away from each other in Brooklyn Heights. Our block consisted of Brownstones. We spoke more about those three characters that night from the track meet before we went to bed.

When we got to school the next day, the same three guys were staring us down from a distance. We looked at them for a second, and then kept moving. Later that day following lunch, we were at Shayna's locker about to go to fifth period. As Shayna closed her locker, the one that called himself Key was standing there leaning on the locker next to hers. Shayna was startled and let out a short gasp. She asked him what his problem was, and why he was sneaking up on her. His pitiful response was "Well just like you run rapidly on that track, you've been running rapidly through my mind." He licked his lips trying to be smooth. Shayna and I leaned back in disbelief of that tired line. We laughed at him as we walked away.

Key continued to follow us down the hall. I noticed a composition notebook in his hand and a pencil behind his ear. I asked him if he was trying to prove something that day by actually having a book in his hand. He said that the book wasn't for school. Shayna laughed sarcastically as she told him that she was not surprised. Key felt the need to continue to tell us that the composition notebook entailed material that no school could teach. He further explained that it was his book of rhymes. I just rolled my eyes because this guy's story was sounding more ridiculous.

We were coming up on Shayna's class; she had English with a teacher named Mr. Johnson. As she was turning in, Key turned in right behind her and said "Oh this is your class?" Shayna replied "Yes!" and asked if he was following her. He claimed that he wasn't and that it was his class also. She asked him why she had never seen him in it. He claimed to have been attending, but missed the last few. All I could think was "Negro please, its April!" I don't know who he thought he was fooling. They both went inside and I made my way to my class, but not before I signaled to Shayna to watch that guy Key.

They found their seats; Key sat behind Shayna. Mr. Johnson slowly rose from his seat and removed his glasses as he looked at Key. Key looked back at him and they had a stare down for a moment. Mr. Johnson said "Mr. Williams". Key replied sarcastically in the same tone, "Mr. Johnson". Mr. Johnson told Key that it was nice of him to join them, and asked him if he would mind telling the class to what they owed the honor of his presence. Key told the class that they didn't owe him anything, but he appreciated their generosity. Mr. Johnson folded his arms and said "Well I'm happy to hear that, now if you would be so kind as to get out." Key wanted to know why he was being asked to leave. Mr. Johnson explained that Key had been absent for a month and a half so he shouldn't try to act like nothing was wrong; "Now unless you have a note stating you had some terminal illness, get out!" He then proceeded to tell Key that if he did not leave, he would have security called to escort him out. Key picked up his notebook and told him that he wouldn't have to worry about calling security. Before he left, he had a few words for Mr. Johnson; "That's a nice tie you have there. When you get a chance, choke yourself." That in turn drew a few laughs and murmurs from some of the class. Mr. Johnson told them to settle down as he continued with his lesson.

About fifteen minutes into the class, Shayna had to go to the bathroom. The bathroom was just down the hall and around the corner. On her short walk she crossed paths with Key who was wandering the halls to pass the time until next class. Key saw her and told her that he knew she couldn't stay away. Shayna gave him a look of disgust and told him to get over himself as she walked into the bathroom. When leaving the bathroom, Key was posted up against the wall next to the door. Shayna noticed him and rolled her eyes as she made her way back to class. As she was walking away, Key shouted "YOU GOT SOME PRETTY EYES!" Shayna replied, "Thanks! My man reminds me every day." Key followed up his compliment by saying "And that thing behind you is crazy." Shayna told him that her man liked that too. Shayna was in a relationship, but her boyfriend graduated from another school a year earlier and things weren't really going too well between the two of them. She only mentioned him because she didn't want to be bothered by Key.

We had track practice after school. As we were getting ready in the locker room, I asked Shayna how things went in Mr. Johnson's class. She told me about Key not lasting a minute before he was kicked out, and how he basically stalked her when she went to the bathroom. I was hoping that he didn't become a nuisance. With the way things were going I had the feeling that he would be at practice too, but thankfully I was wrong. While at practice, Shayna and I spoke about her current relationship with her boyfriend, Darryl. She told me that she was considering breaking up with him. She wasn't getting the type of attention she had become accustomed to in the earlier stages of their relationship, and she felt that he was cheating.

Darryl is the only boyfriend Shayna ever had so she was dangerously attached to him. I honestly felt that she should have left him long before that. I saw him in the mall a year before with some other girl. I was upstairs and I could see them on the level below. He gave the girl a peck on the lips and a hug. He followed that up by grabbing a handful of her behind as they walked away. Without hesitation, I got home and called Shayna to tell her. He managed to convince her that it wasn't him. I never liked Darryl so it was good to hear that she was having a change of heart. Practice was over and the last thing we spoke about was the homecoming dance that was taking place on Friday of that week.

BUSTED

Friday came and we were both at the dance. I wore a purple dress and Shayna wore a sage colored dress. I got a glimpse of us together before leaving and couldn't help but think that we looked like The Joker next to each other. Shayna didn't bother to tell Darryl about the dance. I didn't see the point of having a date to a homecoming dance anyway; it was just a big party. As the night progressed, the fun did as well. The majority of us danced until we couldn't dance anymore. This was high school in the 90s; I can't think of anyone that went to a party and didn't dance. You didn't have to be the greatest dancer of all time to have fun.

Shayna saw me dancing and took it as competition; a friendly competition of course. The DJ put on a Lil Kim song; "No Time". Eventually, we were in the same spot on the dance floor and Shayna wanted to battle me. We went back and forth outdoing each other and soon enough the crowd around us grew bigger. I grabbed a guy near me to add a little flare to my moves; it managed to work in my favor. Shayna folded her arms and laughed. What happened next was so unexpected that it almost killed the vibe, well mine at least.

Some random guy in the crowd behind Shayna must have thought that she needed help. He grabbed her hand, spun her around to face him, and then picked her up. From there, she spun her body 180 degrees while still being elevated with his help. They were now belly to back and both facing me. He put her back down on the floor while holding her waist and she bent over. From that point, they were in a position that resembled someone pushing a lawnmower.

The gym lights were low so I couldn't tell who the guy was right away. I was more impressed with how in sync they were for it to be a random guy. Eventually, someone took a picture and the flash allowed me to see who it was; it was Key. I yelled "KEY!" Shayna got up and turned around to see if it was him. Before she could do anything, security came over and broke everyone up. They would usually break up a crowd because we weren't allowed to dance like that, but that particular time it was to get Key. Key wasn't allowed at the dance. They escorted him out and the party continued.

Shayna and I gave each other a high five and made our way to a vacant table to sit down and catch our breaths. As we were walking back, the guy I danced with was walking behind us. I stopped and asked what he wanted. He asked for my number. I told him it was "867-5309" and he walked away feeling accomplished. When we got to the table, we looked around the room for a second or two. I asked Shayna what that was all about on the dance floor. Shayna asked me what I meant. I gave her a look as if to say don't play dumb. She asked me how she was supposed to know it was Key. I stated that not knowing was the problem, and asked her how she could dance in that manner with just anyone. She accredited it to just having fun. I didn't let her know it, but I took that response as her cry for help regarding the direction her relationship with Darryl was going. I shrugged it off for the night.

I decided to point out how in sync they were on the dance floor. Shayna laughed and couldn't even explain it herself so she accredited it to natural rhythm. I guess that made sense, but I was more focused on her facial expression as she said it. She had a look of content on her face while she ran her fingers through her hair. Shayna only did that when she was nervous or at a loss for words. I asked her what was going through her mind. She had the nerve to ask me what I was talking about, but couldn't look me in my eye as she asked. I knew my sister; that response mixed with her lack of eye contact meant that she was turned on by something. I figured why waste anymore time. I came right out and accused her of liking Key. She gave me a look of disgust and said "Nobody said anything about Key, but it was nice." I asked her what exactly she was referring to when she said that it was nice. She told me to think about the position they were in and then think about what might've been nice. I gave her that same look of disgust she had given me and told her she was nasty as we both busted out in laughter. The DJ put on Junior M.A.F.I.A. "Crush on You" and we were back on the dance floor.

The following Monday at school, we ran into a similar situation while going to class. We got to Shayna's class and Key was standing there with Intellek waiting to go inside. Shayna took her seat; Key took the seat behind her again. As he took his seat Mr. Johnson stared at him, Key stared right back. Mr.

11

Johnson told Key that he needed to leave and that they weren't going to have a repeat of the previous class. Key said "You could've fooled me. If this isn't a repeat, why are you still wearing that same ugly tie?" Mr. Johnson told Key that his mom seemed to like it at the last PTA meeting. That drew a reaction from the class leaving Key feeling embarrassed, but not for long. Key replied "My mom couldn't possibly find anything about you appealing; she's not into sissies. I saw you on TV at the parade in the East Village last weekend dancing to 'It's Raining Men'." That drew an even bigger reaction from the class. Key decided to take his exit on that note.

I was still in my class. One of our teammates informed me that practice was cancelled; coach had an emergency she needed to tend to. My next class was one I had with Shayna. I told Shayna about not having practice and suggested we go to the mall, she liked that idea. When school let out, we went to Basin Mall. Basin Mall is a popular mall in Brooklyn where most students hung out after school. The first store we went to was a department store; we made our way to their shoe section. Shayna would try on some shoes and ask what I thought; I would then do the same. At one point during our shoe shopping, Shayna froze in her tracks and closed her eyes. It looked strange so I walked over to make sure she was okay. She started sniffing and told me that she smelled a familiar scent; we weren't too far from the fragrance counters. After a second or two, it finally hit her. It smelled like cologne she bought Darryl for his birthday the year before. Shayna tried on another pair of shoes and decided to walk to get a feel of them. While she was doing her model turn, her eye caught a glimpse of the fragrance counter. That's when she saw Darryl with his arm around some girl.

Shayna signaled me over to see what she was looking at. When I walked over she asked me if it was Darryl; she wanted to make sure her eyes weren't playing tricks on her. It was definitely him. She walked over to the counter as the attendant was asking him if she could help him with anything else. Darryl told her that they were fine and grabbed the bag. Shayna then said in an angered tone "You sure you and the lady don't need anything else?" Darryl turned around looking like a deer caught in a set of headlights. The dummy was so caught up in being busted that he forgot to take his arm from around the girl. Shayna said "Don't even worry about taking your arm from around her." That's when Darryl immediately removed his arm. His eyes were still bugged out and he was still speechless. The girl with him looked so confused asking him what was going on. I just stood to the side. Shayna continued to look at Darryl with her arms crossed and an angered facial expression.

Darryl was finally able to muster up enough of a vocabulary to say something. The first thing he said to Shayna was "Baby!" The other girl asked him why he was calling her baby. Shayna told her that it was because she was his girlfriend, and then asked the girl who she was. The girl said that she was the woman that was going to smack Shayna if she kept mistaking

13

herself for Darryl's girlfriend. I had to intervene at that point. I looked at the girl and asked "Did you not just hear him call her baby?" We hadn't even heard her name yet and she had the nerve to want to fight over a title. Shayna told me that it was alright and that she would handle it. She then turned back to Darryl and demanded that he explain himself.

Regardless of if he was in shock or not, Darryl had to be the dumbest guy I ever knew. This fool chose to use his chance to explain himself by asking "Aren't you supposed to be at practice?" I couldn't believe it. I also couldn't understand how Shayna could have lowered her standards to such a point. I had witnessed disputes between her and Darryl before, but this one took the cake. Her standards were so low; they might as well have been a sinkhole. I looked back over at Shayna. She had a look on her face in which you could tell she was about to explode. I tried my best to stop what potentially could have happened by telling Shayna to just let it go. She saw all she needed to see in Darryl. The girl with Darryl felt the need to add to it by saying "Yes little girl, run along." She may have been dumber than Darryl.

Shayna kicked the shoes off and charged at the girl. Darryl stepped in the way, but Shayna still managed to get a hold of the girl's hair. All of this was going down while we were still in front of the fragrance counter. The attendant got on the phone and called security to request some assistance. A few seconds later I saw the security guard walking swiftly in our direction.

Shayna still had the girl's hair while Darryl was holding her back. I didn't want to deal with any repercussions so I grabbed Shayna from behind and dragged her back to our bags. I picked up both of our book bags while still holding her with one arm. Darryl was holding his other chick back at the same time. They were both still arguing as the distance between them increased. I finally turned Shayna around and yelled "SHAYNA! WE HAVE TO GO!" We put our shoes on and we left the mall through the department store exit. A bus was just pulling up so we got on right away.

On the bus ride, Shayna was still fuming. I told her that she needed to calm down. She closed her eyes and sat back. Soon after, she started rotating her neck and breathing heavily in an attempt to relax. I sat back and looked around the bus. Shayna finally opened her eyes. She randomly began to blame herself saying things like she knew Darryl was cheating, but didn't do anything. I told her that it was nothing new, and reminded her about the time I saw him with another girl in the mall. She closed her eyes again and started shaking her head. She was disappointed in herself so I gave her some time to gather her emotions. That's when I saw a tear flow down the left side of her face. It hurt me to see her broken and upset.

I pulled Shayna close to me and wiped the tear. From that point she just let it all out; bawling and sobbing. An older lady sitting across from us saw her and asked if she was going to be okay. I rubbed Shayna's arm as a form of solace and reassured the woman that everything was going to be alright. The woman went into her purse and pulled out one of those miniature packages of tissues and handed it to me. I opened the package and pulled one out. As I was handing it back to her, she told us that we could keep it. I thanked her and handed one to Shayna. Shayna wiped her eyes and took another one to blow her nose. That helped her calm down a little. She began to vent some more saying "I was so stupid. How could I be so dumb? Why did I even bother with that fool? It's because I was a fool, that's why. It's whatever! I'm done with him."

Our stop was coming up; we had to transfer to the Subway and catch the 2 train. I pressed the button for the bus to stop. As we got up and started to walk off, Shayna thanked the lady for the tissues again. The lady told her that it was no problem and that she would be okay because God would provide. We walked off of the bus and began to make our way up the block. I decided to give her some words of encouragement. She was a lot more calm and open to listening after letting a lot of the negative thoughts out. I mentioned that I noticed she called herself a fool for dealing with Darryl, and explained to her that it was okay to be a fool. "Darryl was your first boyfriend, and you put up with a lot that he did for a while. We've all been there with someone. You have to just accept the pain and learn from it." I could tell that made her feel a little better, she just needed time to let it set in. All I could do was hope that she didn't relapse and allow him to convince her to let him back in. They had been together since the summer before junior year. That's a pretty long time; therefore it would have been easy for her to succumb to vulnerability again.

It was around 6:00pm when we got in that night. When Shayna walked into her house, her mom told her that Darryl had called a few times. She simply said okay. Everyone called her mother Ms. Kim. Ms. Kim asked Shayna if anything was wrong. Shayna said no, but of course her mother didn't believe that. However, she chose to not push the issue too soon because she did not want to push Shayna away. She simply said that dinner would be ready soon, and then told Shayna's little brother to clean up his toys. Shayna had a five year old brother that came about from her mother's second and current marriage; his name is Shawn Jr. Shayna's dad passed away in an accident at work when she was three. His name was Shane and he worked in construction.

At dinner, Shayna barely touched her food. Meanwhile, Shawn Jr. was going to work on his plate. They were having macaroni & cheese, chicken, and broccoli. Shayna would usually make that particular meal disappear. This gave her mother another opening to ask her if something was wrong. Shayna kept poking at the broccoli with her fork. Her mother attempted to get her attention twice, on a third attempt she called in a louder tone; "SHAYNA!" That startled Shayna causing her to look up immediately. It startled Shawn as well. Her mom asked her again if anything was wrong. Shayna told her again that she was fine.

Her mom asked why she had not eaten anything if nothing was wrong, and expressed concern because Shayna was usually hungry after practice. Shayna told her that practice was cancelled. Her mom asked if that was supposed to make her feel better. If anything, it made her more skeptical. Ms. Kim began to list the clues "You didn't have practice, Darryl calls numerous times, and you come in moping. Is something going on between you two?" Shayna stopped picking at her food and asked her mom if she could skip dinner that night. Her mother approved of the request. Shayna made her way to the steps to go upstairs. Her stepfather, Shawn Sr., was walking in from work. Shawn Sr. worked as a freelance electrician, and was attending law school at one of the top schools in New York City. They said hi to each other and Shayna continued up the stairs.

I got a call from Shayna around 8:00 that evening. I asked her how she was doing. In a depressed tone, she told me that she was okay. She then told me how Darryl called before she got home. I told her that he called me too a little after I had gotten in and that he was looking for her. I told him that he needed to call Shayna because his business was with her. He got very loud and belligerent and started blaming me for what happened at the mall. He then claimed that I was putting ideas in Shayna's head. At that point I just hung up on him.

Shayna told me to hold on because she was getting another call. After about 10 seconds, she clicked back over telling me that it was Darryl on the other line. Caller ID wasn't as prevalent back then so a lot of us didn't have it, otherwise I don't think she would've answered. I asked her what he had to say. She told me that she didn't give him the opportunity to say anything because he didn't deserve to speak. She simply told him that it was over and clicked back over to our conversation. I had to go so Shayna and I ended our conversation also.

THE BREAKDOWN

The next morning, Shayna and I were walking to our bus stop. We took the B52 to school every day. As we were walking, I asked Shayna how she was feeling. She told me that she was better, but still a little upset. While waiting for the bus, I asked her what her plans were from that point on. I incorporated some scenarios. First, I asked her if she was ready to move on without him. She said yes. Then, I asked her how she knew. She said that she just knew. Finally, I asked her what she was going to do if he kept calling her or if he popped up somewhere. She was quiet for a while before saying "We'll just have to cross that bridge when we get to it."

Our bus pulled up. A few stops after ours, it stopped again to pick more people up. Would you believe a few of those individuals were our old friends Key and his crew? I looked down in hopes that they wouldn't spot us sitting in the back. Shayna was already looking down with her mind wrapped around her situation. They sat in the middle section of the bus. Key sat back and put his leg up to get comfortable. His eye must have caught us as he was looking around because he did a double take. He stood up and began walking toward us with a smile on his face. As he was approaching us he said "My dance partner!" Shayna looked up and rolled her eyes. He sat down in the seats parallel to ours and said "What's up? Will I see you in class today?" I looked at him and said "The irony of that question." He looked back at me and told me it was nice to see me again as well. I just rolled my eyes. Key mentioned that he noticed a lot of eye rolling going on and told us to make sure they didn't get stuck; we both rolled them at the same time. The bus pulled up to the school and we all got out.

Key followed us all the way to the front door and kept harassing us in hopes of getting our attention. Thank God for the security guard at the door that was appointed to tell Key to report to the office. He asked the guard what he had to go there for, but we didn't stick around to hear the reason. Key couldn't stay out of trouble so it could've been anything. When the bell rang for first period, Shayna and I parted ways and went to our classes.

On the way into class, Shayna's teacher asked her to deliver something to the office. Shayna was the only one that particular teacher tended to trust. She would willingly take the messenger assignments because she didn't like that class. As she was approaching the office, she ran into Key as he was walking out. She asked him what he was in trouble for that time. Key said "Your guess is as good as mine. They're still pulling stuff up on me from pre-school." Shayna tried to hide her laughter, but could not. She was humored. Key told her that there was something on her face. Shayna started wiping her face and asking him what it was. He said "Well the rest of us usually call it a smile, but the way you act towards me, I didn't think you knew how to make one of those." She twisted her mouth and said "Whatever!" as she proceeded to walk by him. Key told her to hold on and asked her "What are you heading in there for? You finally joined the dark side?" Shayna told him that as long as he was on that side, he would never see her there. Key told her to never say never, then he walked off.

It was lunch time. Shayna and I had gotten lunch from a fast food place called Burger Empire not too far from the school. We got the food to go and brought it back to the school, we ate in the gym. Students would usually go to the gym at lunch to play basketball. We spoke more about her situation, but she eventually didn't want to talk about that anymore. She changed the subject to the track meet we had coming up the following day. She was concerned about her mind not being clear before it. I told her that she needed to just eat and not worry about those things.

Some of the guys playing at lunch were better than some of the players on our school's team. They didn't play for the school because they either couldn't keep their grades up, or they just didn't want to play. It was a shame to see all of that talent going to waste. Key walked into the gym and yelled "I GOT NEXT!" and sat at the bottom of the bleachers. The game ended and Key took the court. To be honest, he was actually pretty good. His coordination and graceful movement on the court explained a lot about his dancing at homecoming. Shayna's eyes were locked in on him the entire time. Mine were too, but I eventually snapped out of it. That was the only way I knew Shayna was staring at him. I told her that she had that look in her eye again. She asked what look I was referring to. It was the same exact look she had after dancing with him at homecoming.

I asked her if she was attracted to him. She said that she didn't know, but she did notice that he had a certain confidence about him. It was almost like everything around him didn't even exist and not too much got him down. I tried to tell her that it sounded like she was giving him a compliment, but she was caught up in a trance again. I yelled "SHAYNA!" She snapped out of it and asked me if it was a crime to look. I told her that in her case a look can lead to other things. She really needed to protect her scattered emotions because anything could look good when you're in a vulnerable state. The game was over and so was lunch.

We were walking down the bleachers and once again Key spotted us. He walked over to the bleachers and picked up the notebook that he was always carrying. I never saw him with a bag, textbooks, or even a sense of urgency, just that notebook. I got the feeling that it was a security blanket. I said "What's up, Key? I see you got your notebook again. Are you going to actually write a note today?" He said "Nope, I'm gonna finish writing my Noah's Ark play for the drama department. I got the perfect part for you. Would you be interested in Donkey #2?" Of course Intellek and Stack appeared out of nowhere and laughed uncontrollably like it was the funniest thing they had ever heard. I ignored them and we all continued walking to our classes.

We didn't have to stop at the lockers that day because we already had our stuff with us after lunch. Key and Shayna's class was closer to the gym than mine so they got to their class earlier than usual. Shayna pointed out that Mr. Johnson wasn't there yet. They both took their seats and just like clockwork Key engaged in flirting with her; "So were you in the bleachers at lunch to cheer me on today?" Shayna turned around and told him to get over himself. She then asked "Why do you want to know, so you can write it in your little diary?" He looked at his notebook and said "I guess you can call it a diary." Shayna asked him why that was. Key explained that a diary is where one usually puts their deepest or innermost thoughts. Shayna looked at the cover of the book and noticed it said "Keynotes". She said "Keynotes? Is that your full name?" He said no, that's where Key's notes go. Shayna asked him what kind of notes he wrote. He opened the book allowing her to take a glimpse, and then quickly closed it back up. That quick glimpse allowed Shayna to only see a bunch of scribbling. Key told her that they were rhymes, and that he was going to be the greatest emcee of all time.

Back in the 90s, hearing someone wanted to rap wasn't like today. Hip-Hop was still elevating so it was impressive if someone had a skill that was on par with what was being produced in the music industry. Nowadays, it's more of a common fad to want to be a rapper, and more fueled by money. That in turn overshadows the ones who are actually skilled. Shayna then asked why his name was Key. Key looked at her with a smile and told her that it was short for Key to the City. He explained by saying "I'm gonna access this city and take it over, but before I do that, I'm gonna be the Key to your heart." Shayna gave him a blank stare and told him to keep his weak player lines to himself.

Mr. Johnson walked into the classroom. He was sorting papers as he walked in and glanced at the class. He did a double take when he saw Key. Key had a big grin on his face to taunt Mr. Johnson. Mr. Johnson looked at him with an angry glare. Key said "How you doin', Mr. Johnson? Are those the last book reports? I came by to turn mine in, but you had already left for the day." Mr. Johnson explained that it was not a stack of book reports, but the most recent class exam, one that Key had missed. Key knew he was in a jam so he pulled an excuse out of mid air. "I knew we were scheduled to take that exam, but I felt it was bias and unfair." Mr. Johnson told him that he could make it up under a few conditions. He had to either have a doctor's note, a note from his parents, or an administrative excuse. Key said "I'll take the doctor's note option." Mr. Johnson asked him why he thought it was all a joke, and then kicked him out again. Key picked up his notebook and left.

Later that day at practice, Coach Robbins explained to us why practice was cancelled the previous day. Apparently her daughter was sick and she couldn't find anyone to take care of her. That immediately caused me to think of how in life we experience certain things taking place just so something else could happen. For example, if coach's daughter got sick and she managed to find someone to take care of her, then we wouldn't have caught Darryl in another one of his lies. At that moment, Coach Robbins pulled me away from my deep thoughts. She had been calling my name for the past ten seconds; "Charmaine! CHARMAINE!" I jumped from being startled and answered "Yes coach?" She told me that I would be running the first leg of the 4x100m relay at the upcoming meet. That took me as well as my teammates by surprise. Coach never asked me specifically to run anything. I didn't know what to say exactly except "Yes, coach!" She then told us to line up for warm ups.

The next day at school we were in our last period of the day. The track meet was away so we were excused from that class. On the bus to the opposing school, Shayna was going into her pre-meet routine. She would usually put in her *Enter the Wu-Tang: 36 Chambers* album, turn the volume up and mellow out. She loved Wu-Tang, especially when she needed to get hype. She was actually a big Method Man fan, but she loved them as a whole. Everyone knew her routine should only be interrupted if it was of dire importance, especially at that point in the season. Those particular meets were the ones that the college scouts attended. Runners had already established themselves for the season and needed to prove they could handle the pressure of an away meet.

When we pulled up to the school, the first thing we noticed was the overall appearance. It wasn't anything special, but it was humongous. It was in a bad neighborhood and had a reputation for having some of the most delinquent students in the entire city. We walked around the outside of the building to the track in the back. During warm ups, some of the students that came to watch the meet began to pile into the bleachers. Shayna and I were warming up together and got a few glimpses of some of the students. They didn't seem like they had much class. I know you shouldn't judge a book by its cover, but this was more instinct than judgment. As part of our warm up, Shayna and I decided to jog an 800; that's two laps around the track.

I could see that Shayna was focused, her eyes stayed forward throughout the whole jog. She was beyond disciplined when it came to track & field. I on the other hand would tend to let my mind and eyes wander during warm ups. As we were finishing our first lap, I managed to get another glimpse at the stands. More people had filled the bleachers and I noticed a very familiar face, but I couldn't remember exactly where I had seen that particular person. Things were also registering a little slower because my mind was still partially focused on warming up. A quarter of the way through our second and final warm up lap, it hit me. The face I saw was the girl that was in the mall with Darryl. I would usually warn Shayna about something like that, but I was afraid that it would cause her to lose focus. Instead, I decided to wait until we got three quarters into the second lap to tell her that I couldn't finish just so we wouldn't cross the girl again. Shayna told me to suck it up and that it was only 100 more meters. I told her that I would rather save it for my event that day. She gave me a look like I was acting strange. I played it off by telling her that I just wasn't used to that much work being an alternate. She bought it and didn't press the issue any further.

The time for the beginning of the track meet was approaching. As things got underway, both of our boys and girls got off to a strong start. The time had come for the 4x100m relay, the event I still don't understand why Coach Robbins wanted me to run in. Either way, I wasn't complaining because it was an event that Shayna and I got to run in together. She was running the anchor position which is the last leg. She usually cleaned up extremely well in relay races. I've seen her in some of the biggest jams due to large degrees of distance between her and her opponent. The positions would look impossible, but she always seemed to get the job done. It was amazing. She didn't need to perform any miracles on that particular day. Our team handled business and got first place.

In the midst of the team's celebration following the win, we ran into a problem. Shayna crossing that finish line drew a lot of attention. Those that knew her praised her performance, and those that were not aware of her skills wanted to know what the big deal was regarding the crowd surrounding her. Of course that meant it wasn't too long before Darryl's other girlfriend became curious, that is if she had not already. She finally got a glimpse of what was going on at the finish line and began walking down the bleachers. She leaned over the barrier and yelled "WHAT'S

28

UP TRACK STAR? YOU BETTER SAVE SOME OF THAT SPEED FOR AFTERWARD CAUSE I'M COMIN' FOR YOU." Shayna turned around to see who it was. As soon as she locked eyes with the girl, her facial expression changed as well. Shayna yelled back "WHY WAIT? COME GET ME NOW, HOE!" I had to intervene before it got out of hand. Shayna wasn't thinking. We were on the girl's turf which meant she had more back up. On top of that, this wasn't the place for that kind of drama. The girl started climbing over the barrier. She didn't take too well to being called a hoe, but I guess the shoe fit. Security came and grabbed her before she could get over the barrier and escorted her out. I grabbed Shayna and started walking her back to the rest of our team. The both of them were still arguing while they were being restrained just like in the mall.

When we got back to our team's spot, Coach Robbins wanted to know what was going on. Shayna was too emotional to express herself. I told coach that a few words were exchanged between Shayna and a critic in the crowd. Coach told Shayna to get her mind back in the right place before the 100 meter event because she needed her. The 100 meter dash was three events away. I tried to take Shayna's mind off of what was going on, but she had lost all focus. I never understood why she let little things bother her for so long. That was probably one of her biggest flaws. I gave her the CD player and she re-entered the 36 chambers. It started to work for a while, but I knew she hadn't tuned all of the distractions out yet because her eyes had not closed.

We both sat against the bleacher barriers trying to relax. As we sat there, three girls walked up behind us on the other side of the barrier. Apparently they were friends with the girl that had a problem with Shayna. They had a message from her; "Simone said to let you know that she'll be waiting for you out front." Shayna didn't hear them due to the music so she took off her headphones and asked them to repeat themselves. I told her to not worry about them because she had a race to focus on. The main instigator amongst the three of them decided to repeat the message; "Simone is waiting for you when you're done with your little race." Shayna replied "Tell her to come tell me herself, and to not send minions. You all can get it too." The girl walked away sucking on a lollipop with the other two following her. This wasn't the Shayna I knew. She was obviously taking the situation with Darryl a lot harder than I thought. I had never heard her using some of the language she was using or picking as many fights.

I had to stop her because it was getting out of hand. I yelled at her "SHAYNA! GET A HOLD OF YOURSELF! WHAT'S WRONG WITH YOU?" Shayna replied "Kill that noise. I'm not trying to hear it." I took a step back in shock because neither of us had ever spoken to one another in that manner. We may have had small arguments, but nothing serious. I asked her "Oh, so you're mad at me now? You're gonna let dumb Darryl cause you to turn into a monster?" Shayna just said "Whatever! I got a race to run." I told her to go ahead because she obviously couldn't be reasoned with. I went to the finish line to wait for her like I usually did.

Coach Robbins called her over and asked if she was ready. Shayna replied yes, and proceeded to set up in lane three. I could see her setting up on the blocks and could tell that she wasn't focused. She was breathing harder than usual, she had her eyes open when she usually started with them closed until the gun went off, and she didn't shake her arms out like she usually did. I couldn't see that race ending well. The runners took their marks, got set, and they were off. Shayna took off like a bullet the way she usually did. Midway through all of her races there's a noticeable ridiculous amount of power in her strides. Her power wasn't so noticeable in that race. As a matter of fact, other runners started to close in on her. Eventually, she was overtaken. Once one passed her you could see the change in her body language. It's almost like she had given up which was hard to believe. At that point she allowed herself to lose all focus and another opponent took advantage. Shayna had run out of time and finished third.

The only other time I saw Shayna finish third or worse was our freshman year. It was so out of the ordinary that everyone on the team was stuck with a look of shock. Nobody knew what to do or how to react. Shayna looked confused and didn't know how to react either. I watched her and waited to see

31

what she was going to do. She began to cry, but attempted to hold back the tears. I walked over to her and hugged her. At that moment her body went limp and she fell to her knees crying even harder. One of our teammates came over to help me pick her up and walk her back over to the team huddle. There was nothing else to do but pack up and head back to the bus, the meet was over.

Before we got back to the bus, we still had that little problem waiting in the parking lot. We didn't need any more drama for that day, and Shayna wasn't even paying those girls attention any more. To avoid any further problems I asked some of the guys on the team to form a convoy-like guard around Shayna as we walked her back to the bus. It worked, but the girls were still making noise and wanting to cause problems. Thankfully it was just noise. They didn't come close and we were able to get back to the bus in one piece.

On the bus ride back, Shayna was quiet. I told her to not hesitate if she needed to talk to me. She was quiet for another maybe fifteen seconds before she let out a big sigh and said "I'm Sorry, Charmaine! I didn't mean to spazz on you." I let her know that it was okay and that I understood where her anger was stemming from. She expressed how she could not believe that she lost the race or the way that she broke down at the end. I told her that it was more than that. She looked at me and asked what I meant. I attempted to explain that it was obvious that she was letting the break up with Darryl effect her overall lifestyle. I started listing all of the changes I had noticed in her up to that point. As I was listing them, she was looking straight forward as if she was in deep thought and just realizing that these things I was telling her were true. Finally, I told her that losing that race and her crying at the end was exactly what she needed.

That statement appeared to have confused her a little so I explained. "The loss was meant to humble you and the cry was supposed to serve as therapy for all of the anger you allowed to build up." She didn't realize it, but after that loss and cry, she forgot all about Simone and wanting to fight her. The solution to all of her problems was to let Darryl go and to let all of that anger go; otherwise she would just experience a downward spiral of pain and stress. We had finally gotten to the school. As we were getting off the bus and walking to our rides, Coach stopped Shayna and told her to report to her office the next day at lunch. Coach looked upset.

TRUE COLORS

The next day at school, Shayna and I were in the class we had together before lunch. She told me that she was feeling a lot better that day. She also told me that Darryl called her after the track meet because he heard about what happened between her and Simone. Their conversation consisted of Darryl asking how she was doing and Shayna simply saying that she was fine and telling him to have a good night. I told her that she had the right idea by staying brief with him in her replies and not allowing the conversation to go on for too long. However, it was going to be a challenge to maintain that mindset because Darryl was more than likely going to try a lot harder.

At lunch time, Shayna made her way to the gym to see Coach Robbins. Her office was upstairs from the gym so you had to walk across the basketball court to get to it. As she walked along the sideline of the court, she received stares and inappropriate comments from the immature boys playing basketball. She ignored them and continued to walk towards the staircase that led to the offices. However, she managed to hear one of them say "Fall back, that's my lady ya talkin' about." Out of curiosity she turned around to see who it was. It was Key holding the basketball and smiling at her as he skyrocketed over all of the other students; Key was 6'5". He said "Go ahead sweetheart, I got this." Shayna just rolled her eyes and walked through the staircase door.

When she got to Coach Robbins' office, she was told to have a seat. Coach got right down to it by telling Shayna that she was very disappointed in how she carried herself at the track meet. She then informed her that there was a scout there. Shayna sat there with her head down looking disappointed. Coach gave Shayna one opportunity to explain what happened. She made it clear that Shayna's behavior was unacceptable, and it had no place on her team. That was one of Coach Robbins' greatest traits as a coach; she never cut anyone slack, and never gave anyone special treatment. I admired her for that. I believe she would have cut Michael Johnson if he was on her team and stepped out of line.

Shayna took a deep breath and told Coach everything. She explained what happened at the mall, the days following that particular altercation, and finally, how things transpired with Simone at the track meet. After hearing all of that, Coach was even more disappointed. I was surprised when she told me that she went into that much detail on the situation with Coach Robbins. There were so many ways she could have abbreviated the story, but I think she was worried that she would lose her spot if she wasn't completely honest.

Coach told Shayna that her way of handling the situation was very immature and very dumb. She then told her that she was letting a boy control her life and that whether he was a boyfriend or not, no one should have that much power over her. Shayna lowered her head again in shame. Coach told her to lift her head up and look at her while she was talking. She finished by telling Shayna that if she was going to let anger get the best of her every time something didn't go her way, she might as well give up on any dreams of success from that point on. A tear rolled down Shayna's face as she told Coach Robbins that she was right and apologized for her behavior. She was beginning to get a clear picture of what her future would look like if she continued to carry herself in that manner. Coach told her that they would work on something to help her control her anger and that she would see her at practice.

Shayna wiped her tear and got up to leave the office. I had just walked into the gym as she was walking out of the stairway door; I waited for her to walk across the court to where I was standing. I noticed that Key was in there again playing ball. As Shayna was walking, he yelled across the gym "ALRIGHT BABY GIRL! I'LL SEE YOU IN CLASS." Shayna looked at him and yelled "I'M NOT YOUR BABY GIRL. STOP CALLING ME THAT!" We walked out of the gym after that.

We had about an hour remaining for lunch. There was a West Indian food spot two blocks up from the school. We decided to get food from there and bring it back to school. We ate the food in a classroom students used for socializing at lunch because the teacher was cool, her name was Ms. Mims. As we sat down to eat, I asked Shayna how the meeting with Coach Robbins went. She gave me all of the details, then she told me about the scout that was there and how she was worried that she may have ruined her chances. I told her that she had nothing to worry about because scouts did not base their decision on one performance. As a form of consolation, I reminded her that she had a great season and a great overall performance at the previous meet. It made her feel a little better, but I can tell she was still concerned.

Lunch was over and we started making our way to our classes. My class was closer to Ms. Mims' classroom so we parted ways there. On Shayna's way to class, she was met in the hallway by Key. He walked up behind her, put his arm around her and said "So what's up, Shay? When are we goin' out?" Shayna pushed him off and verbally expressed her disgust "Don't touch me! Are you stalking me?" Key denied the stalker claim and stated that it wouldn't seem like stalking if they were together. Shayna rolled her eyes and took a step to the side to separate herself from him. She called him rude for not even asking if she was in a relationship before he started pushing up on her. Key told her that he knew she wasn't. He reminded her that she mentioned a boyfriend the first time, but not that particular time. He then added "If you do have a boyfriend, then that's your problem, not mine." Shayna walked away in disgust.

They got to the classroom and Mr. Johnson was standing outside by the door. He said hello to Shayna, she said it back as she walked inside. He then stood in the doorway and crossed his arms preventing Key from walking in. He told Key that he was not welcome in that classroom. Key told Mr. Johnson "Your statement is a matter of opinion. I'm not welcome in a lot places so your statement is also irrelevant." Mr. Johnson pulled out a piece of paper that stated Key was to be formally removed from instruction in that classroom. Key read it and asked what would happen if he went in anyway. Mr. Johnson stepped out of the way and told Key that his two legs could take him anywhere he wanted to go. However, it would then become an issue for security to handle because he was officially no longer registered for that class. Key balled up the piece of paper and threw it in Mr. Johnson's face, then walked off. Mr. Johnson left it on the floor and walked into his classroom.

Later that day after practice, Shayna and I were taking the bus back home. We were talking and laughing about something that happened at track practice. This guy named Edward on our track team wore really long spikes while practicing the 100 meter dash for the next meet. He had forgotten his regular spikes at home that day. Edward wasn't a standout on the team, but he could get you points. He struggled to move as the trial run started, but eventually picked up a little momentum. However, as he began to pick up speed, a few of the spikes got caught in the turf and ripped out of the bottom of his shoe.

The thing about some spikes is that the sole of the shoe is plastic, so the spikes are what provide traction. When Edward's spikes got pulled out, he slid on one foot against the turf for about three to four seconds. He tried to balance himself, but he eventually lost his footing and the front of his shoe caught the turf. It caused him to flip forward and start a pile up involving himself and three of our other teammates that were also in the trial run. Edward looked at the other runners and said "We could always start a bobsled team." They sucked their teeth, got up, and left Edward sitting there.

When Shayna got home, she greeted her mom and brother. Her mom told her that Darryl called three times before she had gotten in. Shayna thanked her and started heading up to her room. Ms. Kim stopped her and asked her what was going on between her and Darryl. Shayna told her mom that she was no longer interested in him. That made Ms. Kim curious as to why. Shayna simply said that it was because he found interest in someone else. Ms. Kim was not aware of what happened at Basin Mall or at the track meet and Shayna preferred to keep it that way. She didn't like her mother worrying. Ms. Kim advised Shayna to tell Darryl how she was feeling if she had not done so already. She then told her that dinner would be ready soon.

Shayna went upstairs and called Darryl. Darryl picked up the phone after one ring and immediately said "Shayna?" Shayna noticed the anxiety in his voice and asked if he was waiting by the phone. Darryl told her that it was all he had done since the day we caught him in the mall. She asked him why he was waiting by the phone; she just wanted to see him squirm a little in his attempt to explain. He claimed that it was because he was very sorry and he never meant to hurt her. Shayna told him that his actions did in fact hurt, but she had gotten past the events that

39

took place. Darryl let out a sigh of relief and asked if he was forgiven. Shayna ignored his question and continued to explain how the situation helped her to mature as a woman, so she was not holding a grudge. You can hear the excitement building in Darryl's tone over the phone as he said "That's great!" Finally, she expressed that her maturation helped her to learn a little more about herself, and helped her to make the decision to not want to be involved with him anymore. In her words; "I no longer have an interest in you, Darryl."

Darryl was quiet for a few seconds. He then began to beg and plead with her to rethink what she was saying. Shayna told him that she didn't have to think any further; it was her final decision. Darryl got quiet again and was beginning to feel embarrassed. In an attempt to maintain a shred of dignity, he went off. "Go ahead, you're tired anyway. I only liked you because you had a big butt, but that was gettin' played out too. Just remember one thing, you're nothing without me." At that moment another voice entered the conversation saying "Will that be all, Darryl? Or is there something else you would like to add?" Darryl replied "Who is this?" Shayna said "Ma? How long have you been on the phone?" Darryl greeted her with an awkward inflection in his voice. "Oh, Hi Ms. Kim! How are you?" Ms. Kim said to Shayna "I was on long enough to hear Darryl's very eloquent speech."

Ms. Kim actually picked up the phone figuring Shayna was on it after calling her name about ten times and not getting a response. She wanted to let Shayna know that dinner was ready. Shayna thanked her mom and told Darryl that if he was still on the line, she wanted to thank him for his time and for showing even more of his true colors, and then hung up.

Shayna's mom was still on the line, and called Darryl's name. Darryl was silent for a moment, but finally answered out of fear. Shayna's mom kept what she had to say brief because she was rather disgusted with the things he said to Shayna, and preferred to not be on the phone with him. She let him know that she no longer wanted him calling her home or trying to contact Shayna. Ms. Kim didn't take disrespect lightly, especially when it was geared toward her family. She mentioned to him that she noticed his obsession with wanting to be a thug and a pimp, and if he thought that she didn't know, then he was more ignorant than the comments he had just made to Shayna. She ended her statement by telling him to tell his mother that she would be in contact with her, and then hung up the phone.

On our bus ride to school the next day, Shayna told me everything that went down in the phone conversation. It made me laugh, but I was more so happy. Darryl had it coming. It felt good to see everyone else finally get a chance to see him for who he really was. The bus stopped and the three stooges got on; Key, Stack, and Intellek. By that point they discovered that we rode the same bus to school so our mornings developed a routine. They would pay their fare, Key would look towards the back and spot us, and then the other two stooges would follow him to where we were sitting. They would take a seat and the harassment would commence.

Key sat down with his notebook on his lap and said "Well I missed breakfast this morning, but you two honey buns are looking quite appetizing so I should be alright." I looked at him and told him exactly how corny he was. He said that his field goal percentage might not be perfect, but he was bound to hit at least one. Shayna looked at him with a disgusted facial expression and told him that he was sick. He realized how his statement sounded and tried to explain that it wasn't supposed to be a sexual reference.

I directed my attention to Stack and Intellek and asked them why they hung out with Key. Intellek said that it was because they were homeboys for life. Key added "That's right, for life. We're about to be bigger than A Tribe Called Quest." Shayna and I were big Tribe fans, but those three characters didn't know that. I told him that he was putting a lot on that comparison, but he didn't care.

Shayna sat there with a disinterested expression on her face and asked Key "So I guess you're supposed to be Q-Tip, huh?" This guy Key was so disrespectful; he had the nerve to say "Q-Tip is going to want be the next Key once I get in the game." Ironically, A Tribe Called Quest released a song the following year called "Phony Rappers". The song described Key's cocky and ignorant attitude perfectly. I just ignored his behavior. Shayna seemed to have taken it a little more seriously and told him to prove it. Stack told Key that he didn't need to prove anything and people needed to pay for their art. Shayna told Stack to chill out because no one was paying to see them. We had never even seen them in the lunch room ciphers. Shayna asked if they even had a name. Key suddenly cut them all off and started spitting a few bars:

Yo Shayna, you look good. Definitely the prettiest girl I've seen in the hood/
A track star, who by far has apparently misunderstood.

My approach wasn't meant to scare you away/
I'm just trying to get to know you and show you what we could be one day.

If that's too much, I can't promise I'll stop trying, I'd be lying/
So you can roll your eyes, mine will stay fixed on your thighs, while you're busy denying.

It's a win-win whether you say yes or no, someday you'll change your mind/
Don't take too much time, and come around when these rhymes pay off my grind.

Stack and Intellek started cheering and hyping Key up. Intellek said "Was that Key or The Notorious B.I.G.?" In my honest opinion, he was solid. His flow was very creative with quality wordplay and bar structure. Apparently I wasn't the only one that felt that way. A few other people on the back of the bus applauded him. I looked at Shayna and I could tell she liked it, but she wasn't going to let him know. I told him that it was pretty good and that his rhyme schemes slightly reminded me of AZ. He wasn't AZ, but he had potential. Some older guy not too far from us told him to not let his talent go to waste. He thanked both of us.

The bus pulled up to the school. We all got off and headed inside. I don't know where the stooges went, but Shayna and I went to class. While Shayna was in class she was daydreaming about what happened on the bus. She wasn't focused so much on his comment in regards to how he looks at her thighs; she was used to that and not just from him. She was more caught up on his actual talent; she found it to be impressive and was quite flattered. However, she didn't realize that her teacher had been trying to get her attention for the past minute or so. She snapped out of her daydream and said "Yes, Ms. Medley!" Ms. Medley was trying to tell her that they wanted her down at the office.

As she walked down the hallway after leaving the classroom, she heard a voice singing LL Cool J's song "Big Ole Butt" with the name in the song replaced with hers "Shayna's got a big ole butt, so I'm leaving you." She turned around and saw that it was Key. He smiled and called her over. She turned her head back in the direction she was walking and told him that she had places to be. He started following her and told her that the only place she needed to be was with him. She ignored him and kept walking. When he caught up to her he said "You're going to the office, right? They called you down there?" Shayna said "Maybe! Why?" Key explained that it was what he was trying to tell her. He was the one that set it up to have her called out of class.

Key had gotten one of the students that worked in the office to send a message to the class with a stamped signature from the principal. She asked him how he pulled it off. He didn't tell her how, he just told her that as much time as he spent in the office, he managed to make friends. Shayna told him to stop wasting her time as she turned around and began walking back to her class. He asked her why she was going back to class when she wasn't even learning anything. She told him that not everyone made it a habit to cut class like him. Key's logic was that with a little over a month of school left, teachers couldn't possibly be teaching anything of significance. Shayna asked him if he had ever heard of regent exams. Regents are the exams required to receive a diploma or matriculate in the state of New York.

Shayna was finally back at her class and about to walk in. Key told her to hold on for a quick second as he took something out of his pocket. She kept ignoring him and didn't turn around to face him, so he put his arm around her head placing whatever he was holding in her face. Shayna jumped back and asked him what his problem was. He told her to just look at what it was.

She took it out of his hand and saw that it was two tickets to an upcoming Nas concert. She was excited, but didn't want to show it. He asked her if she was interested in going with him.

Shayna loved Nas, but she gave the tickets back and told Key that she would think about it. Key asked for her number so he could call her and ask her as the date drew closer. Shayna told him that he wasn't getting her number, especially that easily, but she would take his instead and let him know. Key wrote his number down on a piece of paper. Shayna took it and put it in her pocket. She wanted to know how he managed to get those tickets. Nas was hot and riding off of the success of his debut album *Illmatic* the year before so she knew that they had to be expensive. Key told her that he had connections that got him the tickets. Shayna told him that he seemed to have a lot of connections. He laughed and said that connections made the world go around. He started to walk off and told her that he would see her later. Shayna went back into her classroom. She wanted to go to that concert badly.

Shayna had this starry eyed look on her face throughout the rest of class. She had thoughts running through her mind about technically being serenaded on the bus earlier that morning, the Nas tickets, and the stunt Key pulled to get her out of class. She didn't want to show interest in him, but she was secretly starting to consider it. While her plan was to keep her emotions to herself, they were starting to show. For example, class was over and Ms. Medley was trying to get her attention again as she daydreamed. She eventually snapped out of it and looked around noticing that everybody was gone and the next class was starting to walk in. She looked at Ms. Medley and smiled, then apologized as she collected her books and made her way out of the classroom.

DARRYL'S CHIP

Later that day, Shayna and I were at practice. We had Penn Relays in Philadelphia that coming weekend. Penn Relays is a big track tournament/showcase. Runners ranging from high school to the professional level participate in it annually. There are big name schools and agents watching so you really can't lose if you have a great overall performance. Every year around that time, Coach Robbins would intensify our training. It was no different that year.

During practice, Shayna told me about Key getting her called out of class. I told her that he was crazy and that I still didn't trust him, but Shayna wasn't hearing me. This interest she seemed to have been developing for Key was evidently growing. For example, she told me that I may have seen it as crazy, but she saw it as an act of love, and love makes you do crazy things. I stopped her to ask what she meant by love. I knew she couldn't seriously believe that she was in love. Her response was "I never said I was in love, but Key might be."

I wasn't going to argue that point because Shayna was obviously in denial. She didn't have to necessarily be in love, but she clearly had feelings for him and wouldn't admit it. She made it seem like there were only feelings on his end. Before she went any further, I reminded her about being in that vulnerable stage that one goes through after getting out of a relationship. She needed to be cautious. Coach Robbins called us over. As we were jogging over to the rest of the team, I told Shayna that I hope she didn't end up learning the hard way.

Coach Robbins gave those of us who were selected to compete at Penn Relays our event assignments. From that day on we practiced intensely in those specific events. Shayna got her usual events and I got a spot as an alternate. Being an alternate had its perks; a free trip to Philly and good times with the team. Practice was over, we packed our stuff and we all went home.

The bus ride home felt so relaxing after that strenuous practice. As we were walking up our block, we noticed someone sitting on Shayna's stoop. Once we got close enough we realized that it was Darryl. We both stopped at the bottom of the steps. Shayna asked him "May I help you with something?" Darryl started walking down the steps toward us and told her that he was there to apologize. Shayna asked him if her mother knew he was there. He admitted that Ms. Kim did not know. Shayna told him that it would be best if he kept it that way by going home. We started walking up her front steps. Darryl began pleading with her to work things out, but Shayna didn't even look his direction. He ran up a few stairs behind us and grabbed Shayna's arm demanding in a loud tone that she listen to him. I immediately smacked his hand off of her arm while yelling "GET OFF OF HER!" Darryl backed up and said that he didn't want any trouble.

Shawn Sr. came to the door and asked if everything was okay. Shayna told Shawn that Darryl was losing his mind. Shawn told us to get inside. We walked in and Shawn closed the door behind us, he stayed outside. He told Darryl "Darryl, I don't know what your problem is, but I don't want you back at this house or anywhere near Shayna. Do I make myself clear?" Darryl looked at him and said "Crystal clear!" He then walked away while staring Shawn down. Shawn stared back at him until he was out of sight.

Ms. Kim got on the phone right away and called Darryl's mom to voice her disgust with Darryl's recent behavior. Once they greeted each other, Ms. Kim began to go into what her issue was. Darryl's mom immediately cut her off with a sense of shock in her voice asking her if Darryl was still there. It turns out that she had not seen Darryl for almost a day and was worried. He went out the previous night and never returned home. As Shawn was walking back in the house, Ms. Kim asked him if Darryl was still outside. He told her that Darryl had already left. Ms. Kim relayed the message to Darryl's mom. Darryl's mom told Ms. Kim that she had to go. By having an idea of Darryl's location, she had to go find him. She had some police officers she knew looking for him throughout the day, but they weren't able to find him. Ms. Kim told her that she could call her if she needed help. Ms. Kim told Shawn Sr. to head out in the direction that Darryl walked to see if he could spot him.

Darryl must have run or walked quickly because it was almost as if he had vanished. They searched all night and could not find him. His mom was now at Shayna's with an officer. I was on the phone with Shayna; she was letting me hear everything that was going on. From what I could gather, they were telling the cop about the last time they had seen him or heard from him before we saw him that day on the stoop. Ms. Kim was telling Darryl's mom about the phone conversation the night before. Shayna was getting another call and told me to hold on. When she clicked back over she told me that it was Darryl and she didn't know what she should do. I figured it was important to keep him on the phone so I told her to talk to him and call me back.

When she clicked over, she asked Darryl where he was and told him that his mom was stressing herself out over his absence. Darryl told her that he was aware, and although he didn't want to hurt his mother, he needed a way to finally gain respect. Shayna asked him what he wanted respect for. Darryl started complaining about how he was a laughing stock in the streets. Shayna signaled to her mom to pick up the other phone. Ms. Kim put it on speaker and he could be heard by everyone. Shayna asked him why he was so concerned about the streets. Darryl believed that in his neighborhood, if you weren't respected, you were just a punk taking up space. He said "I got your mom calling me a fake thug and fake pimp. What does that tell you, Shayna?" Shayna told him that she agreed and that he was obviously mimicking behavior he saw on TV. She then asked him if he had a desire to be those things. He had no answer.

In an attempt to finally get a location on him, Shayna asked him where he was. Darryl asked her if she thought he was stupid enough to disclose his location, and that's when it hit him. He asked Shayna why she was so willing to converse after clearly stating that she no longer wanted to talk to him. Shayna said it was because she was worried about his mom. Darryl asked her if she was only concerned about his mom. Shayna told him that his mother's well-being was most important. Darryl became agitated; "SO I DO ALL OF THIS AND YOU'RE STILL NOT EVEN CONCERNED?" Shayna told him that she didn't ask him to do anything, and she was not going to argue with him. Darryl continued to rant before eventually being cut off by his mom. Confused about hearing her voice at Shayna's house, he realized that he was more than likely being heard by everyone. That got him even more agitated. "SO I'M JUST A JOKE TO EVERYBODY? WELL WE'LL SEE WHO LAUGHS LAST." His words were followed by a click as he hung up the phone.

The cop told Darryl's mom that she may have set him off by blowing the cover they had listening in on the conversation. Darryl's mom began to cry; not because of what the cop told her, but because she missed her son. She was now even more worried about him. The officer called the operator to see if they could track recent calls made to the house and their locations. The operator informed them that the call was made from Queens, New York. It was rather peculiar because Darryl's whole life was in Brooklyn. He didn't really know anybody in Queens.

Meanwhile in Queens, Darryl was lurking a few random streets. He was fuming with anger and frustration. He seemed to be serious about getting this supposed "respect and last laugh". He came across a liquor store with that unstable mindset and a chip on his shoulder. He walked in and browsed for a little while. The store clerk kept an eye on him the whole time. Darryl noticed that he was being watched and it only added to his already angered demeanor. He yelled at the clerk "YO SON! WHAT YOU LOOKIN AT? DO WE HAVE A PROBLEM?" The store clerk put his hands up as if to say he didn't want any problems. Darryl stared him down for a second, then continued to walk around the store. A woman stepped to the register to ring her items up. The clerk's attention shifted to the paying customer. Darryl browsed some more.

Not too long after, Darryl began to slowly approach the front of the store. The clerk began to watch him again. Darryl noticed and approached the register yelling "YO! MY MAN! WHAT DID I TELL YOU ABOUT LOOKING AT ME?" The female customer turned around to see an angry Darryl walking up behind her and stepped out of his way. Darryl told her she was wise to move. He was now as close to the counter as he could get. He put his hands on the counter and told the clerk to explain why he kept watching him. The clerk looked at him with a blank stare. He apparently didn't know much English so he was very scared.

Darryl grabbed him by his shirt collar and pulled him closer, then pulled out a switch blade and put it to the man's neck. He told the man "Explain yourself now if you value your life." The female customer suddenly yelled "STOP!", and pepper sprayed Darryl. Some of it got into the clerk's eyes as well. Darryl screamed as he vigorously rubbed his eyes. He tried to make his way to the exit, but not being able to see caused him to walk into a few stocked shelves breaking a number of bottles. The clerk also fell to the floor holding his eyes in pain. The female customer grabbed a bottle and struck Darryl over the head knocking him unconscious, then called the police. An undercover squad car parked not too far away pulled up. It had been placed on the block for numerous problems at that particular liquor store.

The search for Darryl was no longer necessary; he made the task a lot easier. Later that night, his mom visited him at the precinct where he was being held. He was brought up on charges of assault, vandalism, and attempted murder. His mom was informed that his bail would be set at $100,000. She didn't have the money, and she didn't have much to use as collateral. Darryl had to suffer with sitting in jail until his trial date. The date they gave him was three weeks from that night.

The next day at school, Shayna and I were in the class that we had together before lunch. She was telling me about how everything turned out with Darryl. I asked her if she was okay. She just shook her head and said she could not be concerned with him or any of his antics. She felt that Darryl needed help and being locked up may provide that help. I was no fan of Darryl, but jail was no joke. It's even worse when you do not genuinely live the lifestyle that Darryl was portraying. Surprisingly, Shayna was taking it a lot better than I thought she would. I guess she really was completely over him.

PENN RELAYS

After days of tiring and extended practices to prepare for Penn Relays, we had finally made it to the day of departure. We were excused from class on that Friday and took a charter bus to Philly. Everyone was excited to participate, but more excited for the vacation opportunity. On the bus ride we played games, cracked jokes, listened to music, or slept. I asked Shayna if she had heard anything from Key in the past few days; I still couldn't believe the stunt he pulled to get her out of class. Shayna said that other than the bus, he wasn't really around in the locations where he would usually bother us. I thought it was kind of odd, but then again, Key was odd.

We finally arrived at the hotel. We were staying at a hotel a block away from where the events were being held. The events were the next day so we had a day to ourselves in which we were allowed to roam free, to a degree of course. Some of us decided to browse what our part of the city had to offer. The only things we knew about Philly were the references Will Smith made on *Fresh Prince,* and things we saw the previous times we were there. With that in mind, we decided to hit up a spot that sold cheesesteaks. There were about ten of us from the team looking for a cheesesteak spot. We preferred to have a large crowd since we didn't know anyone, and no one knew us.

We had one teammate that had been to Philly on a few occasions to visit family, so he was more accustomed to spots that were safe to try. The only problem was that all of the cheesesteak spots he was familiar with were in South Philly. We were in West Philly so we were forced to take the city bus. When we finally got there, he led the way while we followed and looked around taking in the sights.

The place was pretty nice. It was well lit and appeared to be pretty clean. There was somewhat of a crowd, but it wasn't too bad. Besides, we traveled a long way on the bus so we weren't going to let that deter us. It took some time for all of us to get our orders, but when we finally did, we got two tables and sat back and relaxed. That didn't last long. Before we knew it, someone was yelling from across the room. Not only were they yelling, they were yelling at us. "IS THAT JACKIE ROBINSON HIGH? WHAT'S UP, FAMILY?" It sounded exactly like Key, but I didn't turn around to check because I didn't want to believe it. It just wouldn't make sense for him to be all the way in Philly and at the same exact restaurant. I didn't have to turn around because he made his way over to us and greeted everyone. When he got to me he said "Charmaine, I want to thank you for bringing my wife with you." Shayna looked at him with a disgusted expression mid bite and told him that he was killing her appetite. Key responded by blowing her a kiss.

If there was one thing I knew about Shayna, it was how she responded to the comments of fools. She usually wouldn't dignify comments like Key's with a verbal response. That was new to me. Edward from our team asked Key what he was doing in Philly. Key explained that he had a show that night at a club and invited all of us to watch him perform. Edward asked how we were going to get in being that we were under age. Key told us that as long as we were with him, we were okay. At that moment I reminded everybody that we had a curfew. That seemed to have killed their excitement leaving them all with disappointed facial expressions. Key told them to let him know if they change their minds, and then went back to his table.

We were all done with our food so we began to gather our things to leave. It was getting dark and we couldn't miss our 9:30pm curfew. Curfew was three hours away, but the bus ride back to the hotel was going to take about an hour. When we were walking out, Key left the group at his table and followed us. He met us out in front of the restaurant and asked where we were headed. Edward told him that we were on our way back to our hotel because we had Penn Relays the next day. Key told us that he hoped we did well and asked if we were sure we didn't want to chill with him that night. He also offered to get us back before curfew. We all replied no, but thanked him. All of us refused except Shayna surprisingly. Her argument was "If they have cars, that means no need for bus fare and we can leave anytime we want." Then again, it wasn't too surprising with the way her behavior toward Key had apparently been shifting.

I pulled Shayna to the side and had to tell her that she was risking not suiting up if Coach Robbins found out. It wasn't only a matter of making curfew; it was a matter of sticking with the team. She argued that we were in Philly, so we might as well

58

take in as much as we could. Key agreed that it was a good point. I turned to Key and reminded him that I wasn't talking to him. I turned back to Shayna and asked her how she expected someone from the same place we were from to give us a tour of the same place he was visiting. I also had to remind her that we did not know the guys he was with. She couldn't answer. I wasn't going to let her possibly mess up her chance of performing the next day which could in turn affect her possible future. She looked disappointed, but finally agreed. We parted ways with Key and made our way back to the bus stop.

Halfway through the bus ride back, Shayna looked semi-disappointed. She got over it before we got back to the hotel. It was about 8:15pm when we were getting back to our rooms. I decided that the shenanigans had gone on long enough. Shayna was sitting on her bed going through her bag. I sat down on my bed and asked her what had gotten into her. She decided to play dumb and act like she didn't know what I was talking about. I really wasn't in the mood to play around so I just came out and asked her what I really wanted to know; "Are you interested in Key?" She looked me in my eyes and finally admitted that she was interested in him. I told her that I didn't care that she was interested in him; I just wanted to know why. She told me that she didn't know if it was because she had just gotten out of a relationship like I theorized, if it was his confidence she was attracted to, or if it was the things he had been doing lately to get her attention. Nothing he was doing changed my mind. I still thought he was rude, disrespectful, and didn't deserve her. I can only hope that she did not act solely off of emotion.

The next day we were up early getting ready to head out and prepare for the day. Coach Robbins told all of us to meet in her room. When we got there she told us that we didn't have much time, but she wanted to make sure everyone was accounted for before we boarded the bus. She also had a surprise for all of us. She directed us to a bunch of sneaker boxes in the corner. The athletic department bought the team new sneakers customized with the school colors. Everybody was excited about the surprise, but we had to immediately get to the bus before we started running late.

We arrived at the university where everything was being held and immediately hit the track to warm up. The day was moving by rather quickly. A few of our teammates had their events; some performed better than others. The time had come for Shayna's 100m event. Shayna took her position on the block, and I took my position at the side of the finish line to wait for her to come in. The runners took their marks and were off. The other runners were almost as great as Shayna. Shayna usually burned runners with no problem, but a few of them were neck and neck with her for a quarter of the race. Halfway through the race, she managed to find another gear and create some distance. She was approaching the line and it was now just a matter of finishing strong. When she got to the line, she led with her head and pulled off the win by about a second and a half to qualify for the next round.

I met her at the line to celebrate. She was happy, but didn't like the fact that the race was that close. Knowing Shayna, she only used it to fuel her fire. We went back to our team's meeting spot. We had some time before Shayna's next round so we decided to relax and take pointers from Coach Robbins. Shayna was pacing back and forth throughout Coach Robbins' lecture. Coach Robbins asked her why she felt the need to walk around while she was talking. Shayna told her that it was the new sneakers; she was trying to break them in. Coach asked her if they felt uncomfortable during her last race. Shayna didn't pay much attention to the feel of the shoe as she was running, but since Coach mentioned it, she agreed that it may have been a factor. She decided to change back to her regular running sneakers.

More time had passed and Shayna's next race was approaching. One of our male teammates had placed first in the men's high jump. Shayna was heading over to the blocks to get ready for her next race with a look of focus and determination. She had on her usual sneakers and did her usual pre-race routine. The runners took their marks, got set, and took off at the sound of the gun. That race was a completely different story; Shayna took off and couldn't be touched. She needed to place at least third in that round to make it to the finals. She placed first with a significant margin of victory. She looked a lot happier after that race. There was no time for her to rest because she was running anchor in the 4x100m relay coming up after the next two races.

We made our way back to our team's huddle area where our teammate Denise was on one knee holding on to one of the bleacher barricades. She was apparently sick and had gotten weak over the course of the day. I asked Coach what was wrong with her. Coach said that she wasn't feeling well and had the symptoms of food poisoning. The only thing I could think of it possibly being was the food we had the night before. We all got different meals so it could've been what she ordered. The problem with this situation was that she was the third leg of the relay team. Coach Robbins looked at me and told me to warm up because it didn't look like Denise would be ready. I was placed at first leg and the original first and second legs were moved up in position.

We took our places on the track. To be honest, I was nervous. We trained for any possible changes so it wasn't like I was in foreign territory. However, the competition wasn't the same as when we went up against the local or rival schools, this was technically world competition. I tried my hardest to put those negative thoughts out of my mind as I took my place at the starting line. When the gun went off, we took off. I wasn't performing well enough to maintain a pace with the other runners, but I wasn't falling too far behind either. The time was coming for me to pass the baton. That was all I needed to do and I would have done my part.

I approached our second leg, Vanessa. I yelled "STICK!" as it is customary to do in order to let the next leg know that you're approaching with the baton. As I reached her, there was a bit of a miscommunication. I passed it, but as she began to grip it, it slipped off of her finger tips. The baton dropped causing her to have to turn around and pick it up. She lost all of her momentum. In that brief moment we also lost our third place position. Vanessa tried to regain momentum, but in the process, the fifth place runner closed in on her position. She pumped as hard as she could, but it seemed like she was now running to not lose instead of running to win. She lost control as fifth place entered a tie with her. They approached the third legs at the same time and passed the batons. We then gave up fifth place coming around the corner.

Shayna was waiting in great anticipation for the baton. The third legs were closing in on the anchors. We finally got the baton in Shayna's hand and she took off running as hard as she could. With 100m left, she had a lot of work to do if she wanted to get first. She managed to reclaim fifth place. That must have boosted her confidence because she picked up an immense amount of speed and burned past fourth. Shayna had about fifty meters to go, but the first place position only had about twenty meters remaining. Shayna closed in on third and eventually took it over. She had everyone in the stadium on their feet in amazement as to what they were witnessing. As she closed in on twenty meters, first place crossed the finish line. Second place was not too far ahead. Looking at their positions, Shayna looked as if she could possibly catch her. She came close, but she crossed the finish line just a little under a second after her. We had to settle for third place.

Third place wasn't too bad considering what Shayna did to get us there. She probably got more attention from reporters, onlookers, and scouts than anyone. We walked back to our team's spot to be greeted by Coach Robbins clapping and telling us that we did a good job. Shayna had the final round of her 100m events later on. During the races and events that took place before it, we took advantage of the opportunity to cool down and catch our breaths. Denise still wasn't feeling good and Vanessa was beating herself up for dropping the baton. I really couldn't think of anything to say to her. Coach intervened by telling her to kill the self-pity party and to get her mind back on track.

The last few races had finally passed and Shayna's race was slowly approaching. She was in a corner by herself with her headphones on, eyes closed and mellowing out to whatever she was listening to. The rest of us were watching the other events until it was time. The time for the race had finally come. Coach Robbins tapped Shayna's shoulder. Shayna opened her eyes and got up. She took off her head phones and warm ups and started walking to the starting blocks. I made my way to the finish line. This was it, the main reason Shayna was called to Penn Relays. The runners did their pre-race routines, and then took their positions. They took their marks, got set, and they were off.

Shayna took an early lead and had this look of wanting to destroy everything in her path. She was moving faster than I had ever seen her move. She maintained her lead and crossed the finish line first, but seemed to have pulled something right after.

I walked over to her to congratulate and hug her, but her facial expression let me know that she was in agonizing pain. She was holding the back of her left thigh and was barely able to move. She used me for support and we made our way back to the team. People in the stands and on the track were cheering her on as we walked back. We even saw one big sign in the crowd that read "JACKIE ROBINSON HIGH! FLY, SHAYNA! FLY!" I was impressed at the fact that Jackie Robinson had fans on hand, but that was before I saw who it was. It was Key with that group of guys he was with at the cheesesteak spot. I pointed him out to Shayna. She saw him with the sign and smiled. However, she was more focused on her injury. One of our teammates walked over to help me get Shayna back over to our huddle. That was it for our trip to Pennsylvania. We had the rest of the night to hang out there, but we were scheduled to leave in the morning.

The following morning had arrived. We were all getting our bags downstairs to the bus and I was helping Shayna get around. She was on crutches for the majority of the time. Her injury turned out to be a pulled hamstring. We were finally on the bus to leave. Shayna had a whole two seats to herself; I sat across the aisle from her. For the majority of the ride, we talked about random stuff. Eventually, I changed the subject to Key's latest stunt. I told her that I can see that he was seriously trying to get her attention. Shayna tried to play dumb again and act like she didn't know what I was talking about, so I called her out for being bashful. She turned her head and was smiling hard. I just rolled my eyes at her.

I was curious as to how far she was willing to go. Although she admitted to being interested in him, she was not too eager to let him know. The only thing left for her to do was to stay tuned to see what he would do next to get her attention. I was keeping note of all of his moves. Between getting Shayna pulled out of class, his freestyle serenade, and his sign in the stands at Penn Relays, I would say my favorite would have to be getting her pulled out of class. It took a lot of muscle, energy, guts, and creativity, but that's beside the point. Shayna's response to my question regarding how far she was willing to take it was "We'll just have to see."

CHANGE OF SCENERY

We finally returned home from our trip. Shayna's mom was at the school waiting to pick us up. She was already aware of all of Shayna's accomplishments as well as the injury; they kept in touch over the course of the trip. It felt good to be back in my own space, but I wasn't looking forward to going back to school the next day. I had a bunch of homework that I put off.

The following day at school, Shayna needed help getting around on her crutches so I helped her from class to class. I was excused from being late to my classes because of it. On our way to first period we noticed a few prom posters that were put up by the student government. The prom was a little over three weeks away. Shayna asked me who I was going with. I didn't give the idea of prom a lot of thought so going with someone wasn't on my mind at the time. Shayna hadn't given it full consideration either, but I had an idea of who she would possibly end up going with. It was more than likely going to be Key if his advances persisted; Shayna knew it too. We finally made it to her class.

At lunch, Shayna and I ate in Ms. Mims' classroom. As we ate, we spoke to Ms. Mims about our previous weekend in Pennsylvania. Ms. Mims ran track when she was in high school and always commended Shayna for her skills. She shared stories with us about when she ran, and her trips to Penn Relays. We told her about all of the experiences we encountered while there. Ms. Mims told us that all of her success in track & field stemmed from motivation to get to Penn Relays. It wasn't so much to participate in the events, she just wanted to experience some place away from where she grew up. She said "I love Baltimore, but growing up in that city can be stressful. If we had an opportunity to get out for even a small vacation, we usually took it. A change of scenery was necessary and always welcome."

I was curious as to how she ended up in New York so I asked her what brought her here. At that moment, Key and Intellek walked by the classroom. Ms. Mims stopped in the middle of telling us how she ended up in New York and yelled "KEITH!" They both walked back to the door. Key said "Hey, Ms. Mims! How's everything?" That was the first time Shayna and I heard his real name; I guess we just never bothered to ask. Ms. Mims told him to not play dumb and asked him for his weekly report. Shayna and I gave each other a look of confusion. We had no idea of what a weekly report was. Ms. Mims apparently had a close bond with Key. She had a growing concern with his behavior and the fact that he might not graduate on time. Key had taken an English class with her when he was a freshman; she had a poetry unit and his work impressed her the most. She saw potential in his writing and she felt that it could take him further in life. However, even back then Key was not a disciplined student.

Eventually we learned that a weekly report was homework from all of Key's classes. Ms. Mims would check to make sure he completed all of it, and stayed in contact with his teachers to make sure that he wasn't being disruptive. The idea was working out pretty well in the beginning, but it began to fizzle out. Key didn't have a report for Ms. Mims that day. It was actually the third consecutive week that he had not presented one to her. She asked him if he really wanted her help, or better yet, if he even wanted to graduate. He told her that he of course wanted to graduate. She asked him why he insisted on not doing work and being disruptive in some of his classes if he really wanted to graduate. He asked her if he could talk to her about it at another time. Ms. Mims told him that he may, but she was very disappointed in him. Key greeted us and asked Shayna how her leg was feeling. Ms. Mims cut him off and told him that if he didn't have the time to discuss his future with her, then he wasn't allowed to talk to anyone else. He walked out and met Intellek in the hall and they went on about their business.

Key and Intellek made their way to the gym to play ball. As they were walking, Key had this look of disappointment on his face. Intellek noticed the look and asked him what his problem was. Key told him that it was nothing, but in the back of his mind he was thinking about Ms. Mims and how he had let her down. He knew that there weren't many people that believed he could succeed, but Ms. Mims was one that did and he hated to disappoint her. She always told Key that his success was dependent on letting go of some of his negative mindsets, people around him, and other factors that were hindering his growth. However, Key's behavior was a prime example of bad habits being difficult to break.

A little under an hour had passed and lunch was almost over. Shayna and I started walking to our classes to avoid the after lunch rush of students in the hallway. On our way there, we saw Key walking back towards Ms. Mims' classroom. He didn't even look our direction which was a first. He looked like he was focused on something so we didn't bother to stop him.

When Key finally got back to Ms. Mims' classroom, he knocked to get her attention. Ms. Mims said "Come on in" as she was sorting papers for her incoming class. Key walked in and had a seat in the front of the classroom. The first thing he did was apologize for not having a weekly report to show her for the past few weeks. She told him that he could apologize all he wanted, but it wasn't going to make the work that he was supposed to do just suddenly appear. Key had no response for that. Ms. Mims expressed to him that it hurt her to see someone with so much potential and skill allow it to waste away. It hurt her because she could see the road he was heading down and knew that reality would hurt him even worse once it actually hit. Key told her that he understood what she was saying; it was just that the things being taught in his classes did not interest him. That would usually cause him to get bored and respond negatively. Ms. Mims understood his outlook, but still stressed the fact that his education was necessary to progress. Therefore, unless he had a backup plan to be successful, he had to suck it up and move on.

Key looked at Ms. Mims and told her that he remembered being in her English class when he was a freshman and how she

70

would always compliment his poetry. Ms. Mims actually still had some of his work and would use it for new students each year. She wanted to know what his point was. Key reminded her that she mentioned the need of a backup plan and told her that poetry was his backup plan. He then explained that he had been using his ability to write and manipulate words to establish a career in hip-hop. Ms. Mims took a deep breath and looked at Key. Another second or two passed before she finally said "Okay, let's hear it." Key asked her what she was talking about. Ms. Mims wanted to hear his plan, then she wanted him to recite two poems for her incoming class following lunch.

Breaking down the plan was important in Ms. Mims' eyes; but she was more concerned about why he decided to go the route he was going. In her mind, he was simply settling for a life of being an entertainer. She looked at it as settling because she knew he was capable of a lot more, but he would not apply himself. He told her the plan consisted of him acquiring a manager which he had done, getting shows scheduled for him so that he could gain exposure which he had done, and elevating from there which he planned to do.

Ms. Mims asked him why he chose to do that instead of sticking with basketball or studying more. He claimed that his grades were not good enough for basketball, and studying was useless because he wasn't learning anything. Ms. Mims told him that she heard a completely different story from his coach. She heard that he was meeting the minimum requirements to play basketball, but he was always skipping practices so he was dismissed from the team. She tried to get through to Keith another way; "Keith, when I tell you that you are one of the few students I see potential in, I'm serious. I would go to those games and be utterly impressed with your skills. You had to know that I would be concerned when someone I knew personally was not only absent from the starting lineup, but not even in the gym." Key asked her why she didn't just ask him. Ms. Mims told him that he should have had more respect for himself to not do something that would get him kicked off of the team in the first place. She also explained that she expected him to be a man and be honest.

The bell rang and her students were on the way, some were already outside of her door. Key had one more question for Ms. Mims; "I see your point Ms. Mims, but the reality of the situation is that graduation is in four weeks. All of the potential in the world won't bring my grades back to minimum standing, not to mention already being kicked out of Mr. Johnson's class. How in the world am I going to pull that off?" Ms. Mims asked him if he really wanted to graduate. He gave her a look of confusion, and then told her of course he did. She told him to change his expression because his behavior up to that point said otherwise. The rest of her class had finally made it and were almost seated. Ms. Mims told Key that she would try to pull some strings with the classes he was at most risk in, and she would see if she could get him back into Mr. Johnson's class.

However, she informed him that the part about Mr. Johnson's class would be a long shot. All he had to do in return was share two of his poems with the class. He thanked her and was beginning to feel confident about his situation.

Later on that day we had track practice. Shayna was excused due to her injury so she sat on the side. The whole purpose of the practice was to discuss our last two track meets of the season. One was scheduled for that coming Friday, and the other was going to take place the following week. Coach Robbins asked me to participate in practice as a stand in for Shayna. She just needed an extra body on the field to provide the full feel of the events. Practice was underway, but it wasn't too demanding. We did our stretches, warm-ups, and finally, our simulations for the races. While we were doing our simulations, I could see Shayna sitting on the bleachers watching all of us. We were practicing our relays, I ran the first leg. When I came around the bend to pass the baton, I could see Shayna still sitting there, but this time someone was walking up behind her. After getting a better look, I realized it was Key.

Key must have put two and two together and figured that Shayna was going to be sitting out of practice that day. I guess he saw it as the perfect opportunity to finally talk to her one on one because she wouldn't be able to run or walk away. Key snuck up behind Shayna and put his hands over her eyes while saying "What's up, gorgeous?" Shayna grabbed his pinky finger and bent it back. Key started wincing and told her to let go. She looked up and saw that it was Key and let him go. She should have continued to bend it. Shayna told him that he should be happy that she didn't break it, and to never put his hands on her face again. You can't blame her; there was no telling where his hands had been.

The pain must have worn off of Key's pinky because he wasn't holding it anymore. He finally took a seat next to Shayna on the bleachers and asked her how she was doing. She told him that she was good. He looked at her crutches and inquired about her injury. She told him that the injury wasn't that serious. He tried to ask her how it happened, but she looked at him and asked "Key, did you come over here to interview me or something? You joined the newspaper club and working on an article?" Key leaned back in shock and asked if he caught her at a bad time. He explained that she was coming off as if she wanted to fight, and she was beginning to answer questions with questions. She told him that she was fine.

There actually was something going on with Shayna. Every year around that time, she would experience an inconsistency in her monthly cycle due to her excessive workouts with track. It made her irritable. She was scared out of her mind the first time it happened, but soon learned to cope with it after learning it was temporary. Shayna directed her attention at Key again and asked what his real reason was for being at our practice. Key told her that he wanted to talk to her, but she had made that a little difficult. She asked him what he wanted to talk about. He told her that it depended on if she was willing to listen or if she was just simply going to hear him. Shayna told him that listening or hearing depended on what he said when he finally decided to speak. Key replied "Touché! Okay Shayna, here it is, marry me and I won't take no for an answer." Shayna rolled her eyes and told Key to get away from her. Key told her that if she didn't want that, he would settle for having her as a prom date instead. Her reply to that was "No!" He asked her why not. She told him that it was because she wasn't going. Key asked her again, but that time he said please. She looked at him and paused for a moment before saying "No!"

I was lining up for my next simulation race at practice. Key had so much persistence in his approach, but something seemed different about him throughout that particular attempt to get with Shayna. He was still acting foolish, but a small bit of him seemed a little more mature. Shayna interrupted Key's plea for a prom date by asking if he was even graduating the following month like he was supposed to. Key told her not to worry about that, and that it was being handled. Shayna told him to not try to regulate what she worried about, and that it was her right to ask those questions. Key explained that he was going to graduate; it was just going to take some work. Shayna rolled her eyes and fixed them back on the track.

Key decided to change his approach by asking her if she would go with him if he was graduating. Shayna told him that she probably would not, but if he was, she would need some proof. Key claimed that he could acquire proof, and then asked if they had a deal. Shayna told him to show her and she would give him an answer. Key, with a confused look on his face, asked her what difference it made. Shayna told him her answer was the only difference maker on the whole matter. He didn't have any response to that so he told her he would get the proof.

I finished my race and decided to head back over to them to see what was going on. Key was just getting up to leave. I asked him "Leaving so soon?" He looked at me and said that from the looks of things, it wasn't soon enough. Shayna told him that he was begging for "No!" to be her final answer. He changed his tone quickly and greeted me properly, then left. I asked Shayna what he wanted; she filled me in. I asked her what she would do if he was actually able to provide proof. Shayna said that she would see, but she wasn't worried because being able to graduate with his academic status wouldn't be possible.

MEET THE PARENTS

About two weeks had passed. Senior regent exams were complete, and everyone was getting ready for prom. Track season ended, and Shayna had one of her best performances at our final track meet. She chose a great night to do it because there were a few scouts in the stands. In the midst of all that was going on, we arrived at the scheduled date for Darryl's trial. Shayna, her mom, and Shawn accompanied Darryl's mom to the trial.

From the looks of the situation, Darryl was going to need Johnnie Cochran to win his case. Everything in the case pointed toward him being the aggressor and never being provoked. It didn't help that the prosecution also had surveillance footage. Darryl walked into the courtroom in his inmate jumpsuit and handcuffs. He didn't even look into the audience, he was too ashamed. The judge read him the list of charges. The charges he was facing had changed from the initial ones he had received. He was now facing assault with a weapon, vandalism, and damage of property in addition to other minor charges. The female customer served as a witness and confirmed everything that he was charged with. When it was all said and done, the judge sentenced him to twenty years in prison with a chance for probation. Darryl's mother broke down and fainted. Shawn had to support her limp body.

Darryl was truly an idiot for doing what he did. It was hard to hear that he was going to be locked up, but it was harder to feel sorry for him. Shayna just sat there with a look of disappointment. When they got home, Shayna called me and told me how everything played out. She seemed rather indifferent about the whole situation. I don't think it had fully hit her yet. I could only imagine that when it did, it was going to hit her hard.

The next day we were on the bus on our way to school. For the most part, Shayna was behaving in a normal manner. Just like clockwork, Key and the stooges got on the bus not too long after. They scoped us out and made their way to the back where we were sitting. Key sat near Shayna and reminded her that prom was the following week. He wanted to know if she had made up her mind. Shayna looked at him and told him that she changed her mind, and that she and I would be going together instead. Key looked perplexed. Stack, with a more surprised look on his face asked "Oh! You two get down like that?" I gave him a look of disgust and told him to shut up. Key asked Shayna why she had him do so much to graduate and prove himself. Shayna told him that she did it because he desperately needed an incentive to get out of high school.

Key did in fact take steps toward graduating on time despite his current grades and no longer being enrolled in Mr. Johnson's class. He was actually doing his work. He also followed through on a deal he made with Ms. Mims to visit his teachers during lunch and after school to get extra credit. Ms.

Mims was even able to pull a few strings and get him in a summer school class with Mr. Johnson to make up that credit. All things considered, if he was able to keep up with all of the extra work, it was going to be enough to meet the minimum graduation requirement. Ms. Mims must've really had some juice to pull all of that off. A lot of it was due to a few of the male teachers having a crush on her.

Key was trying to gather his thoughts. He asked Shayna again if she was really serious. Shayna claimed that she was very serious. I could see in Key's facial expression that he was beginning to get upset. He asked her "So that's what you do? You lie?" Shayna looked back at him and said "Excuse me? For your information, I never lied. I said maybe." He asked her how long she knew she was going to say no. Shayna told him that she actually gave the idea some serious consideration. I gave Shayna a look that meant stop playing with his emotions. She got the message and toned it down. I felt sorry for him knowing how hard he had worked for that date with Shayna. I decided to tell him that Shayna and I were not going to the prom as a couple. Stack looked disappointed; he was a pervert.

Shayna asked him for the proof that he had been doing all of this work. Key pulled a paper out of his bag; it was the weekly report that he was scheduled to submit to Ms. Mims at lunch that day. It showed a few of the extra projects and assignments that he had completed. Shayna looked it over and asked him if he was officially graduating with us. He told her that it wouldn't be official until he completed his summer course with Mr. Johnson. We were approaching the school. Shayna handed the paper back to him. A brief moment passed and she said "Purple!" Key looked at her confused and said "Excuse me?" Shayna said "In the event that we go to prom, I would like the color we wear to be purple." Key leaned back in his seat and asked if she was serious. Shayna told him that she felt he had earned it. Key got up from his seat and ran to the front of the bus, then back to his seat. The bus driver told him to knock it off or he would be put off of the bus. Shayna tried to fight a smile that was obviously forming.

At that moment, Stack moved a little closer to me and suggested that he and I go together and make it a double date. I looked at him and told him that the only way he could take me to prom is if he had a license to chauffeur me, and if he was someone that I actually wanted to go with. He moved away from me and claimed that he didn't want to go with me in the first place. When we got to the school, we dispersed into our own individual directions. Key was ahead of all of us trying to get to his class. I couldn't tell if it was because of his new school routine or if he was just excited about Shayna finally agreeing to go to prom with him.

At lunch time Key went to Ms. Mims' classroom to turn in his report. She was impressed with all of the work he had completed thus far. They had a talk about what he wanted to do after high school. He stated that he wanted to continue pursuing his music career. She was very confused as to why the idea of music meant so much to him. He explained that he only saw himself good at two things while growing up; playing basketball and writing rhymes. She asked him what he would be doing if he did not have those two options. He didn't have an answer for her. She asked him if he ever thought about being a doctor or lawyer. He didn't think that her question was serious, but he knew Ms. Mims wouldn't ask if she was not serious. Key never considered any of those professions.

Ms. Mims told him that there was a lot more he could do with his writing. She saw a great degree of character in his personality. She gave him an example of writers like Spike Lee that turned their work into screen plays and even became world renowned actors and directors. She explained that he did not necessarily have to be an actor, but it was very important to broaden his horizons and provide himself with more options. A look of misery formed on Key's face before he told Ms. Mims "With all due respect Ms. Mims, I really don't have a horizon to look upon. If I did, it isn't getting any broader. My dad went to jail when I was a baby, and my mom doesn't even care if I come home or not. All she's concerned about is if I have any extra money." Ms. Mims told him that it didn't mean he had to carry on tradition, and that's why the word "horizons" was plural. He thought about that for a second then nodded his head in agreement. Her point made a lot of sense. He had to leave to get to his next class, but not before thanking her for caring. She gave him a hug and he went on his way.

After school, Shayna and I went to the mall to shop for the prom. We went searching for dresses first. While looking through some of the selections at the first store I asked her how she felt about going to the prom with Key. She just shrugged her shoulders and flipped through more dresses. I asked her what that meant. She told me that she didn't know how to feel given the circumstances. That meant she wasn't expecting him to pull off the grade improvement task so she was clueless on how to feel. It was almost like it hadn't set in, but she wanted to be a woman of her word. It sounded like a good point to me.

We moved to another section of the store to check out other options. I asked her if she still liked him. After all, she did admit to being interested in him at one point. That seemed to get her attention because she dropped part of a gown that she was looking at causing it to fall back into place with the rest of the gowns. She had a confused look on her face as she confessed that that's what was bothering her. She explained that looking back on when she exhibited those feelings; she couldn't tell if it was because of the drama she was going through with Darryl or if she was really interested in Key.

I figured that was the case when I witnessed her going through that time in her life. Shayna let out a sigh with a look as if she was trying to make sense of everything. I told her that she had nothing to lose by just going to prom; it wasn't like they were obligated to carry on a relationship afterward. It was evident that she wanted her emotions to stabilize. It all stemmed from how things ended with Darryl. That was normal though, a break up will place your emotions in a state of disarray. I made it my responsibility to constantly remind her of that.

We moved on to another store because nothing really interested us in the one we were in. However, we kept some of their choices in mind as possibilities. As we were walking through the next store, Shayna came across a blue dress that she thought was nice and pulled it down to get a better look at it. As she looked at it, she said "I think Key mentioned that blue was his favorite color." I gave her a confused look and asked her what that was supposed to mean. Shayna said that it meant she may have found her dress because it looked nice and it was his color. I took the dress out of her hand and told her she wasn't getting it. She asked me what my problem was. I had to remind her that she already proclaimed her preference for purple to be their color. She exhibited a look of embarrassment realizing that she had exposed her true feelings. I told her that she had it bad for Key and that she might be getting the answer she was looking for in regards to if she was really interested in him; she just laughed. She took the dress back from me and brought it to a store clerk to ask if they had it in purple. They actually did so the clerk went to grab it from the stock room.

While the clerk went to get the dress, we sat down and waited. Shayna asked me if I was coming around to liking Key. I told her that I still hadn't gotten over his behavior and language in regards to women that day we met. Shayna nodded her head. I then admitted to her that I noticed a degree of change in his behavior and approach toward her. I wasn't saying that he had in fact changed, but I recognized effort. Effort should be rewarded if it is made with the right motives. Shayna was obviously making him a better person so it might not have been a bad deal. If she decided to allow him to date her, we would just have to see if he could continue that change. Only God knew what would come of that.

The store clerk brought the dress back out and Shayna went to try it on. Shayna looked great in the dress. She was ready to buy it and be done with her search. However, she decided to wait and ask them what their holding policy was. She wanted to finish looking at options in other stores. The store clerk told her that if she decided to reserve it, they could only hold it for an hour. That was only because everything was in high demand with prom season under way. She told the store clerk to hold it and that she would be right back. From there, we went to a few more stores. One other dress came close, but ultimately, she decided to go with her original choice. She purchased new shoes to go with it. I found my dress also; a one strapped black dress with subtle silver accents. I didn't need new shoes; I had enough options in my closet to find something to go with my dress. We finished shopping and made our way back home.

The next day, we had our annual sports banquet at the school around six in the evening. We all got certificates and varsity letters for our participation in our respective sports. The higher caliber athletes like Shayna, the most outstanding players on the basketball, football, and baseball teams, and the best coach were presented with trophies and other forms of honor. The entire ceremony lasted about two hours. Shayna's mom drove us and of course stayed for the festivities. However, there was another guest in the house to support Shayna. It was none other than Key himself. He took a seat next to Ms. Mims. Ms. Mims wasted no time telling him that he should have been receiving awards for basketball.

Shayna received her award and looked good doing so. Key was the loudest person in attendance cheering her on. He was really trying to solidify his position with her. The ceremony ended with a slide show and a few highlight clips of the school sports that season. After the ceremony, Key and Ms. Mims made their way over to our table to congratulate us. Ms. Mims gave us both hugs and caught up with Ms. Kim. Meanwhile, Key told us how proud he was of us without throwing one insult in my direction. He asked Shayna if Ms. Kim was her mom. When Shayna told him that she was, he asked her if he could meet her. Shayna brought him over to Ms. Kim and introduced him as her friend and prom date for that coming Friday. Ms. Kim told him that it was nice to meet him and that he was very handsome. I told her that she didn't have to lie to him. Of course he had a reply; "Now Charmaine, it isn't polite to boast of yourself. We can't all look as handsome as you, my brother." Shayna told him to cut it out. Ms. Kim, still smiling, told Key once more that it was nice to meet him as we gathered our things to leave.

PROM(ISE) NIGHT

Prom night was finally upon us. We were at Shayna's getting ready to leave. I decided to go with a friend from my church named Brandon. We were very close and he was always a respectful gentleman so I figured he would be the best suitor. We were waiting for Key to make his appearance, he had promised an elaborate form of transportation. Brandon and I were in the living room with Ms. Kim, Shawn Jr. was a few feet away playing with his toys. Ms. Kim was asking us how we felt about graduating, our plans after high school, and what else we planned on doing that night. As we were about to answer, the bell rang.

Ms. Kim was about to get the door, but Shawn Sr. walked out of the kitchen telling her not to worry about it and that he would get it. He looked through the window and couldn't tell who it was. When he opened the door he was eye level with someone's chest. He slowly looked up and asked "Who are you?" All we could hear was a voice coming from the foyer saying "Good evening sir or madame." Shawn Sr. said "You've got to be the biggest Jehovah's Witness I've ever seen. And do I look like a madame to you?" The voice paused for a second, and then continued. "It is with great pleasure that I accompany your daughter Shayna to the prom." Shawn Sr. replied "Oh, so you're the boy escorting Shayna." The voice paused for another second, and then continued again, "I want to thank you for the opportunity…" At that point Shawn Sr. just cut him off and told him to kill the act; "I get it, man. What are you, some type of robot?" Brandon and I couldn't help but laugh.

I don't know what Key was doing, but he sounded like a fool. Shawn Sr. walked him to the living room and told him that he could have a seat. Ms. Kim shook his hand and told him that it was nice to meet him again, Key returned the salutation. Shawn Sr. leaned to the side looking at Key and asked him why he could all of a sudden speak like he wasn't constipated. Key replied "I don't know, but that's funny because constipation actually runs in my family." Ms. Kim began to laugh a little. She saw that Shawn wasn't laughing and asked him if he got the joke. Shawn Sr. just looked at Key with a serious face and called him a wise guy, then offered him something to drink.

Shayna finally made her way downstairs with a slow strut. Ms. Kim looked at her and was overwhelmed with happiness. The dress looked better that night than when she tried it on in the store. Key told her that she looked beautiful as he handed her the corsage. She thanked him as he took it out of the box and placed it on her wrist. Ms. Kim told us to hold on as she ran upstairs to get her camera. After taking a bunch of pictures, both silly and serious, we made our way out.

When we got outside we saw this clean black stretched limousine. The only time a limousine would make an appearance in our neighborhood was for a wedding or a funeral. Shayna had to stop and ask how he was able to afford it, Shawn was just as curious. Key explained that he had a cousin who had a friend that gave him a discount for when he did his shows with Stack and Intellek. That's when he explained to Ms. Kim and Shawn that he was an aspiring rapper. They both looked at him with a confused expression. Shayna intervened by mentioning that we were running late and we needed to get going.

On the way to the venue, the four of us cracked jokes and took advantage of the complimentary products in the limo like food, juice, and water. The car had a funny smell, but it wasn't too bad after a while. The ride was smooth and comfortable despite the record breaking potholes New York City had to offer. We had finally reached our destination. The prom was being held in the ballroom of a beautiful hotel. One thing that really caught my eye was the elegance and class of the place. The interior design consisted of replicas of ancient Rome structures and impeccable lighting.

We walked in on Brandon and Key's arms and stopped at a table first to get settled in. We sat down and relaxed for a while. Not too long after we sat down, the DJ played one of my favorite songs; "Give it 2 You" by Da Brat. We all got on the dance floor and danced to that followed by Montell Jordan's "This is How We Do It". After that song, Key and Shayna went back to our table. From where Brandon and I were dancing I could see them talking.

Shayna and Key were just taking a breather. Well, Key was doing the breathing. Shayna took notice and told him that she hoped he wasn't tired after just two songs. Key told Shayna that he would be completely honest by admitting he was not in the best shape at the time. Shayna told him that it didn't look that way when she would see him playing basketball at lunch. Key claimed that it was because he would play against light competition so he didn't need to exert much energy. Shayna expressed that it still didn't explain anything because two songs is a lot less than a half court game of basketball to 16 points. Key just shook his head while slightly looking away because he had no argument for that point. Shayna moved her head into the direction he was looking to cut off his line of sight. She was beginning to not trust his behavior. Key looked back at her and asked her why she was looking at him in that way. She told him that it was because he looked like he was hiding something. He asked what he could possibly be hiding. She told him that he could tell it better. Key looked away again and said that he was going to get some water and asked her if she wanted any. Shayna told him that she was fine.

When Key got back to the table, Shayna was sitting there looking somewhat upset. Another song came on and he asked Shayna to dance, but Shayna wasn't in the mood. Key asked her if it was because she thought he was still hiding something. She just sat there for a few seconds, and then said she had to go to bathroom. As she was walking out she looked in my direction and nodded her head once. That usually meant that she needed to tell me something. I told Brandon to hold on and I went with Shayna to the bathroom.

When we got to the bathroom, I immediately asked her what was wrong. She told me that Key was acting funny and being secretive. I asked her how she got to that conclusion. She explained how he was fatigued after two songs and how he couldn't explain it so something seemed wrong. I admit, something did seem wrong with that. However, we were not completely sure what was going on so there was no real reason to get upset and ruin the night. I had to remind Shayna that she invested a lot of time, money, and patience into preparing for this night so it was really on her if she allowed it to get ruined. She agreed with my point and decided to try another method of figuring out what was wrong. She checked herself in the mirror then we both left the bathroom.

We got back to the ballroom and saw Key and Brandon sitting at our table conversing about something. They both stood up like gentlemen to welcome us back as we approached the table. Key asked Shayna if everything was okay. She smiled and told him that everything was fine; he felt relieved. He was beginning to think the night was over. The DJ played Boyz II Men "On Bended Knee". The timing couldn't have been any more perfect; that was actually Shayna's favorite Boyz II Men song. Key didn't know that, but it aided him in getting back on Shayna's good side. Brandon and I decided to take the breather that time. We just sat at the table and took in the scenery. Shayna and Key's dance started with her arms around his neck and his arms around her waist. As the song progressed, she got closer and laid her head against him while closing her eyes. Key pulled her closer while bringing his head down and gave her a kiss on the top of her head. It all looked very romantic.

When the song was over, Shayna and Key were walking towards the doors of the ballroom. She looked at me again and gave a head nod, but this time it meant that she was okay. They took a walk around the inside of the building and sat down on a couch located in the lobby. Shayna stated that she had noticed something different about him. He asked her what the difference was. She noticed he hadn't been carrying his rhyme notebook around as often. He explained that he had to start leaving it home because it was becoming a distraction. When Ms. Mims got him the deal with all of his teachers, he had to cut a few things out. The notebook served as a distraction in the sense that when he would get bored in class, he opened it and zoned out. Before he knew it, he would miss an entire lesson. Ms. Mims was actually the one that advised it. She knew it would be hard for him, but it would teach him discipline and responsibility. Shayna asked what he did instead when boredom struck without the notebook. Key explained that he started keeping candy or chocolate with him to keep him alert, but the sugar sometimes caused him to crash. Shayna then suggested that he try fruit.

The two of them sat on that lobby couch in silence for a few seconds; it was a nervous type of silence. Shayna broke the silence by asking him if getting tired after dancing was a result of one of those sugar rushes that ended in a crash. Key seemed more open to talking about it that time. He told Shayna that it was actually everything else that made him tired. His life took on some drastic changes in the weeks prior to prom. The changes consisted of sacrifices and a more demanding schedule. Shayna positioned her body in a direction that was facing him a little more and told him to tell her about it. Key seemed a little reluctant to talk about it so Shayna promised him that it wouldn't go beyond the two of them.

Feeling a little more comfortable, Key explained that a lot of it was related to his finances. He hadn't been doing shows or traveling because of the deals he made with Shayna and Ms. Mims. When he didn't do shows, he wasn't making money. His living arrangement wasn't the best either. With his mom being useless and not having a father around, he was the sole provider for the apartment he and his mom lived in. All of that resulted in him having to resort to getting a local part time job at the Burger Empire near the school. With that job, he was barely making it so he would have to work a lot more hours which caused him to get tired often.

Shayna was blown away by the whole situation; speechless to be exact. Key saw the look on her face and told her to not worry about anything because with the school year ending, he could focus on one thing instead of both. He had other worries, but he didn't continue out of fear that it would ruin the night. To ease the mood, he got up and offered his hand to escort her back to the ballroom. As she got up slowly, he asked her if she was okay. Shayna told him that she was okay; it was just a lot for her to take in. Key understood, and reminded her that it would only be temporary. They started walking back to the ballroom.

Shayna and Key got back to the ballroom while the rest of us were in the middle of a soul train line. Brandon and I were about to go down the line. When I saw Shayna I told Brandon that I wanted to go down the line with her; he understood. I signaled Shayna over and she ran over without hesitation. We went down the line doing the goofiest dances you could imagine. It was one thing to do goofy dances, but doing them while you're well dressed always seemed funnier to me.

As the night progressed, the host and faculty chaperones were constantly breaking up couples that were dancing too close. There was one argument that led to a fight which got out of hand. Other than that, they organized games and activities to keep all of us involved. They actually weren't that bad. At first we all wondered why they would interrupt our good time to do group activities like we were kindergarteners. When we found out that there was a possibility of cash prizes and other prizes of value like a pair of new sneakers, it changed everything. One of the games consisted of the DJ calling out a certain color or a certain hairstyle. If we had what he called out, we won a prize.

Prom was approaching an end. We had about an hour left, but some people had already left to get to the after parties. There were parties taking place at student's houses while others were going on in rooms in the hotel. We didn't have any plans, but a few classmates walked by us on their way out and suggested that we check out one of the parties. It was up to Key since it was his limousine. He didn't mind, he actually asked us if we would like to go before we asked him. We all agreed that it was a good idea, but it was midnight so we all called our houses to update our parents first. Once we did that, we gathered our things and left.

We decided to check out the ones in the hotel first. Those actually got out of control quickly; one had already gotten shut down. We decided to go with the house parties instead. The four of us piled into the limousine and told the driver to take us back to Brooklyn. One of the parties most of the students were attending was in Bed-Stuy.

We got to the Stuy and the party was in a Brownstone. People were spilled out onto the sidewalk socializing. We finally got through the crowd of people and into the house. We were two minutes in and I was ready to leave; it wasn't my type of scene. Between the alcohol and not having enough room to get around let alone dance, I wasn't enjoying myself. I told Shayna that we should head back outside, she followed me without hesitation. Brandon and Key walked back out with us. When we got outside we brainstormed what we could do next. We eventually decided to get something to eat and call it a night. As we were making our way to the limo we were cut off by the stooges; Stack and Intellek.

I didn't stop to talk. I said hi, but didn't look at them. Every time they were around, their conversation made me feel like I was losing brain cells. I pulled Brandon along and we both got into the car; Shayna followed us. She didn't want to talk to them either. When we got in, Shayna closed the door behind her. The two of them approached Key very loudly and obnoxiously as usual. Stack did most of the talking. They wanted to know where Key had been and why they had not been doing any shows. Key told them that he had been busy. Stack's facial expressions gave off the impression that he didn't believe Key. He took his attention off of Key and looked at the car asking "So is this your new crew?" Key asked him what he meant by new crew. Stack said "It must be your new crew because it obviously isn't us." Intellek was posted up against a tree zoned out. Key asked Stack if he had a problem with who he hung out with outside of him and Intellek. Stack stated that he had a problem because it was affecting a plan they had as a group to make music and money. Key told Stack that he needed to calm down and respect someone trying to better them self.

Things seemed to be taking a turn for the worst in their conversation. Stack told Key to stop lying and accused him of having an ulterior motive. He said "You changed, son. You're not doing this for yourself. You're doing it for shorty with the big butt." As he said it he pointed at Shayna through the window. Shayna started opening the door telling Stack to watch his mouth. Key pushed the door back closed. He told Shayna to chill and that he would handle it. Stack said "Oh, you'll handle it?" as he stepped closer to Key. Key gently pushed him out of his space. Stack pushed him back. Key didn't retaliate, but his facial expression said that he really wanted to. Stack told him that he changed, but Key denied that claim again. Stack told him to prove that he didn't change by kicking us out of the limo and letting him and Intellek ride somewhere to record. Key told him that he wasn't going to do that. Stack claimed that it was just as he suspected. He then went on a rant about how Key was messing up his money flow by cancelling shows. Intellek verbally agreed by saying "Word!" Key told Intellek to shut up. Intellek went back to resting on the tree. Key told Stack that he needed to check himself. Stack gave a sinister smile and told him he would in fact check himself. Key got in the car and we rode off.

As we pulled off, Key was apparently still bothered by the whole ordeal. Shayna took his hand and held it. He looked down at her hand holding his and then looked at her. Shayna looked back at him and smiled, then rested her head on his shoulder. They didn't let go of each other's hands as the radio played late night slow jams all the way to our destination. I laid back in Brandon's arms. The setting just seemed so perfect and felt great. We finally arrived at our destination; Burger Empire. Key hooked us all up with free meals. We sat there for a while socializing, eating, and joking. When we finished, the limo took us all back home.

The time was 1:45am when we got back to our block. I gave Shayna a hug and told Key good night. Brandon walked me to my door and gave me a hug, then went to his own car and went home. Shayna and Key were outside on her steps for a while after I went inside my house. They looked around in silence for a few moments. They were either nervous or just happy to be around each other. Key broke the silence by asking Shayna if she had a good time that evening. Shayna told him that she enjoyed herself and that she appreciated all he had done. Key cocked his head a little to the side looking confused and said "And you say I'm the one that changed." Shayna laughed a little then looked up at the stars as she told him that it was confirmation that it was a good night. Key told her that he couldn't argue with that.

Shayna gently grabbed his hand and told him that she also wanted to thank him for how he handled the situation with Stack. She liked how he defended her honor and showcased maturity at the same time. Key told her that it was no big deal, but that she was very welcome. Shayna stopped him and told him that it was in fact a big deal, and that it showed how much he had changed. Key smiled and thanked her for her acknowledgement as he gently grasped her other hand. They were now both holding each other's hands. Key looked deeply into her eyes, then slowly leaned in to give her a kiss. Shayna was stiff and looking back into Key's eyes as he was getting closer. At the very last minute before their lips connected, Shayna turned her head causing his lips to hit her cheek. She thanked him again, smiled, and told him that she should be getting inside. She looked up in the direction of her door and saw the curtain in the door quickly close. She looked back at Key and before she could say anything he told her that he saw it too. They both laughed and gave each other a hug.

As Shayna was walking up the rest of the steps, Key watched her and said "Very nice!" Shayna turned around and told him to not ruin a nice finish to a beautiful night. Key claimed that he was talking about the finish of the wood on the door. Shayna didn't believe that, she just rolled her eyes. She finally got her door open and told him good night. Key told her to hold on and asked for her number. Shayna stood there for a second before saying "We'll get there." She then closed the door the rest of the way. Key made his way back to the limo and went home.

NEW BEGINNINGS

I was preparing breakfast the following morning and the phone rang. On the other end was an ecstatic person screaming and saying things like "I CAN'T BELIEVE IT." It only took a second to decipher the voice and realize that it was Shayna. I called out her name twice "SHAYNA! SHAYNA! CALM DOWN!" She calmed down for a second and began to hyperventilate. I asked her if she was alright. After a few more quick breaths, she said "Girl, I'm better than okay. I just opened some mail that came yesterday." I said "And?" There was a dramatic pause for a second or two, then Shayna screamed "I GOT IN." I asked her if she was talking about college. I had a feeling that she was, but I wanted to be sure. She said yes, she was talking about college. We both screamed.

Shayna got accepted to Gainesville University on an athletic scholarship for Track & Field. She had received offers from other schools over the past month in a half. She was flattered by the offers, but she was really hopeful and focused on impressing Gainesville University. She had been to Florida a few times to visit family, go to Disney World, and on one occasion to visit the school. She fell in love with the weather and always mentioned that the scenery reminded her of a paradise. She loved the palm trees, the slower pace of living, and the consistent sun and beaches.

I was proud of her, but then I thought about the fact that she would be leaving. We had been together all of our lives. If we were ever apart, it wasn't for a long period of time. I focused my mind back on the conversation and congratulated her along with suggesting that we do something to celebrate. The plans were made later on. She had to get off of the phone so that she could call some of her other relatives to tell them the news.

We met up later in Coney Island to celebrate on the beach and at the park. My mom and I met Shayna and her family at a restaurant called Frank's where they decided to celebrate. While walking through the entrance door, she rushed us and gave us both a big hug. She was clearly still riding her high from receiving the news that morning. My mom gave Ms. Kim a hug and gave Shayna her gift as Shayna escorted us to seats at the table where she was sitting. Ms. Kim called for everyone's attention so that she could make a toast. She toasted to our accomplishments and expressed how proud she was of the both of us. She touched on how Shayna and I had been friends all of our lives and commended us for doing something positive. She told us that we better not stop there. After eating, Ms. Kim brought out a box of cupcakes from this place called CakeJazz. When we finished, we went out to enjoy ourselves at the park.

Shayna and I took a walk on the boardwalk and discussed what was to come. It was starting to set in that graduation was the following week and after that summer, life was going to change. I asked her if she had shared her big news with anybody outside of her family. She said that the news hadn't gone beyond family yet. I used that as my opportunity to ask her about what happened between her and Key the night before after I went in the house. Shayna told me that they just spoke for a little while on the stoop and that she made sure that was as far as it went. I then asked her what was going on with them at that point in time because they seemed pretty close after prom. She simply smiled and said "Keith has changed" and left it at that. I stopped her at that moment and asked her if she had called him "Keith". She jokingly claimed "I'm just calling him by his name." I didn't need to hear anymore; I had gotten my answer. Shayna never liked to give away too much, but she would drop hints when she was talking to me. It was like a code we had.

We continued our walk. Shayna asked me about what I was planning on doing after graduation and if I had heard anything from the schools I applied to. I applied to some of the top schools in New York City. I really wanted to stay local for a few reasons. I never really traveled, in-state tuition was less expensive, and I wanted to stay close to my mom. My dad left my mom and me when I was young and all we had since then was each other. I never really saw him again at a scheduled time, but New York City is funny. As big as it is, it could also be very small. I've seen him walking on random streets at random times on numerous occasions.

I had not heard from any of the schools yet, but hearing from schools before graduation was considered too early in some cases. I didn't want to wrap my head around that at the moment. I told her that there was no point in stressing myself out over it.

She agreed and said that she was confident that I would be accepted. We both maintained high grades, so that vital portion of the application wasn't a problem. I told Shayna that it was no secret that Key liked her a lot, so I was curious as to how she felt he would take the news that she was leaving. Shayna entered a state of deep thought. After a few moments, she told me that we would know for sure when she told him. I respected that answer. I invited her to join me at church the following day; she wasn't really one to attend church. On occasion, she visited mine and a few others. Her family wasn't into attending church for their own personal reasons. She accepted my invitation. We continued on with our walk and eventually made our way to the park once our food finally digested.

The next day at church we had a program designed specifically for the youths and young adults. I forgot to mention the itinerary to Shayna, but I was sure that she would enjoy it. Being that she did not attend church on a consistent basis, I figured a slight program geared towards our age group would be perfect. The program and sermon was led by a young preacher named Justin. Justin was only a few years older than us so he was able to relate to our generation's culture, the music, temptations, and the worldly distractions. It also consisted of a talent portion that allowed the young people to minister through the gifts God blessed them with. Everyone was very attentive to everything that was being displayed or showcased. Shayna seemed to be tuned in to the talents, but more so into what Justin was saying.

By the end of the program, Shayna was smiling and high off of the message. Our Pastor asked if anyone wanted to say anything before the benediction. I took it upon myself to do just that. My few words consisted of how I was thankful for God's blessings, the church, the support of my family and friends, and the fact that my best friend and I would be moving onto college. I gave the microphone back to the Pastor. He added that the point I made about college was a great and important one. At that point he called all of the young people to the front, but particularly the high school seniors so that he could pray for all of us. That was immediately followed by the benediction.

During the benediction, Justin asked all of us if we knew the definition of salvation. Of course those of us that attended church knew what it was, but a number of the guests that came with members did not; Shayna was one of them. The preacher gave a brief description of it. He stated that it was the act of admitting you were a sinner and asking God for forgiveness which would in turn secure your spot in Heaven when you die. He then asked if anyone was interested in securing their spot. Some raised their hands while others seemed inattentive or confused. The preacher took notice of this and told everyone that he would show them what he was talking about. He told everyone that they were welcome to join him in a prayer and they had to repeat after him; this is known as an alter call.

Shayna looked at Justin like he was crazy. That spiritual high she was on from the sermon seemed to have been interrupted. I told her that her reaction was understandable. I then put my arm around her and told her I would say the prayer with her. Shayna refused and said that she needed some air. She started walking swiftly toward the sanctuary exit, I followed her. I caught her in the vestibule and asked her if she was alright. She told me that she was just confused and everything was sounding a little weird to her. I reassured her that it was okay and that I could explain it to her in depth if she wanted. Shayna just stayed silent.

Church ended after the benediction and my mom met us in the vestibule to check on Shayna. She asked her if she was okay. Shayna said that she was alright, but I knew that she was putting on a front so that my mom wouldn't worry. On the ride home I asked Shayna if she was okay and if she enjoyed herself. She told me that she felt different, but didn't quite know how to explain it. I told her to take her time to gather herself and that she would be okay. I was aware of the feeling of confusion she was referring to, but I wanted to wait until she had a clear head to discuss it. By her not being in the midst of a church environment regularly and the fact that her family didn't promote one, it may have been a bit too much for her. What it looked like to me was spiritual warfare; the act of the absence of God in an individual battling with God's presence being formally introduced. It can cause confusion and overwhelm those that are unfamiliar with

God. Some willingly accept it while others need more of an understanding of what's going on.

It was quiet in the car for another minute or two. All of a sudden, Shayna began to talk about her experiences in churches she had visited. She talked about a few churches where they did nothing but judge her, churches that were not welcoming or hospitable, and even some churches that only wanted money. This served as a contribution to her confusion because a lot of what she heard about Christians was that we were loving and welcoming people. It didn't help that the same things happened to her parents which steered them away from the church as well. She explained that her mother believed in God, but the church was not something she wanted to commit to if those were the type of people she had to deal with.

I knew exactly what she was referring to. I had to explain to Shayna that there were fraudulent figures that posed as Christians, ministers, and people of God. However, their agenda only consisted of getting paid, putting on a fashion show every Sunday, and acting like they were greater than everyone else. In the midst of a fraud's show, the Word of God gets buried. I followed that up by telling her that not all people in the church were like that. I gave her an example of how she never saw me behave in that manner and we had been best friends all of our lives. Shayna nodded her head and agreed that it was true.

I sought some confirmation regarding if she was okay by asking her again. She simply said "Yes, I'm okay." I asked her if she ever felt like that during any of her other visits to our church. She said that she never had, and it was just something about that day. I proposed that we go again someday to see if it had the same effect. She told me that she would think about it. Thinking about it wasn't a problem at all. Everyone needs to make decisions on their own time and when they feel the most comfortable, especially when it comes to anything pertaining to a relationship with Christ. We finally got back to the block and managed to get a good parking spot. After parking and getting out of the car, Shayna gave us hugs and told me to call her later.

GETTING REACQUAINTED

Our next day at school was our last day at school. We had our graduation rehearsal. Once we were done, we were dismissed for the day. On our way out we received our caps and gowns for the ceremony taking place later that week. After rehearsal, we went to Burger Empire up the street to get some lunch. We walked in and saw Key behind the counter. Shayna yelled in a loud voice "AT 6'5", STARTING AT FRIES. KEITH WILLIAMS!" Key gave her a look as if he wanted to say "Are you serious?" Shayna was just laughing it up. When she finally got herself together, she said "Hi Key!" Key gave her a smirk and asked us how we were doing that day. We told him that we were fine. He told us that he was happy to hear that and noticed our caps and gowns in the bags that we were holding. He congratulated us and told us that he was proud of us. We thanked him. Shayna asked him when his summer school class was supposed to start so that he could finish and be graduates with us. He told us that it started in two weeks and would last the duration of the month. We expressed our excitement for him as well. He thanked us and told us that he couldn't wait for it to be over so that he could quit Burger Empire and go back to doing music and shows. Shayna asked how everything else was going. He simply said that he was surviving. He changed the subject and asked us if we wanted anything to eat. We said yes and ordered. We ate it there so that we could harass him some more until we left. It was all in good fun.

Later that night, Key was closing up. He had a lot more going on than anyone knew. The amount of information that he shared with Shayna at prom wasn't even the half of his worries. He had actually been putting in extra hours and working double shifts on days that he wasn't in school just to stay above water. I didn't say anything earlier in the day when Shayna and I had lunch at his job, but he looked very tired. I just prayed that everything was okay. I asked Shayna if she noticed that he looked a little fatigued. All she told me was that he had been working hard at school and work, but he should get better since school was out.

Key was not only closing at nights, but also opening a few mornings. If that wasn't enough, he had to catch the bus all the way back to his neighborhood; East New York. East New York is one of the most dangerous and most crime-filled neighborhoods in Brooklyn. When he got there, he had to make his way through one of the worst projects which was also where he lived. He got his mail and made his way upstairs. When he got to his apartment and opened the door, it was completely dark. His only means of knowing where he was going was being knowledgeable of his own place and a little bit of light shining in from the hallway. Apparently his lights had been turned off a week before because the bill wasn't paid. As he walked in, despite the lack of light, he saw the same sight that he saw every night. It was a dirty apartment and his mother passed out on the couch in the living room. He just shook his head, then went to his room and went to bed.

He woke up the next morning to find his mother still sleeping. He didn't pay her any mind as he made his way to the fridge; there were a few boxes of cereal on top. Each box had a little bit of cereal left. He poured a bowl, but had no milk. He couldn't care less at that point, he was just happy to have something to eat. All of his other meals were usually taken care of at work. He sat at the table and began eating and looking over the mail that he picked up on the way in the night before. It was the same old thing that they got every day; more bills and junk. However, he came across something that wasn't quite like the rest. It was an eviction notice that notified them to vacate the premises within the next thirty days if they did not pay what they owed in back rent. They were about three months behind. The landlord put it in the mailbox instead of taping it to the door so that the tenants couldn't say they didn't receive it.

Key dropped his spoon into the bowl, got up from the table, and made his way to the living room where his mom was sleeping. He called her once "Ma!" She didn't respond. He then kicked the couch and called her again in a louder tone; "MA!" She moved a little and said in a frustrated tone "What, boy?" Key put the eviction notice in her face and asked her if she was going to stop lying around and finally get a job. She looked at the notice and sucked her teeth. She then dropped the notice, folded her arms, then went back to sleep.

Key was so disgusted with how his mother lived. It had gotten to the point where he no longer even looked at her as a mother. He had become even more frustrated with having to be there more often with her due to his change in schedule. Before the change, he would be doing shows or he would spend time at Stack's apartment so time passed a lot faster. Stack lived in the same building on the floor above his. Key was still paying for all of the utilities, but he was making a lot more doing shows than what he made at Burger Empire. After she dropped the notice, Key asked her if she realized that they could no longer live there. She simply told him to shut up and go away. Key just sucked his teeth and went to his room.

While in his room, he got his notebook that he wrote his lyrics and rhymes in and went downstairs to the project courtyard. Writing was Key's way of relieving stress. As he was leaving, his mother stopped him and asked him if he could pick up some lottery tickets and cigarettes for her. He asked her how she was going to hear the numbers with no electricity for the TV, and then he slammed the door. On his way down, he ran into some guys that he knew from the building on their way to the park. They asked him if he wanted to go play ball with them. He gave them all dap; a type of hand shake used among friends, but declined the offer.

When he got to the courtyard, he began writing vigorously. He zoned out and got whatever feelings he had out of his head and onto the paper. The courtyard wasn't the safest place, even if you lived there. One actually makes them self vulnerable to trouble on the inside, and to outsiders that were lurking the premises. That didn't cross Key's mind because he was too angry to care, he just continued to write. Before he knew it he had gone through three pages. As he was about to go onto the fourth page he felt a hand tap his shoulder. It broke his concentration which startled him and caused him to jump back into a fighting stance.

The hand that touched his shoulder was Stack's. Key's facial expression went from shocked to confusion. He got up from where he was sitting and closed his book. Before saying anything to Stack, he took a step back and looked around in fear. He thought that it may all have been a set up after their last conversation at the after prom party. Key continued to look suspiciously at Stack and asked him what he wanted. Stack told him that he didn't want anything. He saw Key sitting in the courtyard as he was walking back from the store so he made his way over to say what's up. Key looked around again then returned the greeting. Stack noticed how Key was looking around and asked him what was wrong. Key told him that he was being cautious after their last conversation. Stack couldn't believe that he was serious. In Stack's mind, they had been fighting all of their lives and they were always over it the next day. Key knew this, but he was thinking about the look and smile Stack gave after the altercation; he didn't trust the look. Instead of admitting that, he just told Stack that he was right.

Stack took a seat on the bench Key was sitting on. He had a bag of chips and some juice from the bodega he had just come from. As he sat down, he asked Key what he was doing out there. Key sat down and explained that he was just writing some rhymes and getting some stuff off his mind. Stack told him that he and Intellek were doing the same thing. Key told him that it was good that they were writing because in the next month or so they would be able to get back on their usual grind. Stack told him to take his time. That response came as a surprise to Key being that it was the complete opposite of what Stack said the night after prom. Stack claimed to have taken time to think about things from Key's perspective. He told him that he understood where he was coming from and decided to let it go. That was Stack's way of apologizing and Key understood. Key thanked him.

Stack opened his chips and juice. He added to his statement that he and Intellek were only juniors so it would be selfish to hold Key back. Key told him that it had not been easy, but he was in fact going to graduate that summer. Stack congratulated him, but told him to be honest about if he was doing it to graduate, or for Shayna. Key looked at him and said "Of course it's for Shayna. That was the main reason, but it got a little more serious as time progressed." From there he told Stack about everything Ms. Mims did for him.

Stack told Key that he commended him on his dedication and asked him if he at least got some. With a confused look on his face, Key asked "From Ms. Mims?" Stack sucked his teeth and said "Nah, from Shayna." Key came down from that shocked state and explained that he didn't get anything from Shayna. This confused Stack; he expected Key to at least get "some" on prom night. Key told him that the opportunity didn't present itself. Stack accused him of lying. Key asked him how he figured he was lying. Stack reminded Key that they were like brothers which meant one knew when the other wasn't telling the truth. He told Key "Your words don't match your facial expression. Plus, you defended her honor when I called her out of her name. That was the perfect set up to get some." Key was just silent.

Stack took Key's silence as proof to his point and asked him what happened. Key told him that nothing happened. Stack said "Well it's obvious that nothing happened, so do you care to explain why?" Key looked at him and simply said "She's different." Stack spit his juice out and began laughing uncontrollably. He looked at Key and blamed him for wasting his juice. Key looked at him with a straight face and told him that he wasted his juice on his own because he was serious about Shayna being different. Stack told him that he wasn't trying to hear any sentimental garbage. Key expressed that he really cared about Shayna. Stack was still confused, but decided to just go with it. He sat back down and told Key that Shayna really did change him. Key admitted that it was beginning to feel that way. Stack then said "Don't get me wrong, Ms. Mims can get it too." Key agreed as they laughed and gave each other dap one more time.

Key changed the subject because he didn't like the fact that the conversation was getting too sentimental. Since he was being honest, he wanted Stack to be honest as well. He reminded Stack that on the night of prom and the party, he was complaining that Key was messing up the group's money by cancelling shows. However, Key noticed something about Stack's demeanor as they sat in the courtyard that said the opposite. He looked Stack up and down noticing his expensive clothes and told him that it didn't look like he was strapped for cash. Stack took another sip of his juice and smiled. Key stated that his confident smile further proved that he wasn't strapped for cash. Not to mention, he told Key to take his time getting back to the group and making music. Key asked him again if he was going to be honest with him about what he had been doing for money.

Stack put his chips and juice down, then went into his pocket and pulled something out. It was a small bottle. Key looked at Stack then looked back at the bottle which appeared to have some type of substance in it. He asked "What are those, anxiety pills?" Stack explained that it wasn't exactly anxiety pills, but they were very similar. Key gave Stack a worried look and asked if he had driven him to using pills due to the fact that they weren't doing shows. Stack explained that they weren't for him, he was selling them. Key asked him who he was getting to buy anxiety pills. Stack looked at him wondering why he had not picked up on it yet.

The substance in the bottle wasn't even in the shape of pills. It was actually cocaine chopped into little rock-like pieces. Key asked him what he was doing with cocaine. Stack told him that he was making money with it. When Key asked where he got it from, Stack told him not to worry about it, but he could get him in on it if he wanted. Key passed on the offer. Stack told him that if he changed his mind to just let him know. Key grabbed his book, told him that he was cool, and that he didn't want to get in trouble for being out there with him and drugs. Stack told him that was fair enough.

As Key was walking away, Stack told him that if business continued the way it was going, he would not be joining the group when they started recording again. Key turned around and asked Stack if he was serious. Stack claimed that he was very serious. He went on to tell Key that the money he had made in the last two days was more than what they usually made in five shows and he did it all in less time. Key had an expression on his face that showed he was impressed. He then got a hold of his emotions and asked Stack if he expected him to believe that. Stack put the pill bottle away and went into his pocket again, but this time pulled out a big roll of cash. He told Key that it didn't matter if he believed him or not because he was going to get money regardless.

Key began to walk back to the bench. When he got back, his eyes were fixated on the thick roll of money that was wrapped in a rubber band. He looked back at Stack's face, Stack looked at him with a serious expression. Key took note of his expression and it was at that moment that he realized Stack was not joking. He asked Stack how he managed to get that hook up. Stack told him that it was Blizz's product. Blizz was short for Blizzard; a notorious drug dealer in Brooklyn at the time. He was known and feared by a majority of the borough as well as other parts of the city.

Key could not believe what Stack was saying. He asked him if he was crazy for getting involved with Blizzard. Stack nonchalantly replied "Some might see me as crazy." Key told him that the ones that see him as crazy are right and that he wasn't getting involved. Stack told Key that he was crazier for not getting involved with his financial situation being the way it was. That made it sound even more tempting to Key. Key then asked Stack how he even landed a deal with Blizzard. Stack explained that it was because he was a low risk and produced a high reward. The fact that Stack was not of legal age to do time and not usually suspected to be trafficking meant that he wouldn't be harassed as frequently. Key asked him what would happen if he did get caught. Stack explained that he would probably get a minor charge and do some time in a juvenile detention center, but no real consequences. Key asked "So you don't mind getting a charge on your record?" Stack flashed the money again and asked Key if he looked like he cared as he flipped his fingers through the hundred dollar bills in the money roll.

While the two of them were still talking about Stack's new business venture, a fight broke out a few feet away over a game of cee-lo. Guys in the projects were always fighting over a dice game. Stack immediately put the money back in his pocket. The sudden noise made him think that it might have been cops coming around to bust someone for something. Stack told Key that he had moves and sales to make so he had to go. Key asked him to see the money one more time before he left. Thinking about his own financial situation at the time, he was now open to anything. Stack showed him one more time. Key took a deep breath and told him that it was a nice looking amount of money.

They both just gazed at the money. Stack told Key that even if he didn't want to get down with Blizzard, he wanted to at least let help him with some of the bills. Key declined the offer and told Stack that he didn't need any money. Stack told him that he knew he was getting evicted. Key wanted to know where he heard about that. Stack heard it from his mother who heard it from a tenant named Mrs. Rodriguez that lived in their building. Mrs. Rodriguez saw the landlord put it in their mailbox. Key was furious because it meant people knew their business. Stack told him that there was no reason to be upset because he knew that Key was trying to maintain the apartment on his own.

Key was still mad. Stack took a few hundred dollar bills out of the roll and handed it to Key. He told him to use it to get back on his feet. Key was hesitant. Stack insisted that Key took the money and said "We're brothers, man. We look out for each other." Key took the money and gave Stack dap and thanked him. Stack told him that he would catch up with him later. They parted ways; Key went back inside and Stack left the courtyard.

GRADUATION

Graduation day had finally arrived. After four years it seemed so surreal. Our graduation was held at Brooklyn College in Flatbush, Brooklyn. Everybody was dressed in their best and very excited about finally walking. Our parents sat together, but we had not spotted them in the humongous crowded audience yet. The directors and coordinators of the graduation were getting everyone lined up and making sure we were all in the right order for name calling purposes. Our section was set and ready to go.

A few seconds before we marched out, Key walked into our preparation area. Shayna expressed how excited she was to see him by immediately screaming "KEEEEEITH!" A few people turned around to see what all of the commotion was about. Key approached us and asked how we were doing. He gave us both hugs and told us that he just wanted to see us and congratulate us one more time before we walked. He had flowers in his hand for Shayna and didn't look as tired as he did earlier that week. It was time for us to march out so Key was asked to leave and find his seat.

The ceremony began with our principal Ms. Chase addressing the crowd and thanking everyone for attending what she described as a beautiful occasion. She shared a story that explained the importance of pursuing an education beyond our diplomas. She stressed the fact that there was more to explore and accomplish after high school so we should enjoy our milestone, but not be satisfied with it. After she received her applause for her speech, she introduced the valedictorian. Our valedictorian was an obnoxious boy that nobody really took a liking to and I think he knew. He was pompous and always felt the need to talk about how smart he was. We couldn't wait for him to be done. After he was done, our special guest speaker was asked to step to the podium.

Our special guest speaker was an NBA legend. He was big in our city a few years prior to our graduation year because he was playing for the Knicks. He is also a native of the borough. At the time of our graduation he had been traded and was playing for our rival team, but still received a welcoming reception from the crowd. Through a connection of friendship between himself and Ms. Chase, he agreed to talk to us that day.

He stepped to the podium to a standing ovation; some from those that grew up as fans, and others that were star struck. However, nobody in the crowd was louder than Key. Key was a big Knicks fan and a fan of any player affiliated with the Knicks. All you could hear from his section of the crowd was "YOU THE MAN! YOU THE MAN!" Everyone turned around to see who was being so loud. When Key realized this, he looked back at everyone and said "Do you all know who that is?" He looked at Key and simply said "Thank you, brother!" Key said "YOU THE MAN!" one more time before he finally took his seat. The speech entailed his upbringing in Brooklyn and how he was pleased to see a large group of young scholars. He gave us a few tips that got him through college and life. He finished his speech by telling us to keep God first and be thankful for the opportunity we had been presented. That was back when mentioning God in school was acceptable.

The time had finally come for us to walk across the stage. Ms. Chase approached the podium and announced "It is time for the moment we have all been waiting for." The graduation directors directed the first row to stand and make their way to the steps on the side of the stage. From there, the rest of us followed suit. It was time for our row to walk. Shayna's name was called first between the two of us. When her name was called, she got a great reception.

The loudest person making noise for Shayna was Key, but that was because he had an unfair advantage. He was using a noise maker that gave off the sound of a car horn. To this day I don't know where he managed to find that. He was making so much noise that security had to approach him and tell him to give them the noise maker or he would have to leave. Key opted to put it away. When it was my turn to walk across, Key pulled the noise maker out again and blew it as hard as he could. Security didn't warn him that time, they just moved in on him. Key saw them coming and decided to retreat. When I looked into the audience, all I can see was a few men in suits running from different directions, and one tall guy running for the exit.

The graduation proceeded. We were finally down to the last few names. The last three students crossed and shook the hands of the faculty, then took their seats. Once the last student took their seat, Ms. Chase announced "It is with great pleasure that I present to you the Jackie Robinson High School Class of 1995." We all celebrated and hugged one another. Shortly after, we were working our way through the humongous crowd trying to get to the exit.

When Shayna and I got outside, we met up with our families and took advantage of photo opportunities. We took some with family and any friends that we could find passing by. Shawn Sr. advised us to wrap it up as soon as we possibly could because there was going to be traffic. Shayna and I gave each other a hug and planned to meet up when we got back to the block. Before we could part ways and head to our cars, we heard Key's voice in the near distance saying "You were gonna leave without taking a picture with me?" He greeted Ms. Kim and Shawn and gave Shawn Jr. a fist bump. He then got to meet my mom. Key asked if we would mind if he got a graduation picture with us. We did it quickly and had to get moving.

Later that night, our families had dinner together over at Shayna's to celebrate. We were done by 8:00. Shayna and I went outside to sit on the stoop. We were out there for about twenty minutes conversing about random topics before we got a visitor. Key came walking down the block and said "What's up, ladies?" Shayna and I were confused as to what he was doing on our block. Shayna eyed him as he began to walk up the steps and asked him why he wasn't at work. He told her that he was off the entire day. She thought about mentioning what he told her at prom because she figured he would be trying to get as many hours as possible. However, she didn't want to put his business out in the streets. He told her that his finances had been taken care of, for a while at least. He was referring to his little bonus that he got from Stack, but Shayna didn't bother to ask what he meant.

Instead of delving further into why he was even on our block, she told him that it was actually good that he was there. Key mentioned that it was the first time he heard her say that as he walked up one more step to get closer to her. In his mind that meant that he was wearing her down. She told him to calm down and put her hand out to stop him from getting any closer. He asked her why she was so happy to see him. Shayna said "I didn't get a chance to tell you when we were at your job earlier this week, but I'm leaving Brooklyn and going away to college at the beginning of August." August was about a month and a half away from that point. You could tell by the expression on his face that he was utterly disappointed, but he was trying to conceal his emotion. He congratulated Shayna and asked her where she would be going. Shayna told him that she would be running track for Gainesville University. He told her that it sounded like a great opportunity and that he was happy for her.

I didn't take my eyes off of Key the entire time. I was too caught up in his facial expressions. He was obviously hurting on the inside. He told her that they needed to go out or do something before she left. She took him up on his offer. He told her that he would get back to her with the details, but at the moment he had to leave. He was headed to his homeboy's house three blocks up. He had recently bought Live 95 and invited a bunch of people over to play. Key asked us if we wanted to go with him, but we politely declined the offer. He said okay, and told us that he would see us around. When he left, Shayna and I looked at each other and had the same thought. We could both tell that the news of her leaving obviously hurt him.

DATE NIGHT

Around Tuesday of the following week, Key was called into his manager Mr. Jones' office. Just the simple fact that he was being called into the office caused him to fear the worst; losing his job. Mr. Jones told him to have a seat. Key told him that he would rather stand. Mr. Jones gave him a confused look then told him that it was okay if that's what he preferred.

Mr. Jones began to explain the reason for the meeting. "Keith, the reason I called you in is because…" Key cut him off and said "Sir, I need this job. You don't even understand. I can't be fired, at least not right now." Mr. Jones gave him another confused look and asked him what he was talking about. Key asked "You're not firing me?" Mr. Jones asked him why he would do that. Key fell back against the door in relief. Mr. Jones told him to relax, but that time he insisted that Key took a seat. Key wasn't as reluctant to sit down that time.

Key was relieved as he attempted to gather himself. Mr. Jones asked if he was okay to which Key replied that he would be fine. Mr. Jones was finally able to get his point across which was that he had to cut back on Key's hours. That caused Key to go from being relieved to a little upset. He asked Mr. Jones what the purpose of cutting back hours was. Mr. Jones explained that business wasn't flowing too well, and he couldn't pay Key as much.

Thoughts immediately began to flow through Key's mind about his living situation. He said "Mr. Jones I can't accept that.

I have bills, summer school starts next week which would already cut into my work schedule, and I support myself. I really need those hours." Mr. Jones told him that there was nothing he could do for him due to the circumstances. He expressed his sentiments in regards to Key's situation and told him that it was all he could offer at the moment. Key thanked him and left the office.

Later that evening, Key sat in his living room watching TV. He was able to get his electricity back on with some of the money Stack gave him. He wasn't able to get all of the utilities back on, but he made sure he at least paid that one. He was watching *Martin*. It managed to help him forget the things that were stressing him out for a while. He laughed uncontrollably throughout the entire episode. It had gotten to a point where his mother yelled at him from the bathroom to shut up. Key let out a louder fake laugh just to spite her. His mom exited the bathroom and walked to the living room telling him that all of his ridiculous laughter was blowing her high. Key gave her a look of disgust and asked "So you have money to buy weed, but no money to pay a bill?" His mother told him that he needed to mind his business because she didn't have to pay for the weed. Key ignored her.

The commercials were over and *Martin* had come back on. Key's mom asked him if he was going to just sit around and watch TV all night. Key told her that it wouldn't be any different from what she did every day of her life. That must've hit a nerve for his mother; she got upset and told him that he was just like his father and that he would end up just like him. Key told her that if he ever ended up like his dad, it would be a better life than being there with her. He then told her "There's no difference between a state prison and the prison you built around my entire life." She walked further into the living room and closer to him telling him to watch his mouth. He told her that it was too late for her to start acting like a mother. She swung to smack him, but the height difference allowed him to see it coming since she had to reach. He blocked her hand and made his way for the door. On his way out he told her that she was tripping. Midway through the doorway, she told him that since he was going out he could ask Stack for some more weed. That completely angered Key. Selling drugs is bad enough, but selling drugs to loved ones is just heartless.

He didn't have anywhere to go leaving the apartment in anger before, but after that comment his mother made, he directed his attention toward Stack's apartment. He made his way up the building stairs and down the hall to Stack's door. He knocked on the door, but no one answered quickly enough to his liking so he knocked again. This time he heard a woman's voice say "Hold on! Who is it?" Key responded "It's Keith". The door opened and Stack's mom was standing in the doorway. She gave him a hug and said "Keith! I haven't seen you in a while." Key was still fuming. He played it off temporarily so she wouldn't ask questions. He asked her how she was doing. She told him that she was doing well and asked him how he and his mother were doing. He told her that they were doing fine. She then asked him if he was there to see Warren; that's Stack's real name. He said yes and asked if he was home. She told him that he was in his room and invited him in. Key thanked her and walked in. He walked through the kitchen and said hello to Stack's sister as she was feeding her daughter. He finally got to Stack's room.

Stack was in his room watching the end of *Martin*. He put his hand out to give Key dap, but Key smacked his hand away. Stack asked him what his problem was. Key looked at him with an angry expression and said "Take a walk with me." Stack replied "You must be high, I ain't walking nowhere with you looking as angry as you do. I might not make it back." Key told him that it was funny that he mentioned being high. Stack looked confused; he asked Key what he was talking about. Key told him to stop playing dumb. Stack stood up and was now standing toe-to-toe with Key. He told Key he needed to chill and leave. Key made it clear that he was not going anywhere until Stack explained why he sold weed to his mom. As he demanded answers, he balled up his fists. Stack noticed Key's fists and told him that he didn't sell her anything, and he also wasn't going to accept disrespect in his home.

Key wanted him to prove that he didn't sell her anything. Stack told him to control his temper and refrain from making demands if he wanted answers. Key was still upset, but he decided to calm down in order to get what he wanted. Stack wanted to know where Key heard that he sold to his mother. Key explained that it was his mother that told him. Stack had to tell Key to slow down and remind him about what he showed him in the bottle. Key remembered, but wanted to know what that had to do with anything. Stack told him that crack was all he sold, and that he didn't even handle weed. Key asked him if he was telling the truth. Stack explained that he would never sell to his friend's moms because it was foul. Key calmed down and apologized for stepping to him so disrespectfully. They gave each other dap and Key was getting ready to leave.

As Key was leaving, Stack asked him if everything was alright. Key told him that he had a lot on his plate and was just trying to work things out. Stack jokingly suggested that Key relieve his stress by smoking a little bit of what his mom had. Key didn't want anything his mom had because it obviously didn't work for her life or her attitude. Stack agreed that it was true, and then suggested another alternative. He told Key that he knew a lot of his stress stemmed from his financial burdens. His suggestion to Key was that he get down with Blizzard and push weight because it was quick and easy money. Key told him that he would pass and that he didn't want anything to do with drugs. Stack told him to think about how good it felt to pay his bills on time with the money he loaned him. Key began to get anxious and considered what Stack was suggesting. He asked Stack what he needed to do if he chose to be a part of it. Stack told him that all he had to do was tell him whenever he was ready. Key thought about it for a second, then left.

The next day, Shayna and Key went on the date they scheduled to have before she left for school and his schedule picked up again. He met her at her house around the afternoon. They started the date with a walk on the Brooklyn Promenade. It was right in her neighborhood so it was relaxing and inexpensive. From there, he took her to Empire. Empire was the name of the most popular skating rink we had in Brooklyn. They got on the Subway and made their way from Brooklyn Heights to Crown Heights. Key managed to get them into Empire for free. He and the DJ worked together earlier that year at one of his shows so he snuck them in through the back. They stayed there for about three hours. While there, they managed to bump into a few people from school and even got into a skate off.

By the time they left Empire, it was only 6:00PM. He asked Shayna if there was anything else she wanted to do, but Shayna had no ideas. With no plans set in stone, Key suggested they go to movies. They couldn't decide what they wanted to see between 'Batman Forever' and 'Friday'. Key immediately got the idea to do what people had been doing for years at the theater. Theaters had matinee deals, but back then we had another version of the matinee. We would leave one movie, and then simply go to another theater playing the other movie we wanted to see. Sometimes the scheduling was so perfect that one would end while the other was starting. Nowadays you can pull it off, but security is tighter.

They saw one movie, and then ran through the hallway to catch the other. They must have been seen that particular day because an attendant approached them with a glow stick when they got settled in. He asked them to see their tickets. Key told Shayna to get up as he showed the attendant the ticket. The attendant took out his flashlight to check it. Just as he did, Shayna swung her purse over her shoulder and acted like she mistakenly hit the flashlight out of his hand and they both ran. They probably would've just been asked to leave the theater, but they felt it was more fun to cause a commotion.

It was 8:30PM and they were out of plans. It didn't matter because they both agreed that it was getting late. However, they decided to get something to eat on the way back because they had not eaten in a while. They went to a local pizza spot not too far from me and Shayna's block. Key wanted to do the gentlemanly thing and offer to pay, but Shayna told him that he didn't have to. Key insisted and held Shayna's hand telling her that it was okay. She thanked him and allowed him to proceed. It was a nice gesture, but he offered it before he even knew the final total which he ended up being a little short of. He stood on line with the money he had while searching his pockets for some more. He was beginning to feel embarrassed. Shayna asked him if he had it. Key let out a nervous laugh and quietly told that he didn't. She intentionally told him in a slightly loud tone "Since you paid for everything else today, let me get this." They actually paid for their own tickets, but she could see that he was embarrassed.

They got their meals to go. They made their way back to her house and sat on the stoop. She went inside to let her mom and Shawn Sr. know that she was home, and then went back outside to join Key. He asked her if she enjoyed the day. She told him that it was one of the more fun days she ever had as they began to eat their food. Key told her that he was glad that she enjoyed it. She rested her head on his shoulder and took one of his cheesy bread sticks. He asked her what he was supposed to eat once he wanted a breadstick. She laughed as she ate it, then took one of hers and fed it to him. As she was bringing the breadstick upward to feed him, he let out a big growl and bit down like he was going to bite her finger. She screamed from being startled then laughed. She rested her head back on his shoulder.

At that moment Key was content with life. All of the things that were causing him stress were non-existent, but he did not want it to stop there. He wanted to feel it more and on a consistent basis as oppose to what he went through at home and at work. Shayna interrupted his thought process by asking him about his recording career that he was trying to establish and how it all worked. He told her that he, Intellek, and Stack usually opened up at small clubs for bigger artists. One thing she always wondered was how well it paid because he gave off the impression that he was living it up. He told her that to a degree, the three of them were in fact living well. The money wasn't outstanding, but at that age, the money they were getting was great. Bills and utilities were always taken care of. He went on to explain that the limousines and the image they were portraying were for the public.

A majority of the time, the cars and women weren't for them; they were just on the itinerary that night so they got to enjoy the perks. Shayna then asked him about the time she saw him in Philly; and who he was opening for that night. He told her that it was an after party for a Fugees concert that took place that night. Key's manager who is also his cousin convinced the promoter to let the three of them perform as one of the opening acts. Shayna was impressed, but now also confused. She wanted to know why Stack was so upset the night of prom if they weren't getting as much money as it seemed. Key explained that Stack's attitude that night was a prime example of the personalities that made up their three man group; Key did it for the love of the art, Intellek did it for the exposure with hope to expand, and Stack did it for the money and fame. He was upset at the time because the money stopped flowing and he wasn't informed on when it would start up again. He then told Shayna that he and Stack were back on speaking terms. She told him that it all made sense.

They were just about finished with their food. He asked Shayna what she would think if he moved to Florida too. She asked if he was talking about with her. He told her that it wouldn't necessarily be with her, they would just be in the same place. She wanted to know why he would do that. He stated that a change of scenery wouldn't be bad, she wouldn't be alone down there, and it may even be a better situation than what he had in New York. She admitted that he had good points, but in the end, it wouldn't matter what she thought because that type of decision should be personal.

Key simply nodded his head. While her head was still on his shoulder he pulled her forward and put his arm around her. She looked at him and he looked back down at her. They stared at each other and began to get closer. They shared a quick kiss on the lips and smiled at each other. She looked at his watch and realized that it was after 10:00. She told him that they should call it a night. He agreed and they got up. He gave her a hug good night and she went inside. He picked up the bags and threw them in the garbage cans at the bottom of the steps.

BOILING POINT

The following morning, Key was back at work with one of the most disinterested facial expressions and demeanors one could imagine. He was three hours into his shift when he decided that he no longer wanted to be there. His mind was racing with thoughts of everything that he was struggling with. A mental imbalance had developed within him between the beautiful date he had with Shayna the night before and the frustration of that morning. He lashed out at a customer and went on a rant causing him to be sent home early by Mr. Jones. He walked out complaining that his hours had already been cut, so losing a few more from being sent home weren't going to make much of a difference.

Back at Shayna's house, the mailman had just delivered the mail. Shayna was walking by the door when he dropped it off so she went to retrieve it. There were a few magazines, bills, and other things addressed to her mom and Shawn. Closer to the bottom, she came across something addressed to her from 'Redd's Island'. Redd's Island is an island within the city that consists of a few jail facilities; we just call it 'The Island'. Its main purpose is to hold convicts that have a sentence of a year or shorter, or inmates that are set to be transferred to an actual prison. Shayna didn't know anybody being held on The Island so she didn't trust it. She brought it to her mom first. Ms. Kim opened it and went directly to the end to see who it was from.

The letter was from Darryl. It turns out that he was being held on The Island until they transferred him to one of the state's correctional facilities. He had to wait to be transferred due to the prisons being over capacitated.

Shayna took the letter outside to read on the stoop. A part of her didn't want to read it because of what it may have possibly entailed. She didn't have any animosity toward Darryl; she just didn't have feelings for him anymore. She finally gathered up enough courage to read it. The letter read:

Hey Shay,

It's been a while, but then again you tend to lose track of time behind these walls. You also tend to learn a lot being confined. I realize now that a lot of the stuff I learned in here could have been learned on the outside. One of the things I learned and became aware of was my immature behavior. With that said, I want to apologize for the ways I acted and the things I did that negatively affected you. I know its summer time so I know you've finished school. I wanted to congratulate you on graduating. I don't know what you plan on doing now that you're done, but I pray God blesses you in your future endeavors.

I know that may come as a shock to hear from me, but it all stems from my renewed relationship with Christ. My mom has been visiting me often and ministering to me with different scriptures. It's what has been helping me to get through some of the things I have to endure in here. I don't know what your schedule consists of, and I don't have a set day for transfer, but I just wanted to extend an invitation to you and your family to visit if you all would like. If you do, the address is the same as the one on the envelope the letter was delivered in. God bless!

-Darryl

Shayna sat out on the stoop for a while thinking. The mailman had dropped off our mail as well. Our doors had mail slots, so the mail carrier usually pushed it through the slot and went on about their day. I picked it up from the foyer floor and opened the front door to see what was going on outside; I hadn't been out yet for the day. I looked up and down the block and saw the usual sights; kids running around, a hydrant busted open, and people taking in the comfortable weather on their own stoops. As I was looking around, my eye caught Shayna sitting on her stoop. I decided to go over and ask her how her date went.

When I got to her stoop, she looked like she had a lot on her mind so I asked her what was wrong. I thought something may have happened on the date. She didn't say anything; she just showed me the letter. I read it and immediately understood her pain. On another note, Darryl's words gave off the impression that he had genuinely changed while being incarcerated. I asked her how she felt about it. She told me that she wasn't sure how to feel yet. I put my arm around her and reassured her that I was there for her. The blank look on her face remained. The only time I would see that expression on Shayna's face was when she was going through something with Darryl. Naturally, I couldn't help but think "Here we go again." I didn't even bother to ask any further questions regarding her date with Key.

Speaking of Key, he wasn't doing any better. He had just gotten home from being dismissed from work. He walked in on his mom sleeping on the living room couch again. He stormed into the living room with anger already built up and yelled "MA!" She woke up in a state of shock asking Key what his problem was. Key asked her why she lied about Stack giving her the weed she had gotten high off of two nights prior. Her reply was "Maybe it wasn't Stack, maybe it was somebody else." She then turned over and closed her eyes again. She was so nonchalant about it like nothing mattered. Key looked down at her and grabbed the blanket she was using. He threw it across the room then walked out.

Key went to his room and grabbed some fresh clothes to change into from his uniform. In the midst of his anger, his left thumb caught a nail on his drawer when he was slamming it closed. The nail left a small gash. Although it was small, it was very deep. Key was now even more enraged, not to mention in excruciating pain. He ran to his sink to wash the cut out. When he turned the faucet knob with his good hand, the faucet spit out a glob of brown water that was sitting in the pipes followed by a hissing sound. The water had been turned off in their apartment due to a delinquent bill. Key grabbed some rubbing alcohol and left the apartment. He made his way upstairs to Stack's place.

When he got to Stack's, he asked him if he could use their water to clean out his cut. Stack let him in right away. Stack asked Key what happened as Key was running water and soap over the open wound. Key told him how his thumb got caught on the nail. He finally finished washing the cut out. Stack opened the bottle of alcohol and poured it straight out of the bottle onto Key's thumb. Key let out a slight grunt from the pain. He looked at Stack angrily and asked him if he had ever heard of using a cotton ball to dab the alcohol. Stack looked back at him like he couldn't be serious and told him "I haven't heard of that method, but I know of many women and children that have." Key ignored his sarcastic comment and posted himself up against the sink looking furious. Stack told him to calm down and that it was a joke. Key explained that he wasn't upset over his comment. The blood finally stopped running which allowed Key to wrap his thumb.

Stack wanted to know what was going on. Key explained everything from not being able to pay for he and Shayna's entire meal the night before, to the issue at work that morning and the water being shut off in his apartment. Stack expressed his sympathy for Key. Key told him that he was sick of all of it and that starting his summer school course the upcoming Monday wasn't going to make things any easier. Stack asked him what he was going to do. Key just stood there for a while. He then looked at Stack and simply said "I'm ready!" Stack told him that he needed to be clear about what he was talking about so that they were on the same page. Key looked away with a distressed expression on his face and told Stack "You know what I'm talking about."

EXECUTIVE DECISIONS

Stack set Key up with a meeting to be introduced to the organization. The meeting wasn't going to be directly with Blizzard. Instead, it was someone under Blizzard. The idea was to make sure Key could handle the business and for them to know who they were getting involved with. The meeting was scheduled for that afternoon. Key was told to be at the Marine Park basketball courts at 4:00. Someone was supposed to be there that would be able to identify him based on information Stack gave them.

Shayna and I were still on her stoop. She had finally begun to express her thoughts about the letter. She was mostly confused due to the fact that she had not heard from Darryl in a long time, and when she finally did, he wasn't even the same person. I asked her what she planned to do from that point. Shayna sat back quietly for a little while before telling me that she believed him. She also told me that if given the opportunity, she would visit him. I told her that if she was serious, she should contact Darryl's mother to find out when she would be going to visit him again. Shayna felt that it was a good idea. We went inside and Shayna made the call. Darryl's mother was actually planning to visit him that coming Sunday after church. Shayna told her that Sunday would be fine and that she would meet her at her house. Darryl's mom extended an invitation to Shayna to attend church with her. Shayna thanked her for the offer, but politely declined. Darryl's mom told her that it was okay, and that she would see her on Sunday.

With a great degree of curiosity clouding her mind, Shayna was considering the different possibilities of what the visit could produce. She pondered what she and Darryl would talk about, how he may look, and what could possibly happen from there given the possibility that his change was genuine. I asked her what she meant exactly by her comment of "What could possibly happen from there." Shayna explained that she just didn't know what to expect. If I didn't know any better, I would've thought that she was saying she still had feelings for him. I knew Shayna too well to not be able to read between the lines of that statement. I personally think the way their relationship ended left their connection too wide open, but that was just my theory. Only time and Shayna's visit to Darryl would provide a better perspective on if my theory was correct.

4:00PM came around and Key had just walked into the park. He posted up against the gate that surrounded the courts. He looked around for a while trying to look as normal as possible. From his right, he heard a voice yell "YO!" He looked in the direction that the voice came from. The guy that yelled it looked at Key and said "Yes, you!" Key said "What's up?" The guy asked him if he wanted to run with them because they were a man short of five players. Key told him that he was okay, and that he wasn't there to play. The guy asked him why he would be at the court as tall as he was and not be dressed or want to play.

Key told him to just get somebody from the losing team when the current game was over. The dude told him that he needed a big man. Key gave in and decided to play.

The current game was over and Key took off his shirt to get ready to play in the upcoming game. The guy gave Key dap and told him to man the paint. Key was perfectly fine with that. Every now and then he would look around in an attempt to locate whoever he was there to meet. He was so distracted by this that he let the guy he was defending beat him with a basic move on the very first play of the game. The guy that recruited Key grabbed the ball and asked Key if he knew how to play. Key told him yes, and explained that he was just distracted. The guy told him to get his head in the game. As Key got more comfortable and allowed his mind to clear, he had become the go-to guy on the team scoring most of their points. In the end they won 16-9. They went on to win three more consecutive games following that one. They had eventually gotten knocked off of the court due to some of the other players getting tired. They sat on the bench following the loss to catch their breaths and rehydrate.

The guy that asked Key to play with them joined them on the bench after posting up against the gate for a while. He apparently wasn't ready to leave the court and was upset about their loss. When he got to the bench he complimented Key on his game and asked him if he played for anybody. Key thanked him and told him that he wasn't playing for any teams at the moment. He then advised Key to get involved with some of the summer tournaments in the city. Key nodded his head in agreement and said he would consider it. The guy mentioned that he had never seen Key in the area. Key stated that he was just there for the day. The guy replied "Yeah, that's what Stack told me." Key looked at him and immediately understood at that point that the meeting was underway.

Key wasted no time asking the guy what he needed to do from that point. The guy picked up his duffle bag and told Key "Frank's in Basin Mall is a more convenient location for those fries when you're in the area. It beats getting on the Subway to go to Coney Island." That was all he said before he walked out of the park. Key was confused as to what he meant. He jogged after the guy to get some clarification, but before he reached him he changed his mind. He didn't know who he was dealing with so he figured it wouldn't be wise to run up on him. He decided to stay and play a few more games before leaving the park. He figured he could ask Stack to verify the comment later on.

Shayna and I made a trip to Basin Mall the next day to pick up a Batman action figure for her little brother. His sixth birthday was approaching, Wednesday of the following week to be exact. Shayna ended up getting him two instead of one. She could never help but spoil Shawn Jr., she loved him. While we were walking out of the store we saw Key walking down the hallway. Shayna yelled "KEITH!" Key turned around and smiled when he saw Shayna. He walked in our direction and asked us what we were doing there. Shayna told him that she was picking

145

something up for her brother. She then asked him what he was doing there. Key told her that he was just browsing. Shayna asked him why he wasn't at work. He told her about how Mr. Jones had been cutting his hours.

It seemed as though none of us had any immediate obligations. Shayna suggested that we all browsed together. I personally didn't mind, but Key politely declined the offer. He explained that he needed some time to think a few things over. Shayna told him that it was okay and to contact her when he got a chance. Key laughed and told her that would be feasible if he had her number. Shayna was withholding that phone number like it was top secret information, but she always had good reason to do so. She told him that he's getting closer to getting it, but that he probably wouldn't need it because they always seemed to bump into each other. He replied "True indeed!" We said our goodbyes and parted ways with him.

Key continued to walk through the mall with a destination in mind; he just wasn't sharing that information with us. He went straight to Frank's located in the small corridor where there wasn't much mall traffic. When he walked in, he looked around for the guy he played ball with the day before. The guy wasn't in there so Key took a seat. He sat there for a while before remembering the guy mentioned fries in his message. Key looked up at the menu board from his table. Soon after, he got up and went to order some fries. He got the fries and went to sit back down.

He wasn't picking up on any clues, but he was enjoying the fries. He stayed there for about an hour and a half and began to grow impatient. The manager approached his table and asked him if everything was to his satisfaction. Key looked at him and told him that he was fine. As the manager smiled and began to walk away, Key quickly called him back. When the manager got back to his table, Key asked him if he had seen the guy he was looking for. He described him as Puerto Rican and about six feet tall with a Caesar (low haircut). The manager told him that a lot of people walk in and out so Key needed to be a little more specific. Key told him to not worry about it. He picked up his fry cup, threw it in the garbage, and left Frank's.

TRIVIAL PURSUIT

Sunday had finally come. Shayna arrived at Darryl's house around 10:00AM to meet up with his mother and drive out to 'The Island'. His mother went to the early service because visitation hours ended at 4:00PM on Sundays. They caught up on what was going on in each other's lives on the drive there. Darryl's mom congratulated Shayna on graduating and her scholarship. Shayna thanked her and commended her on the strength she exhibited since Darryl had gotten locked up. Darryl's mom explained that she wouldn't have been that strong without God. Shayna just nodded her head. His mom wanted to know what made her want to pay a visit all of a sudden. Shayna told her about the letter and felt that at least one visit was customary.

They finally arrived at the jail. They went through the customary security procedures; providing ID, giving up any phones, pagers, CD players, make up products, cigarettes, lighters, and pretty much anything else you can think of. They were then asked to sit in the waiting room until they were called to visit with Darryl. After going through a few metal detectors and providing proof that they weren't concealing anything in their mouths or their shoes, they were escorted by bus from the central facility to the holding facility where Darryl was located. The visitation area was an open space. It was a big room set up with tables and chairs. The room was surrounded by guards to ensure safety and limit any extracurricular activity between the visitors and inmates.

Shayna and Darryl's mom sat at their assigned table and waited for Darryl. The wait wasn't too long. Darryl came out of the holding area in his jumpsuit and handcuffs escorted by a correctional officer. Shayna stood there in shock. She and Darryl's mom stood up as he was approaching. When he finally reached the table, the guard removed his handcuffs. He kissed his mom and hugged her for a while. When they released from their hug, Darryl's mom took a step to the side to give Shayna some room. Darryl and Shayna looked at each other for a while. Darryl actually didn't know Shayna was visiting him that day. He reached out for a hug and she was receptive to it. The three of them took their seats after that.

Darryl's mother opened up with a prayer like she usually did for Darryl's visits. They prayed everything in Jesus' name and proceeded with the visit. The officer informed them that they had a maximum time of an hour and a half. The visits usually consisted of Darryl's mom updating Darryl on what was going on in the world along with a Bible study. However, she allowed the two of them to talk first and have the Bible study for toward the end.

Shayna started the conversation by asking Darryl how he had been. Darryl said that he was blessed and asked how she was doing. She told him that she was doing great and about her upcoming relocation to Florida. He congratulated her and told her that it was a blessing. She thanked him then mentioned how she noticed the changes he had made through the words in his letter and his overall demeanor. He told her that just like he said in his letter, he had learned a lot from being incarcerated. He realized that he was stupid and being locked up may have been for the best. He wasn't necessarily referring to the twenty years part, just the humbling experience.

There was a young girl crying and hugging a young guy at another table not too far away, it appeared to be her boyfriend. It caught Shayna and Darryl's attention causing them to both look over at the couple. Darryl told Shayna that looking at the couple reminded him of them. He further explained that being locked up helped him to understand where he went wrong in their relationship. Shayna replied "You went wrong when you made the turn into that other girl's driveway." Darryl's mom gave Shayna a look of shock. Darryl was shocked as well. Shayna apologized to Darryl's mom and reworded her statement; "I meant you went wrong when you decided that you wanted to be a player." Darryl couldn't argue with that and told Shayna that she was absolutely right.

He admitted that he didn't know better before, but through proper insight and guidance from the Bible stories his mom had been sharing with him, he was able to go about approaching and handling a relationship a lot better. The only problem at that point was that he would have to wait twenty years for another opportunity. Shayna simply told him that she hoped he was successful when he got the opportunity to prove himself. He paused for a second with a perplexed look on his face and then thanked her. He was expecting a different answer; one that involved the two of them.

They were beginning to run low on time so Darryl's mom decided to intervene with a lesson. She decided to go over a story regarding relationships. She felt it would be great to continue their conversation as well as incorporate a word from God. Darryl's mom broke down not only their relationship, but the marriage between Christ and the church. She read from the passage of Ephesians chapter 6, verses 22-33. It references the marriage between a woman and man and how it should be played out. It continues by comparing that marriage to the church's relationship with Christ. She concluded the lesson by telling Shayna and Darryl that their relationship fell apart because one half conformed to outside habits bringing about a weakness in their connection; very similar to the church of Laodicea in the book of Revelation. God was not pleased with the Laodiceans because they lived their lives on the fence or in a lukewarm manner. This meant that they didn't make it clear who they served; God or the world.

Darryl's mom equated the lesson with Darryl's behavior and Shayna's overall reaction. She explained that no one was perfect, and that they should thank God that they could at least still share the bond of friendship. Everyone has the privilege to remain friends after a falling out, but not too many are blessed with the wisdom and maturity to handle that privilege correctly. She ended with a prayer. They gave Darryl a hug and that concluded the visit.

Back in Brooklyn, Key had just arrived at Burger Empire to start his shift. He clocked in and went straight to his register to relieve the person working before him. The employee that he was relieving told him that Mr. Jones wanted to see him immediately. Key sucked his teeth in frustration and made his way to Mr. Jones' office. He knocked on the door. Mr. Jones was on the phone, but told Key to step inside and sit down. He told the person on the other end that he would call them back.

As Mr. Jones hung up the phone, Key told him that he heard he wanted to speak to him. Mr. Jones turned his chair around to face Key. Key told him that if he was going to fire him for going off on that customer, then he should just do it instead of wasting his time. Mr. Jones asked him if he wanted to be fired. Key asked him what kind of question that was. Mr. Jones told him that he seemed to have everything figured out and that he must be able to read minds. Key rolled his eyes and let out a frustrated sigh. Mr. Jones told him that he wasn't fired, but he could be if he didn't lose his attitude. Key sat up and gave a fake smile while sarcastically asking Mr. Jones "Is this better?" Mr. Jones told Key that he was not sure what had gotten into him lately, but he couldn't have it affecting his business that was already on the decline.

Ultimately, he told Key that he was off of the registers and was going to be working on the floor sweeping, mopping and taking out garbage. Key asked him if that was all. Mr. Jones told him that he was free to go unless he had something he wanted to add to the conversation. Key said "Yeah, I'd like to add that at your age you should be able to tie a tie, your clip is showing." Key then walked out of the office. As the door was closing, Mr. Jones yelled "THE MOP IS IN THE BATHROOM."

Key walked back out into the restaurant's general area. He wasn't in any rush to clean any floors so he sat down at one of the table with an infuriated look on his face. He began to rock his chair back and forth while looking around the restaurant. As he looked around, his eyes caught something of great interest. He immediately looked back in the direction of what caught his attention. It was the guy connected to Blizzard that he played ball with two days before. The guy was sitting at one of the restaurant's tables staring back at him.

Key looked around before deciding to get up and walk over to the table. The dude put up his index finger as a non-verbal gesture to tell Key to stop where he was. Key stopped in his tracks. The guy then said "Yo, my man! Assistance please?" Key looked around. The guy said "Yes, you!" Key walked over to him and asked him what he needed. He told Key that his burger was terrible. Key told him that he would get the manager for him; the guy told him that it wouldn't be necessary. He got up from the table and made his way to the exit. As he was walking out, he said to Key "Just don't miss the call." Key was confused. The guy walked outside and passed a payphone. Key looked around, and then went outside. He stared at the payphone for a second and it began to ring.

He began to walk towards the phone. As he was walking, he became so nervous that his palms instantly began to sweat. He looked around, then wiped his hands on his pants and picked up the phone. He said "Hello!" The voice on the other end had a deep tone. It said "Don't quit your day job." A clicking sound followed and the call was disconnected. Key looked at the phone, and then hung it up. The door for Burger Empire opened a few feet away. Mr. Jones leaned outside and yelled "KEITH! YOU'RE PUSHING IT!" Key just rolled his eyes and walked back into work.

NEW COACH, NEW SYSTEM

Later that night, Key got in at around 7:00PM. He sat in his living room and turned the TV on. As he was turning channels looking for something to watch, he suddenly heard a knock at his door. He walked to the door and asked who it was; it was Stack. Key opened the door just a little and asked him what was going on. Stack asked him if he could come in. Key opened the door and let him in; they both went to the living room. Stack was there to give him a message from Blizzard's organization. The message was "Continue flipping burgers if you want an empire." Key asked him what that was supposed to mean. While they were on the subject, he asked "Why is it that every time I talk to someone connected to Blizzard it feels like I'm talking to The Riddler?" Stack told him that it was just the way Blizzard operated and that he hadn't even seen nor met Blizzard in person yet. Key asked him if he could elaborate on the message. Stack told him to sit down so he could explain.

The position at Burger Empire was stressing Key out, but he needed it more than he thought according to Stack. Key asked Stack how Blizzard could possibly know what he needed. Stack told Key to not say anything, but he had gotten word that Blizzard already had an operation in motion and it involved Key. Key wanted to know how he could possibly be involved in anything and he had not even spoken to anybody. Stack explained to Key that was one thing he had to learn in the game they were now a part of. "No one talks, we all just understand."

Key wanted to know what he had to do from that point since he was officially involved. Stack explained that the operation would entail Blizzard's product being sold at the same time Key made a transaction at work. The way he was going to do that was to have customers that wanted the product walk in looking to be served by Key. The meal board only had six meals on it so the customer would ask Key for a certain number. Whatever number they asked for would be the amount of bottles of the product they wanted. The most bottles a customer usually got at one time were two, three on very rare occasions.

Anybody could ask for a number meal so to differentiate between the clientele and regular Burger Empire customers, they had to give a code word with their request. Upon hearing the code word, Key would know that he was dealing with the clientele and slip the number of bottles they requested into their bag. The bottles were small and very discreet, a lot smaller than the one Stack showed Key when they were in the courtyard. The code words were "Hot" and "King". For example, if the customer wanted two bottles, they would say something like "Let me get a hot 2." When using "King", they would refer to Key as "King". For example, Key may hear "What's up, King? Let me get a number 3." King could easily be a play on the word "Empire" in the restaurant's name or passed off as slang. In the 90s, King was a term of endearment among some guys. The code word would change overtime in order to keep things fresh and to make sure no one caught on or got suspicious. Any customer of

Blizzard that purchased the product at Burger Empire received a small discount because the price of the meal was included, but they were only allowed to pay with cash.

Key thought about the plan for a second and agreed that it sounded full proof. The only problem was that he was no longer working the register due to being demoted. Stack told him that if he wanted to be a part of the operation, he would have to get the position back. Key knew that Mr. Jones wouldn't give him that position back, not right away at least. Stack told him that Blizzard was planning to start the operation in the next two days and wanted Key to meet with someone a day before it went into effect. If he couldn't do that, they would more than likely move the operation to another location.

Blizzard's organization initially agreed to using Burger Empire because it had one location in Brooklyn so it was very discreet and wasn't really on many people's radar; a perfect set up for his clientele. Key folded his arms and leaned back in his chair thinking about it for a second. He devised a quick plan in his mind and told Stack that he could count him in. He just needed to know where he was supposed to meet the person for the meeting. Stack told him that he didn't have to worry about that because the person would find him. They gave each other dap, and Stack went on his way.

As Stack was walking out, Key's mom was walking in. She was dressed semi-decent. Key looked her up and down and asked her where she was coming from. She told him that she had a date. Key's facial expression went from confusion to disgust as he said "Ill". She rolled her eyes and walked pass the two of them. Stack told the two of them good night and walked out. Key locked the door and said to his mom "You know seeing you on your feet is a completely strange sight. I'm surprised you still remember how to walk." She told Key to shut up and went into her room.

The next morning Shayna and I were over at her house. We were in her room with Shawn Jr. She was packing for her move to Florida that was coming up in three weeks. While helping her fold clothes and pack her suitcases, the topic of her visit to see Darryl came up. She told me about how he was a completely different person, but she didn't know if she should believe it just yet. Due to their history she didn't know what was real with Darryl and what wasn't.

I was shocked to hear what she was saying. What I had been telling her throughout her entire relationship with Darryl was what she was finally beginning to see. I guess it took some time apart and a little personal growth for her to understand. There was one point in time when he could do no wrong in her eyes. I asked Shayna if things between them were okay. She told me that things were fine as far as she knew. As we packed some more, it was starting to set in that Shayna was really leaving. I was going to miss my partner in crime. We decided to take a break from packing for the day. The three of us went downstairs to watch TV and get something to eat.

That same day was Key's first day of summer school. That meant before he could take on the next step of Blizzard's organization initiation, he had to face his old friend Mr. Johnson. He got to school and was making his way to class. On his way to class, Ms. Mims stopped him in the hallway as he was walking by her classroom. She hugged him and told him that she was proud of him. She then reminded him that all he needed to do was get along with Mr. Johnson and knock out that final class. He thanked her as he hugged her back then went on his way.

He finally got to Mr. Johnson's class where students were still walking in. It was a small class, summer classes usually were. Mr. Johnson was sitting at his desk. As Key walked in, he looked around to check out who else was taking the class. When his eyes got to Mr. Johnson, they looked at each other for a while. Key said "What's up, Mr. Johnson?" Mr. Johnson responded "Keith!" Key took his seat. The class began with an ice breaker. Mr. Johnson told the students to introduce themselves one by one and share something about them self.

He told the class "Before we begin, I noticed some new faces and recognize some old ones. Let's see if we can all be successful this time around." Key sat back and rubbed his hands together, but kept his head down. He felt like Mr. Johnson was picking on him, but he ignored it because he was trying to do the right thing. When it was his turn to share something, he said "Second chances don't come around everyday so we should recognize them and be thankful." Everyone in the room looked

confused, but they nodded along anyway. What Key was actually
doing was playing mind games with Mr. Johnson. It was the
beginning of a diabolical plan to get through the summer course
by any means necessary. After two hours and going over what to
expect for the next month, class was over.

Key was headed to work. At some point during his walk,
he was adjusting the strap on his book bag when a man walking
behind him with a newspaper bumped into him. The man
claimed responsibility for not watching where he was walking
and apologized. Key told him that it was okay and kept walking.
The man called him back asking if he could help him. It was an
older man that appeared to be in his seventies. Key told him that
he couldn't because he had somewhere he needed to be. The man
told him that it wouldn't take long, and that he just needed some
information. Key looked at his watch then told the man to hurry
up. The man thanked him and showed him a page of his
newspaper. He pointed at something on the paper and said "I just
needed to know if you were in." Key looked at the man and the
comment Stack made about someone finding him immediately
came back to mind. He told the man "Yes!" The man said
"Thank you, young man." He then proceeded to walk off.

Despite the fact that he knew what had just taken place,
Key was still a little confused. He was more shocked at the fact
that he got caught again by another one of Blizzard's employees.
He still couldn't believe that he never knew where they were
coming from. He was now verbally committed to being down

with Blizzard. The next step of his journey was to get his cash register position back. He was confident that the plan he compiled the night before would be effective.

He finally got to work and went straight to Mr. Jones' office. Mr. Jones was on the phone. Key walked in with a tear running down his eye saying "Mr. Jones, I'm sorry. I was wrong and I messed up." Mr. Jones covered the receiver of the phone and told Key that it wasn't a good time. Key replied "There won't be a better time, I'm telling you sir. Things haven't been easy at home and my financial situation is the worst. I need my regular job back. I'll do whatever it takes. I have nowhere else to go." Key started to cry some more. Mr. Jones told the person he was talking to that he would call them back. He walked around the desk and gave Key a hug and told him that it would be alright. He told Key that he had been in the same position before and he knew what he was going through. He gave Key his original position back because he felt Key had showcased maturity by apologizing and claiming responsibility. He helped Key stand up straight and told him "Pride will get you but so far in this world. You're becoming a man and I'm proud of you." He then told Key to go wash his face and take the drive through window and they would talk about his register later.

Key went to the bathroom to rinse his face off. In the process of doing that, a voice could be heard from inside the stall saying "Great performance, now it's time to work." The person walked right by Key and left the bathroom. It was the Puerto

Rican guy he played basketball with; he still didn't know his name. Key dried his hands as fast he could in an attempt to catch him and ask how he knew what was going on. By the time he got out of the bathroom, the guy was walking out of the restaurant. It was probably for the best. As Key was getting deeper into the system, he was starting to accept the non-verbal communication aspect.

Key took his place at the drive through window. He took his first order of the day and told the customer to drive up to the window to complete the transaction. The car that pulled up to the window was an all black SUV with tinted windows. The window rolled down and the driver handed over a folded twenty dollar bill. Key took the money and as he was putting it into the cash register, he noticed a smaller piece of paper that was folded within the money. He gave the customer their change and told them to have a nice day. He immediately looked at the paper as they drove off. It was a note that had the next day's date on it and Blizzard's name. Key put the piece of paper in his pocket and went back to work.

Over the course of the week, Key got acclimated to his new joint position. At first he was nervous, but he quickly learned that mistakes weren't allowed in that position. Meanwhile, Shayna and I continued to enjoy the time she had left before she went away. Friday night of that week, Shayna and I went to Coney Island. That used to be what most Brooklynites did on Friday nights; Coney Island was our hang out spot. They usually had fireworks and other festivities. We always had a good time. We had just gotten ice cream and were walking on the boardwalk. Just like old times, we ran into the three musketeers; Key, Intellek, and Stack.

Stack ran up to us saying in a loud voice "FAMILY REUNION!" Shayna looked at him with a disgusted expression as she usually did. They had not seen each other since prom night when he insulted her. Stack asked her if she was still mad at what he said that night. She told him to not ask questions he already knew the answers to. Stack said life goes on; Shayna just ignored him. She said hi to Intellek and Key. I said hi to them as well. Key gave Shayna a hug and asked what we were doing out there. I told him it was the same thing they were doing; chilling in Coney Island on a Friday night. Key asked us if we wanted to hang out with them. We figured why not? From there we continued our night with them.

In the midst of our walk, Stack disconnected from our group after seeing someone he apparently knew. The rest of us continued to walk along the boardwalk. Shayna asked Key how his class was going. He told her that it was going well and that he was looking forward to completing the final upcoming three weeks. She expressed how proud of him she was then asked him how things were going at work. He told her that it had picked up and his financial situation was a little better. Shayna was happy to hear that as well. Key asked her how she was doing. Shayna told him that she was doing great, and that she was looking forward to going to school to run again. Key told her that if that was the case, he would race her to a sign a few meters ahead of us. Being Shayna, she of course accepted the challenge. They ran ahead and left myself and Intellek walking behind. Intellek and I weren't friends or even associates so that would usually be an awkward situation. Surprisingly, it wasn't. On our walk, I learned that aside from hanging out with Key and Stack, Intellek was actually a gentleman and a profound poet. He just happened to put that poetic skill toward being an aspiring artist in the group the three of them had formed.

Intellek and I spoke for a little while. He was the one that initiated conversation starting with "So how you doin' this evening?" It surprised me at first, but I couldn't go on without responding. I told him that I was doing fine. He proceeded to make small talk by asking me if Shayna and I were actually related in any way because we seemed so close. I explained to him how we pretty much were, just not by blood. As our conversation continued, Intellek showed that his name wasn't simply a stage name. He actually possessed a great degree of intellect and impressed me with how knowledgeable he was on different subject matters. I even got him to tell me his real name; Jamal. I asked him why he wasn't doing more with his academic gift. He told me that he wasn't quite sure what he wanted to do yet. I then asked him why he hung around with Stack and Key since he seemed like he had so much more to offer. He told me that they were the realest friends he had. He met Stack one day in a Math class, and Stack introduced him to Key after a freestyle cipher they had in the cafeteria. Key was impressed with Intellek's skill and from there, they all got close.

In the midst of our walk, Intellek stopped and told me that he remembered seeing Shayna on Redd's Island visiting somebody. I asked him why he felt the need to share that. He told me that it was because he meant to say it earlier in our conversation, but only remembered at the moment. That must have been exactly what Shayna and Key were talking about up ahead because they stopped walking. Apparently Key told her that Intellek mentioned seeing her on 'The Island' when he was there visiting his brother. Shayna wanted to know why Key felt that was important. Key told her that he didn't know she knew anyone on 'The Island'. She told him it was because she never mentioned it and asked him if it was a problem. Key told her that it wasn't a problem. He then asked her who she knew there. I don't know why he was that curious. For all he knew, she could've been visiting family. Either way, he was acting suspicious.

As Intellek and I were getting closer to them, I asked him if he mentioned it to Key. He told me that he did. I was starting to put two and two together; them stopping in their tracks, Intellek telling me he saw Shayna on Redd's Island, and then finally telling me that he mentioned it to Key. My only remaining question was if he told Key who she was visiting. He told me that he mentioned that it was some guy. At that point it was a no brainer. I could tell from Shayna's body language that it had to be the topic of the conversation. When we caught up to them all we heard was "What difference does it make if I have an ex-boyfriend that's incarcerated?" Key told her that it made no difference. Shayna told him that it must make a difference because he wouldn't have mentioned it. Key told her that she was right and they should just drop it. I asked if everything was okay. Shayna told me that everything was fine.

We continued our walk. All of a sudden we heard footsteps approaching us from behind at a rapid pace. We immediately turned around and moved to the side just in time to see Stack being chased by six guys. Shayna pulled me out of the way and forcibly walked the both of us a good distance away from what was going on. Key and Intellek started running too. As they were running, Key asked him what he did. Stack told him that he would explain later.

IT'S OFFICIAL

The following Monday, Shayna and I were out in the city shopping for things she needed for school. It was a nice day so we walked across the Brooklyn Bridge instead of taking the train. We went to a few stores; a couple of them were sporting goods stores. She needed new sneakers for her upcoming season along with some other items just in case she didn't like the school's equipment. In the process of searching for those items, the subject of me hearing back from schools came up. I had heard from one school, but it was a school I placed as my last resort. I still had time to hear back from my top choices. I changed the subject to what happened the night before.

I wanted to get the details of the conversation Shayna and Key had about Darryl. Shayna told me that Key was just being nosy because Intellek told him that she was visiting a guy on 'The Island' around our age. I told her that I thought it was pure jealousy which in some aspects was not a problem. It was easy to think that he was being nosy, but it was also a way of thinking that he couldn't control his emotions on the matter because he cared. Shayna said that whatever it was, he had the wrong approach. I couldn't argue with that. We finally finished at the store and went on our way.

Back at Jackie Robinson High, the second week of summer school was underway. The teacher's lounge was full of teachers getting coffee and other energy enhancing supplements.

167

Teachers never want to be there over the summer, but the extra money is always an attractive incentive. Ms. Mims and Mr. Johnson were among those teachers. He was getting coffee and she was eating her breakfast. He sat down at the table where she was eating and asked her how she was doing. She told him that she was great and asked how he was. He said that he was doing better since he ran into her for the day. She rolled her eyes and went back to eating. Ms. Mims knew that Mr. Johnson and a few of the other male teachers were quite fond of her, but she wasn't interested in any of them. She also preferred to not have a relationship with someone she worked with.

Mr. Johnson had made numerous attempts to get Ms. Mims' attention over the course of their time working at the school. That particular day, he attempted to sway her with tickets to an upcoming Anita Baker concert. He managed to get a hold of some information that confirmed that she was a big Anita Baker fan. For a second she got excited, but she wouldn't show it for the sake of not letting him know that she would in fact be interested.

Ms. Mims politely declined his advance and his offer. Mr. Johnson didn't know what to say, but he didn't want to lose her attention. He made another attempt at small talk by asking "You're not a fan of Anita?" Ms. Mims told him that she never said that. That made Mr. Johnson want to know why she didn't want to attend. She asked Mr. Johnson if that was his way of asking her out on a date. He wasn't expecting her to ask that so he nervously said "Well, yeah!" Ms. Mims told him that was exactly why she didn't want to go, she wasn't interested in a date.

She got up from the table to go wash her Tupperware in the sink. He got up and walked behind her asking her why she didn't want to. At that moment, she was turned off by his persistence and lack of respect for boundaries. She reiterated that it was simply because she didn't want to. Mr. Johnson got upset; you could see it in his facial expression. He said "So that's your game? You make deals to get your students some help, and then act like the person helping you out doesn't exist?" That got the attention of some of the other teachers.

Ms. Mims was insulted by his attack on her character. She replied "Excuse me? I make deals to get my students help because they need the help. If you thought you were getting something out of it, that's your own personal problem and you shouldn't be working with these students." Mr. Johnson told Ms. Mims that she had no right to tell him who he should and shouldn't be working with because she didn't know anything about him. Ms. Mims told him that just based on his behavior, she knew that he was immature with a sick mind and needed to get his priorities in order. Mr. Johnson flashed a creepy smile and told Ms. Mims that she was absolutely right and that he did need to check his priorities. He started to slowly walk backwards as he made his way to the lounge door, but never let his eyes off of Ms. Mims. He finally walked out of the room. All of the teachers looked at each other and at the same time, gathered their stuff and ran out of the lounge. The type of smile he gave usually meant that the discussion wasn't over and that he might be back. Nobody was interested in waiting to see what he would do next.

If Mr. Johnson was going to do something like they thought, it wasn't going to happen at that very moment. When he left the lounge, he went back to his classroom. His students were already assembled. Some were talking, some were sleeping at their desks, and others were reading. Mr. Johnson got to his desk and slammed a book down. Everybody immediately turned around, found their seats, or woke up. Key was slouching in his seat just watching Mr. Johnson carry out his anger. He didn't want to pay Mr. Johnson too much attention because he already read into his behavior. Not paying Mr. Johnson any attention would give him a better chance of not having to deal with him.

The class had an essay assignment due that was given to them before the weekend. Mr. Johnson looked out into the classroom and everyone just looked back at him. He said "I know you all were given an assignment so I don't know what you're waiting for." A few of the students that were intimidated by Mr. Johnson's mood swing immediately got up to turn their assignments in. The rest of the students soon followed their lead. Key remained seated and waited for everyone to sit down to turn his in. He already made up his mind that he wasn't going to change just because Mr. Johnson was having a bad day.

Key finally got up to turn his assignment in as the last student was heading back to their seat. Mr. Johnson looked at him as he turned it in and said "You still feel the need to be the center of attention, huh Mr. Williams?" Key ignored him and went back to his seat. Mr. Johnson told Key that he must have been running out of jokes. Key laughed and told Mr. Johnson that he would leave the jokes to him. Mr. Johnson accused Key of losing his edge. Key replied "Since we're questioning character, would you mind if I ask you if you're on your period?" Some of the class started snickering. Key told Mr. Johnson to listen to the other students, and then asked him if it sounded familiar.

Mr. Johnson informed Key that kind of insult was what he was looking for from him. Key replied "It's always a great feeling when you find something you were looking for." Mr. Johnson announced to the class that in the wake of Key's creative verbal responses, the class would have a creative writing essay due the next day in addition to the homework they would already be getting.

The school day was finally over and Key was headed to work. He was making his way up the few blocks he had to walk carrying his book bag on one shoulder as he always did. He finally got to work and put his stuff in his locker in the break room. He then washed his hands and made his way out to the register. He handled three customers before managing to get an on again off again acquaintance as his fourth. It was the Puerto

171

Rican guy that worked for Blizzard. The guy made his order to go and was served. As he was walking away from the counter he told Key to take his break. Key tried to explain that he had just gotten there, but the guy ignored him and kept walking towards the exit. Key watched him walk out, and then looked around to see if Mr. Jones was around. When he realized that the coast was clear, he told his coworker that was working the drive through to cover him for two minutes.

Key went after the guy and asked him what he needed. The guy said "First, who do you work for?" Key was confused as to why he was asking that. The guy told him "You work for Blizz. That means if Blizz tells me to tell you to take a break, you just take a break. End of story!" Key didn't like how he was being spoken to, but he ignored it because he didn't have much time. The guy finally gave his reason for being there. He told Key that Blizzard needed him to put in more hours. The agreement up to that point was that Key would only work when he had a shift because he didn't want things to look too obvious, but Blizzard needed the operation to be more lucrative. Key told him that the shift time was out of his control. The guy told him that he would have to learn to control it or be relocated in the operation. Key opted to find a way to make it work within the restaurant because being relocated was risky.

Mr. Jones walked outside and asked Key what he was doing. Blizzard's employee walked off with his food. Mr. Jones wanted to know who the guy was. Key told him that it was just an old friend. Mr. Jones told Key that he was going to have to do better than that if he thought it was okay to leave his post. He apologized to Mr. Jones and started walking back inside. Mr. Jones stared Key down as he walked back in and asked him who he worked for. Instead of Key giving a straight answer, he told Mr. Jones "You're right, sir. It won't happen again." Hearing the same question twice from two different parties over the course of five minutes was throwing off Key's thought process. They both went back inside the restaurant. A few feet down the block, Blizzard's employee put the food he bought next to a sleeping homeless man.

Later that evening around 9:00, Shayna and I were just getting back to the block from shopping in the city. We gave each other a hug and we went to our houses. At around 11:30PM, Shayna was walking back into her room after taking a shower. She lied down on her bed for a minute. As she was lying down she began to hear a clicking sound; it was coming from the direction of her window. She got up and turned her light off, then went to the side of the window. That's when she realized the clicking was from pebbles hitting the glass. She looked down from the side to see who it was only to find out that it was Key. She opened the window and asked him what he was doing there. Key told her that he had to talk to her about something. She asked him what it was. He told her that he needed to talk to her in person and asked if she could meet him at the front door. She told him that she would be right down.

When Shayna got downstairs, Key was at the middle of the stoop. She met him on that step and looked back up at her window. Shayna asked him how he knew which window was hers. He told her that he just got a few pebbles and hoped for the best. Shayna asked him if he was crazy. He told her that crazy might be the most accurate description. She asked him if he was feeling okay. At that moment Key just blurted out "I want to be your man." Shayna's eyes opened wide. This time he asked if she was okay. Shayna told him that she was okay, but a bit confused as to where it was all coming from. Key asked her to sit down so he could further explain, but Shayna didn't want to sit down with the clothes she was planning on sleeping in. He told her that it was fine.

Key began to explain that his behavior at Coney Island stemmed from the thought of hearing she was visiting some guy in prison that looked to be around our age. He admitted that he was wrong for jumping to conclusions and that he was just a little jealous. Shayna told him that his jealousy was his own personal problem. Key agreed with her point, but explained that jealousy was only going to become more of a problem if he didn't have her by his side. He told her that he needed her badly and that he was sure of that because it was an unfamiliar feeling, but it felt so right. Shayna was moved by his words and told him that she didn't know what to say. Key told her to say that she would help him solve his problem by making him happier than he had ever been. Shayna had gotten a little weak and began to feel around for the steps behind her. Key caught her by her back and arm and asked her if she was okay. She told him that she was fine, and that she just needed to take a seat after all. Key reminded her about her clothes getting dirty, but she said that she would change when she got back in.

Shayna took a seat on the stoop and Key sat next to her. She started to explain that she would be lying if she said didn't have feelings for him as well. Key suggested that they stop holding back the mutual feelings and create something beautiful. Shayna told him that as ideal as that sounded, she couldn't just make a decision that big at that very moment. That's the type of decision you give a lot of thought and consideration. Key understood her logic, but didn't know if it would make much of a difference. He figured that whether she gave it thought or not, her true feelings were that she wanted to be with him as well. In other words, even if she wasn't ready for that type of commitment, the thought of wanting to be together would still be present.

Key was basically suggesting that they cut out the middle process and did what they both felt. Shayna admitted that he made a compelling point, but she still wasn't comfortable making a decision of that nature without giving it some thought. She then went on a rant about how she was leaving for school, how it's only been a few months since she got out of her last relationship, and how she was just starting to really enjoy a life of not being emotionally committed to anyone. Before she could get to the next thing on her list, Key pulled her close and gave her a long deep kiss.

Shayna was slowly captivated by the feeling and soon began to kiss him back. Key slowly released and told her "You could have a million reasons to not pursue a relationship with me, but that's all they'll be if you continue to allow fear to cancel out your heart." Shayna looked into Key's eyes and asked him what his heart was telling him at that very moment. He said that it was telling him that she was his destiny. He then reminded her that his feelings for her changed his entire outlook on life and motivated him to take his education and future more seriously.

All of the games and playing hard to get that Shayna was doing was like a code. That night it seemed like Key's words were delivered in the right combination to crack that code. I say that because Shayna decided that Key proposed a good idea and eventually said yes to being his girlfriend. They had become an official couple. Key put his arm around her and they sat outside for a little while talking about what being together meant, and what the future could possibly hold for them. They also talked about other random topics. One of those random topics was what happened at Coney Island. Shayna wanted to know what went down after her and I separated ourselves from them, and what Stack did to get chased in the first place.

STACK'S ON DECK

Key explained what Stack did as a drug deal that almost went bad. That was the moment Shayna learned that Stack was in fact dealing drugs, but it didn't surprise her. The thing about Stack was that he was the loud and flashy type. He showed off a lot, wore expensive clothes, jewelry, and flashed his pager for the world to see that he had money. Shayna and I always noticed this about him, but didn't say anything. The problem was that it didn't add up. He was only sixteen and we knew he didn't have the type of job to afford the merchandise he was walking around with. He used to do the same thing when the three of them were traveling and doing shows, but to a lesser degree.

On the night we were at Coney Island, Stack was making a transaction with one of his customers. The deal was going over well, but Stack developed a sense of greed. The method in which his deals usually were carried out was an exchange of the money and the product in a single motion of both parties' hands. The customer would usually trust him because they had done business many times before. In that particular transaction, Stack exchanged with the customer using a different hand motion. He managed to grip the money and keep the product. After managing to do that, he took off running. The customer ran after him with his friends that weren't too far away following suit. That's what led to the chase.

Shayna made it clear that she was not surprised about Stack. She told Key about all the signs and hints she picked up on about him over the course of time. Key told her that Stack always had that mentality. As soon he got a little bit of money, he had to let the world know by buying something expensive. Shayna stated that he sounded very insecure to which Key confirmed that he was. Shayna got a little more comfortable in Key's arms as they sat on the stoop and told him that she needed to ask him a question. He told her that she could ask him anything. She asked him why he still hung out with Stack if that was the type of lifestyle Stack lived. Key explained that he and Stack grew up together so he was more than a friend, they were like brothers. Shayna told him that it was understandable, but it said something about his character to be associated with someone involved in illegal activity. Key asked her what exactly she felt it said about him. Shayna simply said "Birds of a feather flock together."

Key moved a little to the side and looked down at Shayna; Shayna looked back up at him. Key asked her if she was insinuating that he was dealing drugs too. Shayna told him that she was only stating general facts. She then turned the question around on him and asked him if he would tell her if he was dealing drugs or doing something illegal. He asked her why she thought he would keep something like that from her. She stated that there were many reasons to keep something like that a secret. Key couldn't argue with that. Shayna sat there still waiting for an answer. Key replied "No, I wouldn't keep something like that from you." She looked at him for a while as a test to see if he could look her in her eyes and keep a straight face while he stated his claim. He must have had a good poker face because Shayna dropped the interrogation. She went on to ask why Stack felt the need to do that if he had done deals with that particular customer before. Key told her that according to Stack, it was fun and gave him a rush.

The two of them went back to their relaxed position. It wasn't too long before Key requested if he could ask a question also; Shayna was okay with that. Key asked her what caused the demise of her last relationship. Shayna took a deep breath and told Key that Darryl cheated on her. Key expressed sympathy by telling her that he was sorry to hear that. She told him that he didn't need to be sorry because he didn't do anything and it was in the past. He then asked her if she minded him asking how Darryl ended up in prison. She told him that Darryl was just like Stack in the sense that he made some foolish decisions and that's where they landed him. Key said "Well yeah, that's usually what happens." Shayna replied "Exactly! Stack better stop believing that he's untouchable." Key had a blank look on his face. Her words obviously hit home.

Shayna asked him if work and his financial situation were continuing to stabilize since their conversation about it at Coney Island. He told her that things were still going well and that he hoped it stayed that way. Shayna was happy to hear that. It was getting late so she suggested that he start making his way back home because he had school in the morning. He agreed and they both got up. They gave each other a hug and kiss and Key started walking back down the steps. As he was walking down, she told him that she might stop by his job some time during the week after visiting Ms. Mims at the school. He told her that he would be looking forward to it. They said good night one more time. He went on his way and Shayna went back inside.

A few days later, Stack was working a corner not too far from his building. He never worked directly in his own courtyard or on his own block. It was now Thursday and he had apparently pulled his stunt a few more times between the night at Coney Island and the present day. He did it despite being warned by someone in the organization. He was told that if he had done it again, he would face consequences because he was throwing off Blizzard's flow of business. Stack didn't pay the warning any attention, or the fact that he may run into those disgruntled customers again.

His stunt didn't go over the way he had planned on that particular day. When making his faulty transaction he turned to run, but turned his ankle at the same time. To make it worse, he wasn't selling to the average crack head. These were fully functioning guys that just loved to get high. They didn't take too well to his attempt to scam them. One of the guys stood over Stack while he grimaced in pain and accused him of trying to cheat them, then punched him square in his face. A few more guys jumped in and began kicking him in his face, ribs, and stomach. The assault went on for about a minute and a half before Pablo, the owner of the bodega Stack was dealing in front of, came out with an axe. He told all of the guys to back up. When they took a step back you could see the damage they had done to Stack. His left eye was swollen and he more than likely had a broken bone or two that couldn't be seen past his clothes.

The lead guy told Stack that it served him right and grabbed the money and the product that Stack dropped. Just then, the police rolled up. Their car jumped the curb and everybody scattered. Pablo ran back into his store. Stack tried to get up and run but his turned ankle and battered body would not permit it. The cops handcuffed him and called an ambulance to the scene. As crooked as cops were in that neighborhood, I'm surprised that they didn't take him down to the precinct in the condition he was in.

Back at Burger Empire, Key managed to find a way to get extra hours. A few days prior to that Thursday, Key worked out a deal with some higher ups in the organization. He proposed that he get one of his coworkers to quit. Then, he would convince Mr. Jones to let him pick up the shift with a sob story about how he could use it for his struggles and financial situation. In return, he would give his coworker six weeks pay to cover him. When Blizzard heard about the idea he approved it under two conditions. If it didn't work, Key would be relocated immediately to avoid any possible suspicions. The other condition was that the six weeks of pay would be coming out of

Key's pocket. Key told the messenger that it would not be a problem.

Key had a coworker that he noticed did not really want to work. He would always show up late, slack around most of the time, and usually just looked for ways to burn time until he got off. Key added all of that up and realized that his coworker was just there for the money. That was a better time than any to propose the idea to him. His coworker did not think twice when he saw how much money he was being given at one time. He took the money and told Mr. Jones he was quitting. That's when phase two of Key's plan was put into motion. That managed to be successful as well and he was immediately given more hours. He didn't need the sob story. Mr. Jones was more interested in filling that position before he started to lose money.

Over the course of those few days, Burger Empire was not the only place where business was picking up. Things were heating up between Key and Shayna as well. They were going through that early romantic stage or what some call puppy love. Every day, either Shayna was at his job, or he was at her doorstep. On one of those days, she stopped by his job after seeing Ms. Mims like she promised. She was giving Ms. Mims a last good bye before she went away to school. When she got to his job, he took his break.

She didn't stay long; they spoke at one of the tables for about ten to fifteen minutes. Their conversation consisted of possible plans for the weekend, and how school was going since he was halfway done with his final class. That's where the conversation got a little rocky. Key told her that school was going well the first week, but for some reason the second week wasn't too great. He explained how Mr. Johnson started giving him a hard time again. For the most part, Key didn't reply much to Mr. Johnson, but Mr. Johnson would randomly harass him like he had some type of vendetta.

Shayna became skeptical about what Key told her and asked him when it started. He explained that it started Monday of that same week. She told him that when she went to visit Ms. Mims earlier, Ms. Mims told her about what happened in the lounge. As a result of that, everyone had been watching their step around him. They both came to the conclusion that there was in fact a correlation between the two events. She then suggested that Key talk to Ms. Mims when he got a chance. It was time for Key to get back to work, but he promised that he would talk to Ms. Mims. They gave each other a hug and she went on her way.

Later that night, Key arrived home to find his mother eating a beef patty with juice by candlelight. Key looked at her like she was weird and asked her what her problem was as he laughed a little. She explained that she didn't have a problem and she was just trying to change. He told her to proceed by all means. All of the bills and utilities had been paid so that relieved the two of them of any stress and tension. His mother never bothered to ask where money was coming from and she didn't care either. One of the more important utilities was the phone; it was out of service for a while before Key started working with Blizzard. His mother told him that Intellek had called.

Key put his stuff down and got settled in before calling him back. He couldn't get him at his house so he paged him. Intellek called him back immediately. He told Key that he had been trying to get a hold of him all day; he even tried to call him at his job. That was one of the biggest differences between now and the 90s. House phones were the primary means of communication. The next technological step up was a pager, then a cell phone. If you didn't have a pager or cell phone, you had to wait until you got home to get messages. Even then, you had to have an answering machine to retrieve them.

Intellek sounded a little frantic over the phone. Key asked him what the problem was. He informed him about what happened to Stack earlier that day, and the condition he was in. At the time, Intellek was with him at the hospital. He asked if Stack's mom knew. She was actually the person that informed Intellek about what happened. Key told him that he would be over there as soon as he possibly could.

Key finally arrived at the hospital. As soon as he got to Stack's room, he noticed how battered he was, and then he noticed the handcuffs. He had been handcuffed to his hospital bed. He couldn't leave because he was still under investigation. Key gave Stack's mother a hug. She hadn't stopped crying ever since she got there. She couldn't bear seeing her only son in the condition he was in. It was also how she found out that he was selling drugs. Stack was conscious, but he couldn't talk for too long without feeling pain. One of the kicks he took to his body cracked a rib and part of the rib was pressing into his right lung.

After looking at Stack for a while, Key asked him what he was thinking when he decided to do what he did. That conversation was just a replay of the first time Stack pulled his stunt. Instead of saying it was fun this time, Stack just rolled his eyes and turned his head. Key reminded him that he warned him that consequences would eventually occur. Stack's mom stopped crying and looked at Key in shock. She asked him how he knew about Stack selling drugs. Key sighed as he realized that he had just told on himself. Stack's mom expressed her disgust and disappointment for them by telling them "You two are supposed to look out for each other. You two are like brothers." Key tried to apologize to her. She told him that apologizing didn't get anybody anywhere at that point. The nurse came in and told all of them that they needed to leave because visiting hours were over.

The next day around noon, Ms. Kim and Shawn Sr. called Shayna downstairs to address a concern they had. Shawn had taken notice of Key's late night visits to the stoop over the previous week. He brought it to Ms. Kim's attention and they wanted answers. Shayna sat down and her mother got straight to the point by asking "Is there something going on with you and Keith?" Shayna had a puzzled facial expression. Ms. Kim took her facial expression as a yes. Shayna asked her mother if she was in trouble for that. Her mother told her that she wasn't in trouble for dating, but the fact that she was sneaking around to do so was setting a foundation that would produce problems for her.

Shawn decided to voice his opinion on the matter. He told Shayna that he personally felt it was a bad idea because Key didn't strike him as someone that had much ambition. Shayna asked him how he would know what kind of person Key was. Shawn told her that he and Ms. Kim were only looking out for her best interest. He also reminded her that her last relationship was only a few months over and that she should give herself more time to emotionally heal. Shayna told Shawn that she didn't need anyone telling her when and when not to move on or get over someone or something. She also said that it was her life and if she was going to make mistakes, then she would deal with them. Ms. Kim told Shayna to watch her tone and her mouth. She then told her that it was best that she went to her room and relaxed for a while. Shayna told her mother that she was relaxed and that the two of them were being judgmental.

In Shayna's mind she was being treated unfairly and they were saying that she couldn't make decisions on her own. She also felt it wasn't fair to Key because the way he looked and who he was were two different things. Ms. Kim told her that the speech she was giving wasn't new; it had been given by woman all over the world before they reached college. She then reiterated that they were looking out for her best interest. Shayna rebutted that Key was her main interest and that she was going to continue seeing him. Ms. Kim told her that it was fine and if she felt she was a grown woman, she was free to make grown women decisions. Shayna felt a little uneasy after that response. She was confident, believing her mom was exhibiting trust. However, she was also doubtful and wondered if it was a trick her mother was trying to play. Either way, she asked if she was free to go. Her mother told her she was free to fly if she was capable.

GAME PLAN

Over the next week, a lot had taken place. Shayna and Key continued to see each other on a regular basis. Shayna's parents' disapproval of their relationship seemed to have pushed them closer together. Business continued to go well at Burger Empire for Key and Blizzard, Stack continued to recover, and Intellek and I spent a day in Times Square hanging out. Key continued to push toward graduation, but ran into some unnecessary disagreements with Mr. Johnson. He managed to talk with Ms. Mims about his issues with Mr. Johnson. They both discovered a few interesting facts about him.

Over the course of Stack's recovery, he was visited by a few detectives in search of a statement on what happened the day he was jumped and drugs were found on him. Stack didn't like police so he consistently refused to speak to them. He was finally healthy enough to travel so he was transferred to a juvenile detention infirmary to complete his recovery. While there, he still refused to speak to anyone. The only thing he was willing to discuss was his court date and how much his bail was. A court date had been set for two months from that date, and his bail was set at $25,000. He didn't have that money and his mother didn't either. He would have if he didn't spend it as soon as he got it. He managed to post bail anyway courtesy of Blizzard's organization. Blizzard didn't want to risk anyone snitching so he usually took care of the bail and legal fees for an employee's first offense. After that, they would have to answer for their own mistakes.

Stack's ride had arrived. He couldn't go home because his mother didn't want him there knowing what kind of money was used to get him out. It didn't matter because they weren't taking him home. They were taking him to a meeting point in DUMBO. DUMBO is an acronym for 'Down Under the Manhattan Bridge Overpass'; it's located in Brooklyn. The meeting was in an abandoned warehouse. When they got there, they informed him that Blizzard was upset. Stack was questioned by some henchmen appointed by Blizzard about why he pulled his infamous stunt after being warned. Due to the amount of times Stack pulled his fake transaction, the organization had lost some business on those particular corners and locations. Stack looked pitiful; his upper body was wrapped, his right arm was in a sling, and he had numerous bandages on his face.

His explanation consisted of a lie about him being strapped for cash and just trying to make some extra money. He then promised it would not happen again. One of the guys told Stack that he was right about it not happening again because he was going to make it right. They threatened to break the rest of his ribs and a few other bones if he did not correct his mistake. Stack asked them if there were any specific methods he needed to follow to correct it. One of the men approached Stack slowly and squeezed his injured arm. Stack began to groan in pain with an expression of anguish on his face. The man told him "You want some specific instructions? Specifically, get it done. If business doesn't specifically pick up on your corners within the next two days, we have specific orders from Blizz to show you specifically how serious he is. You specifically understand?" Stack still grimacing in pain told them that he understood. They left Stack and told him to find his own way home. The upcoming Sunday was his deadline.

Back at the school, Key and Mr. Johnson were verbally going at it once again. Mr. Johnson asked him to read something out of the book that they were using for the class. Key had no problem with that. As he was reading, Mr. Johnson kept stopping him to correct his pronunciation of certain words. The only problem was that Key wasn't mispronouncing any of the words. Mr. Johnson would say the word before Key could say it making it seem like Key needed help reading. Key ignored it three times. A fourth time he looked up at Mr. Johnson, but ignored it again. Mr. Johnson did it a fifth time and that was the last straw. Key put the book down and asked Mr. Johnson if he had a problem. Mr. Johnson told him that there was no problem at all. Key replied "If you don't mind, I'd like to read the rest of the passage on my own."

Key picked the book back up and began to read again. He got through about two lines before Mr. Johnson interrupted again by saying "You're supposed to pause when you get to a comma." Key put the book down again, looked at Mr. Johnson and told him "Why don't you try pausing altogether? You seem very anxious to play with me today." Mr. Johnson told Key to watch his tone and remember that he was the student and Mr. Johnson was the teacher. Key was slightly confused because they had gone back and forth numerous times. Mr. Johnson would either come back with a witty remark of his own or bow out gracefully.

The anger filled response from Mr. Johnson was rather strange. Key told him to calm down. Mr. Johnson took his glasses off and got up from his desk. He began to slowly approach Key's desk. Key didn't wait for him to get to the desk; he stood up too. Once he arrived at Key's desk, he looked up at Key and said in a raspy voice "You gonna hit me, punk?" Key noticed the voice change and asked him "Who are you supposed to be? Clint Eastwood?" Mr. Johnson got a little more belligerent. "COME ON, DUDE! HIT ME! HIT ME RIGHT HERE!" He started smacking his face really hard in the spot where he wanted Key to hit him. Key picked up his books and told Mr. Johnson to chill. Mr. Johnson started shaking the desk and yelling. Key slid around him and left the room. Mr. Johnson flipped Key's desk which prompted the rest of the students to collect their books and exit the room also.

Mr. Johnson was the only one left in the room. He started throwing desks and destroying things while yelling "YOU CAN'T HAVE HER.", "SHE'S MINE!" and "YOU WANT TO TAKE HER FROM ME?" One of the students alerted the principal. Key made his way to Ms. Mims classroom. He told Ms. Mims what was going on and they made their way back to

Mr. Johnson's. When they got there, Mr. Johnson was being restrained outside of the room by school security and one of the other male teachers. He was still yelling "HE CAN'T HAVE HER!" His eyes caught Key and Ms. Mims arriving at the scene and he yelled in Key's direction "YOU CAN'T HAVE HER!" Key and Ms. Mims looked at each other, and then looked back at him. Security picked him up and carried him away. Class was dismissed for that day.

Key went back to Ms. Mims class to have his long overdue conversation with her that he promised Shayna he would have. They shared their personal experiences regarding Mr. Johnson with each other. They found a few common denominators; the ultimate one being that he was in love with Ms. Mims. It didn't help that the one person that had a close connection with her was his least favorite student. The behavior Mr. Johnson exhibited was a result of built up jealousy. We later found out that it was also due to a mental balancing medication that he was on, but stopped taking.

The next day was a Friday. I went into the city for a job interview at The Garden and to run some errands. I was still waiting to hear back from the schools, but I figured I would have to work whether I heard back or not. I had an interview with their catering department. Ultimately, my plan was to get into the field of hospitality. From there, I planned on managing, then owning my own business. I figured a job in their catering services would be a good start. I would also get to see Knicks games for free.

The interview went very well. The human resources lady and I bonded even better. I felt like she really liked me, but I would only know for sure if they contacted me. I was leaving The Garden and heading to a store a block over. When I was walking into the store, Intellek was walking out. We greeted each other and I asked him what he was doing there. He was picking something up for his mother, I thought it was sweet. I told him that I was just there to return something. He asked if I minded his company. I told him that it was fine as long as he didn't mind a few more errands. He didn't mind at all.

Running errands turned into just hanging out and making random stops on our walk. I told him that I preferred calling him by his real name; he was actually fine with it. We walked around some more and before we knew it, we were in Times Square. It was crowded as usual so we got the crazy idea to mess with tourists. It wasn't anything too extreme, just harmless fun. For example, we told them that a certain celebrity was somewhere not too far. Word traveled quickly and the tourists flocked to that one area. That in turn cleared up some room on the cluttered street for us to walk. Tourists were usually star struck in New York when they saw a celebrity so the chance of seeing one made them go crazy. It managed to work for us. We spent a few more hours in the city window shopping and getting something to eat before deciding to head back to Brooklyn. Overall, we had a good time. Jamal was great company.

He walked me home to make sure I got home safely, and then made his way home. He lived in East Flatbush, Brooklyn. Before he walked off, he asked me if I was free the next day which was a Sunday. I told him that my time was going to be occupied by church, but that he was welcome to join me. He told me that he respected that and he would, but not that particular Sunday. I told him that it was fine as long as he kept a promise of at least visiting one day. He explained that he attended a church also, but only to keep his mom happy. She stressed over the mere thought of him straying into the world. I told him that I understood her concern because the world was a very influential place. He nodded his head in agreement and looked up at the stars. He then looked at me and told me that he would tell me the first Sunday that he was available.

The next day, Stack was putting together a game plan to fix the problem he had caused. He couldn't think of any ideas because he was too tied up on what the organization would do if he didn't fix it. His main corner was off limits at the moment because it was still under surveillance for drug activity. His arrest brought a great amount of attention to the area. Blizzard had people working Stack's other corners because Stack was now heavily on the police radar. Stack's main goal was to either bring back the customers that were lost, or recruit new ones. He came to the conclusion that recruiting was the best option because the ones that he angered more than likely still wanted to hurt him.

Recruiting wasn't going to be an easy task because he lost the privilege to carry the product; this meant he had no bait.

Key was aware of Stack's predicament. Stack was staying with Key and Key's mother because he had no other place to go. They spent the second night of his two day window coming up with a plan. Stack knew that he was possibly facing the end if he didn't report to the organization with a sure fire plan the next day. Blizzard made sure the organization knew where Stack was staying. Key and Stack had spent two hours thinking up schemes, but came up with nothing. It was around 3:00 in the morning when Stack decided to call it a night and just play it by ear. Key looked at him like he was crazy. He asked him how he could opt to give up when his life was on the line. They didn't know exactly what the organization was going to do per Blizzard's request, but they weren't putting killing Stack over money past them. After all, money is the blood that pumps life into a drug lord's body. It's their gateway to power and respect.

Stack lied down on the couch that served as his bed while he was staying there. He told Key that he wasn't concerned about it anymore as he closed his eyes. Key asked him if he had a death wish; his words were starting to concern him. Stack replied "If my life is supposed to end at that meeting, then so be it. If that's not the way it's supposed to end, then we carry on." Key couldn't bear the mental load that was being produced by Stack's words. He decided to let Stack sleep; he had his own agenda for the following morning anyway. He was planning on meeting Shayna for breakfast before he went to work.

DO OR DIE

The meeting was being held in DUMBO, this time near the warehouse instead of inside. Key and Stack made their way out of their apartment building. As they were leaving, they saw Stack's mom walking into the building. Stack fixed his eyes on her and said "Hi Ma!" She said "Hello, Warren!" and kept walking. Stack asked her if she was ever going to talk to him, but she didn't give a response. He let out a long sigh and kept walking as well, Key followed him. They made their way to the Subway to catch the 3 train. He told Shayna that he would meet her near the Promenade.

Throughout the entire train ride, Stack didn't express any solid emotion. Key couldn't tell if he was in deep thought on the matter, or if he was scared out of his mind. His stop was before Key's. As the stop was coming up, Key told Stack to be careful and to not do anything stupid. Stack didn't respond; he just kept a blank stare as he walked off of the train. Key watched him walk off, but began to think that he could not live with himself if anything happened to Stack. He decided to get off too, managing to slip between the doors before they closed.

Stack walked his few blocks to the meeting place in an alley on Pearl Street. Key followed him, but kept a good distance to make sure Stack didn't notice. The way Stack was acting, I don't think being noticed was going to be a problem for Key. When Stack finally got to the designated spot, he removed the sling that was holding up his injured shoulder. He then put his healthy arm out to the side and yelled "I'M HERE! DO WHAT YOU GOTTA DO!" Key gave up his cover by yelling "NOOOO!" as he ran towards Stack. He grabbed Stack, but made sure he didn't grab him too aggressively and aggravate any injuries. He pushed him close to a wall in the alley and smacked him while asking him what his problem was. Stack told Key to let him go. Key refused to let him go until he started thinking straight. At that moment, a black SUV pulled up letting three guys out.

Key released Stack from his grip and stared the three guys down as they approached. One of them was the Puerto Rican guy that seemed to keep popping up whenever business took place. The other two guys with him were at the last DUMBO meeting. The Puerto Rican guy went simply by Rivera. They had finally learned his name over the course of their time with the organization. Rivera turned his attention to Key and asked him "Shouldn't you be on your way to work?" Key told him that he felt Stack's meeting was more important. Rivera told Key that Blizzard felt his money was more important and that he and Stack were now making him lose even more. Key told him that money wasn't more important than life. Rivera laughed and told Key that he obviously didn't read the fine print when he joined the organization. The three of them began to approach Stack and Key slowly. Key stepped in front of Stack to protect him.

When Rivera reached the spot where they were standing, he was standing toe to toe with Key. Key looked him right in his eye. Rivera told him that he had one more chance to leave and get to work. Key refused again and told him that if he was going to kill Stack, he would have to kill him too. That got Stack's attention. Rivera told Key that he thought he was smarter, and then signaled for the other two guys to get Key out of the way. They both grabbed Key; Key immediately pushed one off and got into a boxing stance while yelling "WHAT'S UP?" to the other. The other one subtly pulled a gun from inside his jacket and replied "You tell me." Key put his hands up and suggested that everyone calm down. Rivera arrogantly asked him why he all of a sudden wanted to calm down when he was just ready to take on an army. With his hands still up in a surrendering position, Key asked Rivera what kind of a stupid question that was.

Rivera must have not taken too well to Key's answer. He slowly approached Key saying "Oh, so you're calling me stupid now?" Key was still looking him in his eyes, but saying nothing. The henchman with the gun told Key that Rivera asked him a question. Rivera grabbed Key by the collar and pushed him against the wall yelling at him to answer the question. Key stayed quiet. He wasn't dumb enough to go into battle unarmed against a fully armed opposition. Rivera told him that he knew he was smart; referring to Key's decision to stay quiet. He let Key go and told him that he should've stuck to rapping and basketball. Key was noticeably angry. Rivera did a 180 to face Stack's direction, then in one swift movement turned back around and punched Key in his right eye. Key fell to the ground holding his eye while Rivera stood over him saying "Learn your place." The punch left a laceration over Key's eye. Rivera added to that by kicking Key in his stomach.

Stack stood up against the wall parallel to the one Key was against with a look of shock. At the same time, Key decided that he wasn't going to be treated like a child. He got up to retaliate, but the guy with the gun pointed it at him causing him to stop in his tracks once again. Rivera told the henchman to hand the gun to him. He then grabbed Key by the neck and told him to open his mouth. Key didn't have much choice. With blood trickling down his face from the cut, he began to hyperventilate. He looked at Rivera and opened his mouth. Rivera placed the gun in Key's mouth and told him that he wasn't as smart as he thought. Stack frantically yelled "WAIT!" Rivera, still holding the gun in Key's mouth, looked at Stack. Stack told him that he was who they came for so they needed to do their job and leave Key out of it. Rivera told both henchmen to restrain Key.

Rivera slowly approached Stack and told him to not think that they had forgotten about him. Stack told him that if they wanted him, he was right there. Rivera, now relieved that they could finally get down to business, asked Stack if he had come up with a solution to his problem. Stack revealed that he had not.

That wasn't the answer Rivera was looking for so he told the henchmen to put Stack in the vehicle. He continued to point the gun at Key just in case Key tried to stop them. Before Rivera got in, he told Key that he had ten minutes to get to work. He closed his door and they pulled off. Key picked up Stack's sling and ran out of the alley to see which direction they drove in. However, it didn't make a difference at the time.

Key looked in both directions rubbing his head trying to figure out what he should do at that point. He eventually reached the conclusion that he should get in contact with Shayna. He found the nearest payphone and called her house. Shayna had finally given him her number during their time of getting closer. Shawn Sr. picked up the phone. When Key asked if Shayna was there, Shawn told him to hold on as he gave the phone to Ms. Kim. Ms. Kim told Key that she went out earlier and had not been back yet. Key asked if he could leave her a message. Ms. Kim granted his request under the condition that he answered a question for her. He asked her what she needed to know. She told him that he could leave his message first.

Key asked her to tell Shayna that he couldn't make it that morning because something came up with work. Ms. Kim told him that she could do that, and then asked him where they were supposed to meet. Key told her that they were meeting at the Promenade and planned to go to breakfast from there. Ms. Kim explained that was actually what she wanted to ask him about. She asked him if he and Shayna were close. Key respectfully replied "Yes ma'am!" Ms. Kim asked him what his intentions were with Shayna. He asked her if he could answer at a later time. Ms. Kim asked him what was wrong with answering at that very moment. He told her that there was just a lot going on at the moment, and it wasn't the best time to have a discussion. He offered to stop by that week. She approved of that idea.

Life only seemed to get more interesting in Brooklyn for us and everyone associated with us as the days progressed. A few days had passed; it was now Wednesday. Key was progressing through his final week of school, but he wasn't himself. He had a change in class instructor due to Mr. Johnson's behavior the week before. The school brought in a teacher at the last minute to complete the final week. The change had a mental effect on Key; but not as much of an effect as not hearing from or about Stack since the day they were in the alley. He entered a state of depression. The only place that could give him answers was the organization. Needless to say, he wasn't getting any information on Stack. Key had begun to expect the worst possible scenario, but refused to fully believe it. Instead, he remained hopeful that he would soon hear from Stack.

On a positive note, the school informed Key's class upon leaving that day that there would be another slight change in their curriculum. A few of the students let out sighs of frustration. They were told that their frustration was understandable and the change would be beneficial to them. The school knew that the change in instructor wasn't their fault, especially so close to completion. With that said, they were in line to automatically pass that course with a grade of A. All they had to do was complete the final days with perfect attendance. They all celebrated and it brought a slight degree of happiness to Key as he left school for work that day.

That night was the night he decided to go to Shayna's to talk to Ms. Kim like he promised. He had informed Shayna that he would be visiting for that reason. When he got to the door, Shayna was there to greet him. She hadn't seen him in almost a week; their meeting at the Promenade the previous Sunday was their last scheduled meeting time. However, they had been in contact through phone calls. Shayna could tell that he wasn't himself and something seemed different in his overall demeanor during their phone conversations.

When she greeted him at the door, she gave him a hug and told him that she missed him. Ms. Kim and Shawn Sr. looked at each other and shook their heads. Shayna did not feel the same amount of love in the weak hug that he gave her. She asked him if he was okay. He told her that he was fine and kissed her forehead. He was unable to completely mask his feelings of pain, so he figured a kiss on the forehead would reassure her that everything was okay. She noticed the bandage over his eye where Rivera's punch formed a gash. She asked him how it happened. He told her that it was a slight accident at work.

It was around 7:00PM and the meeting was about to commence for the four of them. Ms. Kim told Key that she was going to get straight to the point. She got down to business by asking him what his intentions were with Shayna. Key sat there looking in an off direction with a depressed facial expression. His response was "In life, you meet many people. You don't know how long your connection will last with anyone. All you can hope for is a long term relationship in the event that you develop a strong bond with that person. If you lose someone you love, it tears at your heart with an unimaginable pain." Shayna placed her hand on her chest with a look of overwhelming happiness on her face. She began to tell Key how beautiful his words were. Shayna's parents looked at each other, and then looked back at Key and Shayna. Ms. Kim told him that regardless of how profound it sounded, she needed to know if that was his answer to the question or just a result of his apparent state of depression. Key sat back in his chair rubbing his head and let out a deep sigh before telling her that he didn't know. Shayna asked her mom and Shawn if they could have a minute. Ms. Kim approved and excused them.

Shayna got up and led Key to the front door so that they could talk on the stoop. When they got outside, Shayna told Key that if he was trying to make a good impression on her parents, he wasn't really doing a good job. Key wiped his face with both his hands and revealed a distressed look. Shayna began to get even more worried. She told him to just tell her what the problem was because silence wasn't going to help anyone. Key told her that at that particular moment, he really just needed some water.

Shayna took him back inside. She had to guide him because he began to feel a little faint. As they walked through the living room to the kitchen, Ms. Kim asked Shayna if Key was okay. Shayna told her that he was okay, and that he just wasn't feeling too well.

When they got to the kitchen, Key grabbed for a chair to support himself. He wasn't looking too good. Shayna moved a little quicker to get him some water. She brought a glass to him and told him to just relax. Key took one sip and sat back in the chair. About two seconds later, he sat up and asked Shayna where their nearest bathroom was. She told him that it was the room near the front door. Key ran out of the kitchen and past Shayna's parents directly to the bathroom. They could hear him throwing up. Ms. Kim looked at Shayna in search of an explanation. Shayna just shrugged her shoulders as if to say she didn't know what was going on. Shawn Sr. went to the bathroom door. It was open just a little, but he knocked anyway. He asked "Keith, are you sick?" Key told him that he would be okay. He washed his hands, and then rinsed his mouth out. Shawn told him to take his time.

After feeling a little more ready and up to it, Key went back to the living room. He sat back in his seat still not looking too healthy. He had broken a slight sweat, and his eyes were a little lower than before. Ms. Kim asked him what was wrong. He explained that he had been going through a lot lately. She asked him if it was anything he wanted to talk about, but he insisted that he would be alright and that he just needed to go home. He apologized and requested a date to reschedule their meeting. Ms. Kim approved his request. Shayna walked him out and told him to call her as soon as he got in so that she could know he made it back safely. She gave him a hug and kiss on the cheek, then told him to feel better.

As Shayna walked back in, Ms. Kim told her to understand that the discussion wasn't over. Shayna argued that he gave her an answer. Ms. Kim told her that he obviously wasn't in his right mind. As solid and relevant as Key's answer may have sounded, he had a long way to go if he wanted to prove his worth to Ms. Kim. Shayna just sighed and headed for the steps. Shawn Sr. stopped her before she could make her way up. He told her that he needed to know why she was so interested in him and so intensely attached. Shayna stopped and thought for a second before saying "Not many people are willing to change for others. He put in work and changed for me." Shawn asked her how she was so sure about this. She told Shawn that she would just attribute it to woman's intuition. Shawn decided not to dispute that point, and allowed her to continue walking upstairs.

Key on the other hand was headed down the front steps. On his way down, he spotted Jamal walking down my steps. It threw him off to the point of having to wipe his face to make sure he was seeing correctly. He said in a slightly loud tone "Lek, is that you?" Jamal replied "Key! What up, thun?" Key told him that he was on his way home. He asked Jamal what he was doing leaving my house. Jamal looked back up at my door and said "Oh, umm, I was just hangin' out with Charmaine." Key looked at Jamal with a confused look and asked him if he cared to elaborate. That's when I opened my door and said "Hi Key! Good night, Jamal." Key looked at me and waved with a perplexed look on his face, and then looked back at Jamal. Jamal was waving back also. Key looked at him and asked "Jamal? Since when does Charmaine call you Jamal?" Jamal told him that it had been only going on for a little while. Key wanted an explanation as to what was going on between Jamal and I. They had to take the same train to get home so Jamal told him that he would bring him up to speed on the ride. They made their way to the Subway.

By the time they reached the Subway, Jamal had told Key that he and I had been hanging out and getting to know each other. He also killed any speculation that we had been doing anything beyond that. According to him, his exact words were "She's a very wholesome girl, very different from a lot of the girls you see today." Key asked him if he was going to attempt to take it any further than that. Jamal told him that it was possible. He gave Jamal dap and told him that he was happy to hear that. Being that Jamal was the quiet one in their group, the most he would talk to women was on a friendship level because he was shy. Even when they had shows while traveling to different cities, he was always conservative and respectful to the groupies.

I guess in Key's eyes, seeing Jamal with a woman on a relationship level wasn't surprising, just different.

The subject then changed to what was currently going on with the two of them. Key asked Jamal if he had seen or heard from Stack. Jamal apparently hadn't heard from Stack in a while. He tried paging him about two days prior to that day, but never got a response. Jamal then asked Key if he knew anything about what might be going on. Key filled him in on what happened in the alley earlier in the week, and about how he hadn't heard from or about him since then. If school was in progress, this would've played out a lot differently. The three of them would be aware of each other's whereabouts at all times because they were always together during the school year. That's what the summer would do to you in the 90s. No cell phones and social media meant everyone's personal business belonged to them and maybe a small circle of others.

The train was slowly approaching Saratoga; Jamal's stop. Jamal asked Key why he hadn't contacted him to tell him earlier. Key explained that over the course of the week he hadn't been himself, and he was getting by on the small shred of mental stability he had left. He hadn't been in contact with anyone because there was too much at stake with the police and drugs being involved. Key was also concerned about the possibility of his involvement in the drugs being revealed. Jamal began to feel a little uneasy and concerned about Stack. As his stop came up, he let out a deep sigh and told Key to keep him updated. They gave each other dap and Jamal exited the train. When Key finally got home, he called Shayna and they spoke for a little while before calling it a night. He managed to convince her that what he was feeling may have been a result of something he had eaten.

OPERATION RELOCATION

It was Friday; the day of Key's graduation. Shayna, Jamal, myself and of course Ms. Mims were there to support him. We were all so proud to see the result of his maturation. The ceremony was small and held in the cafeteria. There were only thirteen other students along with Key who had delayed matriculation issues. Instead of them walking across a stage like a traditional graduation, their names were called and they were given their diplomas. They then returned to their seats once they received it. There was a solid turnout; a lot of friends and family of the graduates.

The time had come for Key to receive his. When his name was called, we made the most noise we possibly could. He looked in our direction and let out a smile, almost getting emotional. However, even in the midst of his happiness he exhibited a sense of emptiness in his expression. Upon noticing this, I tapped Shayna and asked her if he was okay. Shayna told me that he wasn't feeling well a few days prior and he may have still been getting over whatever it was. That made sense, but the expression I was witnessing was not an expression of ailment. Key looked like he was hurting. We continued to clap as his name was the last one called.

It was now time for the guest speaker to give their speech and congratulate the graduates, Ms. Mims was chosen for that task. Her speech consisted of how proud she was to see the graduates overcome the obstacles that they faced to reach that day. She indirectly put the spotlight on Key by hinting at some of the things he went through, but generalized her statements so it wouldn't seem like she was showing favoritism. She concluded her speech by telling the graduates to stay encouraged and stick with the plan they used to get there. Most importantly, she told them to not let anyone tell them that they could not do something or that it was too late; "It is never too late to succeed because when it comes to success, being late is better than not arriving at all." We all applauded and they recognized the graduates one more time.

When we got outside we all took pictures; all of us as well as Ms. Mims. Shayna suggested that we go out to eat as a form of celebration. Key told us that he couldn't because he had to get to work. Shayna could not believe what he was saying, and told him that he needed to take a day off regardless of penalty to celebrate his achievement. He told her that he really couldn't miss a day. I was watching him tell us this and came to the conclusion that something was definitely wrong with him. Shayna told him that she was sure Mr. Jones wouldn't mind him missing one day and insisted that he call in sick. Key continued to claim that he really couldn't. It really hurt Shayna to hear that. He apologized and told us that he had to go.

I attempted to intervene by reminding him that it was his special day and that he should not allow himself to become a slave to work and labor. I told him "Money comes, and money goes. Don't let it consume 100% of your time because when time runs out, you can't take that money with you." Key agreed that it was true, but continued to repeat that he had to go into work that particular day. He bent down to give Shayna a kiss on her cheek, but she slightly moved as a show of displeasure. Jamal suggested that we ate at Burger Empire, that way we all stayed together and everyone would be happy. Key quickly signaled for Jamal to be quiet. I saw him from the corner of my eye attempting to be discreet. Shayna expressed further disgust by saying that she didn't want to go there to eat, she wanted to do something fun. Key agreed "Yeah! I don't want to celebrate where I work. I promise all of you that I will make it up to you." Key began to walk in the direction of his job leaving us standing in front of the school.

I didn't need any further proof. I told Shayna that Key wasn't telling us something. I turned to Jamal and asked him if he knew what was going on with Key, but he just played dumb and asked what I meant. I could see that he was just protecting his friend. That was a battle I was not going to win right then and there, but I was determined to eventually get some information. Jamal changed the subject by asking if we still wanted to go out. Shayna didn't seem to be in the mood anymore. I convinced her that it was a good idea and it would make her feel better to go out and have fun instead of sulking. We all agreed to go out to the city.

Meanwhile back at Burger Empire, Key was doing his routine thing. The door of the restaurant opened and Rivera

212

walked in. Key hadn't seen him since the alley incident. He walked directly to Key's register and said "Congratulations, graduate!" Key gave him a deadly stare and asked "Can I help you with anything today, sir?" Rivera told him that he wasn't hungry; he just wanted to know how things were going. Key didn't answer him. Instead, he told Rivera "Cut the garbage and tell him where Stack is." Rivera looked at Key with a sinister-like smile and told him that he would take him up on that offer after all. He ordered his food and asked for a 'Stack' of pickles on the side to go. Key almost lost it. He would have if it wasn't for Mr. Jones walking out from the back of the restaurant. Key got Rivera his meal. Mr. Jones didn't know Rivera, he just saw him as a customer. He put his hand on Rivera's shoulder and told him that Burger Empire valued their customers so he came in at the right time to be served by Key. Rivera casually told Mr. Jones "I can agree with that." He then walked out.

Fuming with anger, Key took off his apron and told Mr. Jones that he needed some air and that he was going on break. He walked outside and grabbed Rivera's shoulder from behind. He did not consider that Rivera may have had back up on hand or may have been carrying a weapon. None of that mattered at that point because Key was approaching a boiling point with the whole Stack issue. After grabbing Rivera, he pressed him up against the restaurant glass and yelled "WHERE'S STACK?" He slammed him against the window a few more times demanding that Rivera tell him. Rivera looked to the side and saw Mr. Jones standing in the doorway. He laughed and said "So is this how you value customers, sir?" Key let him go and looked at Mr. Jones, and then walked back into the restaurant even more upset than before. Mr. Jones stared him down as he walked back in. Rivera walked away laughing some more. At the end of the block, he gave his food to the same homeless man that he gave food to before. The homeless man was always there either begging or sleeping. The crazy thing about the whole situation was that Rivera had no idea where Stack was either. We'll get to that later.

Key went directly to Mr. Jones' office because he already knew that he would be summoned. Mr. Jones walked in and saw him sitting there. He told Key that he should fire him right then and there. Key attempted to interject; "Mr. Jones, that was my friend. We were just..." Mr. Jones cut Key off by telling him that regardless of who it was; an employee slamming someone up against a glass is bad for business. Key had no argument for that. He just stayed quiet before asking what his punishment was. Mr. Jones told him to take the rest of the day off because sending him back on the floor would be saying what he did was okay and that would set a bad precedent.

He mentioned that he should've fired him, but he didn't because his numbers had consistently increased over the past few months. Mr. Jones took notice of the fact that Key was ringing up more people than anyone in the entire restaurant. He did not know what it was, but he was not going to let him go; "People must really like you, Keith." Key thanked him for the compliment and told him that he was going to head out.

When Key got home, he got settled in and sat on the couch in his living room reflecting on the day. He decided that he was going to stay in for the rest of the day. He called out for his mom "Ma! I know you were busy taking a nap, but it would've been nice to see you at graduation today." He didn't get a reply so he figured that she wasn't home. While going through the mail on the kitchen table he noticed her purse across the table in the other chair. At that point he figured that she was sleeping as usual. He decided to go in her room and bother her. He planned to disturb her sleep by running into the room frantically yelling that they had to evacuate the building. He didn't think it was mean to startle her because he had told her on numerous occasions about how she slept too much.

He got himself in position to enter the room making as much noise as he possibly could. He put his hand on the door knob and turned it slowly, then he barged in yelling "MA! WE GOTTA GO!" Little did he know, something was already going on in her bedroom. It was actually the reason she was unable to respond the first time he called her. As he barged in, she and Stack's mom were on the bed face down with their hands restrained and tape on their mouths. Within a split second, two guns held by two men in black hoodies and shades were being pointed at Key. Key threw his hands up and with a cracking voice he asked "Yo, what's goin' on?" A third man told him to shut up and sit down. Key was still frozen in the doorway. The man yelled "SIT!" Key moved quickly to the nearest chair. He looked at his mom and Stack's mom on the bed and asked "What's this all about?" The man gave Key a back hand slap across his face, he then told Key to shut up and that they would be asking the questions.

Key had no idea who the guys were. The man introduced himself as well as his associates as employees of Blizzard. He told them that his name was Lex. Key was about to ask him what they wanted, but he remembered that it got him a slap before. Lex told Key that he was sure he knew why he was there. Key, still sitting with his hands up said "No!" Lex told him to not make it harder than it had to be. Key gave him a confused expression. Lex decided to try another method. He asked "Where's Stack?" Key said "Stack? What you mean where is he? Blizzard has him." Lex told Key to lower his tone or he would blow enough bullets in Key's mother's back to match the amount of dollars that Stack had cost Blizzard. Key swore to them that he didn't know anything.

He attempted to explain that the last time he saw Stack was when Rivera and the two other henchmen picked him up. Lex told Key that he didn't like people lying to him because it wasted his time and he valued his time. Key vowed that he wasn't lying, and then asked the man why Stack would hide at home if he was trying to stay out of sight. Lex realized that Key's point made a lot of sense. That should have been common

216

sense. It only meant that Stack must have gotten away and they were getting desperate to find him. They wanted Stack because he held a lot of the organizations secrets and information.

Key put his hands down slowly and said "Hold up! You mean to tell me you all don't know where Stack is either?" Lex told Key that he didn't tell him he could lower his hands. In other words, he was too ashamed to answer. Key asked him why Rivera was at the restaurant that day. Lex told Key that he was there to get him off work a little quicker. They knew Key would retaliate to seeing Rivera in a manner that would get him sent home that day. Rivera didn't know where Stack was either. That's when it all began to make sense to Key. He realized that Rivera was playing a double role by acting like he knew where Stack was, but had another plan in line just in case Key didn't know either. They really just needed Key to be sent home so the other plan was to get under Key's skin at all costs. Key asked them what they would've done if he didn't go home right after work. Lex told him that other plans were in order.

Stack's mom was trying to say something through the tape. Lex told one of the gunmen to remove the tape from both their mouths. They removed it and Stack's mom demanded that someone told her what was going on. She was originally from Trinidad and her accent was always more apparent when she got angry. Key's mom yelled "DRUGS? KEITH, YOU SELLIN' DRUGS?" Key told her to chill and stop acting like she cared because she would have asked how they were getting by on a part-time Burger Empire check a long time ago. Lex told them that he didn't care about their family issues, he just wanted Stack and he wasn't leaving the apartment without him. Key told him that he was not going to find him there, then asked him where he was last seen by the organization.

That was when the truth about Stack, now also known as Houdini, came out. After taking Stack captive, he managed to slip away. Rivera and one of the other guys were sitting in the back of the vehicle with Stack; Stack was in the middle seat. The way Rivera described it was that as they were driving they got to a red light, Stack scratched his nose. At least they thought he was scratching his nose; he was actually taking a small razor blade out of his mouth from underneath his tongue.

In the 90s, keeping a blade under your tongue was common among a lot of guys that ran the streets. They used it as protection, but of course you had to know what you were doing. He took the razor blade and cut the henchman's wrist. As blood began to squirt out of the man's vein, the man began to yell. Stack pulled the guy's arm and pointed it at Rivera's face causing the blood to get into Rivera's eyes. That's when Stack put his healthy arm out the sunroof and pulled himself up and through it. From there, he jumped off of the back of the vehicle and ran. The driver tried to turn the vehicle around to follow him, but Stack was gone. After hearing the story, Key asked "Stack did that?" Lex looked at Key and told him that he was going to help them get Stack back and it wasn't up for discussion. Key told him that he wasn't going to do anything, and if they wanted Stack they needed to find him on their own.

Lex did not take too well to Key's answer. He told him that if that was his attitude on the manner, then he obviously didn't love his mother. One of the gunmen put their gun to her head. Key frantically told them to stop and that he would help. Lex told Key that he knew he was going to help. To make sure of it, he explained that he was going to leave one of the gunmen at his house so that he didn't try to retreat. He signaled to the other gunman to leave with him. He gave Key thirty-six hours to deliver Stack. When they left, Key ran to him and Stack's moms and untied them. As soon as he did, Stack's mom smacked him and told him that he and Stack were stupid for getting involved with drugs in the first place. She then left the apartment. She refused to stay in that building with her daughter and granddaughter where they were vulnerable. They packed up and moved that night.

Key and his mom acquired a new roommate and he didn't waste any time making himself comfortable. He would make trips to the corner store, but that was about as far as he went. The next day was a Saturday. He had his feet kicked up on their coffee table in the living room watching a *Fresh Prince* re-run when Key came in from work. Key's mom no longer stayed there during the day because Key advised her to not be alone with the guy. She would get home around the time Key did. I'm not exactly sure where she went.

Key walked in and told the henchman that he had some dinner if he wanted any; it was some food from Burger Empire. The guy rushed to the kitchen and grabbed the bag off of the table, then ran back to the living room. Key kept his bag in his hand. He then joined the guy in the living room and expressed a need to be honest with him; "I don't like you staying here so the best thing for us to do is compose a plan to get Stack. That way we can all move on with our lives." The man told Key to shut up because he was watching TV. The guy took the burger out of the bag and took a big bite out of it. Key began to eat his too as his mom was walking in. Within two minutes of the guy eating the food, he was knocked out. Key had slipped some grinded horse tranquilizers into the guy's burger. To double check if he was really unconscious, Key smacked him as hard as he could. The guy didn't wake up.

Key rushed into the kitchen and told his mother to pack everything she could as fast as she could. Their thirty-six hour deadline was approaching. They packed all of their vital necessities and were out within twenty minutes. Key had a friend from school whose father was a superintendant in a building in Brownsville, Brooklyn. He told them that he could give them a vacant apartment for the night, but they had to be out by 7:00AM the next morning. Brownsville was worse than his current neighborhood, but it was their only option. He called a cab to pick them up right in front of the courtyard so that they wouldn't be out in the public eye for too long.

When the thirty-six hours was up, Lex returned with the other gunman. When they got to the apartment, they walked in on the gunman that was left there doing aerobics in his underwear. He was sweating profusely. It wasn't that hot, and he wasn't moving that much. The drugs had a slight side effect that caused him to have an outer body experience. When he turned around and saw them, he grabbed his gun and let off two shots. They ducked and ran out of the apartment. When he ran out after them, the other gunman jumped on his back causing him to drop the gun. However he couldn't bring him down. It turned out the horse tranquilizer that Key slipped him was actually PCP. The gunman in his underwear flipped the other one over his back and slammed him to the ground with one arm. He then turned to Lex. Lex picked up the gun that was dropped and shot him in his chest twice. It didn't seem to faze him at first; he kept coming. After a few more steps he began to slow down and finally fell to the floor.

Lex and the other gunman looked at each other, then made their way to the steps and ran out of the building. On a positive note, no stray bullets traveled through any walls or hit anyone. However, people walked out of their apartments about ten minutes after the last bullet. They all walked out to see the man's lifeless body in the middle of the hallway. They immediately went back inside when they saw him, but one called the police. The police arrived deeming it a crime scene and began to ask the neighbors for information. Half of them were not willing to cooperate while the other half didn't even open their doors. The rest of us saw it as a breaking news report on the news.

I had no idea that it was Stack and Key's building, neither did Shayna. I only found out moments after when Jamal called informing me that it was. The victim was still unidentified. I was just praying that it wasn't either of them. I told Jamal that I would call him back. I called Shayna to ask her if she had heard from Key. I didn't want to alarm her, but when she asked why I was asking, I had to tell her what I was seeing on the news. She turned it on and let out a big gasp. I had to tell her to breathe and sit down somewhere. She immediately began to cry. My call waiting indicator began to go off. I told her to hold on and try to relax. As I was clicking over to my other call, I could hear Ms. Kim in the background asking her what was wrong. Jamal was on the other line calling me to tell me that it wasn't Stack or Key. He had paged Key and Key didn't know what was going on in his building either because he wasn't there. I thanked him for the information and told him I would call him right back. He said okay, and I switched back over. Shayna wasn't on the phone anymore.

I called Shayna back. When she answered I could tell that she had been crying a lot. I called her name twice to get her attention. She finally answered in between her sniffling and attempts to catch her breath. I informed her that Jamal had spoken to Key, and that it wasn't him. She asked if I was sure, I told her that I was positive. She began to feel a little more relieved and told me that she would call me later. We hung up and I called Jamal back. I asked him if he was going to finally tell me what was going on with Key. He asked me what I meant. I told him that there was something suspicious between the way he was acting and then a shooting all of a sudden taking place in his building. I knew that the two didn't necessarily have to be connected, but I just had to ask. Too much was going on at one time so I wasn't allowing anything to get past me without speculating. Jamal said that I needed to pace myself and remember that a shooting in East New York was very common; it was only more pronounced at that moment because it was close to Key and Stack. That was true so I didn't press the issue any further for that moment. I was still going to get my answers, but slowly and steadily.

FAREWELL, MY SISTER!

Over the next few days, a few changes had taken place. Key and his mother relocated to Queens. Queens was a lot more expensive, but it was safer. Besides, Key could afford it. However, he had not been back to work and it was now Tuesday. He wasn't going in for the mere fact that they would be looking for him there. He convinced Mr. Jones that he had gotten very ill over the weekend and he wasn't over it yet. At the moment he was safe, but he had to make a trip back to Brooklyn that day to see Shayna off. He knew he was running the risk of getting caught so he called Shayna that morning to tell her that he would meet her at the airport which was also located in Queens. At the time, we didn't know that he was living in Queens. All he told us was that he would already be in the area.

As a going away gift, Shayna's parents gave her a cell phone. She was so excited about it that she put it to use right away. She called me over and asked me to take a trip with them out to the airport. I was free so I took the trip with them; I would have gone anyway. We drove out to the airport talking about how Florida might be, and reminiscing on the times we had growing up. It was official at that point, she was really leaving.

We finally got to the airport. We got her bags checked after standing in a long line, then made our way to the terminal. Just as promised, Key was standing there waiting for her. As we approached him, he waved and smiled at all of us. Out of respect for Ms. Kim and Shawn, he greeted them first by shaking their hands, then hugged Shayna. Ms. Kim asked "How are you, Keith?" Key said that he was fine and apologized for not being able to find a time to reschedule their meeting, but he wanted her and Shawn to know that he loved Shayna. Ms. Kim just nodded her head.

Shayna had about half an hour before she had to board the plane. Key asked her if he could talk to her before she got on. She asked all of us to give her a minute. They walked off and spoke for a while. In the mean time, we just stood at the gate conversing amongst ourselves. Shawn Jr. was beginning to get restless. One upside to our brief wait was meeting Penny Hardaway. I saw this tall guy walking towards our gate. From far away, I really couldn't tell who it was, but as he got closer there was no mistaking it. I almost lost my mind and fainted. Penny Hardaway was and still is my favorite basketball player of all-time. I really can't verbally express how much of a fan I am.

Penny was actually getting on the same flight as Shayna; I was a little jealous at that point. I was trying to calm down and get my emotions in check; but I was at a loss for words. All of those times watching him play and thinking about what I would say if I ever met him, and I didn't know what to say. Ms. Kim walked up behind me and told Penny that she was a big fan and so was Shawn. Key and Shayna realized what was going on and made their way back over to us. Penny turned out to be pretty cool in person which was a relief; some people you grow up admiring turn out to be jerks in person.

The time had come for Shayna to board her flight. Shayna did her rounds of goodbyes. When she got around to me, I gave her the tightest hug I could and told her how much I was going to miss her. We had a sister moment where we both instantly started crying. It took about a minute or two before we managed to gather ourselves. When she got to Key, she looked at him for a little while, then gave him a hug and told him that she loved him. Key looked back at her for a second and gave her a big kiss right in front of all of us, then told her "It was now or never." Shayna gathered her bags and just like that she was off to Florida. Ms. Kim and Shawn didn't like that kiss too much; they spoke about it the entire ride home.

A few days had passed and we were all still getting acclimated to life without Shayna. Key had to go back to work. He dreaded the day he would have to, but the only other option was to quit his regular job at Burger Empire. However, even that wasn't possible because it was tied into the Blizzard's organization. It wasn't like he could just step away from the organization.

When he arrived on the block for work, everything seemed normal. He went inside and went straight to Mr. Jones' office to inform him that he was back. Mr. Jones asked how he was feeling. Key told him that he would be okay and got back to his job right away, both jobs. The clientele must have been in the restaurant every day over the course of Key's absence looking for him. His first customer that day was one of them. It was almost as if there was no break, Key just picked up where he left off.

Picking up where they left off would be a nice way to look at it, but little did Key know, that customer he was serving was more than just a customer. They were actually a spy for the organization. Blizzard set a few of his men up outside of Burger Empire awaiting the day Key returned. That customer got his product and reported to the guys that were waiting for him. Those guys then called Lex and Rivera to inform them.

After Key's shift, he was headed to the Subway. He knew there was a possibility that he may have been followed. He didn't want them to know about his place in Queens so he got on the train, but not to go home. He took the 2 train into Harlem. I'm not sure if Blizzard's employees got so used to driving everywhere that they forgot which train went where, or if they just didn't know the Subway L's to begin with. Either way, they should've been able to tell where he was going just by the train and direction he chose.

Key managed to fool them and ended up getting off at 125th Street. His plan was to blend in with a crowd as long as he could. That area was usually busy so he figured he could lose anybody that might have been following him in no time. From there, he would spend about ten minutes on the street, then head back to Queens. The overall goal was to make any possible followers believe that he lived in Harlem. However, it was kind of hard to disguise his height amongst a crowd.

The plan was going well for a while. He was starting to make his way back to the Subway when he was stopped by two cops. They asked him what his name was and where he was headed. He asked them what business it was of theirs. One of the cops told him to not get smart. Key asked them what they wanted his information for. The other cop told him that he fit the description of someone that was reported causing a problem in that particular area. Key looked them up and down and told them to stop lying, then claimed that he knew they were lying. He then asked "So you mean to tell me that you two got an APB on a man my height wearing a Burger Empire uniform? A restaurant with only one location in Brooklyn, that's who you're looking for?" The cops knew they were wrong so they avoided the question by asking him for his ID. Key didn't have any identification on him so they told him that they would have to take him in for questioning.

Key decided to refrain from fighting it because he figured it would cause a scene. He didn't want to bring attention to himself or attract the attention of the guys he was trying to avoid. They put him in handcuffs and read him his rights, then put him in the car. The car ride to the precinct was a quiet one. When they got to their destination, Key looked out the window and said "Yo! This isn't a precinct." As a matter of fact, they were at Chelsea Piers near Midtown, Manhattan at one of the docks.

They parked next to a yacht. The cops jumped out of the car and grabbed Key out while he was still in handcuffs. They took out their nightsticks and began beating him relentlessly. This went on for a little while before Lex walked out of the yacht telling the cops that it was enough and told them to bring Key inside. Each cop grabbed an arm and dragged him into the yacht. One of the cops removed the handcuffs and told him "That's what happens when you cost Blizzard money."

That was the moment that Key found out Blizzard had more juice in the city than he thought. Those were actual cops, but they also worked for Blizzard. Key didn't even have enough strength to stand up on his own after being beaten with the nightsticks. He was on his knees breathing heavily. Lex walked over to him and asked him if he sincerely thought that he would get away with what he did. He then told him that the only reason he hadn't been killed yet was because Stack was still out there. Rivera was on the yacht also. Rivera told Key that they could still kill him for fun and deal with Stack later. Key was still trying to catch his breath. Lex noticed that Rivera's comment didn't fully grasp his attention so he added a message of his own; "We could kill you for fun, or we could direct our attention to a friend of yours that just moved to Florida." That managed to get Key's attention. He got up and rushed toward Lex. Rivera stepped in front of Lex and pulled a gun as he told Key "Don't let the fun start so early." Key backed off. He was in bad shape; a swollen eye, swollen and cut right cheek, and bleeding from his mouth.

Lex took a seat and asked Key "Why did you think we wouldn't know about Shayna? We know your every move, you can't hide from us. However, you are beginning to frustrate us." Key told them to stay away from Shayna. Lex asked him what he was going to do if they didn't. Key asked them what they expected him to do. He didn't know where Stack was and he had no way of getting in contact with him so the hiding, seeking, and beating was more than likely going to become a cycle. Lex told him that the issue went deeper than Stack at that point. The word from Blizzard was that he was upset with Key for having one of his men killed, and now costing him more money by missing all of those days of work. Lex was referring to the employee that he killed in Key's building.

Key was now in deep. The only words he could muster up at that time were "I should've just played ball." Lex told him that he needed to pay Blizzard back for all of the days that he missed and he would still need to locate Stack for them. If Stack was gone for that long, my guess was that he moved down south. Growing up in New York, whenever someone was in trouble with the law or on the run from someone, they moved down south until things died down. It usually happened to friends of ours too. When they were gone, but their family was still in the neighborhood, that usually meant their parents sent them down to live with family members. It was similar to Will Smith's story on *The Fresh Prince of Bel-Air*.

The amount of money Key supposedly cost the organization within those few days was fifteen thousand dollars. They wanted it by the next day. Rivera was going to pick it up from him at work. As far as the situation with Stack was concerned, they had a special assignment for Key that would be put into motion within the coming days. They allowed Key to go. The first place he went was a nearby street vendor to get some ice. He managed to come across a vendor that was actually willing to give him some without charging him. The vendor must have felt sorry for Key after looking at how battered his face was. From there, he made his way back to Queens.

The fifteen thousand dollars that he was ordered to pay the next day wasn't really a problem because Key wasn't stupid with his money. A reason for this was that he learned the value of a dollar while struggling before he worked for Blizzard. In the short two months that he was working the Burger Empire-Blizzard operation, he accumulated a little over one-hundred thousand dollars. He put one-hundred thousand of it away in a safe place. That financial wisdom that he acquired helped him make the decision to not pay it all at one time. He understood that it was always better to act like you don't have money; that's how you don't go broke.

The next day, I was at home getting rid of some old papers from the school year. I figured I might as well be productive and get some stuff out of the way. While I was going through the papers, my house phone rang. I figured my mom would get it so I didn't pick it up. I guess she figured I would get it too because it continued to ring. When I realized that she wasn't going to answer it, I got up as fast as I could and ran to the nearest phone. However, it was too late and it went straight to the answering machine. I picked it up anyway. The conversation was going to be recorded, but I could always delete it afterward. It was the woman from Human Resources at The Garden's catering services. She was calling to congratulate me and inform me that I had gotten the job. I was ecstatic, but had to remain professional. I thanked her excessively and got all of the information I needed for my first day and orientation. After I hung up, I went crazy in my bedroom and told my mom. She had already heard since the conversation was recorded on the answering machine.

I had to call Shayna and tell her the news. She seemed just as excited to hear from me when she realized that it was me on the line. She told me that she was missing everyone. I let her vent a little before I shared my news. Her new coach was already putting them to work with very intense practices, and she still didn't have any real friends yet. She took up about ten minutes getting me updated on her life. Finally, I was able to tell her about the job. She was excited to hear that too and immediately went into how I could get a ball player or get another chance to meet Penny. It was just good to hear her voice again, I missed her already. At some point in our conversation, Key managed to become the topic. Needless to say she was missing him too.

Shayna had a lot going on with her track team. The training started earlier than the semester to make sure the runners were conditioned for the upcoming season. Shayna was already getting praise from some of the coaches for the trial times she was posting. She was the only freshman that was giving the seniors legitimate competition. As a result, they placed her in simulation sprints against some of the seniors for the coaches to get a sense of who the strongest runners were. She turned out to be one of the strongest. I was proud of her. I knew she would blow their minds.

NO TIMING LIKE GOD'S TIMING

The following day, I had a date with Jamal. He took me out to lunch at an up skill restaurant in Manhattan to congratulate me on my new job. I felt it was a pretty fancy gesture for a new job position, but he thought otherwise. He told me that it was worth celebrating because it was a step closer to achieving my goal. The food was great and the date was even greater. Jamal was making all of the right moves and saying all of the right things to keep my attention. I started to feel like I could get used to the things he was doing if we were in a serious relationship. However, it was up to him to propose that idea. When a man really wants you, he'll let you know. After lunch, he took me to the movies to see 'Clueless'. He knew I was a big fan of the show. I told him that I was planning on sharing the news about my job at church that coming Sunday and asked if he would like to join me. He said that he would be honored to be there when I made the announcement.

Back in Brooklyn, Key was going into work. The first thing people noticed was his face. A lot of the swelling had gone down from icing it all night, but some of the bruises were still noticeable. His story to those who asked was that he was in a fight. His break time came around and Rivera arrived to pick up the money. Key only gave him five thousand and told him that he would have to work on the rest. Rivera told him that he would have to explain that to Lex as he put the money in his pocket. He then revealed that he was also there to inform him about the

234

special new assignment they had for him. Key's new assignment was working Stack's old corners in addition to his position at Burger Empire. They knew that Key didn't want to work the corners so they were doing it as punishment for the trouble they felt he caused. The only way he could get out of it was to deliver Stack. They still believed that Key was bluffing about not knowing Stack's whereabouts. The organization knew that the conditions were dangerous because Stack's corners were still being monitored by police and angry customers.

Jamal and I had finally gotten back to my place after our day out. We talked on my stoop for a little while about miscellaneous topics. It was still fairly early; the streetlights hadn't even come on yet. My mom had just gotten home from work. She said hello to both of us and told me that she needed help preparing dinner. She asked Jamal if he wanted to stay for dinner. Jamal respectfully declined because he had to get back home. Mom went inside and Jamal and I got up because he was about to leave. I told him that I had a great time and thanked him for treating me to lunch. He told me it was no problem and invited me into his arms for a hug. I gave him a hug. As we were releasing he gave me a kiss on the cheek followed by a smile and a "Good night!" He looked back for a second as he walked down the steps thinking he was so smooth. He was, but I wasn't going to let him know and make his head swell.

The weekend had finally arrived and Key was headed to work. He was now working the corners during the morning and his shift at Burger Empire in the afternoon. Key didn't have any type of practice working corners. He wasn't familiar with the hand to hand transaction technique, the behavior of customers on the streets, the dangers to look for, or even how to recognize an undercover cop disguised as a customer. It was all a set up constructed by Lex that stemmed from his frustration with Key. That didn't matter because Key had an advantage that balanced out the war with Lex. Key was the type of guy that faced adversity all of his life, but always made things work. He was capable of quickly adapting to a new environment. Therefore, whatever came at him on those corners, he simply placed himself in that role and imitated what he had seen in the courtyard growing up.

His first day on the corner wasn't that bad. The only mistake he made was forgetting to make sure somebody from the organization relieved him when it was time for him to go. Blizzard had his corner workers work in shifts to keep a fresh face on the block, and to keep the undercover cops off of their trail. I don't blame Key for leaving. If I didn't have to be out there any longer for that day, I would've left quickly too. Key made his way to Burger Empire and his first day on the corner was in the books. He picked up on a few of the necessary skills quickly. When he got to Burger Empire, someone standing outside of the building called his name. Key ignored the person. He didn't care if the man knew his name because he didn't trust anyone.

When he got settled in and at his station, the same guy that was calling him outside approached his register. He said to Key "I'm sure you heard me calling you outside." Key replied "And I'm sure you saw me ignore you outside." The guy told Key to watch his mouth. Key looked angry. He shrugged it off then asked the man "What meal can I drop on the floor before I serve it to you today, sir?" The man smiled and told Key that he would have the same meal that Shayna was planning to have after practice that day. Key looked at him with the deadliest of stares. The guy noticed that Key didn't like that too much. Not liking it too much was putting it lightly; Key was fuming. He automatically presumed that the guy worked for Blizzard.

The man took a moment to introduce himself. He went by the title of "The Custodian". His name meant that he cleaned up any mess pertaining to criminal activity and made it appear as if nothing ever happened. He was hired by Lex as a security figure and was sent there to give Key a warning. He informed Key that he was going to be watching his every move as well as the moves of everyone associated with him. He was obviously good at what he did because Shayna did finish practice around that time every day. Out of fear for Shayna, Key asked the man what he wanted. "The Custodian" told Key "I just want you to know that I'm here." Key was now in a position where he was no longer only working to support himself, his mother, and their security. He was also working to protect Shayna as well. Shayna didn't know what kind of danger she was in. She didn't even know that Key was involved in that lifestyle. He had to continue to keep it a secret from her as well as make sure they didn't harass her while she was at school. Stress was becoming a factor, and Key didn't know what to do to escape it.

It was 6:00PM and I was just getting back in from running a few errands. I called for my mom to see if she was home; she was in the kitchen. As I was walking in, I stepped on some mail that was on the floor of the foyer. She was home all day, but I guess she hadn't gotten around to picking it up. There were a few loose pieces, but there were three pieces wrapped in a rubber band with a post-it note that said "We have been out of town for the past month and seem to have gotten some of your mail." It was signed "McIntosh". The McIntosh's were our next door neighbors. One of the pieces that were in the rubber band was a big envelope from my top school of choice. The wait was finally over. I learned that I had been accepted and that it was delivered three weeks prior to me finding out. That may have been the best weekend of my life.

I shared the news with my mom first. She was so overjoyed that she started crying and had to take a seat. I sat there with her for a while embracing her as we thanked God. I was at a loss for words and in awe of how God was working. I then made my vital phone calls; Shayna and Jamal. Shayna and I stayed on the phone for about an hour talking about how she was proud of me and giving me more updates on how she was doing with her new team. I was missing her and I could tell she was missing me and everybody in Brooklyn. I called Jamal and he was excited as well. His exact words were "At the rate your blessings are coming, I'm gonna go broke congratulating you." He said that jokingly of course. He congratulated me then said that God is always on time. He had that right.

I carried that celebration into the day after when I went to church. I decided to present a testimony on how I had been blessed over the course of that week. Jamal was in attendance like he promised he would be. As I was presenting the news about each blessing, the elders expressed how proud they were in their facial expressions and head nods. No one was happier than I was. Everything was working out so well.

On Wednesday of that same week, I had my orientation and some training up at The Garden. I was given a tour of the facility, introduced to the employees, and given an idea of how the work day would flow once I got into the groove of things. The training wasn't intense, but I was told that it would pick up in a little over two months if the basketball lockout that was taking place that year didn't persist. I wasn't concerned about that. All that mattered was that I was working and I was in a field that I desired to be in. God always grants us the desires of our hearts. I was informed that my first day would be the following Monday along with some more training.

Down in Florida, Shayna was still getting acclimated to her new environment and trying to enjoy her second week on campus. I called her that weekend. She told me about how she was still excelling at the practices. One coach even told her that if she kept improving her times, she could possibly qualify for an Olympic trial. I was at a loss for words when she told me that. The Olympics were the following year so I began to imagine seeing her winning gold medals and how amazing it would be. However, she also had bad news. Apparently there were some girls down there on and off the track team that did not seem to like her; it was almost to the point where it would stress her out at times.

I didn't take too well to hearing anything regarding harm being done to Shayna. One day during our freshman year of high school, there were some sophomores that decided to flex on us simply because they were older than us. There were three of them; they cornered us in the bathroom before lunch. Understanding that we were outnumbered, we refused to let them get the first swing or do any talking. We just started swinging. The numbers disadvantage caught up to us, but only for a brief moment because one of them slipped. While that particular one was on the ground, Shayna kicked her in her mouth while she was grappling with another. We must've been loud enough to draw a crowd because some other girls walked in and instigated the altercation. In turn, that got the attention of security. They entered the bathroom and broke it up. Shayna and I avoided suspension because we were able to successfully claim self-defense.

It seemed like history was slightly repeating itself in Shayna's first year of college and the year had not even begun. She told me about an incident one day after practice; she laid some clothes out on her desk to change into after a shower. When she got back to her room to change, she found that her favorite pair of jeans had been sabotaged with paint. Immediately, she thought that it was her roommate, but she found a note saying "You're bound to turn heads in these, freshman!"

The way she described the rooming arrangements for athletes was much different from the rooming arrangements for students that were not athletes. Students lived in dorms, apartments, and off-campus apartments. Student athletes lived in houses on campus designated to their team. When joining Gainesville University's track team, Shayna was assigned to a room with a teammate who was also a freshman. The two of them later became close acquaintances. That note was a dead giveaway that it was most likely one of the senior runners named Sabrina. Leading up to that incident with the jeans, Sabrina expressed her dislike for Shayna. Shayna beat her in a simulation race and the girl was supposed to be one of the best on the team.

Shayna confronted her on the matter. The girl had the nerve to say it was part of a hazing process. Shayna expressed that she didn't care for or about any form of hazing; "Sabrina, I know you have a personal problem with me. It can get very personal if you want to go that route. Just try me! You better

241

respect my personal property and that's not up for discussion." After hearing all of that, I was ready to go down there at that very moment. That wasn't all though. She told me about a recurring issue that she had with some girls on and off campus.

There were some girls that weren't too fond of a city girl from New York and her style, so they were jealous of her. Meanwhile, others seemed to admire Shayna's style. The jealous ones secretly admired her as well. It's like they wanted her style, but either couldn't pull it off or didn't get as much attention as she did when they tried to duplicate it. I told her that it would probably get better once the school year began and students started to move in. I figured that she might meet some other people from New York that attended the school.

Shayna's parents planned to take a trip down there later in the week to pay her a visit and bring her any necessary items that she needed, but couldn't carry on the plane. I told her that I was going to make the trip with them and that I would have her back if anything did happen. She told me not to worry about that because we were going to be having too much fun when I got there. For the rest of our conversation we spoke about how campus life was. I wanted to get an idea of what it may feel like although I was going to be commuting every day. We also spoke about Key and Jamal. She even suggested the idea of a double date one day. She had been keeping in touch with him as much as she could, but was only able to contact him through his pager. I figured it was his crazy work schedule.

WELCOME BACK!

The following week had come and Key had completed another week on the corners. The second week didn't prove to be as easy as the first. One particular day, he had to run from the cops when the corner got hot. He was moved to another corner a few blocks away where he got into a fight; he won. Somebody found out that he was holding drugs and tried to get him for the product and the money. It was a slight scuffle that turned into an all out bout. When Key got the better of the guy he left the corner for the day. Lex happened to be riding around the neighborhood with Blizzard that day for a meeting they had in Red Hook. Blizzard noticed that Key's corner was vacant and wanted to know why no one was there.

Lex paged Key to find out where he was. Key called him back asking what he needed. Lex asked him "So you make your own schedule now?" Key told him that they didn't pay him enough to be fighting in the streets. Lex made the situation seem like more than what it was because Blizzard was there. He said in a loud tone "So you don't like how much you're being paid?" Blizzard couldn't hear what was being said on Key's end so it just seemed like Key was being lazy and insubordinate. Blizzard told Lex to hang up the phone. In Blizzard's mind, hanging up the phone after making your point was a bigger statement and had more of an impact. It placed fear in the employee's heart because they didn't know what to expect next.

Blizzard was upset with Lex. He told Lex "You're about as dumb and as much of a liability as the employees you hire." Lex really didn't have an argument; he was responsible for approving Stack and had a hand in approving Key. In Blizzard's eyes, that proved to be irresponsible decision making by Lex. Lex attempted to explain how things went wrong, but Blizzard cut him off and told him to save it because there was no way he could explain himself. He then told Lex that he would've gotten rid of him a long time ago if they weren't brothers. Lex looked out the window feeling disappointed in himself.

The meeting they were headed to was a meeting with some other big named drug kingpins in Brooklyn. It was similar to the mafia style meetings that entailed a bunch of families. Blizzard knew that the madness caused by Stack and Key had probably spread throughout the borough by that point, maybe even further. He was concerned about it making him look like a laughing stock being that he was the head of one of the top three drug empires in Brooklyn. It turns out to that he was right.

As soon as the heads of the drug empires sat at the table, one of them said "Hey Blizz, I heard you brought the circus to town early this year." Everyone laughed except for Blizzard. Another kingpin added "Lighten up; it's not your fault that the odds were 'Stacked' against you." That brought about more laughs. Blizzard looked at Lex who was standing on the side with the rest of the second in command members. He put his gun on the table and told everyone "If amateur hour is over, I'd like to get down to business." One of the other top three leaders called for attention and told Blizzard to calm down. From there they got down to business.

The following Monday was my first official day at work. I was thrown into the middle of everything right away because an event was being held at The Garden and they were short staffed. I was put to work with supervision. I understood basic protocol and proper hygiene technique. The only thing I really needed assistance with was the company's particular method of running things such as communication, cues, body language, and other things of that sort. Overall, it was an easy day. I had to mentally prepare myself to understand that they wouldn't all be that way as my work days progressed.

Everyone within our circle tends to have life events that bounce off of each other. I guess that's what gave us the social balance that we managed to develop. The particular life event I'm referring to is my first day of work turning out to be the same day as Key's last day of work. Key was working his shift at Burger Empire on Monday afternoon; it was just another ordinary work day for him. That is until a SWAT team came barging through the restaurant entrance telling everyone to get on the floor. There was no escape if anyone tried; more police were out in the streets and had already covered the back exit.

Everybody was on the floor. The cops had guns drawn in anticipation of anybody trying anything funny. One police officer walked in after everything was under police control and told all of the employees to stand up and announced that he was looking for Keith Williams. Mr. Jones walked out of his office after hearing the commotion and asked them if they had a warrant. The officer showed him the warrant, and then went about his business.

It didn't take the officer long to figure out who Key was with his name tag sitting right on his chest. The officer asked if he was Keith Williams. Keith told him "Why don't you go look at everybody else's name tag and then come back to me if you don't find another Keith." The officer laughed and told Key that it would be in his best interest to cooperate in order to avoid an ugly situation. One of Key's coworkers said "Yo! Come on, Keith! Just go, son. I aint tryin' to get shot out here today." Keith looked at him and sucked his teeth. The officer said "That's what I thought." He grabbed Key and pressed him up against the wall. He then frisked him and found all of the money he made for Blizzard that day. He also found one of the bottles of the product Key tried to get rid of not too far away on the floor. He showed Key the bottle, but Key claimed that it wasn't his, and that they didn't even find it on him.

That was enough evidence to book Key and close down Burger Empire for the day and the duration of the investigation. The investigation was due to an anonymous tip that was given stating that Key was selling cocaine inside the restaurant. They placed Key under arrest, read him his rights, and took him to jail. This time he actually went to jail and not the Piers. None of us knew he had gotten arrested or was sent to jail because there was no way of contacting him aside from his pager. We didn't even know he had moved to Queens yet either. I just remember hearing Shayna and Jamal saying that they couldn't get him on his house phone.

A few days had passed before we found out what happened. I got a call from Jamal the day before Shayna's parents and I left for Florida. He told me that he went by Burger Empire and it was shut down. He also told me that his brother saw Key on Redd's Island as an inmate. The news was coming so fast that it was confusing me. I asked Jamal what Key did. He told me about the whole drug raid and how Key was selling drugs out of the restaurant. That was when I learned the truth about what happened to Stack and how he disappeared. Key was apparently transferred from a precinct to Redd's Island with no option for bail. I had to take a seat and allow everything to sink in. I knew something was going on with Key and that confirmed it.

Jamal told me that he was going to try to get more information the next time he went to visit his brother. The most he knew at that time was that Key was denied bail and his visitors had to go through a very intense screening. I didn't know what to think. I was going to see Shayna in under twenty-four hours and I was probably going to have to break the news to her. She more than likely wasn't going to hear it anywhere else.

Key was aware of the charges that he was facing, and the restrictions he had. While he was incarcerated, he got acquainted with Jamal's older brother; Jerome. Jerome got locked up after being found guilty of sexually assaulting a woman. Jamal told me about the case and how he wasn't given a fair trial. The night of the assault, Jerome was by their grandmother's house which was in the vicinity of the alleged crime. He went to pick up some lemons for her at a grocery store up the street from them; she was sick and needed them for her tea. When leaving the store and preparing to cross the street, a police cruiser cut him off in the crosswalk. The cops jumped out with their guns telling him to put his hands up. When he did, they grabbed him and slammed him on the hood of the car. The lemons fell out of his pocket and they arrested him before throwing him into the car. The girl that claimed to have been assaulted picked him out of a line up. He had never even met the girl. To make it even worse, the evidence in the trial proved to be inconclusive, but he was still found guilty and received a sentence of twenty-five years to life.

Jerome developed a few connections in the three years that he had already spent there. He told Jamal that he would look out for Key. Key and Jerome got to know each other and discussed their lives. One of the topics of their conversation was Shayna. Key told Jerome about how he was in a relationship, and how Shayna didn't know he was in jail because she was away at school. He was concerned and didn't know how to tell her everything that happened. It was mainly because she didn't know that he was selling drugs. If you can recall, he lied when she asked him if he did. Jerome took it upon himself to give Key some advice. He told Key that Shayna not knowing about what he had done may have been the best opportunity for a fresh start. He further explained to him that a lie is going to simply be a lie, and a relationship built on a lie always crumbles.

He advised Key to tell Shayna the truth about everything that he did or was involved in from the very beginning up to that point. His theory was that if she stayed with him, it meant she really loved him. However, if she didn't stay with him, then it was better to live with a clear conscience. Key asked him why she would want to stay with someone that is potentially looking at life in prison. Jerome told him to look to God because he hadn't been sentenced yet, he was just being held until trial. He also told Key "God's timing is perfect timing, so He'll tell you if you're meant to do time on this rock." The rock he was referring to was Redd's Island.

As their conversation continued, one of the correctional officers called Key and told him to follow him. Key got up and made his way up the stairs to follow the officer. Key asked the officer what was going on. The officer told him that he had a visitor. Key told the officer that he wasn't allowed to have visitors. To Key's knowledge, no one knew he was in there except his mother and Jamal. The officer never looked at Key. He simply told him that he wasn't responsible for knowing the restrictions of each prisoner; he was just there to escort him to the visiting area. Key stopped walking and advised the officer to stop too. He said frantically "It's a setup. It's a setup. They came to kill me." Key attempted to run back to the general population area, but when he got back to the door, another officer grabbed him. Now both officers were carrying him to the visitation area.

Key was starting to believe that the cops may have been in on it; he tried to fight them off. More cops were called and now there were about four attempting to get a hold of him. One threatened to taser him if his behavior persisted. Key kept trying to tell them no one knew he was in jail so it was a set up. All he could think of was being shot and killed as soon as he walked through the visitation door. They continued to drag him out so Key was now putting up more of a fight. They had him in a chokehold, half nelson, and an arm bar. As they got through the door he was relieved to have passed the first test of not getting shot.

Once they made it into the visitation area, Key calmed down. He expected the type of set up with the dividing windows and phones, but it was quite the contrary. It was the same visitation area that Shayna met Darryl in. They told Key which table to report to. When they pointed to it, the visitor was already there; it was Stack. Key looked as if he had seen a ghost. He walked over slowly still trying to make sense of everything. When he finally reached Stack he gave him dap and a hug, but didn't know what to say first, he was just happy to see him. He finally said "You're alive!" Stack put his arms out and told Key that he was very much alive. Key asked him what he was doing there and how he knew he was incarcerated. Stack stated that he knew what was going on with Key the past few months and he also thanked him for looking out for him in the alley that day.

Key did not want to hear any more sentimental banter; he wanted to know what was going on. He asked Stack how he was allowed to visit him and where he had been. Stack told Key that the answer to both of his questions was that he was working with the police. Key demanded an explanation as to what that meant. Stack explained that after he escaped from Rivera and the henchmen, he stayed under the radar for a few days by living in Central Park with some homeless people. He began to realize that he couldn't hide forever. He was looking for a way to stay out of sight, but with protection. That day came when he overheard two cops on beat patrol walking through Central Park. They were talking about how the city was working on taking Blizzard and a few other kingpins down. Stack stopped them and immediately told them that he may be able to help them. He got a deal in writing. He promised to give them information on Blizzard if they could get his record expunged and provide him with security.

Cops would usually take the person offering the deal and bring them in for questioning, but those two particular cops were desperate to move up their ranks. I guess they figured that Stack's information would more than likely help them. Stack was taking a big risk by trusting the cops. They could've easily gone back on their word and taken his information then thrown him in jail. He must have gotten some rookies that weren't tainted by the ways of the job yet. Key realized that Stack was basically saying he was in a witness protection program for being a snitch in the Blizzard investigation.

That may have explained where he had been, but not why he was there to see Key or how he was able to override Key's visitation restriction. When Key asked him why he was there to see him, Stack replied "How do you think you got here?" Key looked at Stack confused and asked him what he was talking about. Stack told him that the information the cops requested was a big fish in the organization, not someone just working a corner because corner workers came a dime a dozen. Key's facial expression slowly changed from confusion to anger. Stack realized that Key had finally caught on and told Key to hear him out before he reacted.

Key jumped across the table and started strangling Stack. He then picked Stack up by his neck, slammed him onto the table and strangled him some more. The guards quickly intervened in an attempt to break them up yelling "NO TOUCHING!" They finally separated them, but Key was still trying to get to Stack. Key kept yelling "YOU SNITCHED! YOU SNITCHED!" Stack tried to gather himself and told Key to calm down. Key asked him how he was supposed to calm down when his life was on the line. Meanwhile, he was still trying to break free of the officers to get to Stack. It turned out that Stack overrode the restriction because it was all a part of a plan by the police.

While the officers had Key somewhat restrained, Stack explained to Key that being imprisoned was for his own good. His reasoning was that it was only a matter of time before Blizzard's organization killed him on the outside. Key rebutted by asking Stack if it ever occurred to him that he could die on the inside also. Stack stood there with a lost look on his face. Key yelled "IDIOT! DO YOU EVER THINK THINGS THROUGH?" Stack told him to relax and he would tell him the plan if he sat down and listened. Key calmed down and they both took a seat. Stack explained that the plan was to use Key as bait. If he testified against Blizzard, it would solidify Blizzard's organization being taken down and grant Key his freedom.

Key made it clear to Stack that he wasn't making any deals. Stack told him that he would have to if he wanted to get out. Key reminded Stack "I wouldn't have to worry about getting out if it wasn't for you and the selfish deal you made. I'm not snitching." Stack called him crazy. Key told Stack that he had a lot of nerve and that he was the one losing his mind. Growing up they saw the police harass everyone and proved on many occasions that the majority of cops couldn't be trusted.

Key began to explain what he saw down the line if he made a deal with the cops. "Blizzard is gonna get some Johnnie Cochran type of lawyer, beat the case, and I'll still be in here because they found his product on me. You know what will

253

happen after that? Blizzard is gonna get someone to kill me in here. So I'm dead whether I'm in or out. I'd rather die with my dignity if it's inevitable. Not to mention, when Blizzard finds out that I'm locked up and his money can't bail me out, he's going after my family and more than likely Shayna too."

Key got up from the table and told the officers that he was ready to go back. They took him back and Stack left. Stack was now in a tough position. He needed Key's testimony for the both of them to get off; he more so wanted it for himself. Stack always had a selfish mindset. His ridiculous plan to get Key incarcerated just to get Blizzard off of his back was proof of that.

AFTERMATH

The next day was the day we were leaving to visit Shayna. We left around 5:00AM. It ended up being a long ride and not because the drive was fifteen hours, but because I couldn't concentrate. I was pondering different ways I could possibly break the news to Shayna while trying to keep a normal demeanor sitting in the car with her parents and Shawn Jr. I figured music would help me find that balance; something really smooth and easy going. I listened to my D'Angelo *Brown Sugar* CD. I had one headphone in and left the other one out just in case Ms. Kim or Shawn tried to get my attention. The plan was to stay for the weekend. Work wasn't an issue because I was still in the training process and the training was set to continue the following Monday.

After the long and exhausting drive, we finally arrived in Gainesville, Florida where her school was located. We were staying in a hotel not too far away so we checked in before going to see her. When we finally got to the school, we got directions to where the Track & Field House was and made our way there. Shayna had just gotten back from eating dinner in the Commons. We knocked on her door and her roommate answered. Ms. Kim told her that we were looking for Shayna. Shayna, being goofy, peeked around the corner like she was shy. When she saw us, she hid again. Ms. Kim saw her and yelled "BABY GIRL!" as she ran to her. The rest of us introduced ourselves to the roommate; her name was Danielle. Ms. Kim introduced herself after hugging Shayna. When Shayna and I saw each other, we both screamed in excitement and gave each other the tightest hug.

It had only been a few weeks, but it felt like months had passed. She picked Shawn Jr. up and gave him a hug, then made her way to Shawn Sr. to give him a hug as well. We spoke in her room for a while before she suggested that we go out and look at the campus. We took in the sights of the campus as we walked, but we were also very hungry. We hadn't eaten much on the drive. Shayna suggested a pizza place that was located on the campus. It sounded good to us so we made our way over there.

It wasn't the best pizza, but I remember it tasting like the most delicious thing I had ever eaten after the long drive. I went right through mine in no time. Shayna asked her parents if we could be excused from the table because she wanted to show me something; Ms. Kim allowed it. We walked outside and Shayna told me that she received a letter the day before. When I asked her who it was from, she pulled an envelope out of her pocket addressed from a New York correctional facility. I immediately thought Key may have written her, but then I remembered that he wasn't in a correctional facility. I was a little on edge still trying to figure out how to tell her what was going on.

The letter was from Darryl; he had finally been transferred. He was congratulating Shayna one more time for getting into Gainesville University, and letting her know that he was praying that God blessed her with more success. I told her that it seemed like a nice gesture and he seemed to be genuinely changing. She disagreed and told me that she knew Darryl. Her perception on the matter was that he was still in search of a relationship and wouldn't stop until he got it, even if he was incarcerated. I figured that was the best opportunity to tell her what was going on with Key. As we continued our walk I asked her if she could remember when she last spoke to Key. She told me that it was some time the week before, but she tried to page him a few times after as well.

I opened up by telling her that he moved to Queens and that was why she couldn't get him on his house phone anymore. I explained why he had to move to Queens and all the details in between; from him and Stack in the alley to how his financial situation all of a sudden got better. Finally, I told her that he had been arrested and was in jail. The news hit Shayna as hard as it hit me when Jamal first told me. Shayna began to get dizzy and expressed a need to sit down. She took one step and fainted. I caught her and yelled for someone to get help. I told someone else that her parents were inside and to let them know what was going on. Her parents got to us in no time.

School security arrived and sealed the area off until an EMT was able to get there to transfer her to the school medical center. After being checked out by a doctor, we were told that she was suffering from a lot of stress, but she would be okay. She was ordered to take it easy for a few days. Ms. Kim didn't know what really caused it so she accredited it to the move, new environment, and Shayna still getting accustomed to the changes.

Shayna stayed at the hotel with us that night instead of her room so that we could look after her.

We took advantage of sharing a room that night to sort things out and come up with a way to deal with what was going on. Shayna had her mind set on going back to New York with us when we left the following Sunday. She kept saying that she needed to see him and that he needed her. I had to tell her to calm down and think; Key didn't even know that Shayna knew, so there was obviously a reason he didn't reach out to her. I figured it was because he already told her that he didn't sell drugs and didn't know how to break the news of his incarceration to her. I asked her how she was feeling about the fact that he lied to her. Shayna just sat there looking angry and confused, and then a tear fell from her eye. I gave her a hug to console her.

Shayna devised a plan to get back to New York with us. She planned to ride off of the doctor's orders about avoiding stress and convince her parents that a week at home would really help. I told her it was a good plan, but she wouldn't be able to see him due to his visitation restriction. She said that she would deal with that once she got there, but she just had to be there for him. The way she was acting was the same way she acted whenever Darryl did something dumb. Shayna would act without thinking and get so caught up in picking up the pieces before doing what was best for her. I saw her go through it before and I refused to let her make the same mistake again. I told her that it was not a good idea to rush back home, and that it was better to

258

hear from him first. I felt that Key needed to be a man and tell her everything that had been going on. Only then would she get an idea of where he stood and if he respected her enough to want to correct his mistakes. She had a day and a half to think about it.

The next day, her mind was made up. She told Ms. Kim that evening that she wanted to spend the week before classes at home to relieve whatever stress may have been plaguing her. Ms. Kim agreed that it sounded like a good idea, but wanted to know how she planned on getting back to school. "Shayna, a plane ticket isn't like a bus ticket." Shayna explained that it was exactly what she planned; she was going to take a bus from the Port Authority the following Saturday to make it back for Monday classes. Ms. Kim told her that if she could go and be back for classes, then she could take the trip back with us. She also reminded Shayna that she was responsible for buying her own bus ticket. Shayna told her that it would be fine.

Hearing their conversation was bittersweet. I didn't agree with Shayna's decision, but it wouldn't be the first time we bumped heads. We had both made a few decisions against the advice we gave each other over the course of our friendship, but we learned from our mistakes and moved on. The sweet feeling was the thought of having her back around for a week. The rest of the night, Shayna and I hung out in her room with Danielle watching TV. I helped her pack her bags for the week. I was curious as to how Shayna managed to be excused from track practice for an entire week. She told me that she would speak to

259

the coach in the morning and she would be excused if she presented a doctor's note upon her return. She planned on getting one by going to the doctor for her annual physical before she left New York.

Just like that, we were headed back home the next day. We got back to the block around 10:00PM. We unpacked and I was ready for bed, but Shayna was ready to go to The Island at that very moment. I hated to admit it, but she was starting to lose her mind. She wanted to make a trip to The Island late at night; a trip that wasn't going to be short. We had to get on the Subway then transfer to the bus. Altogether it was going to take at least an hour. If it wasn't for the fact that visiting hours ended at 2:00 in the afternoon on a Sunday, she would have stopped at nothing to get out there and see him at that very moment.

I did not like the direction things were heading, and it gave me a bad feeling that it would get worse as the week progressed. Sadly, my prediction was accurate. The Island had no visiting hours on Mondays and Tuesdays so that prolonged Shayna's wait. She was beginning to look like she was going through withdrawals. She would get easily frustrated and become anti-social. If she was trying to sell the whole "A trip back home would help relieve stress" theory to her mom, she was blowing her cover.

When Wednesday arrived, Shayna got up early in the morning to take the trip out to The Island. I caught her leaving her house when I was heading to school to pick my courses for the upcoming semester. I had to tell her to get a hold of herself. She didn't even have a plan for if she got there and her request to visit him was denied. She was shaking and obviously not thinking straight; I couldn't bear to see her like that. She was exhibiting the behavior of an addict that couldn't get their drugs. At that moment I promised her that I could get her a ride there the next day as well as a form of communication with him. She asked me how I would be able to do that. I told her not to worry about that; all she had to do was promise to relax and spend the day at home. Shayna closed her eyes and exhaled as she reluctantly agreed.

With her decision to stay put for a day, it gave me time to come up with a plan. Jamal was headed out to meet with his brother that day. I called him and asked him to tell Jerome to relay a message to Key. I needed Key to know that Shayna and I were planning a visit, and anything that Key wanted to tell Shayna he needed to tell Jerome that night. My plan was to get Shayna and go up there the next day with Jamal and allow her to get anything off of her chest; Jerome would then deliver that message to Key. That was all I had for the time being.

The next day, Shayna and I took the train over to East Flatbush and met Jamal at the station. He and his cousin were waiting downstairs in a car to drive to The Island. When we got there we were checked in, frisked, and told to wait until we were called. Our chance finally came to meet with Jerome. When he came out to the table, he dapped Jamal up then greeted us. Jamal

261

introduced Shayna as his friend and Key's girlfriend, and he introduced me as "The special lady in his life". I was caught off guard for a second. I did not expect that, but I was flattered by it. Jerome and Jamal spoke for a while before we finally got down to business. Key's message to Shayna was "I miss you and I'm thankful for a woman like you. The fact that you came all the way back to visit me shows how much you love me. I'm sorry for not telling you the truth from the beginning. I didn't know how to handle it back then, but I want to change."

It went on for a while about the details I had already shared with her. He finished his message by telling her that he didn't know things were going to end up with him incarcerated, but he wanted her to have something. He had $95,000 back at his new apartment in Queens in a hidden place. He wanted her to take 40,000 of it. The other 55,000 was going to be for him and his mother.

The reason behind giving her the money was that in the event that it was found and proven to be connected to Blizzard's product, he planned to tell the cops that he had already spent it. He also preferred to let someone he loved have it than for it to be seized by the authorities. He planned to use the other portion that he designated for him and his mother for legal fees and to keep him on his feet if he were to get through the trial successfully. Speaking of which, his case was scheduled for two months from that point. Meanwhile, with Key refusing to make a deal with the police, Stack was scheduled to face his original court date the following week.

In regards to Key's offer, Shayna accepted the money and told Jerome to tell Key that she forgave him and still loved him. All I could do was shake my head. I could not believe that she would be so naïve as to place herself in the midst of all of that madness. Honestly speaking, Shayna was not one to handle relationships well. With her record slowly approaching 0-2 with Darryl and now Key, I was convinced that relationships were her kryptonite. She surrendered all of her strengths, morals, and values, and lowered her standards in exchange for what she perceived to be happiness. It was always hard to watch. We didn't have much time left for our visit so I decided to talk to her about it later.

Our visiting time was over and we thanked Jerome for all of his help. On the ride back home, I told Shayna that accepting the money was a bad idea, but she wasn't hearing me. She was convinced that the decisions she was making were for the best of their relationship. I could not sit there and let her think the things she was doing were okay anymore. It was like she was brainwashed. I told her she needed to snap out of it and that she sounded ridiculous. Shayna claimed that I didn't want her to be happy and that I was wrong. I wanted to tell her a little more about how I felt, but I remembered that she was leaving in two days and I didn't want us on bad terms. I stayed quiet and decided to let her have that battle. I made sure to tell her that I loved her before going into our houses that night.

It turns out that we weren't the only ones looking for Key. Blizzard finally found out that he was incarcerated just a few days before we got back to New York. As always, his first instinct was to bail Key out and keep his mouth shut. When he found out that bail was prohibited, he decided to call in a favor from someone in the judicial system. It turned out to be too big of a favor so he did the next best thing; he called in a favor from someone on the inside. He told one of the inmates to give Key a warning.

One day when they were out on the yard playing basketball, Key was in the middle of a game when he got an elbow to the back of his neck. Getting elbowed was common in a basketball game on the yard so Key just got up and walked it off. If he showed that he couldn't take pain, inmates would see him as soft and harass him everywhere else on the prison grounds. He had to prove that he could take care of himself. He got back in position on the court and went right back at the inmate who elbowed him. He drove down the lane for a dunk and ran the inmate over. The inmate got up and pushed Key, Key punched him in retaliation. A few other inmates jumped in and started punching and kicking Key. Jerome saw it with his crew from a distance, but only watched. He and Key had an agreement; they didn't get into each other's drama unless it was life threatening.

That way they didn't make any of their problems on the inside bigger than what they were, or bring new enemies to each other.

By the time they were done with Key, he was left on the ground with a cut under his eye. One of them said "Message from Blizz; keep your mouth shut." Key got up and replied "Tell Blizz to die slowly." then he walked off of the court. It was a known street fact that Blizzard had people killed in jail. I don't know what Key was thinking, but it wasn't wise. Maybe a life behind bars was starting to change him. Maybe he was just trying to not appear as weak. Either way, "Die slowly" wasn't something Key would usually say, not even to Mr. Johnson. He was never graphic or gory in his comebacks.

Later that night as Key was sleeping in his cell, the guys that jumped him on the court went in for another round. They got in with Blizzard's muscle again. Blizzard seemed to know about half of the correctional officers on The Island. He knew the one that was monitoring Key's cell block that night. The officer let them into Key's cell. Key heard the gate opening and woke up. When he saw the guys walking in, he tried to get up. When they realized that he was getting up, they rushed him and pinned him back down to the bed. There was one that served as the leader, his name was Flea. Flea pulled out a shank and put it to Key's neck. Key looked him right in his eyes. He never blinked and never allowed his eyes to wander in any other direction. Flea said "So you're a tough guy, huh?" Key just kept his eyes on him and replied "Not as tough as your mom." Flea didn't like that too much. As a result, he pressed the shank into Key's neck just a little. A thin stream of blood began to flow down Key's neck.

The deeper Key got into this beef with Blizzard, the more he began to show shades of his old self, or someone completely worse. Personally, I would say he was worse because he had developed the mindset of a cornered pit bull. As the thin stream of blood traveled down his neck to his chest, Flea reminded him about his "Die slowly!" comment. He told Key "Why don't you die slowly first? That way you can tell me how it is and I'll relay the message to Blizz." Key told him to do what he had to do. Flea expressed that he would have, but Blizzard ordered him to only deliver a warning. The correctional officer told them that their time was up and they had to go. Flea took the shank off of Key's neck and smiled as he walked out. The rest of the guys walked out behind him.

Key's cell mate looked down at him from his bunk and asked him if he had a death wish. Key wiped his neck with his shirt and laid back down. He was thinking a lot differently at that point. Before, he would keep his mouth shut and did what he was told to protect his family and Shayna. Being imprisoned tainted his way of thinking causing him to lose all track of wisdom. He was now bent on revenge and wanted Blizzard personally.

TRUST ISSUES

Shayna used the day before leaving for Florida to visit Key's mom and pick up the money. I still didn't understand why she was going through with it. In her mind it made sense to get it and claim it before the cops got it. No one knew about the money except Key and now Shayna. However, I'm sure Blizzard speculated that Key had some hidden. Shayna had never met Key's mom so my guess was that it was interesting. She went to the address that Key gave her. They were staying in an expensive apartment in Astoria, Queens.

Shayna found the building and made her way to the apartment. When she knocked on the door, she got a "Who is it?" Shayna gave her name and identified herself as Key's girlfriend. Key's mother didn't know who she was nor was she expecting anyone, but she knew that Key was seeing someone. She opened the door with the chain still attached and asked Shayna what she wanted. Key's mother didn't trust anyone because of the situation they were in. Shayna stated that she was there to pick up what Key left. His mom didn't know what she was referring to so she told her to stop wasting her time. Shayna explained that she was on The Island the day before and got a hold of him. Key's mom quickly unchained the door and pulled Shayna in. She asked Shayna if anyone followed her there. Shayna didn't know, but then again she didn't know she was supposed to be incognito. Key's mom introduced herself as Ms. Williams.

Key's mom wanted to know what Shayna was referring to when she mentioned something that Key left. Shayna explained the conversation they had through Jerome. Before telling his mom how much it was or even the fact that it was money, she went over to the hiding place he left it in. It was under a few floor panels located under the dining room table. Shayna put on some leather gloves that she brought with her and pulled up the panels. Underneath the panels was a duffle bag. Key's mom just watched in curiosity still trying to figure out what was going on.

When Shayna opened the bag, Key's mom gasped at the amount of money she saw. Shayna told her to relax then gave her the details regarding how much money it was and that she was advised to take forty thousand of it. Key's mother exhibited a degree of concern. She said "Hold on, I don't even know you. How do I know you're not taking more than what he said to take?" Shayna asked her if she was accusing her of lying. Key's mom explained that she just didn't trust anyone that she was meeting for the first time, especially if money was involved. Shayna explained to her that she and Key were in a relationship so whatever money she took from the bag would still be his; she was simply going to hold it until the case was settled. Key's mom didn't have a response to that.

Shayna continued to count the money until she got her share, but his mother still didn't trust her. She told Shayna that if she believed any money she took would still be Key's as she stated, she might as well leave all of it because it wasn't going anywhere. Shayna let out a sigh of frustration. While trying to maintain her composure, she told Ms. Williams that she was not going to leave anything behind because that wasn't Key's order. Key's mom asked Shayna who she was going to listen to; Key or the parent? Shayna asked her if that was a trick question. Ms. Williams replied "Do I look like The Riddler to you?" Shayna told her that she was going to get her money and go because she had things to do.

Ms. Williams told her to drop the bag as she pulled a knife out of the sink. Shayna got up from her chair and told Ms. Williams that she was crazy if she thought she would show up without protection. Shayna then pulled out a switchblade similar to the one Radames put in Tupac's nose in the movie Juice. As she held the blade she said "Now Ms. Williams, I don't know you, and as time passes I'm losing interest in getting to know you. Keith sent me over here to do a job. Do you think he wants to find out the scene turned bloody between the two of us?" Ms. Williams put her knife back in the sink then looked at Shayna and said "Smart girl, Keith is gonna need that."

Shayna put her money in a bag and told Ms. Williams that it was nice to meet her; she just wished that it was under better circumstances. They shook hands and Shayna started walking towards the door. Ms. Williams watched her walk away and said "Keith always had a thing for 'poison'." Shayna continued walking and replied "He shows me how much he loves it too." Ms. Williams told her to watch her mouth and have respect for her presence. Shayna rolled her eyes.

As Shayna was getting closer to the door, she noticed the doorknob moving as if someone was trying to enter the apartment. She ran back to the kitchen where Ms. Williams was still standing. She zipped up the bag with the rest of the money and gave it to Ms. Williams. She then instructed Ms. Williams to be quiet and follow her. They made their way to the fire escape that was outside of the kitchen window. They were on the seventh floor. They got down two flights before hearing someone yell "HEY!" from their apartment window. Ms. Williams asked who it was. Shayna told her that she didn't know and to just keep moving. Ms. Williams complained the whole way down about Shayna allowing someone to follow her to the apartment. Shayna eventually told her to shut up or she would run out of energy faster.

They finally got to the bottom and began running up the street. Of course Ms. Williams could not keep up with Shayna so that held them back. God was definitely on their side at that moment because Shayna came up with a life-threatening idea. She ran into the street in front of an oncoming yellow cab causing it to stop short and almost run her over. They got in and took off making their way back to Brooklyn. Ms. Williams had some family in Bushwick, Brooklyn so she stayed there for the time being. They didn't get a look at the guy that got into the apartment, but it was more than likely somebody working for Blizzard.

Back in Brooklyn, Shayna asked Shawn Sr. if she could talk to him about something. He told her that she didn't have to ask. She asked him how Law school was going. He just so happened to be working on some homework at the time. He told her that it was going well, but he was ready to graduate. Shawn was scheduled to graduate the following spring. Shayna asked him if the point he was at in school permitted him to handle cases. He told her that he was only allowed to do simulated scenarios as part of class. She asked him if he knew anyone that would be able to handle a case. At that point Shawn began to get suspicious. He took his glasses off and looked at Shayna, then asked her if she had done something. She explained that she didn't, but she knew someone that may need some legal advice and direction.

Shawn put his books to the side and gave Shayna his undivided attention; he did not have a good feeling about the direction of her questions. The first question he asked was what her friend did. She told him that she could not disclose that information. He reassured Shayna that she could trust him, and that he couldn't recommend anyone that could help unless he knew the severity of the crime. She told him that her friend was brought up on charges for money laundering, conspiracy, possession of cocaine with intent to sell, distribution and drug trafficking along with a few other charges she could not remember. Shawn told her that he did know someone that handled drug cases, but he was not going to recommend them. Instead he advised her to let that friend go because he did not see an association with someone living that lifestyle ending well. Shayna did not like that answer.

In an attempt to still get what she wanted, she tried another method. She went the route of being pitiful. She said in a saddened tone "But it's my friend and I'm really worried about them." Shawn replied "If it's not Charmaine that's been brought up on those charges; which I'm sure it isn't, you'll live." He continued to tell Shayna that she's on the right track and has an opportunity that a lot of kids her age did not have. He was referring to receiving a scholarship to get an education while doing what she enjoyed most. Shayna thanked him and went to her room.

The next day was Saturday and Shayna's day to head back to school. She packed her bags and was headed out the door. I went with her to the Port Authority to give her company as she left. We were on better terms than the previous time we spoke. I was going to miss her all over again. When the time came for her to get on the bus, we hugged and she boarded. I stayed until her bus pulled off, then I went home.

At one point on her bus trip back down to Florida, Shayna had to transfer at a bus station in Georgia. Police were in the parking lot with K9s and their sirens still flashing. Shayna's heart dropped into her stomach. She had not done anything, but she immediately thought that if she was followed to Key's apartment, she could have easily been followed anywhere else. The bus driver gave everyone instructions on where they needed to go once they left the bus. He then got off of the bus and opened the cargo area for the passengers to retrieve their bags. As people began to get off of the bus, a cop said "Not so fast!" The bus driver asked them what the problem was. The officer told the driver that they needed to check everybody and see identification. Apparently, there had been a number of serial stabbings along the east coast. The assailant had a style of attacking at rest stops and bus stations. They would wait for their victims in a bathroom stall and they would become just that, a victim.

The driver informed the passengers of this. Shayna knew that she did not kill anybody, but she was carrying the money in one of her bags and was worried that they may find it in the search process. The officer walked onto the bus and greeted everyone. He informed them that all of the women and children were free to go because the attacker was described as a man. One by one, all of the women got off of the bus, but had to present ID to prove this. Shayna was relieved. However, she was developing a sense of paranoia.

When the officers were done with their searches, everyone got on the next bus and continued on to Florida. Shayna had finally gotten back to school and settled in. Class was scheduled to start on Tuesday. The first place she went was her coach's office to check in. She explained that she forgot to get a doctor's note like she promised she would, but she could get one from the school physician that suggested she take time off. Her coach approved of that.

School had begun for Shayna. My courses were scheduled to start the following week. Stack had his case that same week with charges similar to Key's. He was found guilty, but was only sentenced to do five years in a juvenile detention center along with community service. I don't think he understood how blessed he was. He was given a minor penalty despite being of legal age in the state of New York to be tried as an adult. He must have gotten a good judge that day.

ON YOUR MARK!

Shayna's first few days at school were going well. As I suspected, she had a better selection of people to befriend once classes began. Her main associate was still her teammate/roommate, Danielle. They managed to get two classes together and had lunch often. One day when they went to lunch, she mentioned that she remembered Shayna from Penn Relays earlier in the year. They were in the same final race; Danielle placed fourth.

The first week of classes went well and Shayna was excelling even more with the track team. Her practices were becoming more intense, but she was taking each of them on like they were just a jog in the park. She had one practice during the second week in which she was placed in a race with three seniors a sophomore, and two juniors. She won by a small margin, but that was irrelevant once it set in that she had beaten three seniors. Not every race she had against seniors was like that, but the few that were got the attention of the coaches. I wasn't surprised when she would call me with updates. I remember when we were younger and had races on the block with some of the other kids. She would get all of the boys upset because they could never keep up with her.

As time progressed, she found more people to associate with on campus. She found a few people from New York, a few classmates that she networked with through group projects, people from study groups, and some of Danielle's friends. She still didn't get along with Sabrina. They went at each other a lot on the track at practice. It was exactly what Shayna needed because it was making them the two best runners on the team. Shayna did not like her, and the girl didn't want to be shown up by a freshman so they had consistent motivation.

There was a track & field tournament scheduled for the end of that month in Orlando; two weeks from that time. Shayna and Sabrina were among the runners handpicked by the coaches to represent the women in a few events. Shayna was fine with it as long as Sabrina stayed out of her way. She actually took it as a chance to show Sabrina up. Even though they would both be representing Gainesville University, they would be placed in some of the same races together like the 100-meter dash. That was the event that they both specialized in, and the event that they battled the most in during practices.

Shayna planned to bury Sabrina in the 100 meters on a big stage and kill any debates about who was better. There was only one problem; Shayna and Sabrina were also chosen to represent the school in the 4x100m relay. The problem was figuring out who would run the anchor leg. They were both accustomed to running the anchor leg, but the spot usually went to Sabrina on Gainesville's team. That meant the debate of who was the best was going to be settled before they even got to the tournament.

The coaches decided to run some simulation races to determine who would get the spot. The final simulation they conducted was a relay. Every other simulation up to that point proved to show a similar result between the two of them. They picked two teams in which Shayna and Sabrina served as anchors. Shayna wasn't too fond of the idea because a relay's results were dependent on other runners as well. However, she knew complaining wasn't going to get her anywhere. She shook her emotions off and vowed to win regardless.

As the race began, Shayna's team was losing. Her team's second leg closed the gap a little, but it wasn't enough. By the time the third leg got the baton, the race was close with Sabrina's team still holding the lead. Shayna's team's third leg evened it up which set up a perfect scenario for Shayna and Sabrina; a straight away with even positioning. They both took off with their hands out waiting for the baton. Sabrina received hers, but Shayna's third leg struggled to hand it off to her. That gave Sabrina about two paces of a head start, but Shayna didn't let that bother her. The lead changed about two or three times. In the end, Sabrina won by the tip of her sneaker. When the result was announced, Shayna was shocked.

She called me that night and told me all about it. I asked her how she handled it simply because I was aware of her temper. Surprisingly, she just nodded her head and moved on. She did not congratulate Sabrina or shake her hand, she just slowly walked away. She could not believe that she had lost. Shayna could take a loss, but losing to Sabrina brought about an incomparable internal pain.

Shayna wanted another chance badly and soon. She also mentioned that the third leg on her team was a friend of Sabrina's. She was basically insinuating that the baton transfer was a set up. I told her that it was best to let that theory go because if that was the case, then she would have thrown the race way before passing the baton. She let it go eventually, but stressed for days over the loss. It was official at that point; Sabrina was going to be running the anchor and Shayna would be the third leg at the tournament in Orlando.

Things were still pretty ordinary for the rest of us in Brooklyn. Jamal started his senior year of high school, Ms. Kim and Shawn continued on with their lives, Ms. Williams was still hiding out in Bushwick, and I was beginning my own college journey as well as continuing my new catering job at The Garden. Blizzard was still harassing Key in any possible way he could, and Key was still taking on any challenge Blizzard presented. His visitation restriction had been upgraded to immediate family and appointed lawyers. He had been getting a lot of visits from federal agents looking to get a confession or testimony out of him, but he never gave them anything. One day he was visited by a lawyer representing Mr. Jones. Mr. Jones was taken into custody as well when Key got arrested. He was seen as an accessory to Key's crime and possibly going to face time.

When Mr. Jones' lawyer visited Key, he broke down what Key needed to know about Mr. Jones' case. He told Key that if he admitted that Mr. Jones had nothing to do with Blizzard or the distribution of drugs in his own restaurant, then Mr. Jones could walk free. In Key's mind, it wasn't that simple. Key had already said he had nothing to do with Blizzard to every lawyer and agent that questioned him. He felt that providing a statement saying Mr. Jones had nothing to do with it would incriminate his claim. Needless to say he refused to cooperate with Mr. Jones' lawyer.

Mr. Jones' lawyer asked Key how he could allow someone who gave him a job and numerous chances to go to jail for something he was responsible for. He also reminded Key of Mr. Jones' age and how hard it could be for him to survive in jail while he had a family that needed him. Key looked at the lawyer with a smirk and said "You're good. You picked the right career path." The lawyer told Key that it wasn't a game and he wasn't trying to send him on a guilt trip. Key replied "I'm sure you'll be able to come up with something for Mr. Jones, but I'm not giving you a testimony." Key got up and was escorted back to his cell.

I spoke to Jamal some time during that week. He had gone to visit his brother and came back with some news regarding Key. Jerome told Jamal that Key was changing a lot. His theory was that the amount of fights and altercations Key had been in may have played a big role in that change. According to Jamal's update, Key was sounding worse than the disrespectful guy he was when we first met. I always heard stories about prison changing people, but Key's change sounded almost scary. The first thing I did was call Shayna. I was more worried about

279

her being involved with this new character than I was about Key's well-being.

I described everything Jamal told me to Shayna. However, it may not have been the best time to talk about it. She was still dealing with losing her race. She now had these two stressors on her mind, but I was not going to withhold that kind of information from her. Shayna digested everything I told her about Key and said that he may just be reaching a boiling point. She then defended his actions by saying that she would be reacting the same way if she was trapped behind bars. I had to remind her that he had not even been there two months yet, and a transition like that should not take place that soon. Shayna did not comprehend the point I was making. I elaborated by telling her that she may be dealing with someone that was unstable. I figured that in the event that his case was dropped, that was what she was going to have to deal with.

Shayna was just so sure of her "relationship" that she was not even hearing what I was trying to tell her. She told me that I was unable to see what she was seeing and that Key was perfectly fine. Shayna wasn't sounding too stable either. I pointed out that she was defending Key and had not even spoken to him to gain her own perspective on his new behavior. She claimed that she could say the same thing about me. In a sense that was true, but I wasn't pointing the finger at Key. I was simply providing her with the information I received from our only source. She told me that she was not worried about Key or his case because once it all blew over they would go back to being happy.

The way Shayna was speaking made no sense and was very unfamiliar; this was not my sister. I asked her if she was at least worried about his health with all of the fights he had been in. She expressed that she was definitely concerned and wanted him out of there as soon as possible. That's when it hit me; Shayna had convinced herself that she was in love with Key. Therefore, the situation he was facing was causing a mental dysfunction. It did not help that she was forced to handle all that was going on from a thousand miles away by herself. I had already come to the conclusion that she was delusional a long time before, but that phone conversation confirmed it. I say that because Shayna always considered my advice before giving a rebuttal. That particular phone conversation sounded more confrontational than conversational. She told me that she had to go because she had had a quiz the next day and needed to study. We hung up and I just prayed for her.

GET SET!

The day of the Orlando tournament had arrived. Shayna was pumped up for her events and ready to go. She managed to clear her mind of everything going on back home, and the race she lost to Sabrina. She started her day with her traditional routine of listening to Wu-Tang by herself on the bleachers with her eyes closed. That is until she was interrupted by Sabrina. She tapped Shayna's leg and startled her. Shayna and I are closer than Siamese twins, but even I never interrupted her preparation routine. Sabrina seemed to know that it would upset Shayna. What made it even worse was that Sabrina did not really have anything to say after getting Shayna's attention. All she said was "Hope you're ready."

That upset Shayna to the point of wanting to fight Sabrina. That was exactly what Sabrina wanted. Sabrina knew that anybody behaving in a disorderly fashion during the meet would be automatically disqualified by their coach, Coach Batts. Coach Batts would take a runner out of their races as a form of discipline. He knew that they would not make the same mistake if they wanted to race again. He also knew that the rest of the team would be upset with them for costing the team points. He was a former military sergeant. Shayna was aware of those consequences, but she let her emotions get the best of her as usual. As Shayna began to get loud, Coach Batts was not too far away and heard her. She got off of the bleachers and started to walk toward Sabrina. Danielle caught her and tackled her covering her mouth.

Shayna was still going off with Danielle's hand over her mouth, but did not get enough words out to get herself into trouble. Whatever she said was muffled, but she was obviously angry. Coach Batts began to approach them so Danielle was trying to tell her to shut up. She then began to fight Danielle off. Coach Batts got closer and Danielle said "We're just playing, Coach. There's a fight part in a song and we were just reenacting it to get hype." She was telling Coach Batts all of this while they were still wrestling. Coach Batts told them both to get up. When they got up, he told them that he did not care how they chose to get pumped for the races, but he didn't want to see anything like what they were doing on his time. They both apologized. I believe that was the moment when Shayna remembered Coach Batts' disorderly conduct rule.

Shayna picked up her CD player and headphones that came off in Danielle's attempt to keep her quiet. She thanked Danielle for looking out for her and her opportunity to race that day. Sabrina was a few feet away with a few of her minions with their arms crossed. They were upset that their plan to get Shayna in trouble had failed. Shayna and Danielle had taken notice of this. Danielle escorted Shayna away and told her that Sabrina was scared. It was the only explanation as to why she would try to get Shayna out of her events that day. She also explained to Shayna that Sabrina was the type to look out for her own image before the good of the team. Danielle was basically telling Shayna to use Sabrina's selfish mindset against her; beating her would be like cutting off a snake's head.

The tournament was underway and the individual races had begun taking place. Gainesville University was among the top schools in leading positions. Shayna and Sabrina were doing well in their respective events. The time for the 4x100m relay was approaching. Coach Batts assembled the runners and gave them a pep talk. He reminded them of what was most important and refreshed them on minor techniques. The runners then lined up and took their marks.

As the race got under way, the runners were pretty even. Gainesville slowly fell to third as they approached the second leg. The second leg closed the gap just a little. Shayna's leg was coming up. When the second leg passed Shayna the baton, she took off. She was in top form managing to close the gap. She then formed an even larger gap by taking a large lead. The only thing on her mind was making sure her performance upstaged whatever Sabrina would do as the anchor. She also wanted to be responsible for putting the team on top.

Shayna was approaching Sabrina with about sixty meters separating her and second place. She handed the baton off to Sabrina and Sabrina took off. The way Sabrina ran, she didn't seem to need the help of the lead Shayna gave her, but it didn't hurt. Sabrina ran with the same amount of speed and power Shayna ran with in the third leg. As a result, Sabrina and

Gainesville University finished in first by a solid seventy meters. The entire crowd was in awe of what they had just seen. It was one of the greatest performances to say the least. The rest of the team was at the finish line waiting to celebrate as Sabrina crossed.

All four runners congratulated each other. Shayna and Sabrina congratulated each other as well, but never made eye contact. Coach Batts walked over clapping his hands to get everyone's attention. He told them that they all did well and that they needed to make their way back to the team huddle area to prep for the next few events. Sabrina had a high jump event while Shayna had a 200 meter sprint. She also had a long jump event with Danielle. She placed third, and Danielle placed first in the long jump. Even though it wasn't Shayna's regular event, she still hated to lose. She quickly got over it and moved on to preparing for her next event. Sabrina however placed first in her event and had to let everyone know. Coach Batts did not like his athletes exhibiting boastful behavior so when she realized that he was around, she would quickly shut up.

A few more events had taken place. There was only one more event scheduled before Shayna and Sabrina's 100 meter dash event. That gave Shayna a little bit of time to relax before she had to report to the line. She went back to listening to her music. She changed the CD from *Enter the Wu-Tang: 36 Chambers* to Method Man's *Tical* album in order to get herself hype. She had a special song for that particular race; "Bring the

Pain". Nothing got her more hype for her biggest races than listening to that song.

The time had arrived for the race. Shayna and Sabrina approached the line with the other runners. A few of the runners had done their starting line routines. Some prayed, some jumped around to get their last minute jitters out, and others simply did a few stretches. The line official told them to take their marks, get set, and before the gun went off, Shayna accidentally had a false start. In track and field, a first false start would warrant a warning for the runner. Any subsequent false starts by that runner would result in an automatic disqualification. What usually happens when a runner has a false start is the other runners would take off right after as a reflex. That's exactly what happened.

When the runners got back to their places, Sabrina said to Shayna "You have to wait for the gun." Shayna ignored her and got back into position. The official told them to take their marks, get set, and the gun went off. Shayna and Sabrina had taken commanding first and second place leads respectively. Shayna had the lead over Sabrina by an inch, but the distance between them and third was about twenty meters by the time they reached the fifty meter mark. The race had now become a battle between the two of them. There were two times when they were in a neck and neck tie. By about seventy-five meters, Shayna had gained that inch lead back and added another inch before maintaining it. By the time it was all said and done, Shayna had won the race by

1½ meters. She crossed the finish line and celebrated with a scream. It sounded like a stress relieving scream.

When Sabrina crossed the finish line she gave Shayna a hug. Shayna did not return the love; she pushed Sabrina off. Sabrina asked her what her problem was. Shayna said "Don't front for the crowd." She then turned her back on Sabrina and continued to celebrate with the rest of the teammates. Coach Batts saw what Shayna had done and took note of it. That was actually why Sabrina gave Shayna that fake hug. She knew Shayna had a temper, but she also knew she would keep it real which is what she did when she pushed her off. She exploited Shayna's bad temper and used it to make Shayna seem arrogant and unsportsmanlike in front of Coach Batts. It was becoming a game of chess between the two of them; thank God Shayna had Danielle to guide some of her moves.

When they got back to the huddle area, Coach Batts mentioned Shayna's behavior. He usually put his athlete's on blast so that they could remember their mistake. He told her that no matter what kind of differences she may or may not have with a teammate, she should never let it show on the track. He wanted unity on and off of the track among his athletes. He told her that he would talk to her some more about it at a later time because they needed to prepare for other events. Being that it was a tournament, a lot of the events were process of elimination until they got down to the best of the best.

By the end of the tournament, Shayna's school won second place. It wasn't exactly what they expected or what Coach Batts wanted, but they accepted it and moved on. If the scores were solely based on Shayna, Sabrina, and some of the other senior's events, it may have been a different story. They congratulated the other teams, gathered their things and began making their way back to the bus. They had a two hour trip back to the campus ahead of them.

When they got on the bus, everyone was heading to their seats. Once everyone was settled in, Coach Batts asked Shayna to join him up front. Shayna already knew what he wanted to talk about. He started by telling her that she needed to go over the guidelines of the team and remind herself of how they function as a unit. Shayna apologized for her behavior, but Coach Batts told her that apologizing was unnecessary. He did not want to hear the words "I'm sorry" from anyone because in his personal experience, people were likely to repeat their mistake. Instead of saying sorry, he would rather they just show change with their actions. Shayna nodded her head and told the coach that she understood.

The bus took off and Coach Batts continued his lecture to Shayna. He sat back and told her that he was aware of her temper before he even recruited her to attend the school. It turned out that he was at the track meet when Shayna got into it with the girl that Darryl was cheating on her with. When he told Shayna that he was there, she put her hand over her face and shook her head in shame. He told her that there was no need to be embarrassed. He reassured her that if her temper was that much of a deterrent to how great she could be, he would not have asked her to join his team. That made sense to her; she looked back up and took in the rest of what he had to say.

Coach Batts wanted to get to know Shayna a little more so he dug a little deeper. He asked her if she was aware of her temper. Shayna admitted that she was very aware. He told her that it was not necessarily a bad thing because every athlete needs that fire and aggression to get them to the next level. However, they also need wisdom and a leveled head. If it was only about aggression and power, then athletes with muscle would be the only ones that were successful. He was trying to make her understand that she was very skilled, but if she could not control herself, opponents would see that as a weak point and use it against her.

Shayna thanked Coach Batts for his advice, but she was curious as to why he was telling her all of this. He told her that it was because he could see her in Atlanta the following year competing in the 1996 Olympic Games. She expressed that she was flattered and she knew she was fast, but she had not thought about the Olympics, not yet at least. Coach Batts told her that was what he was there for; "I'm not here to only help you improve your running techniques. I'm here to mentor you and help you to become the best." Shayna asked him what made him so sure that she could make it to Atlanta. Coach Batts explained that he knew because it was the same way he ended up in the military.

Apparently, Coach Batts saw a lot of himself in Shayna when he was her age. He was from Camden, New Jersey, one of the highest ranked cities for crime in the nation. He was known in his neighborhood as the fast kid that had a temper. People always encouraged him to run track. He took the advice and ran in high school after figuring he had nothing else to do. He was a force to be reckoned with on the track; pretty much unbeatable. However, one day he found it boring and did not want to run anymore so he quit the team. After leaving his team, he used his running ability for a life of crime.

He started hanging out with a group of guys that spent their lives getting in trouble. One day he allowed them to talk him into setting up a shoplifting operation. The plan was for one of them to steal something from a store; Coach Batts would intentionally dress like the one who did the shoplifting. The shoplifter would run around a corner where Coach Batts was waiting, and just like a relay, Coach Batts would see them and take off. Meanwhile the shoplifter would get in a car with the rest of the guys. The cops would be looking for a guy that ran so they would automatically pursue Coach Batts. However, they could never catch him.

He and his friends would pull off the scam at the mall or just regular stores on the street. Coach Batts would always meet them back at one of their houses. They would split up whatever they got whether it was money or merchandise they could pawn, and Coach Batts would get a share. He was 16 hanging out with guys in their early 20s. He was not home most of the time so his mother eventually put him out. She told him that if he did not want to be home, then he did not need to be home. She was trying to raise him as well as his younger brother and did not want him being a negative influence. He would usually spend nights on one of the guy's couches.

Eventually, the cops caught onto their scheme and began to monitor the types of spots they would hit. They narrowed it down to a few spots that could possibly be their next target. Their next target was an electronic store. One of them stole a few items on a store rack and ran out of the store. Just as planned, he turned the corner and went straight to the car; that was Coach Batts' cue. Coach took off and a police car came around the corner so fast that it was drifting. He looked back and saw the car and began to run faster. As he turned back in his initial running direction, he was clotheslined by a cop that was waiting for him. Getting clotheslined is the act of someone putting their arm out and catching you across the front of your neck and chest. As a result, your entire upper body gets pushed back and your lower body kicks up causing you to land on your back. Coach Batts tried to tell the officer that he did not do anything, but the cop told him to shut up. Another cop car came around the block and blocked the getaway car in.

Coach Batts and everyone in his crew were charged and had a lot of the other robberies with a similar description linked to them. Some of them were ones that they were not responsible for, but they did not have much of a defense. In the end, they were all sentenced to do time. By the time Coach Batts was released, he was nineteen and didn't feel like going back to school. He was embarrassed to be that age in high school; he also felt that he could not do it so he joined the military. While he was enlisted he learned discipline, received his GED, ran track, and received a higher education degree from Gainesville University. His degree gave him an officer position of Sergeant and eventually a job as the school's track coach.

He explained to Shayna that it was why he was so militant and serious about discipline. He did not have anybody to warn him about where his behavior would land him, and he didn't want someone else to go through the same thing. Anybody that did try to warn him was not hard enough on him. Shayna asked him how things were with his mother ever since then. He told her that things had gotten better and she was proud of the man he had become.

Shayna asked him what she needed to do to get to Atlanta. He told her that she just needed to follow his directions and work on changing her attitude. She told him that she felt she could do that. He was pleased with her answer. After his lecture, Coach Batts informed Shayna that she was not the first runner that Sabrina targeted. He explained that Sabrina was a very fast and skilled runner, but she fueled herself on the weaknesses of others. What he meant was she would do anything to stay on top. Sabrina was also very clever. If she knew she couldn't beat you, she would break you down mentally. That was exactly what she seemed to do to Shayna, but Shayna's raw talent is what kept her ahead of Sabrina figuratively and literally when her technique was smothered by her attitude.

The last thing Coach Batts shared was that the other seniors that were top performers came into the program the same time Sabrina did. He told Shayna to look at the girls at the back of the bus and describe what she saw. Shayna looked back for a few seconds then told Coach Batts that they were all just talking. He then asked her if she noticed anything about how they may have been sitting or wore their clothes or styled their hair. Shayna's mouth dropped and said "They're like quadruplets." Coach Batts said "Exactly! Now when they came in as freshman, they were four completely different individuals. Sabrina was the only one out of the four of them to dress, talk, and act that way. You get what I'm saying now?"

It was at that moment that Shayna realized what he meant by how Sabrina breaks people down. She had broken those girls down to the point of making them her loyal followers. They may have even been faster than Sabrina, but allowed themselves to believe that she was the best. Coach Batts told Shayna that her attitude and refusal to conform to Sabrina showed how much of a competitor and independent thinker she was. That was the main reason he wanted her on his team. He told her to keep it up and not let Sabrina get to her. They continued the bus ride back to school.

<u>GO!</u>

As Shayna found a new mentor and someone to talk to in Coach Batts, Key found someone to talk to as well in regards to his situation. He spoke to a lawyer after some advice from Jerome. Jerome told him that unless he wanted to run the risk of representing himself at the big case in two weeks, he needed to speak to a lawyer for advice on what was wise. Key's request to see a lawyer was eventually granted.

The lawyer he met with was one in which the court appointed to him. The lawyer suggested that Key settle for a deal to receive a lesser sentence. Key made it clear that he did not want any time at all, and that he was planning on fighting the case to get his freedom. The lawyer informed him that there was too much evidence against him to assemble a defense in two weeks. Key attempted to explain that they could not possibly have anything on him because the bottle the SWAT team found containing the cocaine was not in his possession. The lawyer removed her glasses and looked at him like he was crazy. She told him that if that was his only defense, then he definitely should have spoken to a lawyer sooner. The bottle they found was in fact on the floor after Key threw it away, but that also meant his finger prints were on it. Not only that, they had gotten a hold of some other bottles that were found in the vicinity of the restaurant that were more than likely dropped by Blizzard's clientele. Those bottles had Key's fingerprints as well as cocaine residue on them.

Key put his head down into his hands in disbelief of what he was hearing. He not only had to explain his fingerprints on the bottles containing cocaine, but also whether he was working for someone or on his own. It had become a web that was only getting bigger. The lawyer asked him what he was thinking by not seeking legal advice. He explained that he did not know because he had never been in that type of situation before. She told him that if he pinpointed Blizzard as the core distributor, she could possibly get five years taken off of his sentence. His confession would be of great help to the investigation geared toward bringing Blizzard down that was already in progress. The investigation had been open for three years before all of this happened, but Blizzard always found a way to slip through their fingers.

After taking a moment to think about it, Key told the lawyer that she could forget it and that he wanted all of the years taken off of his potential sentence. She reiterated that she could not do that. Key told her that he knew for a fact that she could. He then accused her of low-balling him with the five year offer. Key's theory was that if the information he had on Blizzard was so vital in bringing him down, then it was definitely worth more than five years. He told the lawyer "My life is on the line here. The only thing you all have to worry about is finding other ways to bring him down if I don't collaborate with you. So the deal is a clean record or I have nothing else to say." The lawyer threw another offer at him, "I can possibly try for ten years." Key told her that she obviously did not want his testimony that badly. She told him that ten was as high as she could go. Key told her that if that was all she could do, then they needed to send in another lawyer. He got up and asked to be brought back to his cell.

The lawyer started to gather her things. Before the door closed behind Key and the officer, she yelled "WAIT!" They re-entered the room. She told him that she could add protection to the ten years. He asked her what she was going to protect him from. She claimed that she could provide him with protection on the inside of the jail. He stated that it would not be necessary because he could handle himself. She said "Think for a second. With the trial in two weeks, Blizzard is going to make more attempts to keep you quiet." Key folded his arms and asked her how she knew that Blizzard had people harassing him on the inside if he never mentioned it. The lawyer was briefed on what he had been going through since being incarcerated. Key told her "If you have the pull to provide me with protection on the inside from your position on the outside, then there's something you're not telling me." Key figured that she could provide more than a measly ten years. He told her that if she wanted his testimony she would have to get him cleared of all charges.

When Key got back to the general population area, he saw Jerome hanging out in front of his cell talking to one of the other inmates. He went over to Jerome's cell and asked the other inmate to excuse him and told Jerome he needed some advice. The other inmate walked away and Jerome asked Key what he needed. Key told Jerome about his conversation with the lawyer and asked what he would have done. Jerome told him that he did the right thing. He explained to Key that he had to play chess with legal authority because they were set on the game plan of low effort, high reward. He told Key "If your testimony against Blizzard is that vital, they know where to find you." That was actually Key's other problem; he was concerned about what the lawyer said in regards to him making it to the trial. Blizzard did not want him to testify so he would do everything to stop him from making it there. Jerome told him that the only thing that may serve as protection was solitary confinement. Key asked him what he needed to do to get there. Jerome didn't know because he had never been there, but he knew it had to be bad.

Solitary confinement could be a period of a week or even two. It all depended on the severity of what the prisoner did. It was also used for prisoners that proved to be suicidal or a danger to themselves. Key began to brainstorm how he would get there and stay there for the duration of time until the trial. He looked up at the upper level of the general population area. He saw Flea and the rest of the guys that worked for Blizzard congregating. Flea was telling corny jokes, but getting laughs from the rest of Blizzard's employees. Key instantly got an idea.

It was dinner time for the inmates. Key was sitting with Jerome and their associates when he saw Blizzard's employees getting their food. He saw what table they chose to eat at out of the corner of his eye. He went up to see if he could get seconds.

As he was walking away from the table, he told Jerome in a low tone "Don't get involved." Jerome was taking a bite of some bread at the time and looked confused so he kept an eye on Key.

Key managed to get his seconds. Instead of walking back to his table, he made a left in the direction of Flea and his crew. As soon as he got behind Flea, he smacked him in the back of his head with the metal tray. You could hear the sound resonate throughout the cafeteria; "BONG!" The hit immediately caused Flea to experience dizziness and a faint feeling. Flea turned around to try to gather himself, but he was dazed. When he turned around, Key hit him again across his forehead with the tray leaving a gash. Flea's crew tried to jump in, but Key began to swing the tray like a mad man. He got two of them across their heads and kicked another before the rest of them jumped on him and started beating him up. Flea was on the ground unconscious.

The guards took a while to intervene. When they did, they tasered Key and some of Flea's crew and restrained them. This got the attention of the other inmates and they began to get rowdy. When the full story surfaced about how it started and what happened, Key was sent to solitary confinement for two weeks. In his mind it was a double reward; he got revenge on Flea, and the protection he wanted. The only problem with that was with every action there is always a reaction.

Blizzard got word of what happened. He decided to hurt Key as much as Key hurt his business on the inside of the jail; he ordered retaliation. During Key's first week in solitary confinement, there was a brawl. Blizzard's minions pulled off a sneak attack on Jerome and his associates. One guy walked by Jerome as he was talking to someone at his cell. He took off his shirt then quickly turned around and wrapped it around Jerome's neck and said "You roll with Key, right?" Jerome's friend punched the guy that was strangling him. That in turn brought both crews to a rumble. In the midst of the brawl, someone pulled out a shank and cut Jerome across his neck. The fight went on for a few more seconds before the guards were able to separate everybody. When things got under control, Jerome was in the middle of the floor in a pool of his own blood. From there he was rushed to the prison infirmary.

Jamal and his family had gotten word and rushed over to the jail. When they got there, they were told that he was in critical condition after losing a lot of blood. Jamal was distraught. His grandmother immediately began to pray out loud as she held his hand and his mother's hand. She asked God to restore Jerome's health and to keep the family strong. They were all crying; him, his mother, and his cousins. The only one not crying was Jamal's father. He always served as the rock in the family's time of pain, but he was just as hurt. An officer approached them once they were all a little more stable and informed them that it was an act of retaliation. Jamal was even more upset being that Jerome wasn't even supposed to be incarcerated.

FRUITION

Shayna called me the night after. She wanted to get an update on everything that was going on in New York. She would call me on a nightly basis for updates unless she was tied up with homework or too tired after practice. She told me about Coach Batts and Danielle and about her tournament in Orlando. It made me happy to know that she now had two people looking out for her best interest. While she was updating me on what was happening on her end, I sensed a different kind of tone in her voice. She sounded a little depressed so I asked her what was wrong. She tried to tell me that she was fine, but I told her that she knew better than that to think I couldn't read her. She finally told me that not having a firsthand perception of what was going on in New York was bothering her. She was beginning to get frustrated with not being able to speak to Key.

I didn't want to tell her about Jerome because more bad news was the last thing she needed. I wanted to make her feel a little better so I told her that Key managed to get some protection until the day of the trial. She was happy to hear that and it changed the subject. She mentioned that she really wanted to be there for the trial. I advised her to not concern herself with that because it would only serve as a distraction from school and track. That may have already happened based on what she told me next. She had gotten a D on a test, and she had a rough practice earlier that day in which she almost got into a fight with Sabrina. She had actually been dealing with Sabrina well since the tournament up to that day. She just allowed Sabrina to get under her skin.

I could not do anything about that all the way from New York which bothered me. Usually when one of us fell behind in a class, we would help each other study and provide some encouragement. I told her that I would pray for her and that she needed to talk to Coach Batts for a little bit of therapy. She was reluctant at first, but eventually agreed. I had to get back to a paper I was writing for my Humanities course. We said our goodbyes, and just as I was about to hang up I heard a loud "BOOM" sound through the phone. I yelled "SHAYNA! SHAYNA!" All I could hear was a lot of moving around. I finally heard Shayna yell "WHAT'S GOING ON?" I yelled her name again, but apparently she was not holding the phone anymore. Finally I heard her voice, it sounded like she was far away from the phone. She said "CHARMAINE! CALL MY MOM." The phone cut off before she could finish saying "Mom", but I knew what she said.

My heart was racing as I tried to dial her house number. I even began to feel a little faint. I did not know what was going on, but I was praying that Shayna was okay. I couldn't even remember the number with all of the thoughts that were running through my mind. I just dropped the phone and ran over to her house. I ran up their front steps and started banging on the door and ringing the bell frantically. The longer it took for them to answer, the louder I got. I started to cry even more with every second that I couldn't get a hold of anyone. I looked down at the street at one point to see if their car was there; it was. I kept banging on the door and yelling "MS. KIM! SHAWN!"

The light inside finally came on and Shawn was running down the steps in pajamas with Ms. Kim behind him tying her robe. They opened the door and Shawn asked me what was going on. I simply said "Something happened to Shayna." Ms. Kim stepped in front of Shawn and asked "What do you mean?" I tried to tell them what happened while attempting to catch my breath. Ms. Kim grabbed both of my arms and kept asking "WHAT? WHAT? WHAT?" Shawn separated us and told Ms. Kim to give me some air. He brought us both inside. We sat down and I finally caught my breath, but Ms. Kim was beginning to breathe heavily. I told them that I was on the phone with Shayna when I suddenly heard a commotion and Shayna yelling for me to call them.

Ms. Kim fell out of her chair onto one knee and began to hold her chest saying "No No No! Please God, no!" I always managed to catch when a member of Shayna's family called on God's name. Shawn Sr. grabbed her and told me to get him the phone from the coffee table. Ms. Kim was still on the ground repeating the word "No!" Shawn Jr. walked down the stairs crying. The commotion must have disrupted his sleep. When he saw Ms. Kim he ran over to her and began to rub her back. Shawn Sr. told me to hold Ms. Kim and to just keep talking to her.

He went into the kitchen and called Shayna's school. No one was in the offices at that time of night so he got the automated operator; that gave him options of departments he could be forwarded to. He picked the option for security. When security answered, Shawn told them that there was something going on at the Track & Field House and that his daughter may be in trouble. Security asked him what his name was. Shawn told them that they could get all of his information after they checked, but for that moment, every second that passed was just another second that she was being harmed. He ordered them to go over to the Track & Field House and give him a report because being a parent and his taxes granted him that right.

I was able to get Ms. Kim to sit up and breathe a little easier, but she was still a little unstable. Security had the nerve to tell Shawn to calm down. Shawn was ready to verbally put them in their place, but he knew that would not get him anywhere and Shayna would still be in trouble. He told security that if something happened to her, then he would have all of their campus badges. Security informed Shawn that someone had gone over to check. Shawn told them that it should not take an argument to get results when someone's life may be on the line.

Shawn stayed on the phone with security; he put it on speaker so that he could sit with Ms. Kim and keep her calm. I sat with Shawn Jr. in another chair. About five minutes passed before security came back on the phone. They said hello to get our attention. Shawn immediately asked them if Shayna was okay. Security informed us that everyone in the house was okay, but they were not able to go directly inside. He explained that they were barred from entering the house because there was in investigation taking place by the DEA. Shawn, in a confused tone asked what the DEA was looking for in their house. Security told them that they were looking for a piece of evidence for a case that may be located in Shayna and Danielle's room.

After putting two and two together, it was what I feared. The DEA of course would be looking for something drug related, and Shayna was in possession of that $40,000 worth of drug money. I started to get scared because of what could possibly happen to her if she was caught with it. I felt that I had to tell Shawn and Ms. Kim what was going on. Before I could get it out, Shawn put another set of two's together. He said "Oh no!" Shayna's mom asked him what was wrong. He explained how Shayna approached him seeking legal advice for a friend before she went back to school. With the series of events that were taking place at that very moment, he thought that in hindsight she may have been talking about herself. He began to blame himself for not reading a little closer between the lines. Ms. Kim asked him what kind of advice he gave her. He explained that Shayna described a friend that had been brought up on charges and he told her to let that friend go because she did not need to be associated with them.

I could not sit there and allow him to beat himself up. I told him that she couldn't have been talking about herself. I explained that the friend she was referring to had already been brought up on charges and Shayna was not facing any. Hearing that made him feel better and relieved him of his panicked state. However, I had to also tell them that the DEA was likely looking for something that was in her possession. Ms. Kim asked me what I was talking about. I explained that the friend she was talking about was Key and about him being incarcerated for drug possession. Shawn asked me what Shayna had to do with that and if she was holding drugs for him. I told him about the money Key gave her, and that they may be seeking it for his upcoming trial the following week. Ms. Kim fainted when she heard that. Shawn and I caught her and brought her to the couch to rest while she was in her unconscious state.

That was too much for one night and it was only getting started. Back at Shayna's room, the agents had her and Danielle against the wall. One of the agents asked which one of them was Shayna. Danielle and Shayna looked at each other, and then looked back at the agent. The agent told them that if neither of them confessed to being Shayna, then they were both being taken in for questioning. Sabrina and her crew were being nosy as usual standing outside of their room watching everything. The agent asked the two of them who Shayna was again. They both just looked at him again. He told them that he gave them a chance and that they needed to turn around because they were under arrest. Shayna immediately admitted that it was her they were looking for. The agents already knew who she was, but they wanted her to verbally identify herself.

As they were pulling their handcuffs out, Coach Batts ran into the room with a robe and slippers. He didn't live too far from the campus and drove over as fast as he could when he heard about what was going on. He ran right past the outside barricade, but was stopped when he got to the room. He asked them what was going on. The lead agent told Coach Batts that he was going to have to leave or he would be arrested for tampering with an investigation. He told them that he was the coach and that Shayna and Danielle were his athletes. The lead agent presented Coach Batts with a warrant to search the premises. He explained that they were looking for a specific amount of money that was tied to a case and may be in Shayna's possession.

Coach Batts looked at Shayna and asked if it was true, but Shayna did not respond. The agent told Coach Batts that they were willing to give Shayna one chance to surrender the money. If she did not surrender it, they would be forced to thoroughly search the room and anything in it. Coach Batts asked the agent if he could talk to Shayna because he may be able to convince her to turn the money over if she had it. The agent told Coach Batts that he would not be able to do that, and that he was already being nice by not tearing the room up. Coach Batts told the agent that Shayna would hand it over if it was in the room. The agent told him that he would need to hear it from her and she would need to hand it over within the next ten seconds.

According to the agent, all Shayna had to do was hand over the $40,000 and they would call it a night. Instead of surrendering the money, Shayna whispered "He's gonna go to jail." Coach Batts gave her a confused look and asked her who she was talking about. Shayna whispered again, "I can't let him go to jail." The agent told Coach Batts that he had heard enough and ordered his team to find the money. Danielle and Shayna were ordered to stand outside of the room so that they didn't get hurt. Within ten minutes they found the money in a vent behind Shayna's bed. However, they trashed Shayna and Danielle's room as well as some of their belongings.

Shayna was arrested and spent the night in a holding cell. She was charged with tampering with evidence, conspiracy, trafficking, and being an accessory to Key's crime. She was eventually transferred to a holding cell in New York. She had officially earned a place in Key's case. I guess she got what she wanted when she said she wanted to be there for him. Except instead of being there for him, she was now there because of him. In addition to that, she was facing a separate case for her charges.

Security came back to the phone and called for Shawn's attention. He asked Shawn to confirm that his daughter's name was Shayna; Shawn confirmed. Security informed him about what had gone down and gave him the number of the precinct where Shayna would be held. She was more than likely going to call the house first. Ms. Kim was still unconscious with a wet washcloth across her forehead. I was in disbelief, but more so mad at myself for not doing more to prevent this from happening. It was eating me up inside to the point where I couldn't sleep that night. I just wanted to see Shayna and make sure she was okay.

In the midst of all that was going on, I couldn't help but wonder how the DEA knew about the money. Someone had to inform them because they even knew the exact amount. Something just wasn't adding up, but it eventually began to make sense when we heard that Ms. Williams had a visitor at her cousin's house in Bushwick. Her visitor turned out to be the DEA agent that led the team into Shayna and Danielle's room. His name was Agent Wilson.

Agent Wilson had been following Key since he started working for Blizzard. He was working undercover and made his first appearance the day Key played basketball with Rivera at Marine Park. Rivera was the target Agent Wilson was initially following, but he decided to get a following on Key as well. He figured anyone linked to Rivera could be just as helpful. The plan was to follow someone that was fresh in the organization because a tenured employee wouldn't give up information as easy as a newcomer.

The day he showed up in Queens, he did in fact follow Shayna. He knew Shayna was close to Key and had been following her in hopes of getting new information. He could have gotten to Shayna and Ms. Williams quicker when he chased them down the fire escape, but he let them go for their own protection. Make no mistake; he didn't have their best interest at heart. He needed to scare them out of that building out and of Queens because Blizzard knew they were there. He feared that Blizzard would eventually send someone over there as a message to Key. Ms. Williams' relocation had to be sudden instead of planned to avoid being easily tracked. He was using them as bait to get to Key and bring Blizzard down. He took a note of the cab they got into and tracked down the driver to find out where he dropped them off. That's how he found out Ms. Williams was hiding in Bushwick.

When he arrived at Ms. Williams' cousin's house, he told Ms. Williams that she needed to go with him for questioning. Ms. Williams told him that she didn't need to do anything and that he needed to leave their house. He told her that if she didn't cooperate, she would be arrested. She asked Agent Wilson if he thought she was stupid. She told him that she knew he couldn't just walk in and arrest her, and she needed to be charged with something. He told her some lie about her and Key's life and freedom depending on her answering a few questions. She cracked instantly and told him "If this is about the money, I already spent some and I'll surrender the rest if I need to." He didn't even know about the money yet, he just wanted information about Key.

Agent Wilson told her that he was only going to ask her a few questions regarding Key's whereabouts before he was incarcerated; who he was associated with, how he made ends meet on his Burger Empire salary, and who the girl was that she was with in Queens. Ms. Williams looked at him and asked "You're the one that was in the apartment?" He told her that was neither here nor there at that point and that he now wanted to discuss the money she was referring to. Ms. Williams played dumb asking him what he was talking about. He told her "Lying to a federal agent was a federal offense under section 1001 of Title 18 of the United States Code, punishable by a five year sentence." He could have thrown any numbers at her.

Ms. Williams began to get scared. Agent Wilson knew that he had her exactly where he wanted her. He then told her that he could have a team of agents in their house by the evening to search for the money. He was bluffing, but Ms. Williams did not know that. Her cousin told her "If you have any money hidden in my house, you need to give it to him because I don't want the cops destroying my place, especially if they don't plan to clean up afterward." Agent Wilson looked at Ms. Williams and said "Your cousin is right; we're not cleaning anything up and you'll still be going to jail." Ms. Williams began to breathe a little heavier, before finally giving in.

She escorted Agent Wilson to the room she was staying in and gave him the bag of money. They emptied the bag out onto the bed and counted $45,000. Since she already admitted to spending some of it before, he asked how much she spent and where she spent it. She told him that it was $10,000 and that it was mostly spent on clothes and material things. Agent Wilson told her that he was willing to look the other way on her shopping spree if she told him about the possibility of more money. She hesitated for a while. Agent Wilson reminded her about the five year jail sentence and that more charges could be added for spending the money, having possession of the money, and serving as an accomplice to the crime. Hearing that was enough for Ms. Williams to give up Shayna and the other $40,000.

Her decision wasn't too surprising. Ms. Williams was just being herself; selfish and enjoying the life of handouts. She had just as much to do with the crime as Shayna did. She wouldn't have even known about the money if it wasn't for Shayna and Key. Agent Wilson packed up the $45,000 and began to make his way out. Before he left he told her that he needed one more thing. He pulled a tape recorder out of his pocket. He hit the stop button, thanked her for the confession, and then asked her to turn around and he handcuffed her. She asked him why she was being arrested if she gave up the money and didn't lie. He told her she wouldn't be charged for lying, just the other stuff. She reminded him that he promised she wouldn't be affected if she cooperated. Agent Wilson replied "Did I say that?" He then escorted her out past her cousin with the bag of money on his shoulder and gave her a small lecture on the importance of getting promises in writing.

Hearing about this was bittersweet. Ms. Williams got what she deserved, but Shayna was still in trouble. She was scheduled to be back in New York the day following her arraignment in Florida. Shawn and Ms. Kim were given updates on where she would be located. She was ultimately going to be transferred to StockPoint Correctional Facility; an all female prison in Manhattan. Her bail was set at $25,000.

LET'S MAKE A DEAL

Key had finally been released from solitary confinement and escorted back to his regular cell. The inmates were socializing in the general population area. He walked pass Flea's cell on his way back, it was only three cells down from his. They stared each other down as Key passed. Flea still had a bandage on his head and stitches from the metal tray beating. He gave Key a smile as Key walked by with the correctional officer. The first thing Key did when he got back to his cell was look over the railing at the first floor in the direction of Jerome's cell. Jerome was usually hanging out during the inmate leisure time. Key could see directly into the cell. The first thing he noticed was that Jerome's bunk was fully made like no one had been there. He ran downstairs to the cell and looked inside in a panic. He asked Jerome's friend where Jerome was. They gave Key the details about the brawl and Jerome being transferred to the infirmary.

Jerome had been in the infirmary since that day. His condition had been upgraded from critical to stable, but the prison doctor reported that there was a chance that he could go back to critical without a blood transfusion. Key couldn't believe what he was hearing. He fell back against the wall next to Jerome's cell holding his head. He immediately thought about Jamal and felt guilty knowing that retaliation would not have occurred if he had not done what he had done.

While leaning against the wall and trying to make sense of everything, he looked up at the second floor and saw Flea hanging over the railing smiling back down at him. Key stared him down for a while. Flea's pompous look after what his crew had done was enough to fuel the motivation behind Key's next move. He changed his mind about holding out for a better deal with the lawyer. He felt Blizzard had gone too far so he decided that he was going to testify and take Blizzard and anyone affiliated with him down. Key was angry enough to do it for free so he planned to put in a request to speak to his appointed lawyer again.

It was a Friday and the case was scheduled for the Monday after that weekend. Getting in contact with the lawyer was not going to be a problem. She had stopped by almost every day while he was in solitary in an attempt to get him to change his mind. His request for the lawyer wasn't going to be necessary. A couple of hours had passed and Key was informed by an officer that the lawyer stopped by and wanted to see him later in the day. He asked the officer to ask the lawyer if they could meet when the prisoners were sent out onto the yard. With Jerome out, Key knew that he would be next and would be an easy target out on the yard.

When the time came for the inmates to go outside, Key was escorted to the visitation area. He was so sure that she would attempt to give him just a little more of an offer than the last time; that seemed to be her pattern. Key was ready to take whatever she offered, but he was wise enough to not let her know that. The two of them sat down and the first thing the lawyer said was "Okay Mr. Williams, you win! You wanted your record expunged? You got it. All I need is your testimony." Key asked her if she was serious. She replied that she was as serious as a crowd's response to a bad comedian.

Key needed specifics. He asked her if when she said expunged, she meant completely wiped out as if it never happened and he could simply walk out. She asked Key if there was another definition for the word expunged. He told her that if he could get that in writing, they would have a deal. She took the legal document stating that very agreement out of her bag and presented it to Key. Key read the document over and it in fact stated everything they discussed. He got an overwhelming feeling at the thought of finally being free of everything.

He asked her for a pen so that he could sign it. As he was about to sign it, he stopped and asked her what made her change her mind. She told him "I haven't been a lawyer long, but I know that sometimes you have to lose a battle before you win the war." She was more focused on getting Key's testimony to propel her career than she was worried about looking weak for losing a bargaining debate with an inmate. Key told her that he could respect that and mentioned that he had one more request before he signed the paper. She let out a deep exasperating sigh at the thought of what else Key could possibly want. However, she remained professional and remembered how close she was to the testimony. She asked him what he would like. Key asked her if she would be able to get him to see Jerome once they were done with her visit. That turned out to be a light request for her, she knew the warden of the specific jail that Key was being held in personally.

The lawyer told him that she would be able to do that. He signed the document and asked for her name. He realized that he had never gotten it despite the number of visits they had together. She told him that he could call her Liz. Upon finally signing the documents, they shook hands and had an officer escort them to the infirmary. Key had to be shackled at the wrists and ankles first. On the way there, she asked who Jerome was. Key explained who he was and why he was in the infirmary.

When they got to the infirmary, they were directed to where Jerome was being tended to. Key could see Jamal sitting next to Jerome's bed as they walked in. They had not seen each other since Key got locked up. Key said "Lek! What's up, man?" Jamal got up and gave him dap. Key asked him how Jerome was doing. Jamal told him about the blood transfusion and that being the reason he was there. Jamal and Jerome had the same blood type so he was there to give blood. Key told him that he hoped it was a success. Jamal thanked him and asked him what he was doing there. He told Jamal that he was there to visit Jerome to which Jamal thanked him for his support.

Key knew that he was rightfully responsible for what happened to Jerome so he apologized. Jamal admitted that he was upset with Key when he learned about how it happened, but he let it go once Jerome's condition began to stabilize. Once

Jerome began to stabilize, Jamal and I began to attend church more often together. I helped him look to God and that's what he had been doing ever since. Key told Jamal that he was planning on bringing Blizzard down in the case the following Monday and getting justice for Jerome. Jamal thanked him.

Jamal gave Key a confused look. Key noticed the look and asked him what he was looking at. Jamal told Key that he seemed happy like he was in a good mood. Key told him about the deal he made and that he would be getting out once the trial was over. Jamal congratulated him, but explained that he still couldn't understand how he could be happy regardless of what he was being rewarded with Shayna being in trouble. Key had no idea what Jamal was talking about because he had been cut off from all forms of communication while in solitary.

Jamal explained that Shayna was on her way back to New York and was in police custody. He also told him about his mother being in custody. Key asked why they were being held. Jamal told him "I don't have all of the details, but I know your mom snitched on Shayna and they're both in trouble." Jamal had gotten all of the information from me which I got from Shayna when she finally got a chance to call. Key found himself in a state of shock again. That was the second big piece of bad news he had gotten that day.

Key sat there shaking his head thinking about how he was the cause of that as well. He began to regret getting them involved with the money. He asked Jamal if he knew where they

318

were being held. Jamal told him that they were at StockPoint. Key was relieved to know that they were at least in the city instead of somewhere upstate. Liz had to leave the prison to tend to some other business so Key had to go back to his cell. He told Jamal that he would see him Monday at the trial. Key had a whole night of thinking ahead of him.

Meanwhile, over at StockPoint, I was with Ms. Kim and Shawn Sr. waiting for Shayna to be brought in. We were promised that we could visit with her once she was put into the system and paperwork was complete. I didn't care how long it took; I just wanted to see her. Another hour had passed before we were informed that she had arrived. We had to wait another hour after that for her paperwork and prints to be completed and registered before we could see her. We had to talk to her through a glass. I didn't know how to react, seeing her like that was too much to handle. I remember crying at first and not being unable to look at her for too long.

Ms. Kim had not said much since the night we found out that Shayna was arrested. Each day would go by and she would do what she usually did; housework, tending to Shawn Jr., and working. I wasn't used to her being so quiet, it was kind of creepy. Shayna broke the silence between all of us by saying "Hello!" in a very timid tone. I had not completely gotten control of my emotions yet, but Ms. Kim looked like she was about to lose control of hers. Shawn decided to take control of the situation by asking Shayna if she was okay. Shayna told him that she was as good as she could be given the circumstances. He then asked her what happened. She told him that she had nothing to do with any drugs; they just linked her to Key based on money they claim to have found in her possession. She wasn't admitting to anything just in case the visitation room was bugged.

I was still an emotional wreck, but Shayna's statement was enough to break Ms. Kim's silence. She said "I told you from the moment you decided that you wanted to pursue a relationship with that boy that it was a terrible idea. Did I not, Shayna? I don't tell you these things for my health. I tell you these things for your health, but you obviously don't want to be healthy." Shayna had no response to that. She began to cry and told Ms. Kim that she was right. Ms. Kim asked her what she was crying for. Shayna said that she just wanted to go home. Ms. Kim told her that she could imagine that she did, and continued to tell her how disappointed she was. Shayna put her head down in shame. With a stern look and angered tone, Ms. Kim said "Sit up straight and be a woman." She reminded Shayna of how much she wanted to be a woman when she was running around with Key, and feuding with her and Shawn Sr. about dating him. "He doesn't love you. We love you. People that love you wouldn't get you thrown in jail." Finally, she asked Shayna if she was beginning to see Key for whom he really was.

By that point even I was sitting up straight and no longer crying. Ms. Kim's words put me in check and she wasn't even talking to me. She finished her statement by telling Shayna to go back to her cell, gather her things, and then wait there for an officer to escort her out. She was going to bail her out. Shayna asked her if she was serious. Ms. Kim explained that just because she was disappointed, it didn't mean she no longer loved her. Ms. Kim then got up and asked an officer where she could post bail. The officer told her that it could be handled at the front desk. She thanked the officer and told us to follow her to the front desk. I told Shayna I would see her later and followed Ms. Kim and Shawn.

As we were walking through the hallway, Shawn asked Ms. Kim how they were going to bail her out, they couldn't afford it at the time with their salaries. He wasn't making enough as an electrician and Ms. Kim was working as a nurse at Shawn Jr.'s school. The majority of the money they were making was going towards Shawn's Law courses. Ms. Kim told him that there was always a way and that she refused to leave Shayna in jail overnight. In the end they opted to put their house up as collateral to cover the cost of the bail. They were only at risk of losing the house if Shayna fled the country. They would get the deed to their house back once Shayna was done with the trial.

Shayna got back to her cell and started to gather things in preparation of the officer's arrival to escort her out. As she was sitting on her bunk, she received dirty looks from other female inmates that were either interested in her or just trying to intimidate her. She did her best to ignore them. She looked across the facility at the other cells that ran parallel to hers and noticed Ms. Williams in one of them. Shayna left her cell and made her way around to Ms. Williams' cell. Ms. Williams was sitting on her bed. Shayna stood in the doorway of her cell and said "What'd they get you for?" Ms. Williams quickly got up from her bed saying "Shayna! What are you doing here?" Shayna told her that the DEA somehow found out about the money and it landed her in jail. Ms. Williams put on an act to make it seem like she was shocked. Shayna expressed that she didn't understand how the DEA could possibly know about it when only the three of them had knowledge of it. Key wouldn't benefit from getting them both thrown in jail or causing his own money to get confiscated. Shayna wanted an explanation.

All of a sudden, Ms. Williams went on a long tangent about how Shayna did not know how hard she had it growing up and raising a son on her own. Shayna was confused. Ms. Williams continued on about the pressures she's always been under, and how much pressure she was under when Agent Wilson backed her into a corner. Shayna eventually said "Shut up! You're not a woman, all I see is a punk and you're right where you belong for making deals with cops." Shayna walked away and headed back to her cell.

She passed a few other inmates socializing as she made her way back. One of them slapped her behind. Shayna turned around and yelled "HEY!" The one that did it smiled and winked at her, but Shayna wasn't dumb enough to retaliate and end up getting jumped by the rest of them. She went back to her cell and sat down. The officer had finally gotten to her cell and told her that she was free to leave. Shayna got up and followed the officer out. They passed that same group of inmates on their way out. Shayna looked at the one that disrespected her and pushed her, then ran for the exit ahead of the officer. The disrespecting inmate lost her balance and hit her elbow against a bar on the bed. Shayna joined us out in the lobby and we went home.

When Shayna got home they all sat down and Ms. Kim's lecture continued. When Ms. Kim was finally finished, Shawn went about composing a plan to get Shayna some legal assistance. He mentioned that he personally knew a professor at his school that could handle the case she was brought up on charges for. He gave the professor a call.

As Shawn tried to set up legal representation for Shayna, Ms. Kim sat in the living room with Shayna telling her that she needed to look out for herself when she was called to the stand that following Monday. She told her to answers all questions in a manner that would serve as beneficial to herself. Shawn was done with his phone call and told Shayna that she would be going to school with him that following Tuesday to talk with the lawyer he set her up with. As for Monday's trial, he told her that she needed to look out for herself as Ms. Kim advised.

Shawn wanted to know everything that happened when the DEA raided her room; from verbal interactions to physical action that took place. She told him that she didn't tell them anything. Shawn asked her again just to be sure and she gave him the same answer. Hearing that she didn't say anything to the DEA was like music to Shawn's ears. If Shayna did not tell them anything, then nothing could be used against her. In other words, her defense would be a lot easier to compose. He then told her that if she was asked about anything pertaining to Blizzard, Key, or the money, she needed to just say that the agents found it in her room. He reminded her that there was nothing actually linking her to the money. They didn't find it in her bag or any of her other personal belongings. For all the DEA knew, the money was there before she even moved in.

This lifted Ms. Kim as well as Shayna's spirits. They were beginning to feel a little more confident. Shawn continued to tell her that she needed to focus on turning everything on the DEA. There were no rules against doing that. As a matter of fact, many people had won cases and gotten out of trouble by not having said anything and using it to their advantage. Shayna told Shawn that Ms. Williams might have said something about the two of them and the money to the DEA. Shawn told her to turn it on Ms. Williams too by claiming that she did not know what she was talking about. It wouldn't be a lie because Shayna was not there when Agent Wilson visited Ms. Williams.

RUMBLE IN THE JUNGLE: ROUND 1

The day of the trial had finally arrived and everyone was in attendance. People that I had not seen in a while and people that I had only heard of had shown up. Stack, Ms. Williams, Key, Shayna, Mr. Jones, Lex & Rivera, and the infamous Blizzard. That was the first time most of us had seen Blizzard. He was intimidating to say the least which I think everyone expected after hearing so much about this figure that always managed to elude authority. He was about an inch or two shorter than Key, but built like a linebacker. He apparently had quality taste in suits.

Cameras were everywhere outside of the courtroom. Media was swarming to get coverage after hearing that Blizzard may be going down. I had not seen that much coverage for a trial since O.J. Simpson's earlier that year. It was actually pretty amazing and I was blessed to capture it live. Key had just been escorted into the courtroom. His eyes caught Shayna's for a second as she sat next to us. As he walked by, he mouthed "I'm sorry." Shayna looked away.

The case of the State of New York vs. Keith Williams was underway. The prosecution for the DEA presented their case against Key. They stated that Key should be found guilty of possession of narcotics (cocaine) with intention to sell, money laundering, conspiracy, the distribution of cocaine, and drug trafficking. They called for him to be punished to the fullest extent of the law. The judge requested the reports they filed. As he skimmed the reports, he told the prosecution to proceed.

The prosecution made a case to the court about how the city of New York needed people like Key off of the streets. They claimed that the activity that he was engaged in was only killing others and halting the advancement of society. He continued by telling the court that it was only a matter of time before a child got a hold of what he was putting out into the streets. Key's lawyer, Liz objected on the grounds that the prosecution was making predictions about her client based on their personal opinion. They also had no presentable proof that those things would have happened. The objection was sustained and the judge told the prosecution to stick to the facts.

The case was already very entertaining. The prosecution slandered Key's name as much as they could. They built on that until they ran out of facts. For example, they went on a ten minute onslaught of how Key was not only a negative influence on the community, but also disrespectful to authority. They piggybacked off of that by stating that history had shown us that violators of authority only served as a problem to the community. I personally felt that statement was like a slap in the face to every revolutionist in history.

People in the courtroom were expressing their opinions by either nodding their heads in agreement or showcasing distaste through groans. They also mentioned that Key was better off behind bars where he could not fill the streets with his poison.

It was beginning to sound like the DEA and the prosecuting attorney were in cahoots with Blizzard to make it seem like Key was manufacturing and selling the product on his own. I couldn't tell what was going to happen next, but things were not looking good for Key.

When the prosecution was finally done expressing their thoughts of Key, they called their first witness to the stand. They claimed that their witness would be able to vouch for their claims. The first witness that the prosecution called to the stand was Warren James, we knew him better as 'Stack'. Key got up from his slouched position and turned around to see if they were actually talking about the "Warren James" he thought they were talking about. When he saw Stack walking up to take the stand he gave him a look of disgust and called him a sellout. The judge banged his gavel and told Liz to control Key or he would be held in contempt of court. Liz reminded Key that he needed to relax if he still wanted that deal.

As Stack took the stand, they made him promise to tell the whole truth and proceeded with their case. The first question they asked him was if he knew Key. Stack confirmed that he did in fact know Key. When asked how long he knew him, Stack replied that they had known each other since they were six. The prosecutor asked Stack if he would consider Key to be a brother. Stack told the prosecutor as well as the court that he considered himself and Key to be brothers at one point in time. When the prosecutor asked Stack why he no longer felt that way, Stack told them that he could no longer align himself with someone that was contributing to the demise of the community.

Stack had to be joking; at least I hoped he was. Shayna, Jamal, Key, and I just sat there with our mouths open in shock. I looked over at Key and could tell that he was itching to say something, but he held his tongue for the sake of his case. The prosecutor asked Stack to elaborate on what he meant in regards to his claims against Key. Stack told the court that Key was always a quiet individual and the fact that he was selling drugs made perfect sense. My favorite line of Stack's testimony was "It's usually the quiet ones and the ones you least suspect." Key just sat back in his chair shaking his head and anticipating his opportunity to testify.

The prosecution concluded their questioning with Stack. They asked him how it made him feel to see someone he knew all of his life turn to a life of crime that resulted in the demise of others. Liz objected again on the grounds that there was no proof of Key killing anyone. She also stated that a witness' personal feelings toward her client should not be used against her client in the trial. The objection was sustained and the judge told the prosecutor that it was his last warning. As a result, Stack could no longer answer the question and was told that he could step down. Stack stepped down, buttoned his suit jacket, and smiled at Key as he passed him to go back to his seat.

At that point I was just hoping that Key's lawyer brought her A-game. The prosecutor reminded the court that Stack was someone considered to be very close to Key. He turned back to the judge and said "If Key could hurt someone so close to him, he obviously did not care for anyone or anything." Liz objected again on the grounds that it was hearsay. The objection was sustained, but it wasn't as much of a violation as the others because Stack was considered a credible source. It was rather ironic; lies being considered credible.

The prosecutor followed up his questioning of Stack by presenting a piece of evidence to the court. It was the bottle that was found at the restaurant during the raid. He also presented other bottles that were said to be found in the vicinity of the restaurant. The prosecutor explained that he had a sample of the product that Key was poisoning the streets with. When he presented it, he asked the judge to take notice of the report and a copy of Key's prints taken at the precinct when he was originally arrested. The report was supposed to prove that Key's fingerprints were the ones that were in fact on the bottle. The judge put his glasses on and studied the report. As the judge looked over the reports, the prosecutor shared them with the court using an overhead projector. People began murmuring amongst themselves to which the judge demanded order. I personally began to worry; all of the evidence was pointing at Key and Blizzard was beginning to look untouchable.

The judge told the prosecutor that if he had anyone else to call to the stand; he needed to do so at that time. The prosecution's next witness was Martin Jones; better known to us

329

as Mr. Jones, Key's boss from Burger Empire. Mr. Jones swore to tell the whole truth and nothing but the truth. The first question to Mr. Jones was how he knew Key. Mr. Jones told the court that Key was one of his employees at Burger Empire. The prosecutor asked him to describe Key as an employee. Mr. Jones stated that Key was one of his better employees. He admitted that they bumped heads at times, but he looked past their differences because he knew how badly Key needed the job. When asked why Key needed the job so badly, Mr. Jones stated that Key always talked about how he and his mom were suffering financially.

The prosecutor turned to the court and told us to look at Mr. Jones. He told us that Mr. Jones was a man with a family and his Burger Empire restaurant was his only means of income to support them. He then stated that because of Key's actions, the restaurant had been closed down and Mr. Jones was facing a separate trial. He was going to have to explain why the distribution and purchase of an illegal substance was taking place in his establishment. Meanwhile he was facing financial problems. The prosecutor added "This hard-working man saw another man struggling with financial woes and gave him a chance to get on his feet, only to be knocked off of his own and put into the same situation." The audience responded again. The prosecutor's wording of the situation was very profound and convincing.

The questioning continued. He asked Mr. Jones if he was aware that the sale of narcotics was taking place in his restaurant. Mr. Jones stated that he had only become aware when the DEA raided his restaurant. The prosecutor stopped him in the middle of his statement. He turned to the court and stated that it was a shame Mr. Jones had to find out he would lose his business at a point where he could do nothing about it. He added that no one should have to live like that. His questioning with Mr. Jones concluded with him asking if he felt someone that sold drugs was fit to live among society. Mr. Jones told the court as he looked at Key "Drugs have no place in the streets or in my restaurant." He was then told that he could step down.

Judging from who was in the courtroom, I figured that the prosecutor was going to call Shayna next. I could not have been more wrong. The next person called to the stand was Sandra Williams. She was better known to us as Ms. Williams; Key's mom. As she got up to take the stand, Key yelled "WHAT?" The judge banged his gavel and told Key to settle down. Key continued to express his anger; "Nah Ma! I gave you everything, and you violate me by siding with the beast?" The judge banged his gavel again and told Key that it was his last warning and if he couldn't control himself, he would be removed from the case permanently. Liz requested that the judge and the court be patient with Key because emotions were high being that it was the first day, and loved ones were involved. The judge allowed it and ordered a fifteen minute recess for everyone to gather their emotions.

In the fifteen minute break, Liz pulled Key aside and reminded him of the importance of being patient. Key was fuming with anger. It was going to take more than her words to calm him down. She took him to the vending machine to buy him a candy bar. While looking for some change, she accidentally dropped a quarter. The candy bar was working for the time being. He was calming down and she was able to at least talk to him about his attitude. She managed to get his attention by reminding him of what a life in prison would entail if he could not keep his emotions under control. He promised to try his best. She told him that he would need to do more than try or he was going to lose his opportunity to testify which meant a life behind bars. That was going to be important especially in a situation where his mother was testifying against him.

The fifteen minute break was over and everyone was beginning to re-enter the court room. The prosecution picked up where they left off with Ms. Williams. He asked her how she was doing. She stated that she was fine. He then asked her what she knew about Key, but he referred to him as "The defendant". Ms. Williams told him that Key was her son. The prosecutor asked her if it was okay to assume that she knew him well. Ms. Williams asked what kind of question that was. The prosecutor told her that just because two people are related did not mean that they knew each other. Ms. Williams agreed with that theory.

The prosecutor asked her how well she knew Key. She told him that they did not really see much of each other once he got involved with rapping. The prosecutor stopped her and made a verbal note of the fact that Key was a rapper. He then asked what kind of rapper Key was. She honestly didn't know because she never took the time to listen to his music or go to his shows. She took a wild guess based on whatever rapper she may have heard of. She told the prosecutor "He rapped like the rapper, NWA." The prosecutor reminded the court of the content in NWA's music. Liz objected on the grounds that Ms. Williams' statement was obviously coached because NWA was a group, not a solo artist. The objection was overruled because the content of the music was seen as more relevant to the point being made than the actual artist.

A radio was brought into the courtroom in which an NWA song was played that focused on the disrespect of police and authority figures. Liz blurted out "Your Honor, is this claim really going to stand. It makes no sense to claim that Key's music is like NWA's if the court can't hear an example of Key's music as well." The judge asked the prosecutor if he had any of Key's music to share. He didn't have any music by Key so he was asked to surrender that claim or lose his opportunity to continue questioning Ms. Williams.

The prosecutor cooperated and concluded his questioning of Ms. Williams. He reminded the courtroom of the lyrics they had just heard, and claimed that it was similar to Key's behavior toward Ms. Williams when she took the stand. Next, the prosecutor asked Ms. Williams to describe what her relationship with Key was like at that time. She told him that it hadn't been the same since he turned their apartment into a hostile living environment. He asked her to explain in detail how Key managed to do that. She explained how two guys came looking for him and had her at gunpoint. The prosecution stated that there were no further questions. As Ms. Williams walked back to her seat, Key asked her "How much they pay you, Ma?"

It was a pretty convenient place to stop the questioning if you ask me. Ms. Williams sold Key out in exchange for less time on her potential prison sentence. The confession that Agent Wilson recorded was promised to be thrown out if she made Key look like a terrible person when she took the stand. Key was doing a better job of ignoring the lies and attacks on his character. He must have gotten used to the pattern of witnesses. The final witness called to the stand by the prosecution was Shayna. Ms. Kim held Shayna's hand as she got up from her seat to make her way to the stand. Shawn had to grab Ms. Kim's hand to remind her that she needed to let Shayna go. Shayna swore to tell the truth like the rest of the witnesses and her questioning session began.

The prosecutor greeted Shayna as he held a file in his hand. He told her that he had heard so much about her. Shayna maintained her silence. He took a look into the file and told her that she had quite the track record. Shayna was still silent. The prosecutor then said that he only wished he was referring to the greatness she was known for showcasing in track and field. Shayna gave him a look and you could tell she was curious as to where he was going with his questioning. He added that Shayna seemed to be fast in other areas as well. That definitely broke Shayna's silence. She rolled her neck and said "Excuse me? Do you care to elaborate?"

When Shayna responded like that, all I could think was that her temper was about to show itself. However, she looked into the audience and saw Shawn subtly gesturing to her to be patient. She sat up straight and focused more on her posture than the questioning. The prosecutor told her that it would be his pleasure to elaborate. He asked her if she ever dated a young man named Darryl Robinson. Shayna said that she dated someone with that name. The prosecutor said that he would be more specific; he asked her if she dated a Darryl Robinson who was now serving a twenty year sentence. She answered "Yes!" The prosecutor asked if she was currently in a relationship with Key, but once again referring to him as "The defendant". Shayna was quiet for a while; you can see that she was thinking about her answer. She was conflicted by what her mom may have been thinking and what Key may have been thinking. She could not please both so she decided to go with her mom. She answered "No!" Key put his head down on the desk. He was obviously in pain after hearing that.

The prosecutor asked her why they were no longer in a relationship. Shayna looked the prosecutor in his eye, and told him that it was for the same reason he should not have worn brown shoes with a black suit that day; it just wasn't working for her. There were a few snickers from some members of the jury. Shawn was trying to signal to her to not go that route. The judge called for order. The prosecutor let out a slight laugh and told Shayna that he loved a good joke every now and then. He then reminded her of what wasn't a joke; making bad life decisions.

Shayna's temper was trying to rear its head again as she shrugged her shoulders and rolled her eyes. I was getting concerned because it was even closer that time. Shawn gave her a look and signaled for her to relax. Shayna sat up straight again. The prosecutor continued by telling her that bad decisions were the foundation for a life behind bars. He reminded her that both Darryl and Key were behind bars and she made the decision to date both of them. He laid a bombshell on the courtroom with his next statement; "It's kind of hard to determine if your ex-boyfriends were destined to be behind bars or if you were the bad influence in both relationships." The courtroom almost erupted with reactions. It definitely got Ms. Kim upset. She got out of her chair saying "Oh no! He can't talk to my baby girl like that. YOU DON'T KNOW HER!" The judge told her to sit down or she would be removed. Shawn had to grab her and sit her back down.

Shayna wasn't too happy with the claim either. She had done a great job of keeping her temper under control, but she was reaching a boiling point. The prosecutor must have noticed it as well because he continued with his already harsh statement by sharing his theory on the matter. He expressed that he felt Shayna was the bad influence because she had been imprisoned as well. Shayna's foot began to tap rapidly. She was trying to shake off whatever anger she was feeling. Key saw what was going on and asked Liz if there was anything she could do for Shayna. Liz told him that she was only concerned about his case and she wasn't going to get involved in personal business. Key asked her again, but said please. Liz looked at him then yelled "OBJECTION!" She got the attention of the courtroom as well as the judge. She stated that the questions had no relevance to the claims against Key. The prosecutor claimed that it in fact had everything to do with Key. The judge told him that he needed to state the relevance it had to the case and get to the point.

The prosecutor claimed that Shayna must have been familiar with making bad decisions because she made one to land herself in prison. He presented Shayna's biography to the court. It stated how she was a well known track star in the city and state of New York, and known throughout most of the nation for her recent Penn Relay performance. He continued by telling the court that she was even good enough to be recruited by Gainesville University. He added to that by sharing her recent accomplishments at the Orlando tournament in which the school took home 2nd place thanks to her contribution.

The jury and the courtroom became more intrigued as to where he was going with his statement. He concluded his statement by saying "Shayna's reign of greatness came to an end when she decided to hold some money for Key; money that he made while selling cocaine at Burger Empire. She was kicked out of school when it was found in her dorm room amongst her things." People began talking amongst themselves in the courtroom after hearing this. The prosecutor asked Shayna if it was true. Shayna stopped shaking and moving. She looked at the prosecutor, grabbed her microphone closer and said "Nope!"

The courtroom occupants began murmuring again. The prosecutor reminded her that she was under oath. Shayna reminded him that he needed to get his facts straight before questioning her character or accusing her. The prosecutor approached the stand and asked Shayna if $40,000 was or was not found in her room. Shayna claimed to not know how much money was found in her room. He told her that meant she was admitting that money was in fact found. Shayna told him that money could be found anywhere. She went even further by using an example of a quarter she found next to the vending machine during the fifteen minute recess. She asked what his point was. He gave Shayna a smile and told her that she was quite clever, but he would like to get back to the facts. Shayna just looked at him in silence. He told her that $40,000 was found in her room at Gainesville University. Shayna told him that it was nice to hear.

At that moment I began to feel a little better about Shayna's temper because she managed to actually use a wiser approach. He told her that the money was found amongst her things. She then turned the questioning on him by asking him which one of her things it was found among. He looked through the file and told her that it was in a vent on her side of the room. Shayna said that the vent did not belong to her so it could not be considered to be "among her things." He asked her if she put it there. She explained that in order to put it there she would have to know it existed. He asked her if she was telling the court that she had never seen the bag as he pointed to it. She told the prosecutor that she saw a bag like that once on Canal Street going for about five dollars if you bought two. Somebody in the courtroom yelled "THAT'S A GOOD DEAL." The judge banged his gavel.

The prosecutor told her that she must have seen that particular bag that he presented as evidence because it had her fingerprints on it. The murmurs in the courtroom began again. Shayna sat back quietly and confidently because she knew the bag could not have had her prints. She wore gloves whenever she handled it; from the time she got it from Key's apartment to when she hid it at school. She asked the prosecutor if he had proof that the bag had her prints. He knew he didn't so he fiddled with Shayna's file again and claimed that he was sure that it was in the file.

After another minute, the judge intervened. He asked the prosecutor if he had anything proving that she had been in possession of the bag at any point. The prosecutor said that he in fact did. He told the court that Ms. Williams was Shayna's accomplice in the harboring of the money. The judge asked Ms. Williams if that was true. Ms. Williams confirmed it and said that they split the money up before Shayna went back to school. Shayna told the judge that she didn't know the woman that was making the accusations against her. The judge asked her how it was possible to be dating someone and not know their parents. Shayna told him that Key never introduced them and that things were very different where we came from. Your family is either very distant or very close, there's rarely ever and in between.

In order to explain her point, Shayna used Key and their relationship as an example. She told the judge and the court that her and Key spent a great amount of time together, but he never introduced her to his mother because they did not have a close relationship. The judge looked at Key and asked him if that was true. Key confirmed that it was true by saying "My mother and I never had a close relationship. She never loved me and I eventually accepted that. That's why I never brought friends around her. She is an embarrassment and a dead beat." He looked back at Ms. Williams as he said "dead beat". Ms. Williams gave him an angry look in return. The judge told Ms. Williams that she didn't seem to be hurt by Key's claims. She responded by putting on some sunglasses and running out the courtroom with crocodile tears. Key told the judge that she would be okay because she was right in her element; putting on a show to make others feel sorry for her.

The questioning by the prosecutor wasn't over, but you can tell that he was getting frustrated. He directed his attention back to Shayna and asked her if her claims were true, then how was it that she was spotted climbing down the fire escape of their Queens apartment with Ms. Williams by an agent. Ms. Williams walked back into the courtroom saying "There you go. Explain that, heifer." The judge banged the gavel and told Ms. Williams that he would not have his courtroom turn into a circus. He dismissed her from the court house and ordered that she be escorted back to jail. Shayna asked the prosecutor what he was talking about. The prosecutor asked Agent Wilson to stand up and tell the court what he was referring to.

Agent Wilson backed the prosecutor's claims. Shayna stated that to be leaving any building in Queens where Key stayed, Key needed to actually live in Queens. She asked the prosecutor if there was any record of him living there. He couldn't provide any proof. Shayna then turned to Key and asked him if he had a place in Queens that she didn't know about. He replied "I was Brooklyn bred and when it's all over, I'll be Brooklyn dead." The judge warned Shayna about interacting with someone while she was on the stand.

There was no record of Key's Queens apartment because he paid the rent in cash; he didn't have a bank account or a check book. He preferred to pay cash at the time because he didn't want to leave a paper trail. He also avoided signing a lease by making a deal with the landlord to pay six months of rent in advance. Lex and Rivera were sitting right in the courtroom and could have vouched for the prosecution, but it would have incriminated them.

The prosecution had completed their questioning of Shayna and excused her from the stand. As she walked back to her seat, she put her hand on Key's shoulder. It was supposed to mean that she had his back. For her to do that in the midst of facing jail time because of him was moving. Maybe she felt sorry that everyone he loved turned on him. When she got back to her seat, Shawn Sr. gave her a hug and told her that he was proud of her.

The judge asked the prosecutor if there was anybody else that he wanted to call to the stand. I couldn't think of anybody else in the courtroom that they could call so it was only a matter of time before Key and Liz got the opportunity to present their case. The prosecutor told the judge that there was one more person that the court needed to hear from; a surprise witness. Jamal and I looked at each other thinking that it could be us, but it wasn't. The prosecutor told the court that he wanted to call Mark Johnson to the stand; a man better known to us as Mr. Johnson, the English teacher. Shayna, Jamal, and I all looked at each other because we knew it was more than likely not going to end well.

I had to admit at that point that the prosecutor was pretty good, just not when it came to Shayna. However, he definitely did his homework by getting Mr. Johnson as a surprise witness. The prosecutor looked at Key and smiled because he knew about the history he had with Mr. Johnson. Key nodded his head as if to say "Well played!" The prosecutor made Mr. Johnson take the oath, then greeted him and asked him if he could call him Mark. Mr. Johnson sarcastically replied that he didn't see why not since everyone else did. He asked him if he knew Key. Mr. Johnson said "Yeah, yeah I know the brother." The prosecutor was about to ask his next question, but was cut off by Mr. Johnson. Mr. Johnson said "He took her from me." He then began to yell "HE TOOK HER! HE DID IT! I KNOW HE DID IT. I LOVED HER, AND HE TOOK HER." Liz asked Key what he was talking about. Key told her that he didn't know.

The prosecutor had realized that the situation was getting further and further out of his control. He immediately requested that Mr. Johnson's testimony be stricken from the record. The judge granted it. Mr. Johnson began to climb over the stand and was moving in Key's direction like a rabid animal. Key got up and prepared to fight Mr. Johnson if he needed to, but that wasn't going to be necessary. The bailiff grabbed and restrained him while calling for backup. The judge asked the prosecutor if he had any more witnesses. He actually had to yell his question because Mr. Johnson began to yell and scream. The prosecutor yelled back to the judge "THE PROSECUTION RESTS!"

The trial couldn't go on under those circumstances, so the judge moved to have everything continue the next day. It took them a while to get Mr. Johnson fully under control. The courtroom had to be cleared immediately because he had broken free of the officer's restraint and grabbed the flag pole. He began to swing the pole like a bat. Around the time he began to get naked was when the final occupants had been removed from the court. Later on we found out he was detained and checked into a mental institution.

RUMBLE IN THE JUNGLE: ROUND 2

In a way, Mr. Johnson's behavior was actually a blessing. Due to the fact that the courtroom had to be cleared, it gave Liz an extra day to prepare a defense. She was ready the first day to a degree. Her original plan was to put Key on the stand because she felt the impact of his testimony would be enough to turn the case away from him and onto Blizzard. Instead, she was now able to bring witnesses of her own and utilize the prosecution's witnesses as well.

Liz and Key spent the night before the trial in the prison visiting area composing a game plan. The night consisted of phone calls and Key practicing his testimony. Liz was able to go beyond the visitation time for the sake of her case. Once Key felt comfortable with the wording of his testimony, he told Liz that he wanted to make a slight change to the deal that they made. She gave him a look of shock and told him that he better not be backing out of it. He informed her that he was still going to follow through with the testimony and actually couldn't wait to bring Blizzard down. He wanted to change what he got out of the deal. Instead of getting his record expunged, he wanted Shayna's record, and everything tied to her to be stricken from the record books.

Liz expressed her confusion as to why he would do something like that. She reminded him that if he did that, he would go back to possibly facing life if he was found guilty. He stated that he was aware of that. She then reminded him that if he was imprisoned, the battles with Blizzard's goons would continue. He explained that he would be able to handle himself and that it would be worth it. Liz, still in shock, removed her glasses and sat back to let it all sink in. She told him that Shayna had a separate case so there were no guarantees that she could pull those types of strings. Key asked her what she could do for Shayna at the moment. At the most, she would only be able to get a few years knocked off of Shayna's sentence.

Key sat back in his chair and let out a sigh. He told Liz that he believed she could do it. He reminded her that she managed to get a deal like that for him so there had to be a way. Liz asked him what his attachment was to Shayna besides the fact that they used to date. He told Liz that she helped him understand what love really meant. He explained that whether it was puppy love or real love, he knew that he loved her and never experienced that type of connection with anyone else.

Key expressed that Shayna's demand for him to work in order to date her was what taught him the value of having a great woman. He finally told Liz that he was unaware that his relationship with Shayna ended, but he was more than likely the reason that she was facing jail time. Therefore, getting her record expunged in exchange for his was the least he could do. Liz nodded her head and was apparently moved by what Key said. She asked him to excuse her as she left the room.

Liz left the room to make a call to her connection in the New York City court system; the one that managed to get her the deal for Key. She told them that the deal would now consist of Shayna's record being wiped clean. The connection didn't mind, they were more interested in Key's testimony bringing Blizzard down for the sake of their career as well. Just like that, the deal now consisted of Shayna's record. She walked back into the room and told Key that it was all set and that she would bring the proper documents to the courtroom the next day. Key got up and gave her a big hug. The officer monitoring the room yelled "NO TOUCHING!" causing Key to let go immediately. He was placed in solitary that night as an extra precaution for his safety.

Back at Shayna's house, she and her parents were discussing what went on that day and preparing for the second day. The tension between Shayna and Ms. Kim had deteriorated a little. She was proud of the way Shayna carried herself and how she managed to control the temper that she was so notorious for. Shawn was proud of her as well, and even more excited to be in the midst of the drama in the court room. He was jumping up and down and getting excited like basketball fans watching Jordan in his prime.

Ms. Kim told Shayna that she would have to keep the same mindset going into the next day just in case she was called up again. She told Shayna to think about herself because no one would look out for her more than she did. Shayna told them that she felt she could do that. Ms. Kim needed confirmation on if Shayna was truly broken up with Key. She asked Shayna if she was no longer with Key for herself or for the fact that she and

347

Shawn advised her to break it off. Shayna told them that she wasn't really over him because that kind of thing took time.

Ms. Kim wanted her to be done with him completely. Shayna stated that she couldn't simply turn her feelings on and off. Ms. Kim told her that he obviously turned his feelings on and off when it came to her; otherwise she wouldn't be in the situation that she was in. Shayna told Ms. Kim that she did not understand their relationship and it was unfair for her to accuse Key of not loving her. Ms. Kim rubbed her face in frustration and asked Shayna "When are you going to realize that he does not love you? The sooner you realize that, the sooner you can grow up."

Shawn's level of excitement had decreased at the sight of another fight between Shayna and Ms. Kim. He suggested they call it a night because the case was the next day. Shayna excused herself from the living room. Ms. Kim was on her way to the kitchen when Shawn asked her to take a walk with him. Ms. Kim was upset and declined. He asked again and said please, she accepted that time. It was a chilly night so they got their coats. They walked around the block twice as Shawn tried to explain to Ms. Kim that he understood what she was trying to do for Shayna, but her approach was wrong. He told her that she was actually pushing Shayna away. He then reminded her of when they were her age and the mistakes they made. Ms. Kim was receptive to what he was saying and eventually agreed to go a little easier. She told Shawn that it was a major change for her to

348

see her "baby girl" growing up and making independent decisions.

The next morning we all made our way back to the court house and had an even bigger struggle getting pass the media. The drama from the day before made it one of the highest rated productions watched on TV, and that was before Mr. Johnson got his fifteen minutes of fame. There was an even bigger crowd inside the courtroom that day. A lot of the faces that were there the day before had returned, but new faces had shown up as part of Liz's team of witnesses. She managed to get a hold of a few key figures to help her case.

Liz opened her up her case by introducing herself and Key as her client. She told the court that she was there to prove that the recent statements made regarding Key were false and an attack on his character and good name. She stated that the information presented by the prosecution was an act of desperation, and a prime example of how the so called proper authorities had made the City of New York a prison for young men and minorities. She got some murmurs from the courtroom early on with that statement. It was a very true statement that still holds true to this very day. Young black men have become public enemy number one in the city.

In an attempt to set up her case, Liz presented the court with Key's book of rhymes. It was still in his apartment from the night when Lex killed one of his own men. Liz decided to counter the attack that was made on Key's music and presumed mental state the day before by reading some of his work for the court. She asked the judge if she could proceed. The judge granted her request.

Liz started by reading a few lines from a piece Key wrote entitled "Love Lesson". The lines read:

"A beautiful flame that bears our name/
A beautiful sight that burns so bright, and can't be tamed."

"I refuse to hide the fact that your presence in my life has had an affect/
We've had ups and downs that brought about smiles and frowns which helped us to connect."

The courtroom seemed to enjoy it so far. Liz was going to stop there and let that point go out on a high note, but she decided to gain more momentum. She read a few lines from another one entitled "Unburied Treasure". The first two bars read:

"When God made you, He constructed an image of perfection/
A sculpture so well put together, I have yet to see one better, but you're my preferred selection."

The crowd seemed to like that one even more. Someone in the back even gave it a few finger snaps. I was captivated by it myself. Stack was sitting two rows in front of us sucking his teeth and expressing the highest degree of hate. Meanwhile, Key was sitting in his seat nodding his head. He raised his hand as a humble gesture of gratitude to the court. He then gave Shayna a quick look as a way to let her know that the words were about her. Shayna smiled a little and bashfully looked down at her lap. I could tell that she was overwhelmed with joy.

Liz realized that she had the court on her side and decided to build on her momentum by using a trick that the prosecution used against them; presenting the character of the witness. She asked the court if the words that they had just heard sounded like the words of a ruthless authority hating thug. She was referring to how the prosecution and Ms. Williams attempted to portray Key the day before. The prosecutor objected on the grounds that simply hearing a few lines wasn't enough to support Liz's claim. Liz countered the objection by stating that she at least supported her claim with music he had actually written. The objection was overruled and Liz was asked to continue.

Liz continued by calling her first witness to the stand. She told the court that since they were on the subject of Key's music, she wanted to call someone to the stand that knew Key and his music better than anyone. Her witness was Stack, it shocked the court. I was very curious to see what she had in mind. Stack took the stand and was greeted with a snarling look by Key. After taking his oath, Liz asked him if he could rap. Stack being a proud man answered the question in a proud manner. Liz told him that she knew he could rap and she in fact knew that he was pretty good. Stack took it as a compliment and responded with cocky gestures. Humility was never one of his strong points.

Following that question, Liz signaled for the bailiff to bring the radio over to her. After wheeling the cart over to her, Liz looked back at Stack and asked him who the better rapper was between him and Key. Stack of course said he was better than Key. Liz then stated "If you're better than Keith, then according to the prosecution, it would mean that you're even more violent and more thuggish than Keith. After all, to be better than someone, you have to be better than them in every aspect." Stack let his arrogant attitude get the better of him by telling Liz that she was correct.

Now I'm no lawyer, but I, as well as everyone else in the court could clearly see what Liz had just done. She capitalized on it perfectly with a follow up statement. She turned to the court and reminded us of Stack's statement the day before. She quoted the part about how he could not associate himself with someone that promoted the demise of the community by selling drugs and disrespecting authority. She then brought to the court's attention that he was now boasting about being an even bigger advocate for those things. The murmuring started again. She followed up that statement by saying that they should not trust the word of someone that contradicted them self without even realizing. Liz was good. I looked over at Shawn and noticed he was obviously impressed and taking notes. The trial was better than a movie.

Liz's questioning for Stack continued with a piece of evidence she presented to the court. She took another trick used by the prosecutor which was to incriminate the witness. However, she had actual material from Stack. It was a mixtape that the three of them put together when they first formed their group. There was a song on it entitled "Way of Life". It was a song in which the three of them each had a verse about the way they lived. Liz fast forwarded to Stack's verse; two bars in particular where he said:

"I live life on the edge so don't stand too close/
Because I'll take you down with me, I'm grimier than most."

Liz paused the tape and gave her own interpretation of the lyrics. She told the court that Stack was basically saying he was grimy which when translated meant disgusting, foul, or dirty. Simply put, she was saying that Stack was a foul individual who was willing to take others down with him if he found himself in a losing position. She approached Stack and asked him if that was correct. He told her that it was incorrect and that the line meant that he wouldn't go down without a fight. He was obviously agitated as he told her to step back and to not call him out of his name. Liz told him that his defensive demeanor was giving him away. She asked him "If my interpretation is incorrect, then would the day you and Keith were beat up in an alley by a few of Blizzard's employees help you to remember?"

Rivera began to look very uncomfortable in his seat. Liz asked Stack if they were beaten up in a DUMBO alley by Blizzard's employees, and if he managed to escape and make a deal with the police that landed Key in prison in order to get his own charges dropped. Stack told her that he couldn't recall. Liz asked him if he was sure because she had a police report that stated otherwise. She presented the report to the bailiff to give to the judge. It stated that Stack was charged only a week before his case. Being charged and getting a court date usually took time. This could only mean that he was already under police supervision and presented with charges and a court date before the report was even written up.

The judge was listening to Liz's point and reading the report at the same time. He was displeased with what he was hearing. Liz told the jury that if they needed more proof, then it may please them to know that Stack was currently serving time in a juvenile detention center for being found guilty of charges similar to Key's. She turned to the courtroom and reminded them again of Stack claiming that he didn't want to be associated with someone that was poisoning his neighborhood. That was the end of her questioning with Stack.

She may have finished with Stack, but she definitely wasn't done with her attack. She immediately went into her next witness. She told the court that she would like to call Juanita James to the stand. Juanita James is Stack's mother. As his mother took the stand, Liz told her that she wouldn't hold her up for too long. Liz stated that it was no longer a secret that Key and Stack were long time friends, and it was less of a secret that they both sold drugs. Her question to Ms. James was who they sold the drugs for. Ms. James stated it was for a man named Blizzard. Liz asked her how she knew this. Ms. James told her that she was tied up with Ms. Williams and held at gunpoint for some money, and the gunmen claimed that it was money Stack owed to a man named Blizzard. Liz asked Ms. James if she could identify the man that organized the hold up. Ms. James told the court that she recognized Lex as she pointed to him.

The entire courtroom looked at Lex. Liz ended the questioning at that point. She could've gone into more about Stack, but she didn't want to put Ms. James in a position where she was testifying against her son. Ms. James stepped down and Liz returned to her table to get a sip of her water. I think the water was supposed to be a psychological tactic that meant she felt no pressure. After taking a sip, she told the judge that she would like to call upon a surprise witness. She asked Jerome Gaines to take the stand. I noticed Jamal's face go from relaxed to shocked as he sat next to me. He looked around the courtroom anxiously until he finally saw the backdoors open and two guards escorting Jerome in with a wheelchair. Jamal was still in shock, but then a big smile suddenly formed on his face. To this day he tells me that he wishes his family could've been there, but they saw it on TV.

It was the first time Jerome had been seen on the outside of prison since his sentencing. It was also the first time we learned that the blood transfusion was a success. Jerome was helped to the stand and into the chair where he took his oath. Liz asked him how he was doing. He told her that he had seen better days. She sympathized with him and told the court to take notice of the stitches and bandages along his neck. She asked him if he minded telling the court what caused his physical condition. It was apparently hard for him to speak much because one of his vocal cords had been ruptured in the altercation. When he spoke, it was really deep and raspy.

Jerome explained what happened the day of the incident in a few words; "I was attacked and left for dead." Liz asked him if he had any idea why he was targeted. He explained that as far as he knew, it was retaliation from Blizzard for a fight Key got into with one of his employees behind bars. Liz asked him if he knew Key well. Jerome replied "Well enough!" She told him he could just nod yes or no with the approval of the judge so that he wouldn't have to use his voice. The judge approved of it. She asked him if the guy that cut him actually identified himself as an employee of Blizzard; Jerome nodded yes. She then asked him if the employee harassed Key while in jail on a regular basis; Jerome nodded yes again. Her final question was if he was concerned for his own life when he went back in. Jerome didn't want to seem like a punk, but he wasn't dumb. He nodded yes.

He was blessed to still have his life. When he finished, he was escorted back out. Jamal ran after him.

Liz seemed to be on a roll with her pattern of witnesses. Ms. Mims was called to the stand next. Ms. Mims took her oath and was asked about her views on Key. She stated that Key was one of the brightest, most creative, smartest, respectful, and most poetic students she had ever taught. She followed that with "He may have had problems in school at one point and was easily influenced by peer pressure, but the majority of high school students fit that same description." Liz asked her to share the most remarkable thing she could about Key. Ms. Mims shared the story about Key possibly being held back in his senior year that very year, but managed to accumulate the final thirty credits he needed to graduate. Ms. Mims loved telling that story about Key. Each time she did, she never mentioned the fact that she set up the opportunity for him.

That week was the first time Ms. Mims learned about Key being involved in anything drug related. She was disappointed to hear that he had allowed that degree of peer pressure to get the best of him, but she still had love for him. She just figured it was a simple mistake. In all honesty, they had more of a mother and son relationship than Key had with his own mother. Ms. Mims actually cared about his well-being. Liz was done with her questions for Ms. Mims. That was the part of her plan where she maintained momentum; allowing the jury to hear about Key's accomplishments and how good of a person he really was.

The next witness on Liz's list was Ms. Williams. When I heard Ms. Williams get called, I just knew that it was about to go down. Liz went directly into drilling Ms. Williams with questions. She asked her if Key was her son. Ms. Williams got loud and belligerent asking Liz what kind of question that was. Liz told her that it was a simple yes or no question. Ms. Williams said "Of course Key is my son." Liz asked her what number Key wore in basketball, but Ms. Williams couldn't answer. It was 3 because he was a big John Starks fan. She then asked what teacher Key had the most issues with. If Ms. Williams wasn't kicked out of the courtroom the day before, she may have been able to guess that it was Mr. Johnson, but she didn't know that answer either. Her next question was what Key's favorite meal was, and if she ever cooked it. Ms. Williams tried to avoid the question by asking what the point of Liz's questioning was.

With that answer alone she killed her credibility, at least I thought so. Liz saw that as an opening. She stated that the point she was trying to make was that a mother knows everything about their child; their cry amongst other babies in a nursery, the moment they took their first steps, their favorite color, who they took to prom, and overall who they associate with. She did not let up on her questioning of Ms. Williams just yet. She brought up the claim that Ms. Williams made during the first day of the trial; the one about Key turning the apartment into a hostile living environment.

Liz went back to her bag and pulled out some more documents. They were the most recent bills that were issued to their East New York apartment. She held them up in front of the courtroom and asked Ms. Williams to tell the court how much was owed on the last water bill, but Ms. Williams couldn't answer. Liz asked her if she could tell her how much was owed on the electric bill; Ms. Williams couldn't answer that either. Liz told her that it seemed as if she did not know much about what was going on in her own home. She then asked her if she even knew the names of the companies that sent the bills out. Ms. Williams still couldn't answer. Liz finally asked her what she did for a living. Ms. Williams definitely couldn't answer that.

With a nod of the head, Liz smiled and did a confident forty-five degree turn on the heels of her shoes so that she was facing Key. She asked Key the same questions about how much each bill came to. Key was able to give accurate figures for each of them. She told Key that it seemed like he had more of an idea of the financial matters in the home than his mother did. Key stated that Liz's notion was correct, and that he paid all of the bills in the house with the money he made when he traveled doing shows and working at Burger Empire.

Conveniently, Liz directed her attention back to Ms. Williams and told her that the hostile environment she described sounded like a place she should be thanking Key for allowing her to live in, although it should have been the other way around. Ms. Williams told Liz that she had no right to judge her. Liz informed her that she was not judging her, she was only trying to clear up some facts and she was free to step down because she had no further questions.

Liz followed up her questioning with Ms. Williams by calling Alexander Biggins to the stand; better known as Lex. She chose to go with a method of not wasting time between witnesses because she felt it kept the courtroom captivated and made her look smooth. Her calling of Lex was interesting to say the least, but she was on a roll. Lex took the oath and Liz told him that she was going to get straight to the point. She asked him if he worked for Blizzard. Lex claimed that he worked for himself. She asked him if that meant he made the call to hold Ms. Williams and Ms. James up at gunpoint. Lex claimed that he didn't recall doing that. Liz told him that two witnesses already said otherwise. He countered Liz's claim by saying it was hearsay.

Lex was pretty good so far, Blizzard must have threatened him with something if he wasn't. Blizzard sat quietly in his seat like it was just another day, he was very creepy. Liz told Lex that it would be best if he gave straight answers, and that it would help him to avoid embarrassment later on when more evidence was presented. That's when Liz presented another piece of evidence to the court. It was the bullet that was found in the man Lex shot a few doors down from Key's apartment. He told her that bullets were found in people every day. She told him that he was right about that, but the only difference was that his fingerprints were found on the doorknob of the hallway staircase door. Lex asked her if she was claiming that he was the only one that used those steps. Liz stated "I'm not saying that, but I'd like to point out the fact that you just answered the question that I have been asking." Simply put, Lex had just admitted that he was in fact at the apartment at some point after claiming that his supposed presence there was "hearsay".

Lex was pretty much speechless. Liz moved in on his vulnerability by asking him what he was doing there. Lex pleaded the fifth. The courtroom murmurs began once again causing the judge to demand order. Liz asked him if he would like to plead the fifth on if he worked for Blizzard as well. He told her again in a louder tone "I WORK FOR MYSELF." She told him that was perfectly fine and asked him what he did for a living. Lex told her that he was in sales. She asked him what he sold. He told her that he sold whatever he could. She asked if he could give an example of one item. He told her that he couldn't at the moment because he was in between jobs. She asked him what his last position was. He told her that his last position was cleaning boats down at Chelsea Piers. She finally asked him to explain her why a cleaner of boats would want to hold two defenseless women up at gunpoint. The prosecutor objected on the grounds that Liz was badgering the witness. The objection was sustained.

Liz told the judge that she had no further questions for Lex. She then asked Shayna to take the stand once Lex stepped down. With Shayna being called, it pretty much meant that we were approaching the end. Shayna took the oath for the second consecutive day. Liz began her questioning by sharing that she took note of the attack by the prosecutor on Shayna's character the day before. She then told the court that she felt Shayna was a fine young woman with an outstanding athletic gift, and that it was a shame that her college career ended the way it did. The school had officially expelled Shayna and the NACS (National Association for College Sports) notified her that she could no longer compete. Liz learned of this and told her that if she needed a lawyer to get back into the programs, she would represent her pro bono. Shayna thanked her.

Liz continued by telling the court that the point she was trying to make was that young people like Key make mistakes. She then stated that "As a result, people associated with them get caught in the crossfire. In Shayna's case, she was wrongfully accused of hiding drug money for Key." Liz made sure that she emphasized that it was wrongful to the courtroom. She further pushed the fact that it did not help when people such as the prosecution used young people's mistakes against them instead of acknowledging that we all need second chances in life. Liz told Shayna that she was aware that her and Key were no longer together. She then asked "If your decision to give Key another chance was motivated by one memory, what would it be?"

A tear traveled down Shayna's face. She became overwhelmed as she heard her experiences on what she had been through with school Key being verbally expressed. I think she was just happy that someone outside of her circle understood her pain. She wiped her face and told Liz that if there was one memory, it would be their prom night. She chose prom because it was a night in which he was a gentleman, exhibited trust in her, defended her honor, and made her feel like a woman. Shayna and Key's eyes locked for a while. Shawn grabbed Ms. Kim's hand as they watched Shayna express her raw emotions. They had never seen her do that openly.

Liz took what Shayna said and told the courtroom that she wanted them to acknowledge the type of person her client was; "He made mistakes, but so does everyone else. Despite his faults, he was a person that touched the lives of everyone around him, even the ones that didn't appreciate him." She further explained to the court that it was easy to point out the negative traits of a person, but in the end nothing is really gained from that. She told Shayna that she could step down. As she stepped down, Liz whispered to her "Keith loves you."

HAYMAKER

It was now time for the moment everyone had been waiting for. Liz told the entire courtroom that she would like to call Keith Williams to the stand. Everyone sat up, media that was allowed into the courtroom had gotten into position, and recorders were all ready for what he had to say. Key stepped to the stand, took the oath, and took his seat. Liz asked him if there was something he wanted to share. Key told her that there was. He opened by telling the courtroom that after deep deliberation based on attacks on his loved ones, attacks on him, and threats to the life of the woman he loved, he decided to no longer be a coward.

Key pulled the microphone closer to him and said:

"Ladies and gentleman of the jury and the courtroom, I want to tell you a story about how a man in this courtroom that brought an immense amount of pain to my life and the lives of others in the great city of New York. His name is Ronald Biggins. Many of you may know him by his moniker; "Blizzard". My history with Mr. Biggins began during a low point of my life. I was broke, facing eviction, trying to finish high school, and not getting any help from a woman that called herself my mother.

I went through many days trying to figure out how I was going to get out of my financial crisis. I had just given up my regular means of income which was pursuing a dream with two friends of mine. We formed a hip-hop group called 'Young

Bosses' and our trips were funded by my cousin who also served as our manager. Soon after, I met the only woman that I ever loved, Ms. Shayna Green. When I met Shayna, I was the typical adolescent male and only wanted her for that beautiful body that she was blessed with. Shayna wasn't having it though, and refused to give me the time of day. I begged and pleaded with her regularly to change her mind. I noticed that as each day passed and the more I tried, the better a man I was becoming.

One day Shayna presented me with a challenge. She told me that I could take her to prom if I could graduate on time. At the time, everyone knew that I was way behind in school. I cut class a lot and only started attending school again on a regular basis just to see her. I wanted her as a prom date more than anything in the world so I was willing to do whatever it took. At that point, the only woman I've ever recognized as a mother figure intervened; her name is Ms. Mims, I believe you all saw her earlier. She managed to make a deal with my teachers. The deal allowed me to do extra work in order to graduate on time. I love her and I thank her for actually caring when no one else did.

As good as the deal sounded, I realized that I couldn't juggle both school and a life traveling from place to place doing shows. Ultimately, I chose school. That was when the financial woes began to present themselves. I got a local job working for Mr. Jones, a man that is facing charges because of me. I was stable for a while, but business began to slow down. I was soon facing eviction along with a woman that sat in my apartment doing nothing on a daily basis.

I was presented with an opportunity at the most convenient time by Mr. Warren James. He told me that he was working for Blizzard and showed me how much money he was making selling cocaine. At first I turned it down, but eventually gave in because I desperately needed money. I didn't want to be out on the streets. I told Warren that I was on board, and he relayed the message to Ronald Biggins' organization. That was when I met Antonio Rivera, he's here today sitting next to Alexander and Ronald. I was ready to quit my job with Mr. Jones, but they told me to stay because they were going to have me sell the product out of the restaurant.

When I was informed of this, it sounded like a great idea and a well drawn out plan. It was going well and according to plan, that is until Warren James decided that he wanted more money on his assignments from Blizzard. He began to rob the consumers by taking their money, but not giving them the product (cocaine). I told him it was a bad idea, but he continued to do it until he finally got caught and badly beaten on a corner he was working on. That was when his mother, Ms. Juanita James, learned that he was selling drugs and kicked him out. Being that I looked at him as a brother, I took him in.

Warren was being pursued by Ronald for the money that he cost him when the clientele no longer wanted to purchase the product. I decided to help him come up with a plan to get the money before the deadline. On the day that the money was due, we didn't have a plan. I showed up at the meeting place with Warren even though he was supposed to be there alone. I figured they were most likely going to kill him if he didn't have the money. When Mr. Rivera learned that we didn't have the money, he had two men hold us up at gunpoint, beat us up, and he eventually kidnapped Warren.

As time progressed, Warren was pretty much off of the radar and I began to think that he was dead. That is until the day of my graduation from Jackie Robinson High School; I learned Blizzard's organization had no knowledge of Warren's whereabouts either. I learned of this when Mr. Rivera showed up at my job and we got into an argument causing me to be sent home early. When I got home, Alexander Biggins was in my apartment. He had Ms. Williams and Ms. James tied up. He was threatening to kill them if I didn't tell them where Warren was. We went back and forth for a while until I convinced them that I really didn't know where he was. From there, they gave me thirty-six hours to deliver him.

In order to make sure that I didn't try to flee, they left one of their henchmen at my house. I couldn't possibly deliver Warren so I came up with a plan to get myself and Ms. Williams out of harm's way before the thirty-six hours was up. I went to work and brought some food back for dinner. The henchman was a greedy man so I knew he would go straight for the food. I put a horse tranquilizer in his burger. It was supposed to knock him unconscious and give myself and Ms. Williams an opportunity to pack a few things and get out of there. It knocked him out and we went to Brownsville. I knew someone that worked for the housing authority that would give us a vacant apartment for the evening. It was only later that I found out via breaking news that the henchman was shot and killed, and the drug in his system turned out to be PCP. My personal guess was that Lex or the other henchman shot him when he went back to the apartment to see if I had gotten a hold of Warren.

I went into hiding for a while and told Mr. Jones that I was sick. That didn't sit too well with Ronald Biggins or his organization; I supposedly cost them money by not reporting to work. Shayna had gone away to school so I figured that she would at least be okay being away from me. I didn't want her to be caught in the crossfire. My first day back to work for Mr. Jones and Mr. Biggins went according to plan. Being that it was my first day back, I figured that I had a target on my back. On my way home that night I decided to go into Manhattan instead of straight home to avoid any possible followers. That's when I learned that Ronald Biggins had some corrupt cops on his payroll as well.

I was stopped in Harlem by two on duty policemen claiming that I fit a profile which I knew was nonsense, but I didn't want to draw attention to myself so I cooperated. The cops told me that they were taking me to central booking, but instead took me to Chelsea Piers. When we got there, they brutally beat me with their nightsticks and brought me inside one of the docked yachts to talk to Mr. Alexander Biggins and Mr. Antonio Rivera. They told me that they not only wanted Warren, but the money that I supposedly owed Ronald for not reporting to work. In addition to that, they were trying to pin the murder of that henchman Alexander was responsible for on me. I tried to explain to them once again that I honestly didn't know where Warren was. That was when they threatened to go after Shayna in Florida. I got upset at that point and was going to attack Alexander out of anger, but Mr. Rivera pulled a gun on me.

I agreed to pay the money the next day. I had a little bit of money saved from what I had accumulated working for Mr. Ronald Biggins. I figured I had no choice but to continue to work for him because if I didn't, he'd harm Shayna. They even sent a man known as "The Custodian" to tell me that he was monitoring Shayna's every move. Since I couldn't deliver Warren, they placed me on his old corners in addition to working my position at Burger Empire. They knew I didn't know how to work corners; they just wanted me to get killed. I managed to get the hang of it and my days had begun to consist of days on the corners and nights at Burger Empire. That is until one particular day when the DEA brought a SWAT team to the restaurant and arrested me. They claimed to have gotten an anonymous tip that I was selling drugs inside the restaurant.

I spent many days in jail with no visitation rights until one day when I was told that I had a visitor, it was Warren. That

369

was when he told me that he was in hiding and made a deal with the police in order to get both of our charges dropped. According to him, all I had to do was testify against Ronald Biggins in his trial. I refused because he was the reason I had been thrown in jail and he was only asking me to help him for his own benefit. The reward would also consist of Ronald's organization being taken down. If I didn't testify, Warren was going to be charged. I figured that he was the core root of the situation so he needed to find his own way out.

As I spent more time in jail, I got to know some more of Ronald's employees. The main one went by the name of Flea. He told me that Ronald sent him to deliver a message. The message was that if I testified against him, my loved ones as well as myself would suffer. This scar on my neck is one of the forms of warning. They were given access to my cell on Redd's Island by a correctional officer named Matthew Jamison, he works for Ronald also. Flea put a shank to my neck telling me that I needed to keep my mouth shut about Ronald. He also mentioned that Ronald didn't want me dead; he just wanted to warn me.

The war I was in with Ronald's organization was going on for too long. I believe that Ronald finally got the idea that I would not be intimidated by his scare tactics because from that point, he ordered my death. It had become a matter of if I was actually going to make it to the trial today. As a result of that, I did something gruesome to Flea to get myself thrown into solitary confinement for my own protection. While I was in solitary, an attack was carried out on Jerome Gaines, Jerome's associates, and some of the inmates I had associated with. The attack was a form of retaliation to what I did to Flea. It left Jerome Gaines in critical condition and almost took his life. From that point I decided that I wouldn't allow Ronald Biggins to run my life anymore and that is why I sit before you today, to tell you my story. Ronald Biggins is a menace to society and has been a menace to my family. It is only safe to take him as well as his operation down before anyone else is harmed."

Key looked Blizzard right in his eye as he delivered the last points of his statement. He then looked out into the courtroom and said that although he decided to no longer be a coward that day, Blizzard was the real coward by staying out of the public eye and killing people with his product. Key then looked back at Blizzard and told him that he understood now why he had Lex and Rivera do most of his work; "Although it was a smart move, it was actually because you're not man enough to handle your own business." Liz told Key that would be all and thanked him for his testimony. She told the judge "The defense rests."

FINISH LINE

The judge told the court that if there was nothing else that needed to be discussed, he would hand the case over to the jury to deliberate. The testimony rocked the city's core, especially Brooklyn. As a result, Blizzard, Lex, and Rivera were taken into custody. Blizzard was finally able to be arraigned because the crimes that he was accused of in the past three years were now slightly supported by the testimony. What happened to him from there was in the hands of the city of New York. I spent the days of deliberation praying for Key.

The deliberation took two days. I was surprised that it even took that long. I was sure that with the testimony containing a confession, they would only need a few hours at most for them to agree that Key was guilty. We all made our way back to the court house. Everyone was in attendance once again talking and socializing. The topic of everyone's conversation was the possible outcome. We were all asked to rise to receive the judge. The judge told us that we could all be seated. He then turned to the jury and asked them if they had come to a decision. The lead juror told the judge that they did. He asked the juror to continue as the courtroom was completely silent.

The lead juror told the judge that on the count of money laundering, they found Key not guilty. Even though he used a place of business to make the money, the money made was never disguised as tender accumulated by the restaurant. On the charge of conspiracy, they found Key guilty due to his confession of going into business with Blizzard to sell cocaine. On the charge of possession of cocaine with intent to sell, they found Key guilty. On the charge of distributing and trafficking, they found Key guilty due to his confession of selling it on the corners meaning he served as a transporter to a degree.

The courtroom reacted to the decision with mixed emotion. The judge called for order and thanked the jury for their work. He turned to Key and told him that based on the charges he was found guilty of and the amount of counts for each charge; he would be sentenced to sixty-five years in prison. He would have an opportunity for probation and early release with good behavior. The courtroom went crazy once again. Shayna began to cry so I pulled her close to me to console her. Key just sat there and took it like a man nodding his head at the judge as if to say he understood.

The judge banged his gavel very hard telling the courtroom that he had enough of the collective outbursts. He threatened to clear the courtroom if it happened again. It really didn't matter at that point since the deliberation had been complete. I couldn't have been more wrong; the judge had something else to say. He told the court that while listening to Key's testimony he realized that although Key committed the crime, the threats and attack on his family made some of his decisions justifiable. He made it clear that he didn't condone Key's actions, he simply understood his decisions. He looked at Liz and told her that he was going to see everything that Key did after being beaten up in the alley in Brooklyn as an act of self-defense.

That got the attention of the court immediately because it could only mean good news. The judge told her that as a result of Key being forced to do something against his will to protect his loved ones, he would consider it false imprisonment by Blizzard, Lex, and Rivera. He finally told us that he would be taking forty-five years off of Key's sentence. That left him with only twenty years to serve, and the chance for probation and early release were still included. It was better than what he was given and a lot better than the life sentence he was potentially facing. It was still a lot, but I just thanked God for the sentence being abbreviated.

Key was immediately sent back to his cell, but held in solitary for the night because they planned to transfer him the next morning. Everyone got up from their seats and began to leave the courtroom. It was finally finished and we all went back to our regular lives. I continued school and working at The Garden. The lockout was called off so basketball season had started; that was an upside to a rough couple of weeks. I was able to see free games and I brought Jamal and Shayna along some nights. He was in a much better mood than he had been in the weeks prior to and during the trial because Jerome was recovering well. Shayna began looking for a job to hold her over while she was out of school. Ms. Mims gave her a position mentoring her students from time to time. It didn't pay, but it gave her something to do. Shawn and Ms. Kim continued to support her until she found something. Ms. Kim went back to showing her as much love as she did before.

A few weeks had passed and we were informed that Lex, Rivera, and Blizzard had been brought up on charges of drug manufacturing, cultivation, trafficking, distribution, possession, false imprisonment, murder, assault charges, money laundering, and a slew of other charges. A few months after their arraignments, the general public had been informed that Lex and Rivera were facing life sentences along with a lot of the other employees that were found to be working with Blizzard. Flea had years added to his sentence and the inmate that cut Jerome's neck was put on death row. Finally, Blizzard's sentence was announced. He was only given ten years in prison because he managed to prove that he didn't work directly with his employees and his lawyer successfully placed everything he was accused of on Lex and Rivera.

The city was in disbelief that he managed to pull it off, but I was just happy that it was over. I did not like what it was doing to everyone around me. However, it meant that Key's testimony was slightly in vain. It brought Blizzard's organization down, but he really wanted to take Blizzard down for good. In the midst of the bad news, there was some good news. Jerome was transferred to another prison to serve the rest of his term so that he wouldn't be targeted anymore. He was also given special treatment and excused from general population because of his physical condition. Instead, he spent most of his time in a ward with older and disabled prisoners. It made Jamal's family worry a little less about his day to day life in prison.

Blizzard was sent to prison in late December of that year to begin his sentence. A few days later, New York City and most of the East coast was hit by the Blizzard of '96. The timing couldn't have been more perfect. It was almost as if Blizzard cut off his fellow drug kingpins temporarily because he couldn't make money for a while, and they could.

Around that same time, I was getting ready to start my second semester of school. That wasn't the only work of God that had taken place. Around February of 1996, Shayna had been helping the track team at Jackie Robinson part time. One day she received a letter when she got back home. It was a short letter from Liz that read:

Ms. Shayna Green,

I know that your case regarding the charges you are facing is approaching within the next week. I want to let you know that my offer to represent you pro bono would still be on the table; that is if it was necessary. I'm sorry that I couldn't give you this information earlier, but Keith wanted to surprise you. The testimony he provided for the court was part of a deal to have your record and anything in connection with it removed from the record books. You will not have to report to that trial because it has been dismissed along with the charges.

As a result of this, your expulsion from Gainesville University and ban from the NACS has been lifted. You will need

376

to keep this letter as proof for when you re-register. It just brings me joy to see an athlete of your caliber get a second chance. When you get a chance, contact Keith. I packaged a letter from him along with this one.

-Liz

Key's letter was behind Liz's. It was even shorter, but it was the definition of big things coming in small packages. It was a few lines that read:

Shayna,

    Our beautiful time together went by almost as fast as the time it takes you to run 100 meters. I was actually just informed by Liz that you've officially been given a chance to run a lot more of those. I just want you to know that I love you and can't wait for the day that I see you again. Congratulations in advance on your next race. Don't let outside distractions take you away from what you've been blessed to do like last time. Stay focused, and stay on "track".

Love,
The Key to Your Heart

17606328R00215

Made in the USA
Middletown, DE
31 January 2015